Robert Barr (16 September 1849 – 21 October 1912) was a Scottish-Canadian short story writer and novelist. Robert Barr was born in Barony, Lanark, Scotland to Robert Barr and Jane Watson. In 1854, he emigrated with his parents to Upper Canada at the age of four years old. His family settled on a farm near the village of Muirkirk. Barr assisted his father with his job as a carpenter, and developed a sound work ethic. Robert Barr then worked as a steel smelter for a number of years before he was educated at Toronto Normal School in 1873 to train as a teacher. After graduating Toronto Normal School, Barr became a teacher, and eventually headmaster/principal of the Central School of Windsor, Ontario in 1874. While Barr worked as head master of the Central School of Windsor, Ontario, he began to contribute short stories—often based on personal experiences, and recorded his work. On August 1876, when he was 27, Robert Barr married Ontario-born Eva Bennett, who was 21. (Source: Wikipedia)

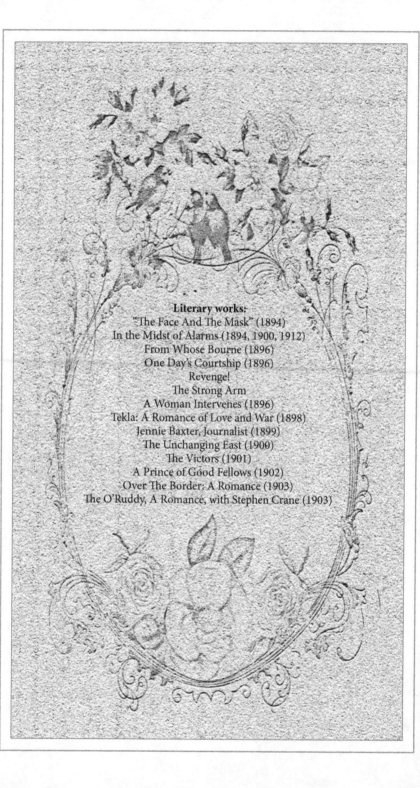

Literary works:
"The Face And The Mask" (1894)
In the Midst of Alarms (1894, 1900, 1912)
From Whose Bourne (1896)
One Day's Courtship (1896)
Revenge!
The Strong Arm
A Woman Intervenes (1896)
Tekla: A Romance of Love and War (1898)
Jennie Baxter, Journalist (1899)
The Unchanging East (1900)
The Victors (1901)
A Prince of Good Fellows (1902)
Over The Border: A Romance (1903)
The O'Ruddy, A Romance, with Stephen Crane (1903)

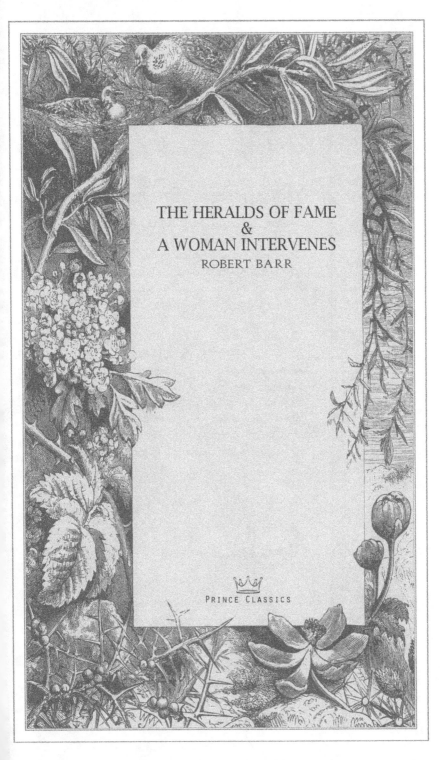

THE HERALDS OF FAME
&
A WOMAN INTERVENES

ROBERT BARR

PRINCE CLASSICS

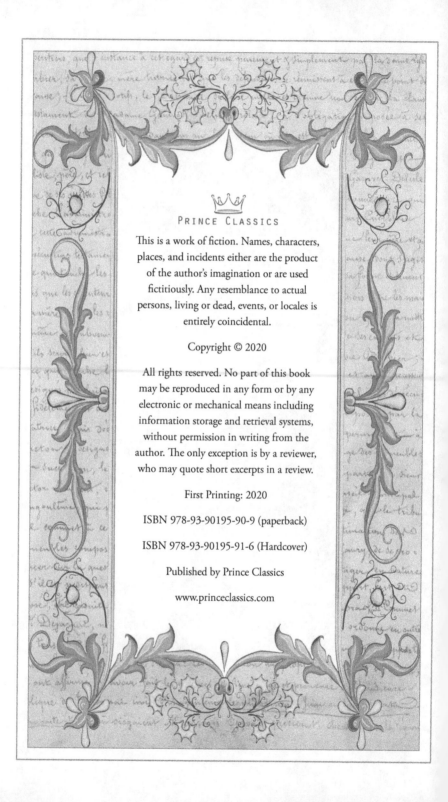

PRINCE CLASSICS

First Printing: 2020

ISBN 978-93-90195-90-9 (paperback)

ISBN 978-93-90195-91-6 (Hardcover)

Published by Prince Classics

www.princeclassics.com

Contents

THE HERALDS OF FAME
&
A WOMAN INTERVENES

THE HERALDS OF FAME

The Heralds of Fame

Chapter I

Now, when each man's place in literature is so clearly defined, it seems ridiculous to state that there was a time when Kenan Buel thought J. Lawless Hodden a great novelist. One would have imagined that Buel's keen insight into human nature would have made such a mistake impossible, but it must be remembered that Buel was always more or less of a hero-worshipper. It seems strange in the light of our after-knowledge that there ever was a day when Hodden's books were selling by the thousand, and Buel was tramping the streets of London fruitlessly searching for a publisher. Not less strange is the fact that Buel thought Hodden's success well deserved. He would have felt honoured by the touch of Hodden's hand.

No convict ever climbed a treadmill with more hopeless despair than Buel worked in his little room under the lofty roof. He knew no one; there were none to speak to him a cheering or comforting word; he was ignorant even of the names of the men who accepted the articles from his pen, which appeared unsigned in the daily papers and in some of the weeklies. He got cheques—small ones—with illegible and impersonal signatures that told him nothing. But the bits of paper were honoured at the bank, and this lucky fact enabled him to live and write books which publishers would not look at.

Nevertheless, showing how all things are possible to a desperate and resolute man, two of his books had already seen the light, if it could be called light. The first he was still paying for, on the instalment plan. The publishers were to pay half, and he was to pay half. This seemed to him only a fair division of the risk at the time. Not a single paper had paid the slightest attention to the book. The universal ignoring of it disheartened him. He had been prepared for abuse, but not for impenetrable silence.

He succeeded in getting another and more respectable publisher to take up his next book on a royalty arrangement. This was a surprise to him, and a gratification. His satisfaction did not last long after the book came out. It was mercilessly slated. One paper advised him to read "Hodden;" another said he had plagiarized from that popular writer. The criticisms cut him like a whip. He wondered why he had rebelled at the previous silence. He felt like a man who had heedlessly hurled a stone at a snow mountain and had been buried by the resulting avalanche.

He got his third publisher a year after that. He thought he would never succeed in getting the same firm twice, and wondered what would happen when he exhausted the London list. It is not right that a man should go on for ever without a word of encouragement. Fate recognised that there would come a breaking-point, and relented in time. The word came from an unexpected source. Buel was labouring, heavy-eyed, at the last proof-sheets of his third book, and was wondering whether he would have the courage not to look at the newspapers when the volume was published. He wished he could afford to go to some wilderness until the worst was over. He knew he could not miss the first notice, for experience had taught him that Snippit & Co., a clipping agency, would send it to him, with a nice type-written letter, saying—

"Dear Sir,

"As your book is certain to attract a great deal of attention from the Press, we shall be pleased to send you clippings similar to the enclosed at the following rates."

It struck him as rather funny that any company should expect a sane man to pay so much good money for Press notices, mostly abusive. He never subscribed.

The word of encouragement gave notice of its approach in a letter, signed by a man of whom he had never heard. It was forwarded to him by his publishers. The letter ran:—

"Dear Sir,

"Can you make it convenient to lunch with me on Friday at the

Métropole? If you have an engagement for that day can you further oblige me by writing and putting it off? Tell the other fellow you are ill or have broken your leg, or anything, and charge up the fiction to me. I deal in fiction, anyhow. I leave on Saturday for the Continent, not wishing to spend another Sunday in London if I can avoid it. I have arranged to get out your book in America, having read the proof-sheets at your publisher's. All the business part of the transaction is settled, but I would like to see you personally if you don't mind, to have a talk over the future—always an interesting subject. "Yours very truly, "L. F. BRANT, "Of Rainham Bros., Publishers, New York."

Buel read this letter over and over again. He had never seen anything exactly like it. There was a genial flippancy about it that was new to him, and he wondered what sort of a man the New Yorker was. Mr. Brant wrote to a stranger with the familiarity of an old friend, yet the letter warmed Buel's heart. He smiled at the idea the American evidently had about a previous engagement. Invitations to lunch become frequent when a man does not need them. No broken leg story would have to be told. He wrote and accepted Mr. Brant's invitation.

"You're Mr. Buel, I think?"

The stranger's hand rested lightly on the young author's shoulder. Buel had just entered the unfamiliar precincts of the Métropole Hotel. The tall man with the gold lace on his hat had hesitated a moment before he swung open the big door, Buel was so evidently not a guest of the hotel.

"My name is Buel."

"Then you're my victim. I've been waiting impatiently for you. I am L. F. Brant."

"I thought I was in time. I am sorry to have kept you waiting."

"Don't mention it. I have been waiting but thirty seconds. Come up in the elevator. They call it a lift here, not knowing any better, but it gets there ultimately. I have the title-deeds to a little parlour while I am staying in this tavern, and I thought we could talk better if we had lunch there. Lunch costs

15

more on that basis, but I guess we can stand it."

A cold shudder passed over the thin frame of Kenan Buel. He did not know but it was the custom in America to ask a man to lunch and expect him to pay half. Brant's use of the plural lent colour to this view, and Buel knew he could not pay his share. He regretted they were not in a vegetarian restaurant.

The table in the centre of the room was already set for two, and the array of wine-glasses around each plate looked tempting. Brant pushed the electric button, drew up his chair, and said—

"Sit down, Buel, sit down. What's your favourite brand of wine? Let's settle on it now, so as to have no unseemly wrangle when the waiter comes. I'm rather in awe of the waiter. It doesn't seem natural that any mere human man should be so obviously superior to the rest of us mortals as this waiter is. I'm going to give you only the choice of the first wines. I have taken the champagne for granted, and it's cooling now in a tub somewhere. We always drink champagne in the States, not because we like it, but because it's expensive. I calculate that I pay the expenses of my trip over here merely by ordering unlimited champagne. I save more than a dollar a bottle on New York prices, and these saved dollars count up in a month. Personally I prefer cider or lager beer, but in New York we dare not own to liking a thing unless it is expensive."

"It can hardly be a pleasant place for a poor man to live in, if that is the case."

"My dear Buel, no city is a pleasant place for a poor man to live in. I don't suppose New York is worse than London in that respect. The poor have a hard time of it anywhere. A man owes it to himself and family not to be poor. Now, that's one thing I like about your book; you touch on poverty in a sympathetic way, by George, like a man who had come through it himself. I've been there, and I know how it is. When I first struck New York I hadn't even a ragged dollar bill to my back. Of course every successful man will tell you the same of himself, but it is mostly brag, and in half the instances it isn't true at all; but in my case—well, I wasn't subscribing to the heathen in those days. I made up my mind that poverty didn't pay, and I have succeeded in

16

remedying the state of affairs. But I haven't forgotten how it felt to be hard up, and I sympathise with those who are. Nothing would afford me greater pleasure than to give a helping hand to a fellow—that is, to a clever fellow who was worth saving—who is down at bed rock. Don't you feel that way too?"

"Yes," said Buel, with some hesitation, "it would be a pleasure."

"I knew when I read your book you felt that way—I was sure of it. Well, I've helped a few in my time; but I regret to say most of them turned out to be no good. That is where the trouble is. Those who are really deserving are just the persons who die of starvation in a garret, and never let the outside world know their trouble."

"I do not doubt such is often the case."

"Of course it is. It's always the case. But here's the soup. I hope you have brought a good appetite. You can't expect such a meal here as you would get in New York; but they do fairly well. I, for one, don't grumble about the food in London, as most Americans do. Londoners manage to keep alive, and that, after all, is the main thing."

Buel was perfectly satisfied with the meal, and thought if they produced a better one in New York, or anywhere else, the art of cookery had reached wonderful perfection. Brant, however, kept apologising for the spread as he went along. The talk drifted on in an apparently aimless fashion, but the publisher was a shrewd man, and he was gradually leading it up to the point he had in view from the beginning, and all the while he was taking the measure of his guest. He was not a man to waste either his time or his dinners without an object. When he had once "sized up" his man, as he termed it, he was either exceedingly frank and open with him, or the exact opposite, as suited his purpose. He told Buel that he came to England once a year, if possible, rapidly scanned the works of fiction about to be published by the various houses in London, and made arrangements for the producing of those in America that he thought would go down with the American people.

"I suppose," said Buel, "that you have met many of the noted authors of this country?"

"All of them, I think; all of them, at one time or another. The publishing business has its drawbacks like every other trade," replied Brant, jauntily.

"Have you met Hodden?"

"Several times. Conceited ass!"

"You astonish me. I have never had the good fortune to become acquainted with any of our celebrated writers. I would think it a privilege to know Hodden and some of the others."

"You're lucky, and you evidently don't know it. I would rather meet a duke any day than a famous author. The duke puts on less side and patronises you less."

"I would rather be a celebrated author than a duke if I had my choice."

"Well, being a free and independent citizen of the Democratic United States, I wouldn't. No, sir! I would rather be Duke Brant any day in the week than Mr. Brant, the talented author of, etc., etc. The moment an author receives a little praise and becomes talked about, he gets what we call in the States 'the swelled head.' I've seen some of the nicest fellows in the world become utterly spoiled by a little success. And then think of the absurdity of it all. There aren't more than two or three at the most of the present-day writers who will be heard of a century hence. Read the history of literature, and you will find that never more than four men in any one generation are heard of after. Four is a liberal allowance. What has any writer to be conceited about anyhow? Let him read his Shakespeare and be modest."

Buel said with a sigh, "I wish there was success in store for me. I would risk the malady you call the 'swelled head.'"

"Success will come all right enough, my boy. 'All things come to him who waits,' and while he is waiting puts in some good, strong days of work. It's the working that tells, not the waiting. And now, if you will light one of these cigars, we will talk of you for a while, if your modesty will stand it. What kind of Chartreuse will you have? Yellow or green?"

18

"Either."

"Take the green, then. Where the price is the same I always take the green. It is the stronger, and you get more for your money. Now then, I will be perfectly frank with you. I read your book in the proof-sheets, and I ran it down in great style to your publisher."

"I am sorry you did not like it."

"I don't say I didn't like it. I ran it down because it was business. I made up my mind when I read that book to give a hundred pounds for the American rights. I got it for twenty."

Brant laughed, and Buel felt uncomfortable. He feared that after all he did not like this frank American.

"Having settled about the book, I wanted to see you, and here you are. Of course, I am utterly selfish in wanting to see you, for I wish you to promise me that we will have the right of publishing your books in America as long as we pay as much as any other publisher. There is nothing unfair in that, is there?"

"No. I may warn you, however, that there has been no great competition, so far, for the privilege of doing any publishing, either here or in America."

"That's all right. Unless I'm a Dutchman there will be, after your new book is published. Of course, that is one of the things no fellow can find out. If he could, publishing would be less of a lottery than it is. A book is sometimes a success by the merest fluke; at other times, in spite of everything, a good book is a deplorable failure. I think yours will go; anyhow, I am willing to bet on it up to a certain amount, and if it does go, I want to have the first look-in at your future books. What do you say?"

"Do you wish me to sign a contract?"

"No, I merely want your word. You may write me a letter if you like, that I could show to my partners, saying that we would have the first refusal of your future books."

"I am quite willing to do that."

19

"Very good. That's settled. Now, you look fagged out. I wish you would take a trip over to New York. I'll look after you when you get there. It would do you a world of good, and would show in the pages of your next book. What do you say to that? Have you any engagements that would prevent you making the trip?"

Buel laughed, "I am perfectly free as far as engagements are concerned."

"That's all right, then. I wish I were in that position. Now, as I said, I considered your book cheap at £100. I got it for £20. I propose to hand over the £80 to you. I'll write out the cheque as soon as the waiters clear away the débris. Then your letter to the firm would form the receipt for this money, and—well, it need not be a contract, you know, or anything formal, but just your ideas on any future business that may crop up."

"I must say I think your offer is very generous."

"Oh, not at all. It is merely business. The £80 is on account of royalties. If the book goes, as I think it will, I hope to pay you much more than that. Now I hope you will come over and see me as soon as you can."

"Yes. As you say, the trip will do me good. I have been rather hard at it for some time."

"Then I'll look out for you. I sail on the French line Saturday week. When will you come?"

"As soon as my book is out here, and before any of the reviews appear."

"Sensible man. What's your cable address?"

"I haven't one."

"Well, I suppose a telegram to your publishers will find you. I'll cable if anything turns up unexpectedly. You send me over a despatch saying what steamer you sail on. My address is 'Rushing, New York.' Just cable the name of the steamer, and I will be on the look-out for you."

It was doubtless the effect of the champagne, for Buel went back to his squalid room with his mind in the clouds. He wondered if this condition was the first indication of the swelled head Brant had talked about. Buel worked harder than ever at his proofs, and there was some growling at head-quarters because of the numerous corrections he made. These changes were regarded as impudence on the part of so unknown a man. He sent off to America a set of the corrected proofs, and received a cablegram, "Proofs received. Too late. Book published today."

This was a disappointment. Still he had the consolation of knowing that the English edition would be as perfect as he could make it. He secured a berth on the Geranium, sailing from Liverpool, and cabled Brant to that effect. The day before he sailed he got a cablegram that bewildered him. It was simply, "She's a-booming." He regretted that he had never learned the American language.

Chapter II

Kenan Buel received from his London publisher a brown paper parcel, and on opening it found the contents to be six exceedingly new copies of his book. Whatever the publisher thought of the inside of the work, he had not spared pains to make the outside as attractive as it could be made at the price. Buel turned it over and over, and could almost imagine himself buying a book that looked so tastefully got up as this one. The sight of the volume gave him a thrill, for he remembered that the Press doubtless received its quota at about the same time his parcel came, and he feared he would not be out of the country before the first extract from the clipping agency arrived. However, luck was with the young man, and he found himself on the platform of Euston Station, waiting for the Liverpool express, without having seen anything about his book in the papers, except a brief line giving its title, the price, and his own name, in the "Books Received" column.

As he lingered around the well-kept bookstall before the train left, he saw a long row of Hodden's new novel, and then his heart gave a jump as he caught sight of two copies of his own work in the row labelled "New Books." He wanted to ask the clerk whether any of them had been sold yet, but in the first place he lacked the courage, and in the second place the clerk was very busy. As he stood there, a comely young woman, equipped for traveling, approached the stall, and ran her eye hurriedly up and down the tempting array of literature. She bought several of the illustrated papers, and then scanned the new books. The clerk, following her eye, picked out Buel's book.

"Just out, miss. Three and sixpence."

"Who is the author?" asked the girl.

"Kenan Buel, a new man," answered the clerk, without a moment's hesitation, and without looking at the title-page. "Very clever work."

Buel was astonished at the knowledge shown by the clerk. He knew that W.H. Smith & Son never had a book of his before, and he wondered how the clerk apparently knew so much of the volume and its author, forgetting that it was the clerk's business. The girl listlessly ran the leaves of the book past the edge of her thumb. It seemed to Buel that the fate of the whole edition was in her hands, and he watched her breathlessly, even forgetting how charming she looked. There stood the merchant eager to sell, and there, in the form of a young woman, was the great public. If she did not buy, why should any one else; and if nobody bought, what chance had an unknown author?

She put the book down, and looked up as she heard some one sigh deeply near her.

"Have you Hodden's new book?" she asked.

"Yes, miss. Six shillings."

The clerk quickly put Buel's book beside its lone companion, and took down Hodden's.

"Thank you," said the girl, giving him a half sovereign; and, taking the change, she departed with her bundle of literature to the train.

Buel said afterwards that what hurt him most in this painful incident was the fact that if it were repeated often the bookstall clerk would lose faith in the book. He had done so well for a man who could not possibly have read a word of the volume, that Buel felt sorry on the clerk's account rather than his own that the copy had not been sold. He walked to the end of the platform, and then back to the bookstall.

"Has that new book of Buel's come out yet?" he asked the clerk in an unconcerned tone.

"Yes, sir. Here it is; three and sixpence, sir."

"Thank you," said Buel, putting his hand in his pocket for the money. "How is it selling?"

"Well, sir, there won't be much call for it, not likely, till the reviews begin to come out."

There, Mr. Buel, you had a lesson, if you had only taken it to heart, or

23

pondered on its meaning. Since then you have often been very scornful of newspaper reviews, yet you saw yourself how the great public treats a man who is not even abused. How were you to know that the column of grossly unfair rancour which The Daily Argus poured out on your book two days later, when you were sailing serenely over the Atlantic, would make that same clerk send in four separate orders to the "House" during the week? Medicine may have a bad taste, and yet have beneficial results. So Mr. Kenan Buel, after buying a book of which he had six copies in his portmanteau, with no one to give them to, took his place in the train, and in due time found himself at Liverpool and on board the Geranium.

The stewards being busy, Buel placed his portmanteau on the deck, and, with his newly bought volume in his hand, the string and brown paper still around it, he walked up and down on the empty side of the deck, noticing how scrupulously clean the ship was. It was the first time he had ever been on board a steamship, and he could not trust himself unguided to explore the depths below, and see what kind of a state-room and what sort of a companion chance had allotted to him. They had told him when he bought his ticket that the steamer would be very crowded that trip, so many Americans were returning; but his state-room had berths for only two, and he had a faint hope the other fellow would not turn up. As he paced the deck his thoughts wandered to the pretty girl who did not buy his book. He had seen her again on the tender in company with a serene and placid older woman, who sat unconcernedly, surrounded by bundles, shawls, straps, valises, and hand-bags, which the girl nervously counted every now and then, fruitlessly trying to convince the elderly lady that something must have been left behind in the train, or lost in transit from the station to the steamer. The worry of travel, which the elderly woman absolutely refused to share, seemed to rest with double weight on the shoulders of the girl.

As Buel thought of all this, he saw the girl approach him along the deck with a smile of apparent recognition on her face. "She evidently mistakes me for some one else," he said to himself. "Oh, thank you," she cried, coming near, and holding out her hand. "I see you have found my book."

He helplessly held out the package to her, which she took.

"Is it yours?" he asked.

"Yes, I recognised it by the string. I bought it at Euston Station. I am forever losing things," she added. "Thank you, ever so much."

Buel laughed to himself as she disappeared. "Fate evidently intends her to read my book," he said to himself. "She will think the clerk has made a mistake. I must get her unbiased opinion of it before the voyage ends."

The voyage at that moment was just beginning, and the thud, thud of the screw brought that fact to his knowledge. He sought a steward, and asked him to carry the portmanteau to berth 159.

"You don't happen to know whether there is any one else in that room or not, do you?" he asked.

"It's likely there is, sir. The ship's very full this voyage."

Buel followed him into the saloon, and along the seemingly interminable passage; then down a narrow side alley, into which a door opened marked 159-160. The steward rapped at the door, and, as there was no response, opened it. All hopes of a room to himself vanished as Buel looked into the small state-room. There was a steamer trunk on the floor, a portmanteau on the seat, while the two bunks were covered with a miscellaneous assortment of hand-bags, shawl-strap bundles, and packages.

The steward smiled. "I think he wants a room to himself," he said.

On the trunk Buel noticed the name in white letters "Hodden," and instantly there arose within him a hope that his companion was to be the celebrated novelist. This hope was strengthened when he saw on the portmanteau the letters "J. L. H.," which were the novelist's initials. He pictured to himself interesting conversations on the way over, and hoped he would receive some particulars from the novelist's own lips of his early struggles for fame. Still, he did not allow himself to build too much on his supposition, for there are a great many people in this world, and the chances were that the traveller would be some commonplace individual of the same name.

The steward placed Buel's portmanteau beside the other, and backed out of the overflowing cabin. All doubt as to the identity of the other occupant was put at rest by the appearance down the passage of a man whom Buel instantly recognised by the portraits he had seen of him in the illustrated papers. He was older than the pictures made him appear, and there was a certain querulous expression on his face which was also absent in the portraits. He glanced into the state-room, looked for a moment through Buel, and then turned to the steward.

"What do you mean by putting that portmanteau into my room?"

"This gentleman has the upper berth, sir."

"Nonsense. The entire room is mine. Take the portmanteau out."

The steward hesitated, looking from one to the other.

"The ticket is for 159, sir," he said at last.

"Then there is some mistake. The room is mine. Don't have me ask you again to remove the portmanteau."

"Perhaps you would like to see the purser, sir."

"I have nothing to do with the purser. Do as I tell you."

All this time he had utterly ignored Buel, whose colour was rising. The young man said quietly to the steward, "Take out the portmanteau, please."

When it was placed in the passage, Hodden entered the room, shut and bolted the door.

"Will you see the purser, sir?" said the steward in an awed whisper.

"I think so. There is doubtless some mistake, as he says."

The purser was busy allotting seats at the tables, and Buel waited patiently. He had no friends on board, and did not care where he was placed.

When the purser was at liberty, the steward explained to him the difficulty which had arisen. The official looked at his list.

26

"159—Buel. Is that your name, sir? Very good; 160—Hodden. That is the gentleman now in the room. Well, what is the trouble?"

"Mr. Hodden says, sir, that the room belongs to him."

"Have you seen his ticket?"

"No, sir."

"Then bring it to me."

"Mistakes sometimes happen, Mr. Buel," said the purser, when the steward vanished. "But as a general thing I find that people simply claim what they have no right to claim. Often the agents promise that if possible a passenger shall have a room to himself, and when we can do so we let him have it. I try to please everybody; but all the steamers crossing to America are full at this season of the year, and it is not practicable to give every one the whole ship to himself. As the Americans say, some people want the earth for £12 or £15, and we can't always give it to them. Ah, here is the ticket. It is just as I thought. Mr. Hodden is entitled merely to berth 160."

The arrival of the ticket was quickly followed by the advent of Mr. Hodden himself. He still ignored Buel.

"Your people in London," he said to the purser, "guaranteed me a room to myself. Otherwise I would not have come on this line. Now it seems that another person has been put in with me. I must protest against this kind of usage."

"Have you any letter from them guaranteeing the room?" asked the purser blandly.

"No. I supposed until now that their word was sufficient."

"Well, you see, I am helpless in this case. These two tickets are exactly the same with the exception of the numbers. Mr. Buel has just as much right to insist on being alone in the room as far as the tickets go, and I have had no instructions in the matter."

"But it is an outrage that they should promise me one thing in London, and then refuse to perform it, when I am helpless on the ocean."

"If they have done so—"

"If they have done so? Do you doubt my word, sir?"

"Oh, not at all, sir, not at all," answered the purser in his most conciliatory tone. "But in that case your ticket should have been marked 159-160."

"I am not to suffer for their blunders."

"I see by this list that you paid £12 for your ticket. Am I right?"

"That was the amount, I believe. I paid what I was asked to pay."

"Quite so, sir. Well, you see, that is the price of one berth only. Mr. Buel, here, paid the same amount."

"Come to the point. Do I understand you to refuse to remedy the mistake (to put the matter in its mildest form) of your London people?"

"I do not refuse. I would be only too glad to give you the room to yourself, if it were possible. Unfortunately, it is not possible. I assure you there is not an unoccupied state-room on the ship."

"Then I will see the captain. Where shall I find him?"

"Very good, sir. Steward, take Mr. Hodden to the captain's room."

When they were alone again Buel very contritely expressed his sorrow at having been the innocent cause of so much trouble to the purser.

"Bless you, sir, I don't mind it in the least. This is a very simple case. Where both occupants of a room claim it all to themselves, and where both are angry and abuse me at the same time, then it gets a bit lively. I don't envy him his talk with the captain. If the old man happens to be feeling a little grumpy today, and he most generally does at the beginning of the voyage, Mr. Hodden will have a bad ten minutes. Don't you bother a bit about it, sir, but go down to your room and make yourself at home. It will be all right."

Mr. Hodden quickly found that the appeal to Cæsar was not well timed.

28

The captain had not the suave politeness of the purser. There may be greater and more powerful men on earth than the captain of an ocean liner, but you can't get any seafaring man to believe it, and the captains themselves are rarely without a due sense of their own dignity. The man who tries to bluff the captain of a steamship like the Geranium has a hard row to hoe. Mr. Hodden descended to his state-room in a more subdued frame of mind than when he went on the upper deck. However, he still felt able to crush his unfortunate room-mate.

"You insist, then," he said, speaking to Buel for the first time, "on occupying this room?"

"I have no choice in the matter."

"I thought perhaps you might feel some hesitation in forcing yourself in where you were so evidently not wanted?"

The hero-worshipper in Buel withered, and the natural Englishman asserted itself.

"I have exactly the same right in this room that you have. I claim no privilege which I have not paid for."

"Do you wish to suggest that I have made such a claim?"

"I suggest nothing; I state it. You have made such a claim, and in a most offensive manner."

"Do you understand the meaning of the language you are using, sir? You are calling me a liar."

"You put it very tersely, Mr. Hodden. Thank you. Now, if you venture to address me again during this voyage, I shall be obliged if you keep a civil tongue in your head."

"Good heavens! You talk of civility?" cried the astonished man, aghast.

His room-mate went to the upper deck. In the next state-room pretty Miss Carrie Jessop clapped her small hands silently together. The construction of staterooms is such that every word uttered in one above the breath is audible in the next room; Miss Jessop could not help hearing the whole controversy, from the time the steward was ordered so curtly to remove the portmanteau, until the culmination of the discussion and the evident defeat of Mr. Hodden. Her sympathy was all with the other fellow, at that moment unknown, but a sly peep past the edge of the scarcely opened door told her that the unnamed party in the quarrel was the awkward young man who had found her book. She wondered if the Hodden mentioned could possibly be the author, and, with a woman's inconsistency, felt sure that she would detest the story, as if the personality of the writer had anything whatever to do with his work. She took down the parcel from the shelf and undid the string. Her eyes opened wide as she looked at the title.

"Well I never!" she gasped. "If I haven't robbed that poor, innocent young man of a book he bought for himself! Attempted eviction by his roommate, and bold highway robbery by an unknown woman! No, it's worse than that; it's piracy, for it happened on the high seas." And the girl laughed softly to herself.

Chapter III

Kenan Buel walked the deck alone in the evening light, and felt that he ought to be enjoying the calmness and serenity of the ocean expanse around him after the noise and squalor of London; but now that the excitement of the recent quarrel was over, he felt the reaction, and his natural diffidence led him to blame himself. Most of the passengers were below, preparing for dinner, and he had the deck to himself. As he turned on one of his rounds, he saw approaching him the girl of Euston Station, as he mentally termed her. She had his book in her hand.

"I have come to beg your pardon," she said. "I see it was your own book I took from you to-day."

"My own book!" cried Buel, fearing she had somehow discovered his guilty secret.

"Yes. Didn't you buy this for yourself?" She held up the volume.

"Oh, certainly. But you are quite welcome to it, I am sure."

"I couldn't think of taking it away from you before you have read it."

"But I have read it," replied Buel, eagerly: "and I shall be very pleased to lend it to you."

"Indeed? And how did you manage to read it without undoing the parcel?"

"That is to say I—I skimmed over it before it was done up," he said in confusion. The clear eyes of the girl disconcerted him, and, whatever his place in fiction is now, he was at that time a most unskilful liar.

"You see, I bought it because it is written by a namesake of mine. My name is Buel, and I happened to notice that was the name on the book; in fact, if you remember, when you were looking over it at the stall, the clerk mentioned the author's name, and that naturally caught my attention."

The girl glanced with renewed interest at the volume.

"Was this the book I was looking at? The story I bought was Hodden's latest. I found it a moment ago down in my state-room, so it was not lost after all."

They were now walking together as if they were old acquaintances, the girl still holding the volume in her hand.

"By the way," she said innocently, "I see on the passenger list that there is a Mr. Hodden on board. Do you think he can be the novelist?"

"I believe he is," answered Buel, stiffly.

"Oh, that will be too jolly for anything. I would so like to meet him. I am sure he must be a most charming man. His books show such insight into human nature, such sympathy and noble purpose. There could be nothing petty or mean about such a man."

"I—I—suppose not."

"Why, of course there couldn't. You have read his books, have you not?"

"All of them except his latest."

"Well, I'll lend you that, as you have been so kind as to offer me the reading of this one."

"Thank you. After you have read it yourself."

"And when you have become acquainted with Mr. Hodden, I want you to introduce him to me."

"With pleasure. And—and when I do so, who shall I tell him the young lady is?"

The audacious girl laughed lightly, and, stepping back, made him a saucy bow.

"You will introduce me as Miss Caroline Jessop, of New York. Be sure that you say 'New York,' for that will account to Mr. Hodden for any eccentricities of conduct or conversation he may be good enough to notice. I suppose you think American girls are very forward? All Englishmen do."

"On the contrary, I have always understood that they are very charming."

"Indeed? And so you are going over to see?"

Buel laughed. All the depression he felt a short time before had vanished.

"I had no such intention when I began the voyage, but even if I should quit the steamer at Queenstown, I could bear personal testimony to the truth of the statement."

"Oh, Mr. Buel, that is very nicely put. I don't think you can improve on it, so I shall run down and dress for dinner. There is the first gong. Thanks for the book."

The young man said to himself, "Buel, my boy, you're getting on;" and he smiled as he leaned over the bulwark and looked at the rushing water. He sobered instantly as he remembered that he would have to go to his state-room and perhaps meet Hodden. It is an awkward thing to quarrel with your room-mate at the beginning of a long voyage. He hoped Hodden had taken his departure to the saloon, and he lingered until the second gong rang. Entering the stateroom, he found Hodden still there. Buel gave him no greeting. The other cleared his throat several times and then said—

"I have not the pleasure of knowing your name."

"My name is Buel."

"Well, Mr. Buel, I am sorry that I spoke to you in the manner I did, and I hope you will allow me to apologise for doing so. Various little matters had combined to irritate me, and—Of course, that is no excuse. But—"

"Don't say anything more. I unreservedly retract what I was heated enough to say, and so we may consider the episode ended. I may add that if the purser has a vacant berth anywhere, I shall be very glad to take it, if the occupants of the room make no objection."

"You are very kind," said Hodden, but he did not make any show of

33

declining the offer.

"Very well, then, let us settle the matter while we are at it." And Buel pressed the electric button.

The steward looked in, saying,—

"Dinner is ready, gentlemen."

"Yes, I know. Just ask the purser if he can step here for a moment."

The purser came promptly, and if he was disturbed at being called at such a moment he did not show it. Pursers are very diplomatic persons.

"Have you a vacant berth anywhere, purser?"

An expression faintly suggestive of annoyance passed over the purser's serene brow. He thought the matter had been settled. "We have several berths vacant, but they are each in rooms that already contain three persons."

"One of those will do for me; that is, if the occupants have no objection."

"It will be rather crowded, sir."

"That doesn't matter, if the others are willing."

"Very good, sir. I will see to it immediately after dinner."

The purser was as good as his word, and introduced Buel and his portmanteau to a room that contained three wild American collegians who had been doing Europe "on the cheap" and on foot. They received the new-comer with a hilariousness that disconcerted him.

"Hello, purser!" cried one, "this is an Englishman. You didn't tell us you were going to run in an Englishman on us."

"Never, mind, we'll convert him on the way over."

"I say, purser, if you sling a hammock from the ceiling and put up a cot on the floor you can put two more men in here. Why didn't you think of that?"

"It's not too late yet. Why did you suggest it?"

"Gentlemen," said Buel, "I have no desire to intrude, if it is against your wish."

"Oh, that's all right. Never mind them. They have to talk or die. The truth is, we were lonesome without a fourth man."

"What's his name, purser?"

"My name is Buel."

One of them shouted out the inquiry, "What's the matter with Buel?" and all answered in concert with a yell that made the steamer ring, "He's all right."

"You'll have to sing 'Hail Columbia' night and morning if you stay in this cabin."

"Very good," said Buel, entering into the spirit of the occasion. "Singing is not my strong point, and after you hear me at it once, you will be glad to pay a heavy premium to have it stopped."

"Say, Buel, can you play poker?"

"No, but I can learn."

"That's business. America's just yearning for men who can learn. We have had so many Englishmen who know it all, that we'll welcome a change. But poker's an expensive game to acquire."

"Don't be bluffed, Mr. Buel. Not one of the crowd has enough money left to buy the drinks all round. We would never have got home if we hadn't return tickets."

"Say, boys, let's lock the purser out, and make Buel an American citizen before he can call for help. You solemnly swear that you hereby and hereon renounce all emperors, kings, princes, and potentates, and more especially— how does the rest of it go!"

"He must give up his titles, honours, knighthoods, and things of that sort."

"Say, Buel, you're not a lord or a duke by any chance? Because, if you are, we'll call back the purser and have you put out yet."

"No, I haven't even the title esquire, which, I understand, all American citizens possess."

"Oh, you'll do. Now, I propose that Mr. Buel take his choice of the four bunks, and that we raffle for the rest."

When Buel reached the deck out of this pandemonium, he looked around for another citizen of the United States, but she was not there. He wondered if she were reading his book, and how she liked it.

Chapter IV

Next morning Mr. Buel again searched the deck for the fair American, and this time he found her reading his book, seated very comfortably in her deck chair. The fact that she was so engaged put out of Buel's mind the greeting he had carefully prepared beforehand, and he stood there awkwardly, not knowing what to say. He inwardly cursed his unreadiness, and felt, to his further embarrassment, that his colour was rising. He was not put more at his ease when Miss Jessop looked up at him coldly, with a distinct frown on her pretty face.

"Mr. Buel, I believe?" she said pertly.

"I—I think so," he stammered.

She went on with her reading, ignoring him, and he stood there not knowing how to get away. When he pulled himself together, after a few moments' silence, and was about to depart, wondering at the caprice of womankind, she looked up again, and said icily—

"Why don't you ask me to walk with you? Do you think you have no duties, merely because you are on shipboard?"

"It isn't a duty, it is a pleasure, if you will come with me. I was afraid I had offended you in some way."

"You have. That is why I want to walk with you. I wish to give you a piece of my mind, and it won't be pleasant to listen to, I can assure you. So there must be no listener but yourself."

"Is it so serious as that?"

"Quite. Assist me, please. Why do you have to be asked to do such a thing? I don't suppose there is another man on the ship who would see a lady struggling with her rugs, and never put out his hand."

Before the astonished young man could offer assistance the girl sprang to her feet and stood beside him. Although she tried to retain her severe look of displeasure, there was a merry twinkle in the corner of her eye, as if she enjoyed shocking him.

"I fear I am very unready."

"You are."

"Will you take my arm as we walk?"

"Certainly not," she answered, putting the tips of her fingers into the shallow pockets of her pilot jacket. "Don't you know the United States are long since independent of England?"

"I had forgotten for the moment. My knowledge of history is rather limited, even when I try to remember. Still, independence and all, the two countries may be friends, may they not?"

"I doubt it. It seems to be natural that an American should hate an Englishman."

"Dear me, is it so bad as that? Why, may I ask? Is it on account of the little trouble in 1770, or whenever it was?"

"1776, when we conquered you."

"Were we conquered? That is another historical fact which has been concealed from me. I am afraid England doesn't quite realise her unfortunate position. She has a good deal of go about her for a conquered nation. But I thought the conquering, which we all admit, was of much more recent date, when the pretty American girls began to come over. Then Englishmen at once capitulated."

"Yes," she cried scornfully. "And I don't know which to despise most, the American girls who marry Englishmen, or the Englishmen they marry. They are married for their money."

"Who? The Englishmen?"

The girl stamped her foot on the deck as they turned around.

"You know very well what I mean. An Englishman thinks of nothing but money."

"Really? I wonder where you got all your cut-and-dried notions about Englishmen? You seem to have a great capacity for contempt. I don't think it is good. My experience is rather limited, of course, but, as far as it goes, I find good and bad in all nations. There are Englishmen whom I find it impossible to like, and there are Americans whom I find I admire in spite of myself. There are also, doubtless, good Englishmen and bad Americans, if we only knew where to find them. You cannot sum up a nation and condemn it in a phrase, you know."

"Can't you? Well, literary Englishmen have tried to do so in the case of America. No English writer has ever dealt even fairly with the United States."

"Don't you think the States are a little too sensitive about the matter?"

"Sensitive? Bless you, we don't mind it a bit."

"Then where's the harm? Besides, America has its revenge in you. Your scathing contempt more than balances the account."

"I only wish I could write. Then I would let you know what I think of you."

"Oh, don't publish a book about us. I wouldn't like to see war between the two countries."

Miss Jessop laughed merrily for so belligerent a person.

"War?" she cried. "I hope yet to see an American army camped in London."

"If that is your desire, you can see it any day in summer. You will find them tenting out at the Métropole and all the expensive hotels. I bivouacked with an invader there some weeks ago, and he was enduring the rigours of camp life with great fortitude, mitigating his trials with unlimited champagne."

"Why, Mr. Buel," cried the girl admiringly, "you're beginning to talk just like an American yourself."

39

"Oh, now, you are trying to make me conceited."

Miss Jessop sighed, and shook her head.

"I had nearly forgotten," she said, "that I despised you. I remember now why I began to walk with you. It was not to talk frivolously, but to show you the depth of my contempt! Since yesterday you have gone down in my estimation from 190 to 56."

"Fahrenheit?"

"No, that was a Wall Street quotation. Your stock has 'slumped,' as we say on the Street."

"Now you are talking Latin, or worse, for I can understand a little Latin."

"'Slumped' sounds slangy, doesn't it? It isn't a pretty word, but it is expressive. It means going down with a run, or rather, all in a heap."

"What have I done?"

"Nothing you can say will undo it, so there is no use in speaking any more about it. Second thoughts are best. My second thought is to say no more."

"I must know my crime. Give me a chance to, at least, reach par again, even if I can't hope to attain the 90 above."

"I thought an Englishman had some grit. I thought he did not allow any one to walk over him. I thought he stood by his guns when he knew he was in the right. I thought he was a manly man, and a fighter against injustice!"

"Dear me! Judging by your conversation of a few minutes ago, one would imagine that you attributed exactly the opposite qualities to him."

"I say I thought all this—yesterday. I don't think so to-day."

"Oh, I see! And all on account of me?"

"All on account of you."

"Once more, what have I done?"

"What have you done? You have allowed that detestably selfish specimen of your race, Hodden, to evict you from your room."

The young man stopped abruptly in his walk, and looked at the girl with astonishment. She, her hands still coquettishly thrust in her jacket-pockets, returned his gaze with unruffled serenity.

"What do you know about it?" he demanded at last.

"Everything. From the time you meekly told the steward to take out your valise until the time you meekly apologised to Hodden for having told him the truth, and then meekly followed the purser to a room containing three others."

"But Hodden meekly, as you express it, apologised first. I suppose you know that too, otherwise I would not have mentioned it."

"Certainly he did. That was because he found his overbearing tactics did not work. He apologised merely to get rid of you, and did. That's what put me out of patience with you. To think you couldn't see through his scheme!"

"Oh! I thought it was the lack of manly qualities you despised in me. Now you are accusing me of not being crafty."

"How severely you say that! You quite frighten me! You will be making me apologise by-and-by, and I don't want to do that."

Buel laughed, and resumed his walk.

"It's all right," he said; "Hodden's loss is my gain. I've got in with a jolly lot, who took the trouble last night to teach me the great American game at cards—and counters."

Miss Jessop sighed.

"Having escaped with my life," she said, "I think I shall not run any more risks, but shall continue with your book. I had no idea you could look so fierce. I have scarcely gotten over it yet. Besides, I am very much interested in that book of yours."

"Why do you say so persistently 'that book of mine'?"

"Isn't it yours? You bought it, didn't you? Then it was written by your relative, you know."

"I said my namesake."

"So you did. And now I'm going to ask you an impudent question. You will not look wicked again, will you?"

"I won't promise. That depends entirely on the question."

"It is easily answered."

"I'm waiting."

"What is your Christian name, Mr. Buel?"

"My Christian name?" he repeated, uncomfortably.

"Yes, what is it?"

"Why do you wish to know?"

"A woman's reason—because."

They walked the length of the deck in silence.

"Come, now," she said, "confess. What is it?"

"John."

Miss Jessop laughed heartily, but quietly.

"You think John commonplace, I suppose?"

"Oh, it suits you, Mr. Buel. Goodbye."

As the young woman found her place in the book, she mused, "How blind men are, after all—with his name in full on the passage list." Then she said to herself, with a sigh, "I do wish I had bought this book instead of Hodden's."

Chapter V

At first Mr. Hodden held somewhat aloof from his fellow-passengers; but, finding perhaps that there was no general desire to intrude upon him, he condescended to become genial to a select few. He walked the deck alone, picturesquely attired. He was a man who paid considerable attention to his personal appearance. As day followed day, Mr. Hodden unbent so far as to talk frequently with Miss Jessop on what might almost be called equal terms. The somewhat startling opinions and unexpected remarks of the American girl appeared to interest him, and doubtless tended to confirm his previous unfavourable impressions of the inhabitants of the Western world. Mr. Buel was usually present during these conferences, and his conduct under the circumstances was not admirable. He was silent and moody, and almost gruff on some occasions. Perhaps Hodden's persistent ignoring of him, and the elder man's air of conscious superiority, irritated Buel; but if he had had the advantage of mixing much in the society of his native land he would have become accustomed to that. People thrive on the condescension of the great; they like it, and boast about it. Yet Buel did not seem to be pleased. But the most astounding thing was that the young man should actually have taken it upon himself to lecture Miss Jessop once, when they were alone, for some remarks she had made to Hodden as she sat in her deck-chair, with Hodden loquacious on her right and Buel taciturn on her left. What right had Buel to find fault with a free and independent citizen of another country? Evidently none. It might have been expected that Miss Jessop, rising to the occasion, would have taught the young man his place, and would perhaps have made some scathing remark about the tendency of Englishmen to interfere in matters that did not concern them. But she did nothing of the kind. She looked down demurely on the deck, with the faint flicker of a smile hovering about her pretty lips, and now and then flashed a quick glance at the serious face of the young man. The attitude was very sweet and appealing, but it was not what we have a right to expect from one whose ruler is her servant towards one whose ruler is his sovereign. In fact, the conduct of those two young people at this time was utterly inexplicable.

"Why did you pretend to Hodden that you had never heard of him, and make him state that he was a writer of books?" Buel had said.

"I did it for his own good. Do you want me to minister to his insufferable vanity? Hasn't he egotism enough already? I saw in a paper a while ago that his most popular book had sold to the extent of over 100,000 copies in America. I suppose that is something wonderful; but what does it amount to after all? It leaves over fifty millions of people who doubtless have never heard of him. For the time being I merely went with the majority. We always do that in the States."

"Then I suppose you will not tell him you bought his latest book in London, and so you will not have the privilege of bringing it up on deck and reading it?"

"No. The pleasure of reading that book must be postponed until I reach New York. But my punishment does not end there. Would you believe that authors are so vain that they actually carry with them the books they have written?"

"You astonish me."

"I thought I should. And added to that, would you credit the statement that they offer to lend their works to inoffensive people who may not be interested in them and who have not the courage to refuse? Why do you look so confused, Mr. Buel? I am speaking of Mr. Hodden. He kindly offered me his books to read on the way over. He has a prettily bound set with him. He gave me the first to-day, which I read ever so many years ago."

"I thought you liked his books?"

"For the first time, yes; but I don't care to read them twice."

The conversation was here interrupted by Mr. Hodden himself, who sank into the vacant chair beside Miss Jessop. Buel made as though he would rise and leave them together, but with an almost imperceptible motion of the hand nearest him, Miss Jessop indicated her wish that he should remain, and then thanked him with a rapid glance for understanding. The young man felt a glow of satisfaction at this, and gazed at the blue sea with less discontent than usual in his eyes.

"I have brought you," said the novelist, "another volume."

"Oh, thank you," cried Miss Duplicity, with unnecessary emphasis on the middle word.

"It has been considered," continued Mr. Hodden, "by those whose opinions are thought highly of in London, to be perhaps my most successful work. It is, of course, not for me to pass judgment on such an estimate; but for my own part I prefer the story I gave you this morning. An author's choice is rarely that of the public."

"And was this book published in America?"

"I can hardly say it was published. They did me the honour to pirate it in your most charming country. Some friend—or perhaps I should say enemy—sent me a copy. It was a most atrocious production, in a paper cover, filled with mistakes, and adorned with the kind of spelling, which is, alas! prevalent there."

"I believe," said Buel, speaking for the first time, but with his eyes still on the sea, "there is good English authority for much that we term American spelling."

"English authority, indeed!" cried Miss Jessop; "as if we needed English authority for anything. If we can't spell better than your great English authority, Chaucer—well!" Language seemed to fail the young woman.

"Have you read Chaucer?" asked Mr. Hodden, in surprise.

"Certainly not; but I have looked at his poems, and they always remind me of one of those dialect stories in the magazines."

Miss Jessop turned over the pages of the book which had been given her, and as she did so a name caught her attention. She remembered a problem that had troubled her when she read the book before. She cried impulsively—

"Oh, Mr. Hodden, there is a question I want to ask you about this book. Was—" Here she checked herself in some confusion.

Buel, who seemed to realise the situation, smiled grimly.

"The way of the transgressor is hard," he whispered in a tone too low for Hodden to hear.

"Isn't it?" cordially agreed the unblushing young woman.

"What did you wish to ask me?" inquired the novelist.

"Was it the American spelling or the American piracy that made you dislike the United States?"

Mr. Hodden raised his eyebrows.

"Oh, I do not dislike the United States. I have many friends there, and see much to admire in the country. But there are some things that do not commend themselves to me, and those I ventured to touch upon lightly on one or two occasions, much to the displeasure of a section of the inhabitants—a small section, I hope."

"Don't you think," ventured Buel, "that a writer should rather touch on what pleases him than on what displeases him, in writing of a foreign country?"

"Possibly. Nations are like individuals; they prefer flattery to honest criticism."

"But a writer should remember that there is no law of libel to protect a nation."

To this remark Mr. Hodden did not reply.

"And what did you object to most, Mr. Hodden?" asked the girl.

"That is a hard question to answer. I think, however, that one of the most deplorable features of American life is the unbridled license of the Press. The reporters make existence a burden; they print the most unjustifiable things in their so-called interviews, and a man has no redress. There is no escaping them. If a man is at all well known, they attack him before he has a chance to leave the ship. If you refuse to say anything, they will write a purely imaginative interview. The last time I visited America, five of them came out to interview me—they came out in the Custom House steamer, I believe."

"Why, I should feel flattered if they took all that trouble over me, Mr. Hodden."

"All I ask of them is to leave me alone."

"I'll protect you, Mr. Hodden. When they come, you stand near me, and I'll beat them off with my sunshade. I know two newspaper men—real nice young men they are too—and they always do what I tell them."

"I can quite believe it, Miss Jessop."

"Well, then, have no fear while I'm on board."

Mr. Hodden shook his head. He knew how it would be, he said.

"Let us leave the reporters. What else do you object to? I want to learn, and so reform my country when I get back."

"The mad passion of the people after wealth, and the unscrupulousness of their methods of obtaining it, seem to me unpleasant phases of life over there."

"So they are. And what you say makes me sigh for dear old London. How honest they are, and how little they care for money there! They don't put up the price 50 per cent. merely because a girl has an American accent. Oh no. They think she likes to buy at New York prices. And they are so honourable down in the city that nobody ever gets cheated. Why, you could put a purse up on a pole in London, just as—as—was it Henry the Eighth—?"

"Alfred, I think!" suggested Buel.

"Thanks! As Alfred the Great used to do."

Mr. Hodden looked askance at the young woman.

"Remember," he said, "that you asked me for my opinion. If what I have

47

said is offensive to one who is wealthy, as doubtless you are, Miss Jessop, I most sincerely—"

"Me? Well, I never know whether I'm wealthy or not. I expect that before long I shall have to take to typewriting. Perhaps, in that case, you will give me some of your novels to do, Mr. Hodden. You see, my father is on the Street."

"Dear me!" said Mr. Hodden, "I am sorry to hear that."

"Why? They are not all rogues on Wall Street, in spite of what the papers say. Remember your own opinion of the papers. They are not to be trusted when they speak of Wall Street men. When my father got very rich once I made him give me 100,000 dollars, so that, should things go wrong—they generally go wrong for somebody on Wall Street—we would have something to live on, but, unfortunately, he always borrows it again. Some day, I'm afraid, it will go, and then will come the typewriter. That's why I took my aunt with me and saw Europe before it was too late. I gave him a power of attorney before I left, so I've had an anxious time on the Continent. My money was all right when we left Liverpool, but goodness knows where it will be when I reach New York."

"How very interesting. I never heard of a situation just like it before."

Chapter VI

The big vessel lay at rest in New York Bay waiting for the boat of the health officers and the steamer with the customs men on board. The passengers were in a state of excitement at the thought of being so near home. The captain, who was now in excellent humour, walked the deck and chatted affably with every one. A successful voyage had been completed. Miss Jessop feared the coming of the customs boat as much as Hodden feared the reporters. If anything, he was the more resigned of the two. What American woman ever lands on her native shore without trembling before the revenue laws of her country? Kenan Buel, his arms resting on the bulwarks, gazed absently at the green hills he was seeing for the first time, but his thoughts were not upon them. The young man was in a quandary. Should he venture, or should he not, that was the question. Admitting, for the sake of argument, that she cared for him, what had he to offer? Merely himself, and the debt still unpaid on his first book. The situation was the more embarrassing because of a remark she had made about Englishmen marrying for money. He had resented that on general principles when he heard it, but now it had a personal application that seemed to confront him whichever way he turned. Besides, wasn't it all rather sudden, from an insular point of view? Of course they did things with great rapidity in America, so perhaps she would not object to the suddenness. He had no one to consult, and he felt the lack of advice. He did not want to make a mistake, neither did he wish to be laughed at. Still, the laughing would not matter if everything turned out right. Anyhow, Miss Jessop's laugh was very kindly. He remembered that if he were in any other difficulty he would turn quite naturally to her for advice, although he had known her so short a time, and he regretted that in his present predicament he was debarred from putting the case before her. And yet, why not? He might put the supposititious case of a friend, and ask what the friend ought to do. He dismissed this a moment later. It was too much like what people did in a novel, and besides, he could not carry it through. She would see through the sham at once. At this point he realised that he was just where he began.

"Dear me, Mr. Buel, how serious you look. I am afraid you don't approve of America. Are you sorry the voyage is ended?"

"Yes, I am," answered Buel, earnestly. "I feel as if I had to begin life over again."

"And are you afraid?"

"A little."

"I am disappointed in you. I thought you were not afraid of anything."

"You were disappointed in me the first day, you remember."

"So I was. I had forgotten."

"Will your father come on board to meet you?"

"It depends altogether on the state of the market. If things are dull, he will very likely meet me out here. If the Street is brisk, I won't see him till he arrives home to-night. If medium, he will be on the wharf when we get in."

"And when you meet him I suppose you will know whether you are rich or poor?"

"Oh, certainly. It will be the second thing I ask him."

"When you know, I want you to tell me. Will you?"

"Are you interested in knowing?"

"Very much so."

"Then I hope I shall be rich."

Mr. Buel did not answer. He stared gloomily down at the water lapping the iron side of the motionless steamer. The frown on his brow was deep. Miss Jessop looked at him for a moment out of the corners of her eyes. Then she said, impulsively—

"I know that was mean. I apologise. I told you I did not like to apologise, so you may know how sorry I am. And, now that I have begun, I also apologise for all the flippant things I have said during the voyage, and for my frightful mendacity to poor Mr. Hodden, who sits there so patiently and picturesquely waiting for the terrible reporters. Won't you forgive me?"

Buel was not a ready man, and he hesitated just the smallest fraction of a second too long.

"I won't ask you twice, you know," said Miss Jessop, drawing herself up with dignity.

"Don't—don't go!" cried the young man, with sudden energy, catching her hand. "I'm an unmannerly boor. But I'll risk everything and tell you the trouble. I don't care a—I don't care whether you are rich or poor. I—"

Miss Jessop drew away her hand.

"Oh, there's the boat, Mr. Buel, and there's my papa on the upper deck."

She waved her handkerchief in the air in answer to one that was fluttering on the little steamer. Buel saw the boat cutting a rapid semicircle in the bay as she rounded to, leaving in her wake a long, curving track of foam. She looked ridiculously small compared with the great ship she was approaching, and her deck seemed crowded.

"And there are the reporters!" she cried; "ever so many of them. I guess Mr. Hodden will be sorry he did not accept my offer of protection. I know that young man who is waving his hand. He was on the Herald when I left; but no one can say what paper he's writing for now."

As the boat came nearer a voice shouted—

"All well, Carrie?"

The girl nodded. Her eyes and her heart were too full for speech. Buel frowned at the approaching boat, and cursed its inopportune arrival. He was astonished to hear some one shout from her deck—

"Hello, Buel!"

"Why, there's some one who knows you!" said the girl, looking at him.

Buel saw a man wave his hand, and automatically he waved in return. After a moment he realised that it was Brant the publisher. The customs officers were first on board, for it is ordained by the law that no foot is to tread the deck before theirs; but the reporters made a good second.

Miss Jessop rushed to the gangway, leaving Buel alone. "Hello, Cap!" cried one of the young men of the Press, with that lack of respect for the dignitaries of this earth which is characteristic of them. "Had a good voyage?"

"Splendid," answered the captain, with a smile.

"Where's your celebrity? Trot him out."

"I believe Mr. Hodden is aft somewhere."

"Oh,—Hodden!" cried the young man, profanely; "he's a chestnut. Where's Kenan Buel?"

The reporter did not wait for a reply, for he saw by the crowd around a very flushed young man that the victim had been found and cornered.

"Really, gentlemen," said the embarrassed Englishman, "you have made a mistake. It is Mr. Hodden you want to see. I will take you to him."

"Hodden's played," said one of the young men in an explanatory way, although Buel did not understand the meaning of the phrase. "He's petered out;" which addition did not make it any plainer. "You're the man for our money every time."

"Break away there, break away!" cried the belated Brant, forcing his way through them and taking Buel by the hand. "There's no rush, you know, boys. Just let me have a minute's talk with Mr. Buel. It will be all right. I have just set up the champagne down in the saloon. It's my treat, you know. There's tables down there, and we can do things comfortably. I'll guarantee to produce Buel inside of five minutes."

Brant linked arms with the young man, and they walked together down the deck.

"Do you know what this means, Buel?" he said, waving his hand towards

52

the retreating newspaper men.

"I suppose it means that you have got them to interview me for business purposes. I can think of no other reason."

"I've had nothing to do with it. That shows just how little you know about the American Press. Why, all the money I've got wouldn't bring those men out here to interview anybody who wasn't worth interviewing. It means fame; it means wealth; it means that you have turned the corner; it means you have the world before you; it means everything. Those young men are not reporters to you; they are the heralds of fame, my boy. A few of them may get there themselves some day, but it means that you have got there now. Do you realise that?"

"Hardly. I suppose, then, the book has been a success?"

"A success? It's been a cyclone. I've been fighting pirates ever since it came out. You see, I took the precaution to write some things in the book myself."

Buel looked alarmed.

"And then I copyrighted the whole thing, and they can't tell which is mine and which is yours until they get a hold of the English edition. That's why I did not wait for your corrections."

"We are collaborators, then?"

"You bet. I suppose some of the English copies are on this steamer? I'm going to try to have them seized by the customs if I can. I think I'll make a charge of indecency against the book."

"Good heavens!" cried Buel, aghast. "There is nothing of that in it."

"I am afraid not," said Brant, regretfully. "But it will give us a week more at least before it is decided. Anyhow, I'm ready for the pirates, even if they do come out. I've printed a cheap paper edition, 100,000 copies, and they are now in the hands of all the news companies—sealed up, of course—from New York to San Francisco. The moment a pirate shows his head, I'll telegraph the word 'rip' all over the United States, and they will rip open the packages and flood the market with authorised cheap editions before the pirates leave New York. Oh, L. F. Brant was not born the day before yesterday."

"I see he wasn't," said Buel, smiling.

"Now you come down and be introduced to the newspaper boys. You'll find them jolly nice fellows."

"In a moment. You go down and open the champagne. I'll follow you. I—I want to say a few words to a friend on board."

"No tricks now, Buel. You're not going to try to dodge them?"

"I'm a man of my word, Mr. Brant. Don't be afraid."

"And now," said the other, putting his hands on the young man's shoulders, "you'll be kind to them. Don't put on too much side, you know. You'll forgive me for mentioning this, but sometimes your countrymen do the high and mighty act a little too much. It doesn't pay."

"I'll do my best. But I haven't the slightest idea what to say. In fact, I've nothing to say."

"Oh, that's all right. Don't you worry. Just have a talk with them, that's all they want. You'll be paralysed when the interviews come out to-morrow; but you'll get over that."

"You're sure the book is a success in its own merits, and not through any newspaper puffing or that sort of thing, you know?"

"Why, certainly. Of course our firm pushed it. We're not the people to go to sleep over a thing. It might not have done quite so well with any other house; but I told you in London I thought it was bound to go. The pushing was quite legitimate."

"In that case I shall be down to see the reporters in a very few minutes." Although Buel kept up his end of the conversation with Brant, his mind was not on it. Miss Jessop and her father were walking near them; snatches of their talk came to him, and his attention wandered in spite of himself. The

Wall Street man seemed to be trying to reassure his daughter, and impart to her some of the enthusiasm he himself felt. He patted her affectionately on the shoulder now and then, and she walked with springy step very close to his side.

"It's all right, Carrie," he said, "and as safe as the bank."

"Which bank, papa?"

Mr. Jessop laughed.

"The Chemical Bank, if you like; or, as you are just over from the other side, perhaps I should say the Bank of England."

"And did you take out every cent?"

"Yes; and I wished there was double the amount to take. It's a sure thing. There's no speculation about it. There isn't a bushel of wheat in the country that isn't in the combination. It would have been sinful not to have put every cent I could scrape together into it. Why, Carrie, I'll give you a quarter of a million when the deal comes off."

Carrie shook her head.

"I've been afraid of wheat corners," she said, "ever since I was a baby. Still, I've no right to say anything. It's all your money, anyway, and I've just been playing that it was mine. But I do wish you had left a hundred dollars for a typewriter."

Mr. Jessop laughed again in a very hearty and confident way.

"Don't you fret about that, Carrie. I've got four type machines down at the office. I'll let you have your choice before the crash comes. Now I'll go down and see those customs men. There won't be any trouble. I know them."

It was when Mr. Jessop departed that Buel suddenly became anxious to get rid of Brant. When he had succeeded, he walked over to where the girl leaned on the bulwark.

"Well?" he said, taking his place beside her.

55

"Well!" she answered, without looking up at him.

"Which is it? Rich or poor?"

"Rich, I should say, by the way the reporters flocked about you. That means, I suppose, that your book has been a great success, and that you are going to make your fortune out of it. Let me congratulate you, Mr. Buel."

"Wait a minute. I don't know yet whether I am to be congratulated or not; that will depend on you. Of course you know I was not speaking of myself when I asked the question."

"Oh, you meant me, did you? Well, I can't tell for some time to come, but I have my fears. I hear the click of the typewriter in the near future."

"Caroline, I am very serious about this. I don't believe you think, or could think, that I care much about riches. I have been on too intimate terms with poverty to be afraid of it. Of course my present apparent success has given me courage, and I intend to use that courage while it lasts. I have been rather afraid of your ridicule, but I think, whether you were rich or poor, or whether my book was a success or a failure, I would have risked it, and told you I loved you."

The girl did not look up at him, and did not answer for a moment. Then she said, in a voice that he had to bend very close to hear—

"I—I would have been sorry all my life if you hadn't—risked it."

A WOMAN INTERVENES

TO

MY FRIEND

HORACE HART

CHAPTER I.

The managing editor of the New York Argus sat at his desk with a deep frown on his face, looking out from under his shaggy eyebrows at the young man who had just thrown a huge fur overcoat on the back of one chair, while he sat down himself on another.

'I got your telegram,' began the editor. 'Am I to understand from it that you have failed?'

'Yes, sir,' answered the young man, without the slightest hesitation.

'Completely?'

'Utterly.'

'Didn't you even get a synopsis of the documents?'

'Not a hanged synop.'

The editor's frown grew deeper. The ends of his fingers drummed nervously on the desk.

'You take failure rather jauntily, it strikes me,' he said at last.

'What's the use of taking it any other way? I have the consciousness of knowing that I did my best.'

'Um, yes. It's a great consolation, no doubt, but it doesn't count in the newspaper business. What did you do?'

'I received your telegram at Montreal, and at once left for Burnt Pine—most outlandish spot on earth. I found that Kenyon and Wentworth were staying at the only hotel in the place. Tried to worm out of them what their reports were to be. They were very polite, but I didn't succeed. Then I tried to bribe them, and they ordered me out of the room.'

'Perhaps you didn't offer them enough.'

'I offered double what the London Syndicate was to pay them for making the report, taking their own word for the amount. I couldn't offer more, because at that point they closed the discussion by ordering me out of the room. I tried to get the papers that night, on the quiet, out of Wentworth's valise, but was unfortunately interrupted. The young men were suspicious, and next morning they left for Ottawa to post the reports, as I gathered afterwards, to England. I succeeded in getting hold of the reports, but I couldn't hang on. There are too many police in Ottawa to suit me.'

'Do you mean to tell me,' said the editor, 'that you actually had the reports in your hands, and that they were taken from you?'

'Certainly I had; and as to their being taken from me, it was either that or gaol. They don't mince matters in Canada as they do in the United States, you know.'

'But I should think a man of your shrewdness would have been able to get at least a synopsis of the reports before letting them out of his possession.'

'My dear sir,' said the reporter, rather angry, 'the whole thing covered I forget how many pages of foolscap paper, and was the most mixed-up matter I ever saw in my life. I tried—I sat in my room at the hotel, and did my best to master the details. It was full of technicalities, and I couldn't make it out. It required a mining expert to get the hang of their phrases and figures, so I thought the best thing to do was to telegraph it all straight through to New York. I knew it would cost a lot of money, but I knew, also, you didn't mind that; and I thought, perhaps, somebody here could make sense out of what baffled me; besides, I wanted to get the documents out of my possession just as quickly as possible.'

'Hem!' said the editor. 'You took no notes whatever?'

'No, I did not. I had no time. I knew the moment they missed the documents they would have the detectives on my track. As it was, I was arrested when I entered the telegraph-office.'

'Well, it seems to me,' said the managing editor, 'if I had once had the papers in my hand, I should not have let them go until I had got the gist of

64

what was in them.'

'Oh, it's all very well for you to say so,' replied the reporter, with the free and easy manner in which an American newspaper man talks to his employer; 'but I can tell you, with a Canadian gaol facing a man, it is hard to decide what is best to do. I couldn't get out of the town for three hours, and before the end of that time they would have had my description in the hands of every policeman in the place. They knew well enough who took the papers, so my only hope lay in getting the thing telegraphed through; and if that had been accomplished, everything would have been all right. I would have gone to gaol with pleasure if I had got the particulars through to New York.'

'Well, what are we to do now?' asked the editor.

'I'm sure I don't know. The two men will be in New York very shortly. They sail, I understand, on the Caloric, which leaves in a week. If you think you have a reporter who can get the particulars out of these men, I should be very pleased to see you set him on. I tell you it isn't so easy to discover what an Englishman doesn't want you to know.'

'Well,' said the editor, 'perhaps that's true. I will think about it. Of course you did your best, and I appreciate your efforts; but I am sorry you failed.'

'You are not half so sorry as I am,' said Rivers, as he picked up his big Canadian fur coat and took his leave.

The editor did think about it. He thought for fully two minutes. Then he dashed off a note on a sheet of paper, pulled down the little knob that rang the District Messenger alarm, and when the uniformed boy appeared, gave him the note, saying:

'Deliver this as quickly as you can.'

The boy disappeared, and the result of his trip was soon apparent in the arrival of a very natty young woman in the editorial rooms. She was dressed in a neatly-fitting tailor-made costume, and was a very pretty girl, who looked about nineteen, but was, in reality, somewhat older. She had large, appealing blue eyes, with a tender, trustful expression in them, which made the ordinary man say: 'What a sweet, innocent look that girl has!' yet, what the young woman didn't know about New York was not worth knowing. She boasted that she could get State secrets from dignified members of the Cabinet, and an ordinary Senator or Congressman she looked upon as her lawful prey. That which had been told her in the strictest confidence had often become the sensation of the next day in the paper she represented. She wrote over a nom de guerre, and had tried her hand at nearly everything. She had answered advertisements, exposed rogues and swindlers, and had gone to a hotel as chambermaid, in order to write her experiences. She had been arrested and locked up, so that she might write a three-column account, for the Sunday edition of the Argus, of 'How Women are Treated at Police Headquarters.' The editor looked upon her as one of the most valuable members of his staff, and she was paid accordingly.

She came into the room with the self-possessed air of the owner of the building, took a seat, after nodding to the editor, and said, 'Well?'

'Look here, Jennie,' began that austere individual, 'do you wish to take a trip to Europe?'

'That depends,' said Jennie; 'this is not just the time of year that people go to Europe for pleasure, you know.'

'Well, this is not exactly a pleasure trip. The truth of the matter is, Rivers has been on a job and has bungled it fearfully, besides nearly getting himself arrested.'

The young woman's eyes twinkled. She liked anything with a spice of danger in it, and did not object to hear that she was expected to succeed where a mere masculine reporter had failed.

The editor continued:

'Two young men are going across to England on the Caloric. It sails in a week. I want you to take a ticket for Liverpool by that boat, and obtain from either of those two men the particulars—the full particulars—of reports they have made on some mining properties in Canada. Then you must land at Queenstown and cable a complete account to the Argus.'

'Mining isn't much in my line,' said Miss Jennie, with a frown on her pretty brow. 'What sort of mines were they dealing with—gold, silver, copper, or what?'

'They are certain mines on the Ottawa River.'

'That's rather indefinite.'

'I know it is. I can't give you much information about the matter. I don't know myself, to tell the truth, but I know it is vitally important that we should get a synopsis of what the reports of these young men are to be. A company, called the London Syndicate, has been formed in England. This syndicate is to acquire a large number of mines in Canada, if the accounts given by the present owners are anything like correct. Two men, Kenyon and Wentworth—the first a mining engineer, and the second an experienced accountant—have been sent from London to Canada, one to examine the mines, the other to examine the books of the various corporations. Whether the mines are bought or not will depend a good deal on the reports these two men have in their possession. The reports, when published, will make a big difference, one way or the other, on the Stock Exchange. I want to have the gist of them before the London Syndicate sees them. It will be a big thing for the Argus if it is the first in the field, and I am willing to spend a pile of hard cash to succeed. So, don't economize on your cable expenses.'

'Very well; have you a book on Canadian mines?'

'I don't know that we have; but there is a book here, "The Mining Resources of Canada;" will that be of any use?'

'I shall need something of that sort. I want to be a little familiar with the subject, you know.'

'Quite so,' said the editor; 'I will see what can be got in that line. You can read it before you start, and on the way over.'

'All right,' said Miss Jennie; 'and am I to take my pick of the two young men?'

'Certainly,' answered the editor. 'You will see them both, and can easily make up your mind which will the sooner fall a victim.'

'The Caloric sails in a week, does it?'

'Yes.'

'Then I shall need at least five hundred dollars to get new dresses with.'

'Good gracious!' cried the editor.

'There is no "good gracious" about it. I'm going to travel as a millionaire's daughter, and it isn't likely that one or two dresses will do me all the way over.'

'But you can't get new dresses made in a week,' said the editor.

'Can't I? Well, you just get me the five hundred dollars, and I'll see about the making.'

The editor jotted the amount down.

'You don't think four hundred dollars would do?' he said.

'No, I don't. And, say, am I to get a trip to Paris after this is over, or must I come directly back?'

'Oh, I guess we can throw in the trip to Paris,' said the editor.

'What did you say the names of the young men are?—or are they not young? Probably they are old fogies, if they are in the mining business.'

'No; they are young, they are shrewd, and they are English. So you see your work is cut out for you. Their names are George Wentworth and John Kenyon.'

'Oh, Wentworth is my man,' said the young woman breezily. 'John Kenyon! I know just what sort of a person he is—sombre and taciturn. Sounds too much like John Bunyan, or John Milton, or names of that sort.'

'Well, I wouldn't be too sure about it until you see them. Better not make up your mind about the matter.'

'When shall I call for the five hundred dollars?'

68

'Oh, that you needn't trouble about. The better way is to get your dresses made, and tell the people to send the bills to our office.'

'Very well,' said the young woman. 'I shall be ready. Don't be frightened at the bills when they come in. If they come up to a thousand dollars, remember I told you I would let you off for five hundred dollars.'

The editor looked at her for a moment, and seemed to reflect that perhaps it was better not to give a young lady unlimited credit in New York. So he said:

'Wait a bit; I'll write you out the order, and you can take it downstairs.'

Miss Jennie took the paper when it was offered to her, and disappeared. When she presented the order in the business office, the cashier raised his eyebrows as he noticed the amount, and, with a low whistle, said to himself:

'Five hundred dollars! I wonder what game Jennie Brewster's up to now.'

CHAPTER II.

The last bell had rung. Those who were going ashore had taken their departure. Crowds of human beings clustered on the pier-head, and at the large doorways of the warehouse which stood open on the steamer wharf. As the big ship slowly backed out there was a fluttering of handkerchiefs from the mass on the pier, and an answering flutter from those who crowded along the bulwarks of the steamer. The tug slowly pulled the prow of the vessel round, and at last the engines of the steamship began their pulsating throbs—throbs that would vibrate night and day until the steamer reached an older civilization. The crowd on the pier became more and more indistinct to those on board, and many of the passengers went below, for the air was bitterly cold, and the boat was forcing its way down the bay among huge blocks of ice.

Two, at least, of the passengers had taken little interest in the departure. They were leaving no friends behind them, and were both setting their faces toward friends at home.

'Let us go down,' said Wentworth to Kenyon, 'and see that we get seats together at table before all are taken.'

'Very good,' replied his companion, and they descended to the roomy saloon, where two long tables were already laid with an ostentatious display of silver, glassware, and cutlery, which made many, who looked on this wilderness of white linen with something like dismay, hope that the voyage would be smooth, although, as it was a winter passage, there was every chance it would not be. The purser and two of his assistants sat at one of the shorter tables with a plan before them, marking off the names of passengers who wished to be together, or who wanted some particular place at any of the tables. The smaller side-tables were still uncovered because the number of passengers at that season of the year was comparatively few. As the places were assigned, one of the helpers to the purser wrote the names of the passengers on small cards, and the other put the cards on the tables.

One young woman, in a beautifully-fitting travelling gown, which was evidently of the newest cut and design, stood a little apart from the general group which surrounded the purser and his assistants. She eagerly scanned every face, and listened attentively to the names given. Sometimes a shade of disappointment crossed her brow, as if she expected some particular person to possess some particular name which that particular person did not bear. At last her eyes sparkled.

'My name is Wentworth,' said the young man whose turn it was.

'Ah! any favourite place, Mr. Wentworth?' asked the purser blandly, as if he had known Wentworth all his life.

'No, we don't care where we sit; but my friend Mr. Kenyon and myself would like places together.'

'Very good; you had better come to my table,' replied the purser. 'Numbers 23 and 24—Mr. Kenyon and Mr. Wentworth.'

The steward took the cards that were given him, and placed them to correspond with the numbers the purser had named. Then the young woman moved gracefully along, as if she were interested in the names upon the table. She looked at Wentworth's name for a moment, and saw in the place next to his the name of Mr. Brown. She gave a quick, apprehensive glance around the saloon, and observed the two young men who had arranged for their seats at table now walking leisurely toward the companion-way. She took the card with the name of Mr. Brown upon it, and slipped upon the table another on which were written the words 'Miss Jennie Brewster.' Mr. Brown's card she placed on the spot from which she had taken her own.

'I hope Mr. Brown is not particular which place he occupies,' said Jennie to herself; 'but at any rate I shall see that I am early for dinner, and I'm sure Mr. Brown, whoever he is, will not be so ungallant as to insist on having this place if he knows his card was here.'

Subsequent events proved her surmise regarding Mr. Brown's indifference to be perfectly well founded. That young man searched for his card, found it, and sat down on the chair opposite the young woman, who already occupied her chair, and was, in fact, the first one at table. Seeing there would be no unseemly dispute about places, she began to plan in her own mind how she would first attract the attention of Mr. Wentworth. While thinking how best to approach her victim, Jennie heard his voice.

'Here you are, Kenyon; here are our places.'

'Which is mine?' said the voice of Kenyon.

'It doesn't matter,' answered Wentworth, and then a thrill of fear went through the gentle heart of Miss Jennie Brewster. She had not thought of the young man not caring which seat he occupied, and she dreaded the possibility of finding herself next to Kenyon rather than Wentworth. Her first estimate of the characters of the two men seemed to be correct. She always thought of Kenyon as Bunyan, and she felt certain that Wentworth would be the easier man of the two to influence. The next moment her fears were allayed, for Kenyon, giving a rapid glance at the handsome young woman, deliberately chose the seat farthest from her, and Wentworth, with 'I beg your pardon,' slipped in and sat down on the chair beside her.

'Now,' thought Jennie, with a sigh of relief, 'our positions are fixed for the meals of the voyage.' She had made her plans for beginning an acquaintance with the young man, but they were rendered unnecessary by the polite Mr. Wentworth handing her the bill of fare.

'Oh, thank you,' said the girl, in a low voice, which was so musical that Wentworth glanced at her a second time and saw how sweet and pretty and innocent she was.

'I'm in luck,' said the unfortunate young man to himself. Then he remarked aloud: 'We have not many ladies with us this voyage.'

'No,' replied Miss Brewster; 'I suppose nobody crosses at this time of the year unless compelled to.'

'I can answer for two passengers that such is the case.'

'Do you mean yourself as one?'

'Yes, myself and my friend.'

'How pleasant it must be,' said Miss Brewster, 'to travel with a friend! Then one is not lonely. I, unfortunately, am travelling alone.'

'I fancy,' said the gallant Wentworth, 'that if you are lonely while on board ship, it will be entirely your own fault.'

Miss Brewster laughed a silvery little laugh.

'I don't know about that,' she said. 'I am going to that Mecca of all Americans—Paris. My father is to meet me there, and we are then going on to the Riviera together.'

'Ah, that will be very pleasant,' said Wentworth. 'The Riviera at this season is certainly a place to be desired.'

'So I have heard,' she replied.

'Have you not been across before?'

'No, this is my first trip. I suppose you have crossed many times?'

'Oh no,' answered the Englishman; 'this is only my second voyage, my first having been the one that took me to America.'

'Ah, then you are not an American,' returned Miss Brewster, with apparent surprise.

She imagined that a man is generally flattered when a mistake of this kind is made. No matter how proud he may be of his country, he is pleased to learn that there is no provincialism about him which, as the Americans say, 'gives him away.'

'I think,' said Wentworth, 'as a general thing, I am not taken for anything but what I am—an Englishman.'

'I have met so few Englishmen,' said the guileless young woman, 'that really I should not be expected to know.'

'I understand it is a common delusion among Americans that every Englishman drops his "h's," and is to be detected in that way.'

Jennie laughed again, and George Wentworth thought it one of the prettiest laughs he had ever heard.

Poor Kenyon was rather neglected by his friend during the dinner. He felt a little gloomy while the courses went on, and wished he had an evening paper. Meanwhile, Wentworth and the handsome girl beside him got on very well together. At the end of the dinner she seemed to have some difficulty in getting up from her chair, and Wentworth showed her how to turn it round, leaving her free to rise. She thanked him prettily.

'I am going on deck,' she said, turning to go; 'I am so anxious to get my first glimpse of the ocean at night from the deck of a steamer.'

'I hope you will let me accompany you,' returned young Wentworth. 'The decks are rather slippery, and even when the boat is not rolling it isn't quite safe for a lady unused to the motion of a ship to walk alone in the dark.'

'Oh, thank you very much,' replied Miss Brewster, with effusion. 'It is kind of you, I am sure; and if you promise not to let me rob you of the pleasure of your after-dinner cigar, I shall be most happy to have you accompany me. I will meet you at the top of the stairway in five minutes.'

'You are getting on,' said Kenyon, as the young woman disappeared.

'What's the use of being on board ship,' said Wentworth, 'If you don't take advantage of the opportunity for making shipboard acquaintances? There is an unconventionality about life on a steamer that is not without its charm, as perhaps you will find out before the voyage is over, John.'

'You are merely trying to ease your conscience because of your heartless desertion of me.'

George Wentworth had waited at the top of the companion-way a little more than five minutes when Miss Brewster appeared, wrapped in a cloak edged with fur, which lent an additional charm to her complexion, set off as it was by a jaunty steamer cap. They stepped out on the deck, and found it not at all so dark as they had expected. Little globes of electric light were placed at regular intervals on the walls of the deck building. Overhead was stretched a sort of canvas roof, against which the sleety rain pattered. One of the sailors, with a rubber mop, was pushing into the gutter by the side of the ship the moisture from the deck. All around the boat the night was as black as ink, except here and there where the white curl of a wave showed luminous for a moment in the darkness.

Miss Brewster insisted that Wentworth should light his cigar, which, after some persuasion, he did. Then he tucked her hand snugly under his arm, and she adjusted her step to suit his. They had the promenade all to themselves. The rainy winter night was not so inviting to most of the passengers as the comfortable rooms below. Kenyon, however, and one or two others came up, and sat on the steamer chairs that were tied to the brass rod which ran along the deckhouse wall. He saw the glow of Wentworth's cigar as the couple turned at the farther end of the walk, and when they passed him he heard a low murmur of conversation, and caught now and then a snatch of silvery laughter. It was not because Wentworth had deserted him that Kenyon felt so uncomfortable and depressed. He could not tell just what it was, but there had settled on his mind a strange, uneasy foreboding. After a time he went down into the saloon and tried to read, but could not, and so wandered along the seemingly endless narrow passage to his room (which was Wentworth's as well), and, in nautical phrase, 'turned in.' It was late when his companion came.

'Asleep, Kenyon?' asked the latter.

'No,' was the answer.

'By George! John, she is one of the most charming girls I ever met. Wonderfully clever, too; makes a man feel like a fool beside her. She has read nearly everything. Has opinions on all our authors, a great many of whom I've never heard of. I wish, for your sake, John, she had a sister on board.'

'Thanks, old man; awfully good of you, I'm sure,' said Kenyon. 'Don't you think it's about time to stop raving, get into your bunk, and turn out that confounded light?'

'All right, growler, I will.'

Meanwhile, in her own state-room, Miss Jennie Brewster was looking at her reflection in the glass. As she shook out her long hair until it rippled down her back, she smiled sweetly, and said to herself:

'Poor Mr. Wentworth! Only the first night out, and he told me his name was George.'

CHAPTER III.

The second day out was a pleasant surprise for all on board who had made up their minds to a disagreeable winter passage. The air was clear, the sky blue as if it were spring-time, instead of midwinter. They were in the Gulf Stream. The sun shone brightly and the temperature was mild. Nevertheless, it was an uncomfortable day for those who were poor sailors. Although there did not seem, to the casual observer, to be much of a sea running, the ship rolled atrociously. Those who had made heroic resolutions on the subject were sitting in silent misery in their deck-chairs, which had been lashed to firm stanchions. Few were walking the clean bright deck, because walking that morning was a gymnastic feat. Three or four who evidently wished to show they had crossed before, and knew all about it, managed to make their way along the deck. Those recumbent in the steamer-chairs watched with lazy interest the pedestrians who now and then stood still, leaning apparently far out of the perpendicular, as the deck inclined downward. Sometimes the pedestrian's feet slipped, and he shot swiftly down the incline. Such an incident was invariably welcomed by those who sat. Even the invalids smiled wanly.

Kenyon reclined in his deck-chair with his eyes fixed on the blue sky. His mind was at rest about the syndicate report now that it had been mailed to London. His thoughts wandered to his own affairs, and he wondered whether he would make money out of the option he had acquired at Ottawa. He was not an optimistic man, and he doubted.

After their work for the London Syndicate was finished, the young men had done a little business on their own account. They visited together a mica-mine that was barely paying expenses, and which the proprietors were anxious to sell. The mine was owned by the Austrian Mining Company, whose agent, Von Brent, was interviewed by Kenyon in Ottawa. The young men obtained an option on this mine for three months from Von Brent. Kenyon's educated eye had told him that the white mineral they were placing on the dump at the mouth of the mine was even more valuable than the mica for which they were mining.

Kenyon was scrupulously honest—a quality somewhat at a discount in the mining business—and it seemed to him hardly the fair thing that he should take advantage of the ignorance of Von Brent regarding the mineral on the dump. Wentworth had some trouble in overcoming his friend's scruples. He claimed that knowledge always had to be paid for, in law, medicine, or mineralogy, and therefore that they were perfectly justified in profiting by their superior wisdom. So it came about that the young men took to England with them a three months' option on the mine.

Wentworth had been walking about all morning like a lost spirit apparently seeking what was not. 'It can't be,' he said to himself. No; the thought was too horrible, and he dismissed it from his mind, merely conjecturing that perhaps she was not an early riser, which was indeed the case. No one who works on a morning newspaper ever takes advantage of the lark's example.

'Well, Kenyon,' said Wentworth 'you look as if you were writing a poem, or doing something that required deep mental agony.'

'The writing of poems, my dear Wentworth, I leave to you. I am doing something infinitely more practical—something that you ought to be at. I am thinking what we are to do with our mica-mine when we get it over to London.'

'Oh, "sufficient for the day is the evil thereof,"' cried Wentworth jauntily; 'besides, half an hour's thinking by a solid-brained fellow like you is worth a whole voyage of my deepest meditation.'

'She hasn't appeared yet?' said Kenyon.

'No, dear boy; no, she has not. You see, I make no pretence with you as other less ingenuous men might. No, she has not appeared, and she has not breakfasted.'

'Perhaps——' began Kenyon.

'No, no!' cried Wentworth; 'I'll have no "perhaps." I thought of that, but I instantly dismissed the idea. She's too good a sailor.'

'It requires a very good sailor to stand this sort of thing. It looks so unnecessary, too. I wonder what the ship is rolling about?'

'I can't tell, but she seems to be rolling about half over. I say, Kenyon, old fellow, I feel horrible pangs of conscience about deserting you in this way, and so early in the voyage. I didn't do it last time, did I?'

'You were a model travelling companion on the last voyage,' returned Kenyon.

'I don't wish to make impertinent suggestions, my boy, but allow me to tell you that there are some other very nice girls on board.'

'You are not so bad as I feared, then,' replied Kenyon, 'or you wouldn't admit that. I thought you had eyes for no one but Miss—Miss—I really didn't catch her name.'

'I don't mind telling you confidentially, Kenyon, that her name is Jennie.'

'Dear me!' cried Kenyon, 'has it got so far as that? Doesn't it strike you, Wentworth, that you are somewhat in a hurry? It seems decidedly more American than English. Englishmen are apt to weigh matters a little more.'

'There is no necessity for weighing, my boy. I don't see any harm in making the acquaintance of a pretty girl when you have a long voyage before you.'

'Well, I wouldn't let it grow too serious, if I were you.'

'There isn't the slightest danger of seriousness about the affair. On shore the young lady wouldn't cast a second look at me. She is the daughter of a millionaire. Her father is in Paris, and they are going on to the Riviera in a few weeks.'

'All the more reason,' said Kenyon, 'that you shouldn't let this go too far. Be on your guard, my boy. I've heard it said that American girls have the delightful little practice of leading a man on until it comes to a certain point, and then arching their pretty eyebrows, looking astonished, and forgetting all about him afterwards. You had better wait until we make our fortunes on this mica-mine, and then, perhaps, your fair millionairess may listen to you.'

'John,' cried Wentworth, 'you are the most cold-blooded man I know of. I never noticed it so particularly before, but it seems to me that years and years of acquaintance with minerals of all kinds, hard and flinty, transform a man. Be careful that you don't become like the minerals you work among.'

'Well, I don't know anything that has less tendency to soften a man than long columns of figures. I think the figures you work at are quite as demoralizing as the minerals I have spent my life with.'

'Perhaps you are right, but a girl would have to be thrown into your arms before you would admit that such a thing as a charming young lady existed.'

'If I make all the money I hope to make out of the mica-mine, I expect the young ladies will not be thrown into my arms, but at my head. Money goes a long way toward reconciling a girl to marriage.'

'It certainly goes a long way toward reconciling her mother to the marriage. I don't believe,' said Wentworth slowly, 'that my—that Miss Brewster ever thinks about money.'

'She probably doesn't need to, but no doubt there is someone who does the thinking for her. If her father is a millionaire, and has, like many Americans, made his own money, you may depend upon it he will do the thinking for her; and if Miss Brewster should prove to be thoughtless in the matter, the old gentleman will very speedily bring you both to your senses. It would be different if you had a title.'

'I haven't any,' replied Wentworth, 'except the title George Wentworth, accountant, with an address in the City and rooms in the suburbs.'

'Precisely; if you were Lord George Wentworth, or even Sir George, or Baron Wentworth of something or other, you might have a chance; as it is, the title of accountant would not go far with an American millionaire, or his daughter either.'

'You are a cold, calculating wretch.'

'Nothing of the sort. I merely have my senses about me, and you haven't at this particular moment. You wouldn't think of trusting a book-keeper's figures without seeing his vouchers. Well, my boy, you haven't the vouchers— at least, not yet, so that is why I ask you to give your attention to what we are going to do with our mine; and if you take my advice you will not think seriously about American millionaires or their daughters.'

George Wentworth jumped to his feet, the ship gave a lurch at that particular moment, and he no sooner found his feet than he nearly lost them again; however, he was an expert at balancing himself as well as his accounts, and though for the moment his attention was occupied in keeping his equilibrium, he looked down on his companion, still placidly reclining in his chair, with a smile on his face.

'Kenyon,' he said, 'I am going to look for another girl.'

'Is one not enough for you?'

'No, I want two—one for myself, and one for you. No man can sympathize with another unless he is in the same position himself. John, I want sympathy, and I'm not getting it.'

'What you need more urgently,' said Kenyon calmly, 'is common-sense, and that I am trying to supply.'

'You are doing your duty in that direction; but a man doesn't live by common-sense alone. There comes a time when common-sense is a drug in the market. I don't say it has come to me yet, but I'm resolved to get you into a more sympathetic mood, so I am going to find a suitable young lady for you.'

'More probably you are going to look for your own,' answered Kenyon, as his friend walked off, and, disappearing round the corner, crossed to the other side of the ship.

Kenyon did not turn again to his figures when his companion left him. He mused over the curiously rapid turn of circumstances. He hoped Wentworth would not take it too seriously, for he felt that, somehow or other, Miss Brewster was just the sort of girl to throw him over after she had whiled away a tedious voyage. Of course he could not say this to his friend, who evidently admired Miss Brewster, but he had said as much as he could to put Wentworth on his guard.

'Now,' said Kenyon to himself, 'if she had been a girl like that, I wouldn't have minded.' The girl 'like that' was a young woman who for half an hour had been walking the deck alone with marvellous skill. She was not so handsome as the American girl, but she had a better complexion, and there was a colour in her cheek which seemed to suggest England. Her dress was not quite so smart nor so well-fitting as that of the American girl; but, nevertheless, she was warmly and sensibly clad, and a brown Tam o' Shanter covered her fair head. The tips of her hands were in the pockets of her short blue-cloth jacket; and she walked the deck with a firm, reliant tread that aroused the admiration of John Kenyon. 'If she were only a girl like that,' he repeated to himself, 'I wouldn't mind. There's something fresh and genuine about her. She makes me think of the breezy English downs.'

As she walked back and forward, one or two young men seemingly made an attempt to become acquainted with her, but it was evident to Kenyon that the young woman had made it plain to them, politely enough, that she preferred walking alone, and they raised their sea-caps and left her.

'She doesn't pick up the first man who comes,' he mused.

The ship was beginning to roll more and more, and yet the day was beautiful and the sea seemingly calm. Most of the promenaders had left the deck. Two or three of them had maintained their equilibrium with a gratifying success which engendered the pride that goeth before a fall, but the moment came at last when their feet slipped and they had found themselves thrown against the bulwark of the steamer. Then they had laughed a little in a crestfallen manner, picked themselves up, and promenaded the deck no more. Many of those who were lying in the steamer-chairs gave up the struggle and went down to their cabins. There was a momentary excitement as one chair broke from its fastenings and slid down with a crash against the bulwarks. The occupant was picked up in a hysterical condition and taken below. The deck steward tied the chair more firmly, so that the accident would not happen again. The young English girl was opposite John Kenyon when this disaster took place, and her attention being diverted by fear for the safety of the occupant of the sliding chair, her care for herself was withdrawn at the very moment when it was most needed. The succeeding lurch which the ship gave to the other side was the most tremendous of the day. The deck rose until the girl leaning outward could almost touch it with her hand, then, in spite of herself, she slipped with the rapidity of lightning against the chair John Kenyon occupied, and that tripping her up, flung her upon him with an unexpectedness that would have taken his breath away if the sudden landing of a plump young woman upon him had not accomplished the same thing. The fragile deck-chair gave way with a crash, and it would be hard to say which was the more discomfited by the sudden catastrophe, John Kenyon or the girl.

'I hope you are not hurt,' he managed to stammer.

'Don't think about me!' she cried. 'I have broken your chair, and— and——'

'The chair doesn't matter,' cried Kenyon. 'It was a flimsy structure at best. I am not hurt, if that is what you mean—and you mustn't mind it.'

Then there came to his recollection the sentence of George Wentworth: 'A girl will have to be thrown into your arms before you will admit that such a thing as a charming young woman exists.'

CHAPTER IV.

Edith Longworth could hardly be said to be a typical representative of the English girl. She had the English girl's education, but not her training. She had lost her mother in early life, which makes a great difference in a girl's bringing up, however wealthy her father may be; and Edith's father was wealthy, there was no doubt of that. If you asked any City man about the standing of John Longworth, you would learn that the 'house' was well thought of. People said he was lucky, but old John Longworth asserted that there was no such thing as luck in business—in which statement he was very likely incorrect. He had large investments in almost every quarter of the globe. When he went into any enterprise, he went into it thoroughly. Men talk about the inadvisability of putting all one's eggs into one basket, but John Longworth was a believer in doing that very thing—and in watching the basket. Not that he had all his eggs in one basket, or even in one kind of basket; but when John Longworth was satisfied with the particular variety of basket presented to him, he put a large number of eggs in it. When anything was offered for investment—whether it was a mine or a brewery or a railway—John Longworth took an expert's opinion upon it, and then the chances were that he would disregard the advice given. He was in the habit of going personally to see what had been offered to him. If the enterprise were big enough, he thought little of taking a voyage to the other end of the world for the sole purpose of looking the investment over. It was true that in many cases he knew nothing whatever of the business he went to examine, but that did not matter; he liked to have a personal inspection where a large amount of his money was to be placed. Investment seemed to be a sort of intuition with him. Often, when the experts' opinions were unanimously in favour of the project, and when everything appeared to be perfectly safe, Longworth would pay a personal visit to the business offered for sale, and come to a sudden conclusion not to have anything to do with it. He would give no reasons to his colleagues for his change of front; he simply refused to entertain the proposal any further, and withdrew. Several instances of this kind had occurred. Sometimes a large and profitable business, held out in the prospectus to be exceedingly desirable, had come to nothing, and when the company was wound up, people remembered what Longworth had said about it. So there came to be a certain superstitious feeling among those who knew him, that, if old Mr. Longworth was in a thing, the thing was safe, and if a company promoter managed to get his name on the prospectus, his project was almost certain to succeed.

* * * * *

When Edith Longworth was pronounced finished so far as education was concerned, she became more and more the companion of her father, and he often jokingly referred to her as his man of business. She went with him on his long journeys, and so had been several times to America, once to the Cape, and one long voyage, with Australia as the objective point, had taken her completely round the world. She inherited much of her father's shrewdness, and there is no doubt that, if Edith Longworth had been cast upon her own resources, she would have become an excellent woman of business. She knew exactly the extent of her father's investments, and she was his confidante in a way that few women are with their male relatives. The old man had a great faith in Edith's opinion, although he rarely acknowledged it. Having been together so much on such long trips, they naturally became, in a way, boon companions. Thus, Edith's education was very unlike that of the ordinary English girl, and this particular training caused her to develop into a different kind of woman than she might have been had her mother lived.

Perfect confidence existed between father and daughter, and only lately had there come a shadow upon their relations, about which neither ever spoke to the other since their first conversation on the subject.

Edith had said, with perhaps more than her usual outspokenness, that she had no thought whatever of marriage, and least of all had her thoughts turned toward the man her father seemed to have chosen. In answer to this, her father had said nothing, but Edith knew him too well to believe that he had changed his mind about the matter. The fact that he had invited her cousin to join them on this particular journey showed her that he evidently believed all that was necessary was to throw them more together than had been the case previously; and, although Edith was silent, she thought her father had not the same shrewdness in these matters that he showed in the purchasing of a growing business. Edith had been perfectly civil to the young man—as she would have been to anyone—but he saw that she preferred her own company to his; and so, much to the disgust of Mr. Longworth, he spent most of his time at cards in the smoking-room, whereas, according to the elder gentleman's opinion, he should have been promenading the deck with his cousin.

William Longworth, the cousin, was inclined to be a trifle put out, for he looked upon himself as quite an eligible person, one whom any girl in her senses would be glad to look forward to as a possible husband. He made no pretence of being madly in love with Edith, but he thought the marriage would be an admirable thing all round. She was a nice girl, he said to himself, and his uncle's money was well worth thinking about. In fact, he was becoming desirous that the marriage should take place; but, as there was no one upon whom he could look as a rival, he had the field to himself. He would therefore show Miss Edith that he was by no means entirely dependent for his happiness upon her company; and this he proceeded to do by spending his time in the smoking-room, and playing cards with his fellow-passengers. It was quite evident to anyone who saw Edith, that, if this suited him, it certainly suited her; so they rarely met on shipboard except at table, where Edith's place was between her father and her cousin. Miss Longworth and her cousin had had one brief conversation on the subject of marriage. He spoke of it rather jauntily, as being quite a good arrangement, but she said very shortly that she had no desire to change her name.

'You don't need to,' said Cousin William; 'my name is Longworth, and so is yours.'

'It is not a subject for a joke,' she answered.

'I am not joking, my dear Edith. I am merely telling you what everybody knows to be true. You surely don't deny that my name is Longworth?'

'I don't mean to deny or affirm anything in relation to the matter,' replied the young woman, 'and you will oblige me very much if you will

86

never recur to this subject again.'

And so the young man betook himself once more to the smoking-room.

On this trip Edith had seen a good deal of American society. People over there had made it very pleasant for her, and, although the weather was somewhat trying, she had greatly enjoyed the sleigh-rides and the different festivities which winter brings to the citizen of Northern America. Her father and her cousin had gone to America to see numerous breweries that were situated in different parts of the country, and which it was proposed to combine into one large company. They had made a Western city their headquarters, and while Edith was enjoying herself with her newly-found friends, the two men had visited the breweries in different sections of the country—all, however, near the city where Edith was staying. The breweries seemed to be in a very prosperous condition, although the young man declared the beer they brewed was the vilest he had ever tasted, and he said he wouldn't like to have anything to do with the production of it, even if it did turn in money. His uncle had not tried the beer, but confined himself solely to the good old bottled English ale, which had increased in price, if not in excellence, by its transportation. But there was something about the combination that did not please him; and, from the few words he dropped on the subject, his nephew saw that Longworth was not going to be a member of the big Beer Syndicate. The intention had been to take a trip to Canada, and Edith had some hopes of seeing the city of Montreal in its winter dress; but that visit had been abandoned, as so much time had been consumed in the Western States. So they began their homeward voyage, with the elder Longworth sitting a good deal in his deck-chair, and young Longworth spending much of his time in the smoking-room, while Edith walked the deck alone. And this was the lady whom Fate threw into the arms of John Kenyon.

CHAPTER V.

Steamer friendships ripen quickly. It is true that, as a general thing, they perish with equal suddenness. The moment a man sets his foot on solid land the glamour of the sea seems to leave him, and the friend to whom he was ready to swear eternal fealty while treading the deck, is speedily forgotten on shore. Edith Longworth gave no thought to the subject of the innocent nature of steamer friendships when she reviewed in her own mind her pleasant walk along the deck with Kenyon. She had met many interesting people during her numerous voyages, but they had all proved to be steamer acquaintances, whose names she had now considerable difficulty in remembering. Perhaps she would not have given a second thought to Mr. Kenyon that night if it had not been for some ill-considered remarks her cousin saw fit to make at the dinner-table.

'Who was that fellow you were walking with today?' young Longworth asked.

Edith smiled upon him pleasantly, and answered:

'Mr. Kenyon you mean, I suppose?'

'Oh, you know his name, do you?' he answered gruffly.

'Certainly,' she replied; 'I would not walk with a gentleman whose name I did not know.'

'Really?' sneered her cousin. 'And pray were you introduced to him?'

'I do not think,' answered Edith quietly, 'any person has a right to ask me that question except my father. He has not asked it, and, as you have, I will merely answer that I was introduced to Mr. Kenyon.'

'I did not know you had any mutual acquaintance on board who could make you known to each other.'

'Well, the ceremony was a little informal. We were introduced by our mutual friend, old Father Neptune. Father Neptune, being, as you know, a little boisterous this morning, took the liberty of flinging me upon Mr. Kenyon. I weigh something more than a feather, and the result was—although Mr. Kenyon was good enough to say he was uninjured—that the chair on which he sat had not the same consideration for my feelings, and it went down with a crash. I thought Mr. Kenyon should take my chair in exchange for the one I had the misfortune to break, but Mr. Kenyon thought otherwise. He said he was a mining engineer, and that he could not claim to be a very good one if he found any difficulty in mending a deck-chair. It seems he succeeded in doing so, and that is the whole history of my introduction to, and my intercourse with, Mr. Kenyon, Mining Engineer.'

'Most interesting and romantic,' replied the young man; 'and do you think that your father approves of your picking up indiscriminate acquaintances in this way?'

Edith, flushing a little at this, said:

'I would not willingly do what my father disapproved of;' then in a lower voice she added: 'except, perhaps, one thing.'

Her father, who had caught snatches of the conversation, now leaned across towards his nephew, and said warningly:

'I think Edith is quite capable of judging for herself. This is my seventh voyage with her, and I have always found such to be the case. This happens to be your first, and so, were I you, I would not pursue the subject further.'

The young man was silent, and Edith gave her father a grateful glance. Thus it was that, while she might not have given a thought to Kenyon, the remarks which her cousin had made, brought to her mind, when she was alone, the two young men, and the contrast between them was not at all to the advantage of her cousin.

The scrubbing-brushes on the deck above him woke Kenyon early next morning. For a few moments after getting on deck he thought he had the ship to himself. One side of the deck was clean and wet; on the other side the men were slowly moving the scrubbing-brushes backward and forward, with a drowsy swish-swish. As he walked up the deck, he saw there was one passenger who had been earlier than himself.

Edith Longworth turned round as she heard his step, and her face brightened into a smile when she saw who it was.

Kenyon gravely raised his steamer cap and bade her 'Good-morning.'

'You are an early riser, Mr. Kenyon.'

'Not so early as you are, I see.'

'I think I am an exceptional passenger in that way,' replied the girl. 'I always enjoy the early morning at sea. I like to get as far forward on the steamer as possible, so that there is nothing between me and the boundless anywhere. Then it seems as if the world belongs to myself, with nobody else in it.'

'Isn't that a rather selfish view?' put in Kenyon.

'Oh, I don't think so. There is certainly nothing selfish in my enjoyment of it; but, you know, there are times when one wishes to be alone, and to forget everybody.'

'I hope I have not stumbled upon one of those times.'

'Oh, not at all, Mr. Kenyon,' replied his companion, laughing. 'There was nothing personal in the remark. If I wished to be alone, I would have no hesitation in walking off. I am not given to hinting; I speak plainly—some of my friends think a little too plainly. Have you ever been on the Pacific Ocean?'

'Never.'

'Ah, there the mornings are delicious. It is very beautiful here now, but in summer on the Pacific some of the mornings are so calm and peaceful and fresh, that it would seem as if the world had been newly made.'

'You have travelled a great deal, Miss Longworth. I envy you.'

'I often think I am a person to be envied, but there may come a shipwreck one day, and then I shall not be in so enviable a position.'

'I sincerely hope you may never have such an experience.'

'Have you ever been shipwrecked, Mr. Kenyon?'

'Oh no; my travelling experiences are very limited. But to read of a shipwreck is bad enough.'

'We have had a most delightful voyage so far. Quite like summer. One can scarcely believe that we left America in the depth of winter, with snow everywhere and the thermometer ever so far below zero. Have you mended your deck-chair yet, sufficiently well to trust yourself upon it again?'

'Oh!' said Kenyon, with a laugh, 'you really must not make fun of my amateur carpentering like that. As I told you, I am a mining engineer, and if I cannot mend a deck-chair, what would you expect me to do with a mine?'

'Have you had much to do with mines?' asked the young woman.

'I am just beginning,' replied Kenyon; 'this, in fact, is one of my first commissions. I have been sent with my friend Wentworth to examine certain mines on the Ottawa River.'

'The Ottawa River!' cried Edith. 'Are you one of those who were sent out by the London Syndicate?'

'Yes,' answered Kenyon with astonishment. 'What do you know about it?'

'Oh, I know everything about it. Everything, except what the mining expert's report is to be, and that information, I suppose, you have; so, between the two of us, we know a great deal about the fortunes of the London Syndicate.'

'Really! I am astonished to meet a young lady who knows anything about the matter. I understood it was rather a secret combination up to the present.'

'Ah! but, you see, I am one of the syndicate.'

'You!'

'Certainly,' answered Edith Longworth, laughing. 'At least, my father is, and that is the same thing, or almost the same thing. We intended to go to Canada ourselves, and I was very much disappointed at not going. I understand that the sleighing, and the snowshoeing, and the tobogganing are something wonderful.'

'I saw very little of the social side of life in the district, my whole time being employed at the mines; but even in the mining village where we stayed, they had a snowshoe club, and a very good toboggan slide—so good, in fact, that, having gone down once, I never ventured to risk my life on it again.'

'If my father knew you were on board, he would be anxious to meet you. Doubtless you know the London Syndicate will be a very large company.'

'Yes, I am aware of that.'

'And you know that a great deal is going to depend upon your report?'

'I suppose that is so, and I hope the syndicate will find my report at least an honest and thorough one.'

'Is the colleague who was with you also on board?'

'Yes, he is here.'

'He, then, was the accountant who was sent out?'

'Yes, and he is a man who does his business very thoroughly, and I think the syndicate will be satisfied with his work.'

'And do you not think they will be satisfied with yours also? I am sure you did your work conscientiously.'

Kenyon almost blushed as the young woman made this remark, but she looked intently at him, and he saw that her thoughts were not on him, but on the large interests he represented.

'Were you favourably impressed with the Ottawa as a mining region?' she asked.

'Very much so,' he answered, and, anxious to turn the conversation away from his own report, he said: 'I was so much impressed with it that I secured the option of a mine there for myself.'

'Oh! do you intend to buy one of the mines there?'

Kenyon laughed.

'No, I am no capitalist seeking investment for my money, but I saw that the mine contained possibilities of producing a great deal of money for those who possess it. It is very much more valuable, in my opinion, than the owners themselves suspect; so I secured an option upon it for three months, and hope when I reach England to form a company to take it up.'

'Well, I am sure,' said the young lady, 'if you are confident that the mine is a good one, you could see no one who would help you more in that way than my father. He has been looking at a brewery business he thought of investing in, but which he has concluded to have nothing to do with, so he will be anxious to find something reliable in its place. How much would be required for the purchase of the mine you mention?'

'I was thinking of asking fifty thousand pounds for it,' said Kenyon, flushing, as he thought of his own temerity in more than doubling the price of the mine.

Wentworth and he had estimated the probable value of the mine, and had concluded that even selling it at that price—which would give them thirty thousand pounds to divide between them—they were selling a mine that was really worth very much more, and would soon pay tremendous dividends on the fifty thousand pounds. He expected the young woman to be impressed by the amount, and was, therefore, very much surprised when she said:

'Fifty thousand pounds! Is that all? Then I am afraid my father would have nothing to do with it. He only deals with large businesses, and a company with a capitalization of fifty thousand pounds I am sure he would not look at.'

'You talk of fifty thousand pounds,' said Kenyon, 'as if it were a mere trifle. To me it seems an immense fortune. I only wish I had it, or half of it.'

'You are not rich, then?' said the girl, with apparent interest.

'No,' replied the young man. 'Far otherwise.'

At that moment the elder Mr. Longworth appeared in the door of the companion-way, and looked up and down the deck.

'Oh, here you are,' he said, as his daughter sprang from her chair.

'Father,' she cried, 'let me introduce to you Mr. Kenyon, who is the mining expert sent out by our syndicate to look at the Ottawa mines.'

'I am pleased to meet you,' said the elder gentleman.

The capitalist sat down beside the mining engineer, and began, somewhat to Kenyon's embarrassment, to talk of the London Syndicate.

CHAPTER VI.

A few mornings later Wentworth worked his way, with much balancing and grasping of stanchions, along the deck, for the ship rolled fearfully, but the person he sought was nowhere visible. He thought he would go into the smoking-room, but changed his mind at the door, and turned down the companion-way to the main saloon. The tables had been cleared of the breakfast belongings, but on one of the small tables a white cloth had been laid, and at this spot of purity in the general desert of red plush sat Miss Brewster, who was complacently ordering what she wanted from a steward, who did not seem at all pleased in serving one who had disregarded the breakfast-hour, to the disarrangement of all saloon rules. The chief steward stood by a door and looked disapprovingly at the tardy guest. It was almost time to lay the tables for lunch, and the young woman was as calmly ordering her breakfast as if she had been the first person at table.

She looked up brightly at Wentworth, and smiled as he approached her.

'I suppose,' she began, 'I'm dreadfully late, and the steward looks as if he would like to scold me. How awfully the ship is rolling! Is there a storm?'

'No. She seems to be doing this sort of thing for amusement. Wants to make it interesting for the unfortunate passengers who are not good sailors, I suppose. She's doing it, too. There's scarcely anyone on deck.'

'Dear me! I thought we were having a dreadful storm. Is it raining?'

'No. It's a beautiful sunshiny day; without much wind either, in spite of all this row.'

'I suppose you have had your breakfast long ago?'

'So long since that I am beginning to look forward with pleasant anticipation to lunch.'

'Oh dear! I had no idea I was so late as that. Perhaps you had better scold me. Somebody ought to do it, and the steward seems a little afraid.'

'You over-estimate my courage. I am a little afraid, too.'

'Then you do think I deserve it?'

'I didn't say that, nor do I think it. I confess, however, that up to this moment I felt just a trifle lonely.'

'Just a trifle! Well, that is flattery. How nicely you English do turn a compliment! Just a trifle!'

'I believe, as a race, we do not venture much into compliment making at all. We leave that for the polite foreigner. He would say what I tried to say a great deal better than I did, of course, but he would not mean half so much.'

'Oh, that's very nice, Mr. Wentworth. No foreigner could have put it nearly so well. Now, what about going on deck?'

'Anywhere, if you let me accompany you.'

'I shall be most delighted to have you. I won't say merely a trifle delighted.'

'Ah! Haven't you forgiven that remark yet?'

'There's nothing to forgive, and it is quite too delicious to forget. I shall never forget it.'

'I believe that you are very cruel at heart, Miss Brewster.'

The young woman gave him a curious side-look, but did not answer. She gathered the wraps she had taken from her cabin, and, handing them to him before he had thought of offering to take them, she led the way to the deck. He found their chairs side by side, and admired the intelligence of the deck-steward, who seemed to understand which chairs to place together. Miss Jennie sank gracefully into her own, and allowed him to adjust the wraps around her.

'There,' she said, 'that's very nicely done; as well as the deck-steward himself could do it, and I am sure it is impossible to pay you a more graceful compliment than that. So few men know how to arrange one comfortably in a steamer chair.'

'You speak as though you had vast experience in steamer life, and yet you told me this was your first voyage.'

'It is. But it doesn't take a woman more than a day to see that the average man attends to such little niceties very clumsily. Now just tuck in the corner out of sight. There! Thank you, ever so much. And would you be kind enough to—Yes, that's better. And this other wrap so. Oh, that is perfect. What a patient man you are, Mr. Wentworth!'

'Yes, Miss Brewster. You are a foreigner. I can see that now. Your professed compliment was hollow. You said I did it perfectly, and then immediately directed me how to do it.'

'Nothing of the kind. You did it well, and I think you ought not to grudge me the pleasure of adding my own little improvements.'

'Oh, if you put it in that way, I will not. Now, before I sit down, tell me what book I can get that will interest you. The library contains a very good assortment.'

'I don't think I care about reading. Sit down and talk. I suppose I am too indolent to-day. I thought, when I came on board, that I would do a lot of reading, but I believe the sea-air makes one lazy. I must confess I feel entirely indifferent to mental improvement.'

'You evidently do not think my conversation will be at all worth listening to.'

'How quick you are to pervert my meaning! Don't you see that I think your conversation better worth listening to than the most interesting or improving book you can choose from the library? Really, in trying to avoid giving you cause for making such a remark, I have apparently stumbled into a worse error. I was just going to say I would like your conversation much better than a book, when I thought you would take that as a reflection on your reading. If you take me up so sharply I will sit here and say nothing. Now then, talk!'

'What shall I say?'

'Oh, if I told you what to say I should be doing the talking. Tell me about yourself. What do you do in London?'

'I work hard. I am an accountant.'

'And what is an accountant? What does he do? Keep accounts?'

'Some of them do; I do not. I see, rather, that accounts which other people keep have been correctly kept.'

'Aren't they always correctly kept? I thought that was what book-keepers were hired for.'

'If books were always correctly kept there would be little for us to do; but it happens, unfortunately for some, but fortunately for us, that people occasionally do not keep their accounts accurately.'

'And can you always find that out if you examine the books?'

'Always.'

'Can't a man make up his accounts so that no one can tell there is anything wrong?'

'The belief that such a thing can be done has placed many a poor wretch in prison. It has been tried often enough.'

'I am sure they can do it in the States. I have read of it being done and continued for years. Men have made off with great sums of money by falsifying the books, and no one found it out until the one who did it died or ran away.'

'Nevertheless, if an expert accountant had been called in, he would have found out very soon that something was wrong, and just where the wrong was, and how much.'

'I didn't think such cleverness possible. Have you ever discovered anything like that?'

'I have.'

'What is done when such a thing is discovered?'

'That depends upon circumstances. Usually a policeman is called in.'

'Why, it's like being a detective. I wish you would tell me about some of the cases you have had. Don't make me ask so many questions. Talk.'

'I don't think my experiences would interest you in the least. There was one case with which I had something to do in London, two years ago, that——'

'Oh, London! I don't believe the book-keepers there are half so sharp as ours. If you had to deal with American accountants, you would not find out so easily what they had or had not done.'

'Well, Miss Brewster, I may say I have just had an experience of that kind with some of your very sharpest American book-keepers. I found that the books had been kept in the most ingenious way with the intent to deceive. The system had been going on for years.'

'How interesting! And did you call in a policeman?'

'No. This was one of the cases where a policeman was not necessary. The books were kept with the object of showing that the profits of the m—of the business—had been much greater than they really were. I may say that one of your American accountants had already looked over the books, and, whether through ignorance or carelessness, or from a worse motive, he reported them all right. They were not all right, and the fact that they were not, will mean the loss of a fortune to some people on your side of the water, and the saving of good money to others on my side.'

'Then I think your profession must be a very important one.'

'We think so, Miss Brewster. I would like to be paid a percentage on the money saved because of my report.'

'And won't you?'

'Unfortunately, no.'

'I think that is too bad. I suppose the discrepancy must have been small, or the American accountant would not have overlooked it?'

'I didn't say he overlooked it. Still, the size of a discrepancy does not make any difference. A small error is as easily found as a large one. This one was large. I suppose there is no harm in my saying that the books, taking them together, showed a profit of forty thousand pounds, when they should have shown a loss of nearly half that amount. I hope nobody overhears me.'

'No; we are quite alone, and you may be sure I will not breathe a word of what you have been telling me.'

'Don't breathe it to Kenyon, at least. He would think me insane if he knew what I have said.'

'Is Mr. Kenyon an accountant, too?'

'Oh no. He is a mineralogist. He can go into a mine, and tell with reasonable certainty whether it will pay the working or not. Of course, as he says himself, any man can see six feet into the earth as well as he can. But it is not every man that can gauge the value of a working mine so well as John Kenyon.'

'Then, while you were delving among the figures, your companion was delving among the minerals?'

'Precisely.'

'And did he make any such startling discovery as you did?'

'No; rather the other way. He finds the mines very good properties, and he thinks that if they were managed intelligently they would be good paying investments—that is, at a proper price, you know—not at what the owners ask for them at present. But you can have no possible interest in these dry details.'

'Indeed, you are mistaken. I think what you have told me intensely interesting.'

For once in her life Miss Jennie Brewster told the exact truth. The unfortunate man at her side was flattered.

100

'For what I have told you,' he said, 'we were offered twice what the London people pay us for coming out here. In fact, even more than that: we were asked to name our own price.'

'Really now! By the owners of the property, I suppose, if you wouldn't tell on them?'

'No. By one of your famous New York newspaper men. He even went so far as to steal the papers that Kenyon had in Ottawa. He was cleverly caught, though, before he could make any use of what he had stolen. In fact, unless his people in New York had the figures which were originally placed before the London Board, I doubt if my statistics would have been of much use to him even if he had been allowed to keep them. The full significance of my report will not show until the figures I have given are compared with those already in the hands of the London people, which were vouched for as correct by your clever American accountant.'

'You shouldn't run down an accountant just because he is American. Perhaps there will come a day, Mr. Wentworth, when you will admit that there are Americans who are more clever than either that accountant or that newspaper man. I don't think your specimens are typical.'

'I don't "run down," as you call it, the men because they are Americans. I "run down" the accountant because he was either ignorant or corrupt. I "run down" the newspaper man because he was a thief.'

Miss Brewster was silent for a few moments. She was impressing on her memory what he had said to her, and was anxious to get away, so that she could write out in her cabin exactly what had been told her. The sound of the lunch-gong gave her the excuse she needed, so, bidding her victim a pleasant and friendly farewell, she hurried from the deck to her state-room.

CHAPTER VII.

One morning, when Kenyon went to his state-room on hearing the breakfast-gong, he found the lazy occupant of the upper berth still in his bunk.

'Come, Wentworth,' he shouted, 'this won't do, you know. Get up! get up! breakfast, my boy! breakfast!—the most important meal in the day to a healthy man.'

Wentworth yawned and stretched his arms over his head.

'What's the row?' he asked.

'The row is, it's time to get up. The second gong has sounded.'

'Dear me! is it so late? I didn't hear it.' Wentworth sat up in his bunk, and looked ruefully over the precipice down the chasm to the floor. 'Have you been up long?' he asked.

'Long? I have been on deck an hour and a half,' answered Kenyon.

'Then, Miss What's-her-Name must have been there also.'

'Her name is Miss Longworth,' replied Kenyon, without looking at his comrade.

'That's her name, is it? and she was on deck?'

'She was.'

'I thought so,' said Wentworth; 'just look at the divine influence of woman! Miss Longworth rises early, therefore John Kenyon rises early. Miss Brewster rises late, therefore George Wentworth is not seen until breakfast-time. If the conditions were reversed, I suppose the getting-up time of the two men would be changed accordingly.'

'Not at all, George—not at all. I would rise early whether anybody else on board did or not. In fact, when I got on deck this morning, I expected to have it to myself.'

'I take it, though, that you were not grievously disappointed when you found you hadn't a monopoly?'

'Well, to tell the truth, I was not; Miss Longworth is a charmingly sensible girl.'

'Oh, they all are,' said Wentworth lightly. 'You had no sympathy for me the other day. Now you know how it is yourself, as they say across the water.'

'I don't know how it is myself. The fact is, we were talking business.'

'Really? Did you get so far?'

'Yes, we got so far, if that is any distance. I told her about the mica-mine.'

'Oh, you did! What did she say? Will she invest?'

'Well, when I told her we expected to form a company for fifty thousand pounds, she said it was such a small sum, she doubted if we could get anybody interested in it in London.'

Wentworth, who was now well advanced with his dressing, gave a long whistle.

'Fifty thousand pounds a small sum? Why, John, she must be very wealthy! Probably more so than the American millionairess.'

'Well, George, you see, the difference between the two young ladies is this: that while American heiresses are apt to boast of their immense wealth, English women say nothing about it.'

'If you mean Miss Brewster when you speak in that way, you are entirely mistaken. She has never alluded to her wealth at all, with the exception of saying that her father was a millionaire. So if the young woman you speak of has been talking of her wealth at all, she has done more than the American girl.'

'She said nothing to indicate she was wealthy. I merely conjectured it when I discovered she looked upon fifty thousand pounds as a triviality.'

'Well, the fault is easily remedied. We may raise the price of the mine to one hundred thousand pounds if we can get people to invest. Perhaps the young lady's father might care to go in for it at that figure.'

'Oh, by the way, Wentworth,' said Kenyon, 'I forgot to tell you, Miss Longworth's father is one of the London Syndicate.'

'By Jove! are you sure of that? How do you know? You weren't talking of our mission out there, were you?'

'Certainly not,' replied Kenyon, flushing. 'You don't think I would speak of that to a stranger, do you? nor of anything concerned with our reports.'

Wentworth proceeded with his dressing, a guilty feeling rising in his heart.

'I want to ask you a question about that.'

'About what?' said Wentworth shortly.

'About those mines. Miss Longworth's father being a member of the London Syndicate, suppose he asks what our views in relation to the matter are: would we be justified in telling him anything?'

'He won't ask me as I don't know him; he may ask you, and if he does, then you will have to decide the question for yourself.'

'Would you say anything about it if you were in my place?'

'Oh, I don't know. If we were certain it was all right—if you are sure he is a member of the syndicate, and he happens to ask you about it, I scarcely see how you can avoid telling him.'

'It would be embarrassing; so I hope he won't ask me. We should not speak of it until we give in our reports. He knows, however, that you are the accountant who has that part of the business in charge.'

'Oh, then you have been talking with him?'

'Just a moment or two, after his daughter introduced me.'

'What did you say his name was?'

'John Longworth, I believe. I am sure about the Longworth, but not about the John.'

'Oh, old John Longworth in the City! Certainly; I know all about him. I never saw him before, but I think we are quite safe in telling him anything he wants to know, if he asks.'

'Breakfast, gentlemen,' said the steward, putting his head in at the door.

After breakfast Edith Longworth and her cousin walked the deck together. Young Longworth, although in better humour than he had been the night before, was still rather short in his replies, and irritating in his questions.

'Aren't you tired of this eternal parade up and down?' he asked his cousin. 'It seems to me like a treadmill—as if a person had to work for his board and lodging.'

'Let us sit down then,' she replied; 'although I think a walk before lunch or dinner increases the attractiveness of those meals wonderfully.'

'I never feel the need of working up an appetite,' he answered pettishly.

'Well, as I said before, let us sit down;' and the girl, having found her chair, lifted the rug that lay upon it, and took her place.

The young man, after standing for a moment looking at her through his glistening monocle, finally sat down beside her.

'The beastly nuisance of living on board ship,' he said, 'is that you can't play billiards.'

'I am sure you play enough at cards to satisfy you during the few days we are at sea,' she answered.

'Oh, cards! I soon tire of them.'

'You tire very quickly of everything.'

'I certainly get tired of lounging about the deck, either walking or sitting.'

'Then, pray don't let me keep you.'

'You want me to go so you may walk with your newly-found friend, that miner fellow?'

'That miner fellow is talking with my father just now. Still, if you would like to know, I have no hesitation in telling you I would much prefer his company to yours if you continue in your present mood.'

'Yes, or in any mood.'

'I did not say that; but if it will comfort you to have me say it, I shall be glad to oblige you.'

'Perhaps, then, I should go and talk with your father, and let the miner fellow come here and talk with you.'

'Please do not call him the miner fellow. His name is Mr. Kenyon. It is not difficult to remember.'

'I know his name well enough. Shall I send him to you?'

'No. I want to talk with you in spite of your disagreeableness. And what is more, I want to talk with you about Mr. Kenyon. So I wish you to assume your very best behaviour. It may be for your benefit.'

The young man indulged in a sarcastic laugh.

'Oh, if you are going to do that, I have nothing more to say,' remarked Edith quietly, rising from her chair.

'I meant no harm. Sit down and go on with your talk.'

'Listen, then. Mr. Kenyon has the option of a mine in Canada, which he believes to be a good property. He intends to form a company when he reaches London. Now, why shouldn't you make friends with him, and, if you found the property is as good as he thinks it is, help him to form the company, and so make some money for both of you?'

'You are saying one word for me and two for Kenyon.'

'No, it would be as much for your benefit as for his, so it is a word for each of you.'

'You are very much interested in him.'

'My dear cousin, I am very much interested in the mine, and I am very much interested in you. Mr. Kenyon can speak of nothing but the mine, and I am sure my father would be pleased to see you take an interest in something of the sort. I mean, you know that if you would do something of your own accord—something that was not suggested to you by him—he would like it.'

'Well, it is suggested to me by you, and that's almost the same thing.'

'No, it is not the same thing at all. Father would indeed be glad if he saw you take up anything on your own account and make a success of it. Why can you not spend some of your time talking with Mr. Kenyon discussing arrangements, so that when you return to London you might be prepared to put the mine on the market and bring out the company?'

'If I thought you were talking to me for my own sake, I would do what you suggest; but I believe you are speaking only because you are interested in Kenyon.'

'Nonsense! How can you be so absurd? I have known Mr. Kenyon but for a few hours—a day or two at most.'

The young man pulled his moustache for a moment, adjusted his eyeglass, and then said:

'Very good. I will speak to Kenyon on the subject if you wish it, but I don't say that I can help him.'

'I don't ask you to help him. I ask you to help yourself. Here is Mr. Kenyon. Let me introduce you, and then you can talk over the project at your leisure.'

'I don't suppose an introduction is necessary,' growled the young man; but as Kenyon approached them, Edith Longworth said:

'We are a board of directors, Mr. Kenyon, on the great mica-mine. Will you join the Board now, or after allotment?' Then, before he could reply, she said: 'Mr. Kenyon, this is my cousin, Mr. William Longworth.'

Longworth, without rising from his chair, shook hands in rather a surly fashion.

'I am going to speak to my father,' said the girl, 'and will leave you to talk over the mica-mine.'

When she had gone, young Longworth asked Kenyon:

'Where is the mine my cousin speaks of?'

'It is near the Ottawa River, in Canada,' was the answer.

'And what do you expect to sell it for?'

'Fifty thousand pounds.'

'Fifty thousand pounds! That will leave nothing to divide up among— by the way, how many are there in this thing—yourself alone?'

'No; my friend Wentworth shares with me.'

'Share and share alike?'

'Yes.'

'Of course, you think this mine is worth the money you ask for it— there is no swindle about it, is there?'

Kenyon drew himself up sharply as this remark was made. Then he answered coldly:

'If there was any swindle about it, I should have nothing to do with it.'

'Well, you see, I didn't know; mining swindles are not such rarities as you may imagine. If the mine is so valuable, why are the proprietors anxious to sell?'

'The owners are in Austria, and the mine in Canada, and so it is rather at arm's-length, as it were. They are mining for mica, but the mine is more valuable in other respects than it is as a mica property. They have placed a figure on the mine which is more than it has cost them so far.'

'You know its value in those other respects?'

'I do.'

'Does anyone know this except yourself?'

'I think not—no one but my friend Wentworth.'

'How did you come to learn its value?'

'By visiting the mine. Wentworth and I went together to see it.'

'Oh, is Wentworth also a mining expert?'

'No; he is an accountant in London.'

'Both of you were sent out by the London Syndicate, I understand, to look after their mines, or the mines they thought of purchasing, were you not?'

'We were.'

'And you spent your time in looking up other properties for yourselves, did you?'

Kenyon reddened at this question.

'My dear sir,' he said, 'if you are going to talk in this strain, you will have to excuse me. We were sent by the London Syndicate to do a certain thing. We did it, and did it thoroughly. After it was done the time was our own, as much as it is at the present moment. We were not hired by the day, but took a stated sum for doing a certain piece of work. I may go further and say that the time was our own at any period of our visit, so long as we fulfilled what the London Syndicate required of us.'

'Oh, I meant no offence,' said Longworth. 'You merely seemed to be posing as a sort of goody-goody young man when I spoke of mining swindles, so I only wished to startle you. How much have you to pay for the mine—

that is the mica-mine?'

Kenyon hesitated for a moment.

'I do not feel at liberty to mention the sum until I have consulted with my friend Wentworth.'

'Well, you see, if I am to help you in this matter, I shall need to know every particular.'

'Certainly. I shall have to consult Wentworth as to whether we require any help or not.'

'Oh, you will speedily find that you require all the help you can get in London. You will probably learn that a hundred such mines are for sale now, and the chances are you will find that this very mica-mine has been offered. What do you believe the mine is really worth?'

'I think it is worth anywhere from one hundred thousand pounds to two hundred thousand pounds, perhaps more.'

'Is it actually worth one hundred thousand pounds?'

'According to my estimate, it is.'

'Is it worth one hundred and fifty thousand pounds?'

'It is.'

'Is it worth two hundred thousand pounds?'

'I think so.'

'What percentage would it pay on two hundred thousand pounds?'

'It might pay ten per cent., perhaps more.'

'Why, in the name of all that is wonderful, don't you put the price at two hundred thousand pounds? If it will pay ten per cent and more on that amount of money, then that sum is what you ought to sell it for. Now we will investigate this matter, if you like, and if you wish to take me in with you, and put the price up to two hundred thousand pounds, I will see what can

110

be done about it when we get to London. Of course, it will mean somebody going out to Canada again to report on the mine. Your report would naturally not be taken in such a case; you are too vitally interested.'

'Of course,' replied Kenyon, 'I shouldn't expect my report to have any weight.'

'Well, somebody would have to be sent out to report on the mine. Are you certain that it will stand thorough investigation?'

'I am convinced of it.'

'Would you be willing to make this proposition to the investors, that, if the expert did not support your statement, you would pay his expenses out there and back?'

'I would be willing to do that,' said Kenyon, 'if I had the money; but I haven't the money.'

'Then, how do you expect to float the mine on the London market? It cannot be done without money.'

'I thought I might be able to interest some capitalist.'

'I am much afraid, Mr. Kenyon, that you have vague ideas of how companies are formed. Perhaps your friend Wentworth, being an accountant, may know more about it.'

'Yes, I confess I am relying mainly on his assistance.'

'Well, will you agree to put the price of the mine at two hundred thousand pounds, and share what we make equally between the three of us?'

'It is a large price.'

'It is not a large price if the mine will pay good dividends upon it; if it will pay eight per cent. on that amount, it is the real price of the mine, while you say that you are certain it will pay ten per cent.'

'I say I think it will pay that percentage. One never can speak with entire certainty where a mine is concerned.'

'Are you willing to put the price of the mine at that figure? Otherwise, I will have nothing to do with it.'

'As I said, I shall have to consult my friend about it, but that can be done in a very short time, and I will answer you in the afternoon.'

'Good; there is no particular hurry. Have a talk over it with him, and while I do not promise anything, I think the scheme looks feasible, if the property is good. Remember, I know nothing at all about that, but if you agree to take me in, I shall have to know full particulars of what you are going to pay for the property, and what its peculiar value is.'

'Certainly. If we agree to take a partner, we will give that partner our full confidence.'

'Well, there is nothing more to say until you have had a consultation with your friend. Good-morning, Mr. Kenyon;' and with that Longworth arose and lounged off to the smoking-room.

Kenyon waited where he was for some time, hoping Wentworth would come along, but the young man did not appear. At last he went in search of him. He passed along the deck, but found no trace of his friend, and looked for a moment into the smoking-room, but Wentworth was not there. He went downstairs to the saloon, but his search below was equally fruitless. Coming up on deck again, he saw Miss Brewster sitting alone reading a paper-covered novel.

'Have you seen my friend Wentworth?' he asked.

She laid the book open-faced upon her lap, and looked quickly up at Kenyon before answering.

'I saw him not so very long ago, but I don't know where he is now. Perhaps you will find him in his state-room; in fact, I think it more than likely that he is there.'

With that, Miss Brewster resumed her book.

Kenyon descended to the state-room, opened the door, and saw his comrade sitting upon the plush-covered sofa, with his head in his hands. At the opening of the door, Wentworth started and looked for a moment at his friend, apparently not seeing him. His face was so gray and ghastly that Kenyon leaned against the door for support as he saw it.

'My God, George!' he cried, 'what is the matter with you? What has happened? Tell me!'

Wentworth gazed in front of him with glassy eyes for a moment, but did not answer. Then his head dropped again in his hands, and he groaned aloud.

CHAPTER VIII.

There was one man on board the Caloric to whom Wentworth had taken an extreme dislike. His name was Fleming, and he claimed to be a New York politician. As none of his friends or enemies asserted anything worse about him, it may be assumed that Fleming had designated his occupation correctly. If Wentworth were asked what he most disliked about the man, he would probably have said his offensive familiarity. Fleming seemed to think himself a genial good fellow, and he was immensely popular with a certain class in the smoking-room. He was lavishly free with his invitations to drink, and always had a case of good cigars in his pocket, which he bestowed with great liberality. He had the habit of slapping a man boisterously on the back, and saying, 'Well, old fellow, how are you? How's things?' He usually confided to his listeners that he was a self-made man: had landed at New York without a cent in his pocket, and look at him now!

Wentworth was icy towards this man; but frigidity had no effect whatever on the exuberant spirits of the New York politician.

'Well, old man!' cried Fleming to Wentworth, as he came up to the latter and linked arms affectionately. 'What lovely weather we are having for winter time!'

'It is good,' said Wentworth.

'Good? It's glorious! Who would have thought, when leaving New York in a snowstorm as we did, that we would run right into the heart of spring? I hope you are enjoying your voyage?'

'I am.'

'You ought to. By the way, why are you so awful stand-offish? Is it natural, or merely put on "for this occasion only"?'

'I do not know what you mean by "stand-offish."'

'You know very well what I mean. Why do you pretend to be so stiff and formal with a fellow?'

'I am never stiff and formal with anyone unless I do not desire his acquaintance.'

Fleming laughed loudly.

'I suppose that's a personal hint. Well, it seems to me, if this exclusiveness is genuine, that you would be more afraid of newspaper notoriety than of anything else.'

'Why do you say that?'

'Because I can't, for the life of me, see why you spend so much time with Dolly Dimple. I am sure I don't know why she is here; but I do know this: that you will be served up to the extent of two or three columns in the Sunday Argus as sure as you live.'

'I don't understand you.'

'You don't? Why, it's plain enough. You spend all your time with her.'

'I do not even know of whom you are speaking.'

'Oh, come now, that's too rich! Is it possible you don't know that Miss Jennie Brewster is the one who writes those Sunday articles over the signature of "Dolly Dimple"?'

A strange fear fell upon Wentworth as his companion mentioned the Argus. He remembered it as J.K. Rivers' paper; but when Fleming said Miss Brewster was a correspondent of the Argus, he was aghast.

'I—I—I don't think I quite catch your meaning,' he stammered.

'Well, my meaning's easy enough to see. Hasn't she ever told you? Then it shows she wants to do you up on toast. You're not an English politician, are you? You haven't any political secrets that Dolly wants to get at, have you? Why, she is the greatest girl there is in the whole United States for finding out just what a man doesn't want to have known. You know the Secretary of State'—and here Fleming went on to relate a wonderfully brilliant feat of

Dolly's; but the person to whom he was talking had neither eyes nor ears. He heard nothing and he saw nothing.

'Dear me!' said Fleming, drawing himself up and slapping the other on the back, 'you look perfectly dumfounded. I suppose I oughtn't to have given Dolly away like this; but she has pretended all along that she didn't know me, and so I've got even with her. You take my advice, and anything you don't want to see in print, don't tell Miss Brewster, that's all. Have a cigar?'

'No, thank you,' replied the other mechanically.

'Better come in and have a drink.'

'No, thank you.'

'Well, so long. I'll see you later.'

'It can't be true—it can't be true!' Wentworth repeated to himself in deep consternation, but still an inward misgiving warned him that, after all, it might be true. With his hands clasped behind him he walked up and down, trying to collect himself—trying to remember what he had told and what he had not. As he walked along, heeding nobody, a sweet voice from one of the chairs thrilled him, and he paused.

'Why, Mr. Wentworth, what is the matter with you this morning? You look as if you had seen a ghost.'

Wentworth glanced at the young woman seated in the chair, who was gazing up brightly at him.

'Well,' he said at last, 'I am not sure but I have seen a ghost. May I sit down beside you?'

'May you? Why, of course you may. I shall be delighted to have you. Is there anything wrong?'

'I don't know. Yes, I think there is.'

'Well, tell it to me; perhaps I can help you. A woman's wit, you know. What is the trouble?'

116

'May I ask you a few questions, Miss Brewster?'

'Certainly. A thousand of them, if you like, and I will answer them all if I can.'

'Thank you. Will you tell me, Miss Brewster, if you are connected with any newspaper?'

Miss Brewster laughed her merry, silvery little laugh.

'Who told you? Ah! I see how it is. It was that creature Fleming. I'll get even with him for this some day. I know what office he is after, and the next time he wants a good notice from the Argus he'll get it; see if he don't. I know some things about him that he would just as soon not see in print. Why, what a fool the man is! I suppose he told you out of revenge because I wouldn't speak to him the other evening. Never mind; I can afford to wait.'

'Then—then, Miss Brewster, it is true?'

'Certainly it is true; is there anything wrong about it? I hope you don't think it is disreputable to belong to a good newspaper?'

'To a good newspaper, no; to a bad newspaper, yes.'

'Oh, I don't think the Argus is a bad newspaper. It pays me well.'

'Then it is to the Argus that you belong?'

'Certainly.'

'May I ask, Miss Brewster, if there is anything I have spoken about to you that you intend to use in your paper?'

Again Miss Brewster laughed.

'I will be perfectly frank with you. I never tell a lie—it doesn't pay. Yes. The reason I am here is because you are here. I am here to find out what your report on those mines will be, also what the report of your friend will be. I have found out.'

'And do you intend to use the information you have thus obtained—if

117

I may say it—under false pretences?'

'My dear sir, you are forgetting yourself. You must remember that you are talking to a lady.'

'A lady!' cried Wentworth in his anguish.

'Yes, sir, a lady; and you must be careful how you talk to this lady. There was no false pretence about it, if you remember. What you told me was in conversation; I didn't ask you for it. I didn't even make the first advances towards your acquaintance.'

'But you must admit, Miss Brewster, that it is very unfair to get a man to engage in what he thinks is a private conversation, and then to publish what he has said.'

'My dear sir, if that were the case, how would we get anything for publication that people didn't want to be known? Why, I remember once, when the Secretary of State——'

'Yes,' interrupted Wentworth wearily; 'Fleming told me that story.'

'Oh, did he? Well, I'm sure I'm much obliged to him. Then I need not repeat it.'

'Do you mean to say that you intend to send to the Argus for publication what I have told you in confidence?'

'Certainly. As I said before, that is what I am here for. Besides, there was no "in confidence" about it.'

'And yet you pretend to be a truthful, honest, honourable woman?'

'I don't pretend it; I am.'

'How much truth, then, is there in your story that you are a millionaire's daughter about to visit your father in Paris, and accompany him from there to the Riviera?'

Miss Brewster laughed brightly.

'Oh, I don't call fibs, which a person has to tell in the way of business, untruths.'

'Then probably you do not think your estimable colleague, Mr. J.K. Rivers, behaved dishonourably in Ottawa?'

'Well, hardly. I think Rivers was not justified in what he did because he was unsuccessful, that is all. I'll bet a dollar if I had got hold of these papers they would have gone through to New York; but, then, J.K. Rivers is only a stupid man, and most men are stupid'—with a sly glance at Wentworth.

'I am willing to admit that, Miss Brewster, if you mean me. There never was a more stupid man than I have been.'

'My dear Mr. Wentworth, it will do you ever so much good if you come to a realization of that fact. The truth is, you take yourself much too seriously. Now, it won't hurt you a bit to have what I am going to send published in the Argus, and it will help me a great deal. Just you wait here for a few moments.'

With that she flung her book upon his lap, sprang up, and vanished down the companion-way. In a very short time she reappeared with some sheets of paper in her hand.

'Now you see how fair and honest I am going to be. I am going to read you what I have written. If there is anything in it that is not true, I will very gladly cut it out; and if there is anything more to be added, I shall be very glad to add it. Isn't that fair?'

Wentworth was so confounded with the woman's impudence that he could make no reply.

She began to read: '"By an unexampled stroke of enterprise the New York Argus is enabled this morning to lay before its readers a full and exclusive account of the report made by the two English specialists, Mr. George Wentworth and Mr. John Kenyon, who were sent over by the London Syndicate to examine into the accounts, and inquire into the true value of the mines of the Ottawa River."'

She looked up from the paper, and said, with an air of friendly confidence:

'I shouldn't send that if I thought the people at the New York end would

119

know enough to write it themselves; but as the paper is edited by dull men, and not by a sharp woman, I have to make them pay twenty-five cents a word for puffing their own enterprise. Well, to go on: "When it is remembered that the action of the London Syndicate will depend entirely on the report of these two gentlemen—"'

'I wouldn't put it that way,' interrupted Wentworth in his despair. 'I would use the word "largely" for "entirely."'

'Oh, thank you,' said Miss Brewster cordially. She placed the manuscript on her knee, and, with her pencil, marked out the word 'entirely,' substituting 'largely.' The reading went on: '"When it is remembered that the action of the London Syndicate will depend largely on the report of these two gentlemen, the enterprise of the Argus in getting this exclusive information, which will be immediately cabled to London, may be imagined." That is the preliminary, you see; and, as I said, it wouldn't be necessary to cable it if women were at the head of affairs over there, which they are not. "Mr. John Kenyon, the mining expert, has visited all the mineral ranges along the Ottawa River, and his report is that the mines are very much what is claimed for them; but he thinks they are not worked properly, although, with judicious management and more careful mining, the properties can be made to pay good dividends. Mr. George Wentworth, who is one of the leading accountants of London—"'

'I wouldn't say that, either,' groaned George. 'Just strike out the words "one of the leading accountants of London."'

'Yes?' said Miss Brewster; 'and what shall I put in the place of them?'

'Put in place of them "the stupidest ass in London"!'

Miss Brewster laughed at that.

'No; I shall put in what I first wrote: "Mr. George Wentworth, one of the leading accountants of London, has gone through the books of the different mines. He has made some startling discoveries. The accounts have been kept in such a way as to completely delude investors, and this fact will have a powerful effect on the minds of the London Syndicate. The books of the different mines show a profit of about two hundred thousand dollars,

120

whereas the actual facts of the case are that there has been an annual loss of something like one hundred thousand dollars—"'

'What's that? what's that?' cried Wentworth sharply.

'Dollars, you know. You said twenty thousand pounds. We put it in dollars, don't you see?'

'Oh,' said Wentworth, relapsing again.

'"One hundred thousand dollars"—where was I? Oh yes. "It is claimed that an American expert went over these books before Mr. Wentworth, and that he asserted they were all right. An explanation from this gentleman will now be in order."'

'There!' cried the young lady, 'that is the substance of the thing. Of course, I may amplify a little more before we get to Queenstown, so as to make them pay more money. People don't value a thing that doesn't cost them dearly. How do you like it? Is it correct?'

'Perfectly correct,' answered the miserable young man.

'Oh, I am so glad you like it! I do love to have things right.'

'I didn't say I liked it.'

'No, of course, you couldn't be expected to say that; but I am glad you think it is accurate. I will add a note to the effect that you think it is a good résumé of your report.'

'For Heaven's sake, don't drag me into the matter!' cried Wentworth.

'Well, I won't, if you don't want me to.'

There was silence for a few moments, during which the young woman seemed to be adding commas and full-stops to the MS. on her knee. Wentworth cleared his throat two or three times, but his lips were so dry that he could hardly speak. At last he said:

'Miss Brewster, how can I induce you not to send that from Queenstown to your paper?'

121

The young woman looked up at him with a pleasant bright smile.

'Induce me? Why, you couldn't do it—it couldn't be done. This will be one of the greatest triumphs I have ever achieved. Think of Rivers failing in it, and me accomplishing it!'

'Yes; I have thought of that,' replied the young man despondently. 'Now, perhaps you don't know that the full report was mailed from Ottawa to our house in London, and the moment we get to Queenstown I will telegraph my partners to put the report in the hands of the directors?'

'Oh, I know all about that,' replied Miss Brewster; 'Rivers told me. He read the letter that was enclosed with the documents he took from your friend. Now, have you made any calculations about this voyage?'

'Calculations? I don't know what you mean.'

'Well, I mean just this: We shall probably reach Queenstown on Saturday afternoon. This report, making allowance for the difference in the time, will appear in the Argus on Sunday morning. Your telegram will reach your house or your firm on Saturday night, when nothing can be done with it. Sunday nothing can be done. Monday morning, before your report will reach the directors, the substance of what has appeared in the Argus will be in the financial papers, cabled over to London on Sunday night. The first thing your directors will see of it will be in the London financial papers on Monday morning. That's what I mean, Mr. Wentworth, by calculating the voyage.'

Wentworth said no more. He staggered to his feet and made his way as best he could to the state-room, groping like a blind man. There he sat down with his head in his hands, and there his friend Kenyon found him.

CHAPTER IX.

'Tell me what has happened,' demanded John Kenyon.

Wentworth looked up at him.

'Everything has happened,' he answered.

'What do you mean, George? Are you ill? What is the matter with you?'

'I am worse than ill, John—a great deal worse than ill. I wish I were ill.'

'That wouldn't help things, whatever is wrong. Come, wake up. Tell me what the trouble is.'

'John, I am a fool—an ass—a gibbering idiot.'

'Admitting that, what then?'

'I trusted a woman—imbecile that I am; and now—now—I'm what you see me.'

'Has—has Miss Brewster anything to do with it?' asked Kenyon suspiciously.

'She has everything to do with it.'

'Has she—rejected you, George?'

'What! that girl? Oh, you're the idiot now. Do you think I would ask her?'

'I cannot be blamed for jumping at conclusions. You must remember "that girl," as you call her, has had most of your company during this voyage; and most of your good words when you were not with her. What is the matter? What has she to do with your trouble?'

Wentworth paced up and down the narrow limits of the state-room as if he were caged. He smote his hand against his thigh, while Kenyon looked at him in wonder.

'I don't know how I can tell you, John,' he said. 'I must, of course; but I don't know how I can.'

'Come on deck with me.'

'Never.'

'Come out, I say, into the fresh air. It is stuffy here, and, besides, there is more danger of being overheard in the state-room than on deck. Come along, old fellow.'

He caught his companion by the arm, and partly dragged him out of the room, closing the door behind him.

'Pull yourself together,' he said. 'A little fresh air will do you good.'

They made their way to the deck, and, linking arms, walked up and down. For a long time Wentworth said nothing, and Kenyon had the tact to hold his peace. Suddenly Wentworth noticed that they were pacing back and forth in front of Miss Brewster, so he drew his friend away to another part of the ship. After a few turns up and down, he said:

'You remember Rivers, of course.'

'Distinctly.'

'He was employed on that vile sheet, the New York Argus.'

'I suppose it is a vile sheet. I don't remember ever seeing it. Yes, I know he was connected with that paper. What then? What has Miss Brewster to do with Rivers?'

'She is one of the Argus staff, too.'

'George Wentworth, you don't mean to tell me that!'

'I do.'

'And is she here to find out about the mine?'

'Exactly. She was put on the job after Rivers had failed.'

'George!' said Kenyon, suddenly dropping his companion's arm and

124

facing him. 'What have you told her?'

'There is the misery of it. I have told her everything.'

'My dear fellow, how could you be——'

'Oh, I know—I know! I know everything you would say. Everything you can say I have said to myself, and ten times more and ten times worse. There is nothing you can say of me more bitter than what I think about myself.'

'Did you tell her anything about my report?'

'I told her everything—everything! Do you understand? She is going to telegraph from Queenstown the full essence of the reports—of both our reports.'

'Heavens! this is fearful. Is there no way to prevent her sending it?'

'If you think you can prevent her, I wish you would try it.'

'How did you find it out? Did she tell you?'

'Oh, it doesn't matter how I found it out. I did find it out. A man told me who she was; then I asked her, and she was perfectly frank about it. She read me the report, even.'

'Read it to you?'

'Yes, read it to me, and punctuated it in my presence—put in some words that I suggested as being better than those she had used. Oh, it was the coolest piece of work you ever saw!'

'But there must be some way of preventing her getting that account to New York in time. You see, all we have to do is to wire your people to hand in our report to the directors, and then hers is forestalled. She has to telegraph from a British office, and it seems to me that we could stop her in some way.'

'As, for instance, how?'

'Oh, I don't know just how at the moment, but we ought to be able to do it. If it were a man, we could have him arrested as a dynamiter or something; but a woman, of course, is more difficult to deal with. George, I would appeal to her better nature if I were you.'

Wentworth laughed sneeringly.

'Better nature?' he said. 'She hasn't any; and that is not the worst of it. She has "calculated," as she calls it, all the possibilities in the affair; she "calculates" that we will reach Queenstown about Saturday night. If we do, she will get her report through in time to be published on Sunday in the New York Argus. If that is the case, then see where our telegram will be. We telegraph our people to send in the report. It reaches the office Saturday night, and is not read. The office closes at two o'clock; but even if they got it, and understood the urgency of the matter, they could not place the papers before the directors until Monday morning, and by Monday morning it will be in the London financial sheets.'

'George, that woman is a fiend.'

'No, she isn't, John. She is merely a clever American journalist, who thinks she has done a very good piece of work indeed, and who, through the stupidity of one man, has succeeded, that's all.'

'Have you made any appeal to her at all?'

'Oh, haven't I! Of course I have. What good did it do? She merely laughed at me. Don't you understand? That is what she is here for. Her whole voyage is for that one purpose; and it's not likely the woman is going to forego her triumph after having succeeded—more especially as somebody else in the same office has failed. That's what gives additional zest to what she has done. The fact that Rivers has failed and she has triumphed seems to be the great feather in her cap.'

'Then,' said Kenyon, 'I'm going to appeal to Miss Brewster myself.'

'Very well. I wish you joy of your job. But do what you can, John, there's a good fellow. Meanwhile, I want to be alone somewhere.'

Wentworth went down the stairway that led to the steerage department, and for a few moments sat among the steerage passengers. Then he climbed up another ladder, and got to the very front of the ship. Here he sat down on a coil of rope, and thought over the situation. Thinking, however, did him very little good. He realized that, even if he got hold of the paper Miss Brewster had, she could easily write another. She had the facts in her head, and all that she needed to do was to get to a telegraph office and there hand in her message.

Meanwhile, Kenyon took a few turns up and down the deck, thinking deeply on the same subject. He passed over to the side where Miss Brewster sat, but on coming opposite her had not the courage to take his place beside her. She was calmly reading her book. Three times he came opposite her, paused for a moment, and then continued his hopeless march. He saw that his courage was not going to be sufficient for the task, and yet he felt the task must be accomplished. He didn't know how to begin. He didn't know what inducement to offer the young woman for foregoing the fruits of her ingenuity. He felt that this was the weak point in his armour. The third time he paused in front of Miss Brewster; she looked up and motioned him to the chair beside her, saying:

'I do not know you very well, Mr. Kenyon, but I know who you are. Won't you sit down here for a moment?'

The bewildered man took the chair she indicated.

'Now, Mr. Kenyon, I know just what is troubling you. You have passed three or four times wishing to sit down beside me, and yet afraid to venture. Is that not true?'

'Quite true.'

'I knew it was. Now I know also what you have come for. Mr. Wentworth has told you what the trouble is. He has told you that he has given me all the particulars about the mines, hasn't he?'

'He has.'

'And he has gone off to his state-room to think over the matter, and has left the affair in your hands, and you imagine you can come here to me and, perhaps, talk me out of sending that despatch to the Argus. Isn't that your motive?'

'That is about what I hope to be able to do,' said Kenyon, mopping his brow.

'Well, I thought I might just as well put you out of your misery at once. You take things very seriously, Mr. Kenyon—I can see that. Now, don't you?'

'I am afraid I do.'

'Why, of course you do. The publication of this, as I told Mr. Wentworth, will really not matter at all. It will not be any reflection on either of you, because your friends will be sure that, if you had known to whom you were talking, you would never have said anything about the mines.'

Kenyon smiled grimly at this piece of comfort.

'Now, I have been thinking about something since Mr. Wentworth went away. I am really very sorry for him. I am more sorry than I can tell.'

'Then,' said Kenyon eagerly, 'won't you——'

'No, I won't, so we needn't recur to that phase of the subject. That is what I am here for, and, no matter what you say, the despatch is going to be sent. Now, it is better to understand that at the first, and then it will create no trouble afterwards. Don't you think that is the best?'

'Probably,' answered the wretched man.

'Well, then, let us start there. I will say in the cablegram that the information comes from neither Mr. Kenyon nor Mr. Wentworth.'

'Yes, but that wouldn't be true.'

'Why, of course it wouldn't be true; but that doesn't matter, does it?'

'Well, on our side of the water,' said Kenyon, 'we think the truth does matter.'

Miss Brewster laughed heartily.

'Dear me!' she said, 'what little tact you have! How does it concern you whether it is true or not? If there is any falsehood, it is not you who tell it, so you are free from all blame. Indeed, you are free from all blame anyhow, in this affair; it is all your friend Wentworth's fault; but still, if it hadn't been Wentworth, it would have been you.'

Kenyon looked up at her incredulously.

'Oh yes, it would,' she said, nodding confidently at him. 'You must not flatter yourself, because Mr. Wentworth told me everything about it, that you wouldn't have done just the same, if I had had to find it out from you. All men are pretty much alike where women are concerned.'

'Can I say nothing to you, Miss Brewster, which will keep you from sending the message to America?'

'You cannot, Mr. Kenyon. I thought we had settled that at the beginning. I see there is no use talking to you. I will return to my book, which is very interesting. Good-morning, Mr. Kenyon.'

Kenyon felt the hopelessness of his project quite as much as Wentworth had done, and, thrusting his hands deep into his pockets, he wandered disconsolately up and down the deck.

As he went to the other side of the deck, he met Miss Longworth walking alone. She smiled a cordial welcome to him, so he turned and changed his step to suit hers.

'May I walk with you a few minutes?' he said.

'Of course you may,' was the reply, 'What is the matter? You are looking very unhappy.'

'My comrade and myself are in great trouble, and I thought I should like to talk with you about it.'

'I am sure if there is anything I can do to help you, I shall be most glad to do it.'

'Perhaps you may suggest something. You see, two men dealing with

129

one woman are perfectly helpless.'

'Ah, who is the one woman—not I, is it?'

'No, not you, Miss Longworth. I wish it were, then we would have no trouble.'

'Oh, thank you!'

'You see, it is like this: When we were in Quebec—I think I told you about that—the New York Argus sent a man to find out what we had reported, or were going to report, to the London Syndicate.'

'Yes, you told me that.'

'Rivers was his name. Well, this same paper, finding that Rivers had failed after having stolen the documents, has tried a much more subtle scheme, which promises to be successful. They have put on board this ship a young woman who has gained a reputation for learning secrets not intended for the public. This young woman is Miss Brewster, who sits next Wentworth at the table. Fate seems to have played right into her hand and placed her beside him. They became acquainted, and, unfortunately, my friend has told her a great deal about the mines, which she professed an interest in. Or, rather, she pretended to have an interest in him, and so he spoke, being, of course, off his guard. There is no more careful fellow in the world than George Wentworth, but a man does not expect that a private conversation with a lady will ever appear in a newspaper.'

'Naturally not.'

'Very well, that is the state of things. In some manner Wentworth came to know that this young woman was the special correspondent of the New York Argus. He spoke to her about it, and she is perfectly frank in saying she is here solely for the purpose of finding out what the reports will be, and that the moment she gets to Queenstown she will cable what she has discovered to New York.'

'Dear me! that is very perplexing. What have you done?'

'We have done nothing so far, or rather, I should say, we have tried everything we could think of, and have accomplished nothing. Wentworth has appealed to her, and I made a clumsy attempt at an appeal also, but it was of no use. I feel my own helplessness in this matter, and Wentworth is completely broken down over it.'

'Poor fellow! I am sure of that. Let me think a moment.'

They walked up and down the deck in silence for a few minutes. Then Miss Longworth looked up at Kenyon, and said;

'Will you place this matter in my hands?'

'Certainly, if you will be so kind as to take any interest in it.'

'I take a great deal of interest. Of course, you know my father is deeply concerned in it also, so I am acting in a measure for him.'

'Have you any plan?'

'Yes; my plan is simply this: The young woman is working for money; now, if we can offer her more than her paper gives, she will very quickly accept, or I am much mistaken in the kind of woman she is.'

'Ah, yes,' said Kenyon; 'but we haven't the money, you see.'

'Never mind; the money will be quickly forthcoming. Don't trouble any more about it. I am sure that can be arranged.'

Kenyon thanked her, looking his gratitude rather than speaking it, for he was an unready man, and she bade him good-bye until she could think over her plan.

That evening there was a tap at the state-room door of Miss Jennie Brewster.

'Come in,' cried the occupant.

Miss Longworth entered, and the occupant of the room looked up, with a frown, from her writing.

'May I have a few moments' conversation with you?' asked the visitor gravely.

CHAPTER X.

Miss Jennie Brewster was very much annoyed at being interrupted, and she took no pains to conceal her feelings. She was writing an article entitled 'How People kill Time on Shipboard,' and she did not wish to be disturbed; besides, as she often said of herself, she was not 'a woman's woman,' and she neither liked, nor was liked by, her own sex.

'I desire a few moments' conversation with you, if I have your permission,' said Edith Longworth, as she closed the door behind her.

'Certainly,' answered Jennie Brewster. 'Will you sit down?'

'Thank you,' replied the other, as she took a seat on the sofa. 'I do not know just how to begin what I wish to say. Perhaps it will be better to commence by telling you that I know why you are on board this steamer.'

'Yes; and why am I on board the steamer, may I ask?'

'You are here, I understand, to get certain information from Mr. Wentworth. You have obtained it, and it is in reference to this that I have come to see you.'

'Indeed! and are you so friendly with Mr. Wentworth that you——'

'I scarcely know Mr. Wentworth at all.'

'Then, why do you come on a mission from him?'

'It is not a mission from him. It is not a mission from anyone. I was speaking to Mr. Kenyon, or, rather, Mr. Kenyon was speaking to me, about a subject which troubled him greatly. It is a subject in which my father is interested. My father is a member of the London Syndicate, and he naturally would not desire to have your intended cable message sent to New York.'

'Really; are you quite sure that you are not speaking less for your father than for your friend Kenyon?'

Anger burned in Miss Longworth's face, and flashed from her eyes as she answered:

'You must not speak to me in that way.'

'Excuse me, I shall speak to you in just the way I please. I did not ask for this conference; you did, and as you have taken it upon yourself to come into this room uninvited, you will have to put up with what you hear. Those who interfere with other people's business, as a general thing, do not have a nice time.'

'I quite appreciated all the possible disagreeableness of coming here, when I came.'

'I am glad of that, because if you hear anything you do not like, you will not be disappointed, and will have only yourself to thank for it.'

'I would like to talk about this matter in a spirit of friendliness if I can. I think nothing is to be attained by speaking in any other way.'

'Very well, then. What excuse have you to give me for coming into my state-room to talk about business which does not concern you?'

'Miss Brewster, it does concern me—it concerns my father, and that concerns me. I am, in a measure, my father's private secretary, and am intimately acquainted with all the business he has in hand. This particular business is his affair, and therefore mine. That is the reason I am here.'

'Are you sure?'

'Am I sure of what?'

'Are you sure that what you say is true?'

'I am not in the habit of speaking anything but the truth.'

'Perhaps you flatter yourself that is the case, but it does not deceive me. You merely come here because Mr. Kenyon is in a muddle about what I am going to do. Isn't that the reason?'

Miss Longworth saw that her task was going to be even harder than she had expected.

'Suppose we let all question of motive rest? I have come here—I have asked your permission to speak on this subject, and you have given me the permission. Having done so, it seems to me you should hear me out. You say that I should not be offended——'

'I didn't say so. I do not care a rap whether you are offended or not.'

'You at least said I might hear something that would not be pleasant. What I wanted to say is this: I have taken the risk of that, and, as you remark, whether I am offended or not does not matter. Now we will come to the point——'

'Just before you come to the point, please let me know if Mr. Kenyon told you he had spoken to me on this subject already.'

'Yes, he told me so.'

'Did he tell you that his friend Wentworth had also had a conversation with me about it?'

'Yes, he told me that also.'

'Very well, then, if those two men can do nothing to shake my purpose, how do you expect to do it?'

'That is what I am about to tell you. This is a commercial world, and I am a commercial man's daughter. I recognise the fact that you are going to cable this information for the money it brings. Is that not the case?'

'It is partly the case.'

'For what other consideration do you work, then?'

'For the consideration of being known as one of the best newspaper women in the city of New York. That is the other consideration.'

'I understood you were already known as the most noted newspaper woman in New York.'

This remark was much more diplomatic than Miss Longworth herself suspected.

Jennie Brewster looked rather pleased, then she said:

'Oh, I don't know about that; but I intend it shall be so before a year is past.'

'Very well, you have plenty of time to accomplish your object without using the information you have obtained on board this ship. Now, as I was saying, the New York Argus pays you a certain amount for doing this work. If you will promise not to send the report over to that paper, I will give you a cheque for double the sum the Argus will pay you, besides refunding all your expenses twice over.'

'In other words, you ask me to be bribed and refuse to perform my duty to the paper.'

'It isn't bribery. I merely pay you, or will pay you, double what you will receive from that paper. I presume your connection with it is purely commercial. You work for it because you receive a certain amount of money; if the editor found someone who would do the same work cheaper, he would at once employ that person, and your services would be no longer required. Is that not true?'

'Yes, it is true.'

'Very well, then, the question of duty hardly enters into such a compact. They have sent you on what would be to most people a very difficult mission. You have succeeded. You have, therefore, in your possession something to sell. The New York paper will pay you a certain sum in cash for it. I offer you, for the same article, double the price the New York Argus will pay you. Is not that a fair offer?'

Jennie Brewster had arisen. She clasped and unclasped her hands nervously. For a small space of time nothing was said, and Edith Longworth imagined she had gained her point. The woman standing looked down at the woman sitting.

'Do you know all the particulars about the attempt to get this information?' asked Miss Brewster.

'I know some of them. What particulars do you mean?'

'Do you know that a man from the Argus tried to get this information from Mr. Kenyon and Mr. Wentworth in Canada?'

'Yes; I know about that.'

'Do you know that he stole the reports, and that they were taken from him before he could use them?'

'Yes.'

'Do you know he offered Mr. Kenyon and Mr. Wentworth double the price the London Syndicate would have paid them, on condition they gave him a synopsis of the reports?'

'Yes, I know that also.'

'Do you know that, in doing what he asked, they would not have been keeping back for a single day the real report from the people who engaged them? You know all that, do you?'

'Yes; I know all that.'

'Very well, then. Now you ask me to do very much more than Rivers asked them, because you ask me to keep my paper completely in the dark about the information I have got. Isn't that so?'

'Yes, you can keep them in the dark until after the report has been given to the directors; then, of course, you can do what you please with the information.'

'Ah, but by that time it will be of no value. By that time it will have been published in the London financial papers. At that time anybody can get it. Isn't that the case?'

'I suppose so.'

'Now, I want to ask you one other question, Miss—Miss—I don't think you told me your name.'

'My name is Edith Longworth.'

'Very well, Miss Longworth. I want to ask you one more question. What do you think of the conduct of Mr. Kenyon and Mr. Wentworth in refusing to take double what they had been promised for making the report?'

'What do I think of them?' repeated the girl.

'Yes; what do you think of them? You hesitate. You realize that you are in a corner. You think Mr. Wentworth and Mr. Kenyon did very nobly in refusing Rivers' offer?'

'Of course I do.'

'So do I. I think they acted rightly, and did as honourable men should do. Now, when you think that, Miss Longworth, how dare you come and offer me double, or three times, or four times, the amount my paper gives to me for getting this information? Do you think that I am any less honourable than Kenyon or Wentworth? Your offer is an insult to me; nobody but a woman, and a woman of your class, would have made it. Kenyon wouldn't have made it. Wentworth wouldn't have made it. You come here to bribe me. You come here to do exactly what J. K. Rivers tried to do for the Argus in Canada. You think money will purchase anything—that is the thought of all your class. Now, I want you to understand that I am a woman of the people. I was born and brought up in poverty in New York. You were born and brought up amid luxury in London. I have suffered privation and hardships that you know nothing of, and, even if you read about them, you wouldn't understand. You, with the impudence of your class, think you can come to me and bribe me to betray my employer. I am here to do a certain thing, and I am going to do that certain thing in spite of all the money that all the Longworths ever possessed, or ever will possess. Do I make myself sufficiently plain?'

'Yes, Miss Brewster. I don't think anyone could misunderstand you.'

'Well, I am glad of that, because one can never tell how thickheaded some people may be.'

'Do you think there is any parallel between your case and Mr. Wentworth's?'

'Of course I do. We were each sent to do a certain piece of work. We each did our work. We have both been offered a bribe to cheat our employers of the fruits of our labour; only in my case it is very much worse than in Wentworth's, because his employers would not have suffered, while mine will.'

'This is all very plausible, Miss Brewster, but now allow me to tell you that what you have done is a most dishonourable thing, and that you are a disgrace to our common womanhood. You have managed, during a very short acquaintance, to win the confidence of a man—there is a kind of woman who knows how to do that: I thank Heaven I am not of that class; I prefer to belong to the class you have just now been reviling. Some men have an inherent respect for all women; Mr. Wentworth is apparently one of those, and, while he was on his guard with a man, he was not on his guard with a woman. You took advantage of that and you managed to secure certain information which you knew he would never have given you if he had thought it was to be published. You stole that information just as disreputably as that man stole the documents from Mr. Kenyon's pocket. You talk of your honour and your truth when you did such a contemptible thing! You prate of unbribeableness, when the only method possible is adopted of making you do what is right and just and honest! Your conduct makes me ashamed of being a woman. A thoroughly bad woman I can understand, but not a woman like you, who trade on the fact that you are a woman, and that you are pretty, and that you have a pleasing manner. You use those qualities as a thief or a counterfeiter would use the peculiar talents God had given him. How dare you pretend for a moment that your case is similar to Mr. Wentworth's? Mr. Wentworth is an honourable man, engaged in an honourable business; as for you and your business, I have no words to express my contempt for both. Picking pockets is reputable compared with such work.'

Edith Longworth was now standing up, her face flushed and her hands clenched. She spoke with a vehemence which she very much regretted when she thought of the circumstance afterwards; but her chagrin and disappointment at failure, where she had a moment before been sure of success, overcame her. Her opponent stood before her, angry and pale. At first Edith Longworth thought she was going to strike her, but if any such idea passed through the brain of the journalist, she thought better of it. For a few moments neither spoke, then Jennie Brewster said, in a voice of unnatural calmness:

'You are quite welcome to your opinion of me, Miss Longworth, and I presume I am entitled to my opinion of Kenyon and Wentworth. They are two fools, and you are a third in thinking you can control the actions of a woman where two young men have failed. Do you think for a moment I would grant to you, a woman of a class I hate, what I would not grant to a man like Wentworth? They say there is no fool like an old fool, but it should be said that there is no fool like a young woman who has had everything her own way in this world. You are——'

'I shall not stay and listen to your abuse. I wish to have nothing more to do with you.'

'Oh, yes! you will stay,' cried the other, placing her back against the door. 'You came here at your own pleasure; you will leave at mine. I will tell you more truth in five minutes than you ever heard in your life before. I will tell you, in the first place, that my business is quite as honourable as Kenyon's or Wentworth's. What does Kenyon do but try to get information about mines which other people are vitally interested in keeping from him? What does Wentworth do but ferret about among accounts like a detective trying to find out what other people are endeavouring to conceal? What is the whole mining business but one vast swindle, whose worst enemy is the press? No wonder anyone connected with mining fears publicity. If your father has made a million out of mines, he has made it simply by swindling unfortunate victims. I do my business my way, and your two friends do theirs in their way. Of the two, I consider my vocation much the more upright. Now that you have heard what I have to say, you may go, and let me tell you that I never wish to see you or speak with you again.'

'Thank you for your permission to go. I am sure I cordially echo your wish that we may never meet again. I may say, however, that I am sorry I spoke to you in the way I did. It is, of course, impossible for you to look on the matter from my point of view, just as it is impossible for me to look upon it from yours. Nevertheless, I wish you would forget what I said, and think over the matter a little more, and if you see your way to accepting my offer it will be always open to you. Should you forego the sending of that cablegram, I will willingly pay you three times what the New York Argus will give you for it. I do not offer that as a bribe; I merely offer it so that you will not suffer from doing what I believe to be a just action. It seems to me a great pity that two young men should have to endure a serious check to their own business advancement because one of them was foolish enough to confide in a woman in whom he believed.'

Edith Longworth was young, and therefore scarcely likely to be a mistress of diplomacy, but she might have known the last sentence she uttered spoiled the effect of all that had gone before.

'Really, Miss Longworth, I had some little admiration for you when you blazed out at me in the way you did; but now, when you coolly repeat your offer of a bribe, adding one-third to it, all my respect for you vanishes. You may go and tell those who sent you that nothing under heaven can prevent that cablegram being sent.'

In saying this, however, Miss Brewster somewhat exceeded her knowledge. Few of us can foretell what may or may not happen under heaven.

CHAPTER XI.

Edith Longworth went to her state-room and there had what women call 'a good cry' over her failure. Jennie Brewster continued her writing, every now and then pausing as she thought, with regret, of some sharp thing she might have said, which did not occur to her at the time of the interview. Kenyon spent his time in pacing up and down the deck, hoping for the reappearance of Miss Longworth—an expectation which, for a time at least, was the hope deferred which maketh the heart sick. Fleming, the New York politician, kept the smoking-room merry, listening to the stories he told. He varied the proceedings by frequently asking everybody to drink with him, an invitation that met with no general refusal. Old Mr. Longworth dozed most of his time in his steamer chair. Wentworth, who still bitterly accused himself of having been a fool, talked with no one, not even his friend Kenyon. All the time, the great steamship kept forging along through the reasonably calm water just as if nothing had happened or was going to happen. There had been one day of rain, and one night and part of a day of storm. Saturday morning broke, and it was expected that some time in the night Queenstown would be reached. Early on Saturday morning the clouds looked lowering, as they have a right to look near Ireland.

Wentworth, the cause of all the worry, gave Kenyon very little assistance in the matter that troubled his mind. He was in the habit, when the subject was referred to, of thrusting his hands into his hair, or plunging them down into his pockets, and breaking out into language which was as deplorable as it was expressive. The more Kenyon advised him to be calm, the less Wentworth followed that advice. As a general thing, he spent most of his time alone in a very gloomy state of mind. On one occasion when the genial Fleming slapped him on the shoulder, Wentworth, to his great astonishment, turned fiercely round and cried:

'If you do that again, sir, I'll knock you down.'

Fleming said afterwards that he was 'completely flabbergasted' by this—

whatever that may mean—and he added that the English in general were a queer race. It is true that he gathered himself together at the time and, having laughed a little over the remark, said to Wentworth:

'Come and have a drink; then you'll feel better.'

This invitation Wentworth did not even take the trouble to decline, but thrust his hands in his pockets once more, and turned his back on the popular New York politician.

Wentworth summed up the situation to John Kenyon when he said:

'There is no use in our talking or thinking any more about it. We can simply do nothing. I shall take the whole blame on my shoulders. I am resolved that you shall not suffer from my indiscretion. Now, don't talk to me any more about it. I want to forget the wretched business, if possible.'

So thus it came about quite naturally that John Kenyon, who was a good deal troubled about the matter, took as his confidante Edith Longworth, who also betrayed the greatest interest in the problem. Miss Longworth was left all the more alone because her cousin had taken permanently to the smoking-room. Someone had introduced him to the fascinating game of poker, and in the practice of this particular amusement Mr. William Longworth was now spending a good deal of his surplus cash, as well as his time.

Jennie Brewster was seldom seen on deck. She applied herself assiduously to the writing of those brilliant articles which appeared later in the Sunday edition of the New York Argus under the general title of 'Life at Sea,' and which have more recently been issued in book form. As everybody is already aware, her sketches of the genial New York politician, and also of the taciturn, glum Englishman, are considered the finest things in the little volume. They have been largely copied as typical examples of American humour.

When Jennie Brewster did appear on deck, she walked alone up and down the promenade, with a sort of half-defiant look in her eyes as she passed Kenyon and Edith Longworth, and she generally encountered them together.

On this particularly eventful Saturday morning, Kenyon and Edith had the deck to themselves. The conversation naturally turned to the subject which for the last few days had occupied the minds of both.

'Do you know,' said the girl, 'I have been thinking all along that she will come to me at the last for the money.'

'I am not at all sure about that,' answered Kenyon.

'I thought she would probably keep us on the tenterhooks just as long as possible, and then at the last moment come and say she would accept the offer.'

'If she does,' said Kenyon, 'I would not trust her. I would give her to understand that a cheque would be handed to her when we were certain the article had not been used.'

'Do you think that would be a safe way to act if she came and said she would take the money for not sending the cablegram? Don't you think it would be better to pay her and trust to her honour?'

Kenyon laughed.

'I do not think I would trust much to her honour.'

'Now, do you know, I have a different opinion of her. I feel sure that if she said she would do a thing, she would do it.'

'I have no such faith,' answered Kenyon. 'I think, on the contrary, that she is quite capable of asking you for the money and still sending her telegram.'

'Well, I doubt if she would do so. I think the girl really believes she is acting rightly, and imagines she has done a creditable action in a very smart way. If she were not what she calls "honest," she would not have shown so much temper as she did. Not but that I gave a deplorable exhibition of temper myself, for which there was really no excuse.'

'I am sure,' said Kenyon warmly, 'you did nothing of the kind. At all events, I am certain everything you did was perfectly right; and I know you were completely justified in anything you said.'

143

'I wish I could think so.'

'I want to ask you one question,' said Kenyon.

But what that question was will never be known. It was never asked; and when Edith Longworth inquired about it some time later, the question had entirely gone from Kenyon's mind. The steamship, which was ploughing along through the waters, suddenly gave a shiver, as if it were shaken by an earthquake; there were three tremendous bumps, such as a sledge might make by going suddenly over logs concealed in the snow. Both Kenyon and Miss Longworth sprang to their feet. There was a low roar of steam, and they saw a cloud rise amidships, apparently pouring out of every aperture through which it could escape. Then there was silence. The engines had stopped, and the vessel heeled distinctly over to the port side. When Edith Longworth began to realize the situation, she found herself very close to Kenyon, clasping his arm with both hands.

'What—what is it?' she cried in alarm.

'Something is wrong,' said Kenyon. 'Nothing serious, I hope. Will you wait here a moment while I go and see?'

'It is stupid of me,' she answered, releasing his arm; 'but I feel dreadfully frightened.'

'Perhaps you would rather not be left alone.'

'Oh no, it is all over now; but when the first of those terrible shocks came it seemed to me we had struck a rock.'

'There are no rocks here,' said Kenyon. 'The day is perfectly clear, and we are evidently not out of our course. Something has gone wrong with the machinery, I imagine. Just wait a moment, and I will find out.'

As Kenyon rushed towards the companion-way, he met a sailor hurrying in the other direction.

'What is the matter?' cried Kenyon.

The sailor gave no answer.

144

On entering the companion-way door, Kenyon found the place full of steam, and he ran against an officer.

'What is wrong? Is anything the matter?'

'How should I know?' was the answer, very curtly given. 'Please do not ask any questions. Everything will be attended to.'

This was scant encouragement. People began crowding up the companion-way, coughing and wheezing in the steam; and soon the deck, that but a moment before had been almost without an occupant, was crowded with excited human beings in all states of dress and undress.

'What is wrong?' was the question on every lip, to which, as yet, there was no answer. The officers who hurried to and fro were mute, or gave short and unsatisfactory replies to the inquiries which poured in upon them. People did not pause to reflect that even an officer could hardly be expected to know off-hand what the cause of the sudden stoppage of the engine might be. By-and-by the captain appeared, smiling and bland. He told them there was no danger. Something had gone amiss with the machinery, exactly what he could not, at the moment, tell; but there was no necessity for being panic-stricken, everything would be all right in a short time if they merely remained calm. These, and a lot of other nautical lies, which are always told on such occasions, served to calm the fears of the crowd; and by-and-by one after another went down to their state-rooms on finding the vessel was not going to sink immediately. They all appeared some time afterward in more suitable apparel. The steam which had filled the saloon soon disappeared, leaving the furniture dripping with warm moisture. Finally, the loud clang of the breakfast-gong sounded as if nothing had happened, and that did more, perhaps, than anything else to allay the fears of the passengers. If breakfast was about to be served, then, of course, things were not serious. Nevertheless, a great many people that morning had a very poor appetite for the breakfast served to them. The one blessing, as everybody said, was that the weather kept so fine and the sea so calm. To those few who knew anything about disasters at sea, the list of the ship to the port side was a most serious sign. The majority of the passengers, however, did not notice it. After breakfast people came up on deck. There was a wonderful avoidance of hurry, alike by officers and sailors. Orders were given calmly and quietly, and as calmly and quietly obeyed. Officers were still up on the bridge, although there were no commands to give to the man at the wheel and no screw turning. The helmsman stood at the wheel as if he expected at any time the order to turn it port or starboard. All this absence of rush had a very soothing effect on the passengers, many of whom wanted only a slight excuse to become hysterical. As the day wore on, however, a general feeling of security seemed to have come upon all on board. They one and all congratulated themselves on the fact that they had behaved in a most exemplary manner considering the somewhat alarming circumstances. Nevertheless, those who watched the captain saw that he swept the long line of the horizon through his glass every now and then with a good deal of anxiety, and they noticed on looking at the long level line where sea and sky met that not a sail was visible around the complete circle. Up from the engine-room came the clank of hammers, and the opinion was general that, whatever was amiss with the engine, it was capable of being repaired. One thing had become certain, there was nothing wrong with the shafts. The damage, whatever it was, had been to the engine alone. All of the passengers found themselves more or less affected by the peculiar sensation of the steamer being at rest—the awe-inspiring and helpless consciousness of complete silence—after the steady throb they had become so accustomed to all the way across. That night at dinner the captain took his place at the head of the table, urbane and courteous, as if nothing unusual had happened; and the people, who, notwithstanding their outward calmness, were in a state of anxious tension, noticed this with gratified feelings.

'What is the matter?' asked a passenger of the captain; 'and what is the extent of the accident?'

The captain looked down the long table.

'I am afraid,' said he, 'that if I went into technical details you would not understand them. There was a flaw in one of the rods connected with the engine. That rod broke, and in breaking it damaged other parts of the machinery. Doubtless you heard the three thuds which it gave before the engine was stopped. At present it is impossible to tell how long it will take to repair the damage. However, even if the accident were serious, we are right in the track of vessels, and there is no danger.'

This was reassuring; but those who lay awake that night heard the ominous sound of the pumps, and the swishing of water splashing down into the ocean.

CHAPTER XII.

Most of the passengers awoke next morning with a bewildering feeling of vague apprehension. The absence of all motion in the ship, the unusual and intense silence, had a depressing effect. The engines had not yet started; that at least was evident. Kenyon was one of the first on deck. He noticed that the pumps were still working at their full speed, and that the steamer had still the unexplained list to port. Happily, the weather continued good, so far as the quietness of the sea was concerned. A slight drizzle of rain had set in, and the horizon was not many miles from the ship. There would not be much chance of sighting another liner while such weather continued.

Before Kenyon had been many minutes on deck, Edith Longworth came up the companion-way. She approached him with a smile on her face.

'Well,' he said, 'you, at least, do not seem to be suffering any anxiety because of our situation.'

'Really,' she replied, 'I was not thinking of that at all, but about something else. Can you not guess what it is?'

'No,' he answered hesitatingly. 'What is it?'

'Have you forgotten that this is Sunday morning?'

'Is it? Of course it is. So far as I am concerned, time seemed to stop when the engines broke down. But I do not understand why Sunday morning means anything in particular.'

'Don't you? Well, for a person who has been thinking for the last two or three days very earnestly on one particular subject, I am astonished at you. Sunday morning and no land in sight! Reflect for a moment.'

Kenyon's face brightened.

'Ah,' he cried, 'I see what you mean now! Miss Brewster's cable message will not appear in this morning's New York Argus.'

'Of course it will not; and don't you see, also, that when we do arrive you will have an equal chance in the race. If we get in before next Sunday, your telegram to the London people will go as quickly as her cable despatch to New York; thus you will be saved the humiliation of seeing the substance of your report in the London papers before the directors see the report itself. It is not much, to be sure, but, still, it puts you on equal terms; while if we had got into Queenstown last night that would have been impossible.'

Kenyon laughed.

'Well,' he said, 'for such a result the cause is rather tremendous, isn't it? It is something like burning down the house to roast the pig!'

Shortly after ten o'clock the atmosphere cleared, and showed in the distance a steamer, westward bound. The vessel evidently belonged to one of the great ocean lines. The moment it was sighted there fluttered up to the masthead a number of signal-flags, and people crowded to the side of the ship to watch the effect on the outgoing vessel. Minute after minute passed, but there was no response from the other liner. People watched her with breathless anxiety, as though their fate depended on her noticing their signals. Of course, everybody thought she must see them, but still she steamed westward. A cloud of black smoke came out of her funnel, and then a long dark trail, like the tail of a comet, floated out behind; but no notice was taken of the fluttering flags at the masthead. For more than an hour the steamer was in sight. Then she gradually faded away into the west, and finally disappeared.

This incident had a depressing effect on the passengers of the disabled ship. Although every officer had maintained there was no danger, yet the floating away of that steamer seemed somehow to leave them alone; and people, after gazing toward the west until not a vestige of her remained in the horizon, went back to their deck-chairs, feeling more despondent than ever.

Fleming, however, maintained that if people had to drown, it was just as well to drown jolly as mournful, and so he invited everybody to take a drink at his expense—a generous offer, taken instant advantage of by all the smoking-room frequenters.

'My idea is this,' said Fleming, as he sipped the cocktail which was

149

brought to him, 'if anything happens, let it happen; if nothing happens, why, then let nothing happen. There is no use worrying about anything, especially something we cannot help. Here we are on the ocean in a disabled vessel— very good; we cannot do anything about it, and so long as the bar remains open, gentlemen, here's to you!'

And with this cheerful philosophy the New York politician swallowed the liquor he had paid for.

Still the swish of water from the pumps could be heard, but the metallic clanking of steel on steel no longer came up from the engine-room. This in itself was ominous to those who knew. It showed that the engineer had given up all hope of repairing the damage, whatever it was, and the real cause of the disaster was as much a mystery as ever. Shortly before lunch it became evident to people on board the ship that something was about to be done. The sailors undid the fastenings of one of the large boats, and swung it out on the davits until it hung over the sea.

Gradually rumour took form, and it became known that one of the officers and certain of the crew were about to make an attempt to reach the coast of Ireland and telegraph to Queenstown for tugs to bring the steamer in. The captain still asserted that there was no danger whatever, and it was only to prevent delay that this expedient was about to be tried.

'Do you know what they are going to do?' cried Edith Longworth, in a state of great excitement, to John Kenyon.

Kenyon had been walking the deck with Wentworth, who now had gone below.

'I have heard,' said Kenyon, 'that they intend trying to reach the coast.'

'Exactly. Now, why should you not send a telegram to your people in London, and have the reports forwarded at once? The chances are that Miss Brewster will never think of sending her cablegram with the officer who is going to make the trip; then you will be a clear day or two ahead of her, and everything will be all right. In fact, when she understands what has been done, she probably will not send her own message at all.'

'By George!' cried Kenyon, 'that is a good idea. I will see the mate at once, and find out whether he will take a telegram.'

He went accordingly, and spoke to the mate about sending a message with him. The officer said that any passenger who wished to send a telegraphic message would be at liberty to do so. He would take charge of the telegrams very gladly. Kenyon went down to his state-room and told Wentworth what was going to be done. For the first time in several days George Wentworth exhibited something like energy. He went to the steward and bought the stamps to put on the telegram, while John Kenyon wrote it.

The message was given to the officer, who put it into his inside pocket, and then Kenyon thought all was safe. But Edith Longworth was not so sure of that. Jennie Brewster sat in her deck-chair calmly reading her usual paper-covered novel. She apparently knew nothing of what was going on, and Edith Longworth, nervous with suppressed excitement, sat near her, watching her narrowly, while preparations for launching the boat were being completed. Suddenly, to Edith's horror, the deck-steward appeared, and in a loud voice cried:

'Ladies and gentlemen, anyone wishing to send telegrams to friends has a few minutes now to write them. The mate will take them ashore with him, and will send them from the first office that he reaches. No letters can be taken, only telegrams.'

Miss Brewster looked up languidly from her book during the first part of this recital. Then she sprang suddenly to her feet, and threw the book on the deck.

'Who is it will take the telegrams?' she asked the steward.

'The mate, miss. There he is standing yonder, miss.'

She made her way quickly to that official.

'Will you take a cable despatch to be sent to New York?'

'Yes, miss. Is it a very long one?' he asked.

'Yes, it is a very long one.'

'Well, miss,' was the answer, 'you haven't much time to write it. We leave now in a very few minutes.'

'It is all written out; I have only to add a few words to it.'

Miss Brewster at once flew to her state-room. The telegram about the mine was soon before her with the words counted, and the silver and gold that were to pay for it piled on the table. She resolved to run no risk of delay by having the message sent 'to collect.' Then she dashed off, as quickly as she could, a brief and very graphic account of the disaster which had overtaken the Caloric. If this account was slightly exaggerated, Miss Brewster had no time to tone it down. Picturesque and dramatic description was what she aimed at. Her pen flew over the paper with great rapidity, and she looked up every now and then, through her state-room window, to see dangling from the ropes the boat that was to make the attempt to reach the Irish coast. As she could thus see how the preparations for the departure were going forward, she lingered longer than she might otherwise have done, and added line after line to the despatch which told of the disaster. At last she saw the men take their places in the longboat. She hurriedly counted the words in the new despatch she had written, and quickly from her purse piled the gold that was necessary to pay for their transmission. Then she sealed the two despatches in an envelope, put the two piles of gold into one after rapidly counting them again, cast a quick look up at the still motionless boat, grasped the gold in one hand, the envelope in the other, and sprang to her feet; but, as she did so, she gave a shriek and took a step backwards.

Standing with her back to the door was Edith Longworth. When she had entered the state-room, Miss Brewster did not know, but her heart beat wildly as she saw the girl standing silently there, as if she had risen up through the floor.

'What are you doing here?' she demanded.

'I am here,' said Miss Longworth, 'because I wish to talk with you.'

'Stand aside; I have no time to talk to you just now. I told you I didn't want to see you again. Stand aside, I tell you.'

152

'I shall not stand aside.'

'What do you mean?'

'I mean that I shall not stand aside.'

'Then I will ring the bell and have you thrust out of here for your impudence.'

'You shall not ring the bell,' said Edith calmly, putting her hand over the white china plaque that held in its centre the black electric button.

'Do you mean to tell me that you intend to keep me from leaving my own state-room?'

'I mean to tell you exactly that.'

'Do you know that you can be imprisoned for attempting such a thing?'

'I don't care.'

'Stand aside, you vixen, or I will strike you!'

'Do it.'

For a moment the two girls stood there, the one flushed and excited, the other apparently calm, with her back against the door and her hand over the electric button. A glance through the window showed Miss Brewster that the mate had got into the boat, and that they were steadily lowering away.

'Let me pass, you—you wretch!'

'All in good time,' replied Edith Longworth, whose gaze was also upon the boat swinging in mid-air.

Jennie Brewster saw at once that, if it came to a hand-to-hand encounter, she would have no chance whatever against the English girl, who was in every way her physical superior. She had her envelope in one hand and the gold in the other. She thrust both of them into her pocket, which, after some fumbling, she found. Then she raised her voice in one of the shrillest screams which Edith Longworth had ever heard. As if in answer to that ear-piercing sound, there rose from the steamer a loud and ringing cheer. Both glanced up to see where the boat was, but it was not in sight. Several ropes were dangling down past the porthole. Miss Brewster sprang up on the sofa, and with her small hands turned round the screw which held the window closed.

Edith Longworth looked at her without making any attempt to prevent the unfastening of the window.

Jennie Brewster flung open the heavy brass circle which held the thick green glass, and again she screamed at the top of her voice, crying 'Help!' and 'Murder!'

The other did not move from her position. In the silence that followed, the steady splash of oars could be heard, and again a rousing cheer rang out from those who were left upon the motionless steamer. Edith Longworth raised herself on tiptoe and looked out of the open window. On the crest of a wave, five hundred yards away from the vessel, she saw the boat for a moment appear, showing the white glitter of her six dripping oars; then it vanished down the other side of the wave into the trough of the sea.

'Now, Miss Brewster', she said, 'you are at liberty to go.'

CHAPTER XIII.

After Edith Longworth left her, Jennie Brewster indulged in a brief spasm of hysterics. Her common-sense, however, speedily came to her rescue; and, as she became more calm, she began to wonder why she had not assaulted the girl who had dared to imprison her. She dimly remembered that she thought of a fierce onslaught at the time, and she also recollected that her fear of the boat leaving during the struggle had stayed her hand. But now that the boat had left she bitterly regretted her inaction, and grieved unavailingly over the fact that she had stopped to write the account of the disaster which befell the Caloric. Had she not done so, all might have been well, but her great ambition to be counted the best-newspaper woman in New York, and to show the editor that she was equal to any emergency that might arise, had undone her. While it would have been possible for her to send away one telegram, her desire to write the second had resulted in her sending none at all. Although she impugned her own conduct in language that one would not have expected to have heard from the lips of a millionaire's daughter, her anger against Edith Longworth became more intense, and a fierce desire for revenge took possession of the fair correspondent. She resolved that she would go up on deck and shame this woman before everybody. She would attract public attention to the affair by tearing Edith Longworth from her deck-chair, and in her present state of mind she had no doubt of her strength to do it. With the yearning for vengeance fierce and strong upon her, the newspaper woman put on her hat and departed for the deck. She passed up one side and down the other, but her intended victim was not visible. The rage of Miss Brewster increased when she did not find her prey where she expected. She had a fear that, when she calmed down, a different disposition would assert itself, and her revenge would be lost. In going to and fro along the deck she met Kenyon and Fleming walking together. Fleming had just that moment come up to Kenyon, who was quietly pacing the deck alone, and, slapping him on the shoulder, asked him to have a drink.

'It seems to me,' he said, 'that I never have had the pleasure of offering you a drink since we came on board this ship. I want to drink with everybody here, and especially now, when something has happened to make it worth while.'

'I am very much obliged to you,' said John Kenyon coldly, 'but I never drink with anybody.'

'What, never touch it at all? Not even beer?'

'Not even beer.'

'Well, I am astonished to hear that. I thought every Englishman drank beer.'

'There is at least one Englishman who does not.'

'All right, then; no harm done, and no offence given, I hope. I may say, however, that you miss a lot of fun in this world.'

'I suppose I miss a few headaches also.'

'Oh, not necessarily. I have one great recipe for not having a headache. You see, this is the philosophy of headaches.' And then, much to John's chagrin, he linked arms with him and changed his step to suit Kenyon's, talking all the time as if they were the most intimate friends in the world. 'I have a sure plan for avoiding a headache. You see, when you look into the matter, it is this way: The headache only comes when you are sober. Very well, then. It is as simple as A B C. Never get sober; that's my plan. I simply keep on, and never get sober, so I have no headaches. If people who drink would avoid the disagreeable necessity of ever getting sober, they would be all right. Don't you see what I mean?'

'And how about their brains in the meantime?'

'Oh, their brains are all right. Good liquor sharpens a man's brains wonderfully. Now, you try it some time. Let me have them mix a cocktail for you? I tell you, John, a cocktail is one of the finest drinks that ever was made, and this man at the bar—when I came on board, he thought he could make a cocktail, but he didn't know even the rudiments—I have taught

156

him how to do it; and I tell you that secret will be worth a fortune to him, because if there is anything Americans like, it is to have their cocktails mixed correctly. There's no one man in all England can do it, and very few men on the Atlantic service. But I'm gradually educating them. Been across six times. They pretend to give you American drinks over in England, but you must know how disappointing they are.'

'I'm sure I don't see how I should know, for I never taste any of them.'

'Ah, true; I had forgotten that. Well, I took this bar-keeper here in hand, and he knows now how to make a reasonably good cocktail; and, as I say, that secret will be worth money to him from American passengers.'

John Kenyon was revolving in his mind the problem of how to get rid of this loquacious and generous individual, when he saw, bearing down upon them, the natty figure of Miss Jennie Brewster; and he wondered why such a look of bitter indignation was flashing from her eyes. He thought that she intended to address the American politician, but he was mistaken. She came directly at him, and said in an excited tone, with a ring of anger in it:

'Well, John Kenyon, what do you think of your work?'

'What work?' asked the bewildered man.

'You know very well what work I mean. A fine specimen of a man you are! Without the courage yourself to prevent my sending that telegram, you induced your dupe to come down to my state-room and brazenly keep me from sending it.'

The blank look of utter astonishment upon the face of honest John Kenyon would have convinced any woman in her senses that he knew nothing at all of what she was speaking. A dim impression of this, indeed, flashed across the young woman's heated brain. But before she could speak, Fleming said:

'Tut, tut, my dear girl! you are talking too loud altogether. Do you want to attract the attention of everybody on the deck? You mustn't make a scandal in this way on board ship.'

'Scandal!' she cried. 'We will soon see whether there will be a scandal or not. Attract the attention of those on deck! That is exactly what I am going to do, until I show up the villainy of this man you are talking to. He was the concocter of it, and he knows it. She never had brains enough to think of it. He was too much of a coward to carry it through himself, and so he set her to do his dastardly piece of work.'

'Well, well,' said Fleming, 'even if he has done all that, whatever it is, it will do no good to attract attention to it here on deck. See how everybody is listening to what you are saying. My dear girl, you are too angry to talk just now; the best thing you can do is to go down to your state-room.'

'Who asked you to interfere?' she cried, turning furiously upon him. 'I'll thank you to mind your own business, and let me attend to mine. I should have thought that you would have found out before this that I am capable of attending to my own affairs.'

'Certainly, certainly, my dear child,' answered the politician soothingly; 'I'm sorry I can't get you all to come and have a drink with me, and talk this matter over quietly. That's the correct way to do things, not to stand here scolding on the deck, with everybody listening. Now, if you will quietly discuss the matter with John here, I'm sure everything will be all right.'

'You don't know what you are talking about,' replied the young lady. 'Do you know that I had an important despatch to send to the Argus, and that this man's friend, doubtless at his instigation, came into my room and practically held me prisoner there until the boat had left, so that I could not send the despatch? Think of the cheek and villainy of that, and then speak to me of talking wildly!'

An expression of amazement upon Kenyon's face convinced the newspaper woman, more than all his protestations would have done, that he knew nothing whatever of the escapade.

'And who kept you from coming out?' asked Fleming.

'It is none of your business,' she replied tartly.

'If you will believe me,' said Kenyon at last, 'I had absolutely no knowledge of all this; so, you see, there is no use speaking to me about it. I won't pretend I am sorry, because I am not.'

This added fuel to the flames, and she was about to blaze out again, when Kenyon, turning on his heel, left her and Fleming standing facing each other. Then the young woman herself turned and quickly departed, leaving the bewildered politician entirely alone, so that there was nothing for him to do but to go into the smoking-room and ask somebody else to drink with him, which he promptly did.

Miss Brewster made her way to the captain's room and rapped at the door. On being told to enter, she found that officer seated at his table with some charts before him, and a haggard look upon his face, which might have warned her that this was not the proper time to air any personal grievances.

'Well?' he said briefly as she entered.

'I came to see you, captain,' she began, 'because an outrageous thing has been done on board this ship, and I desire reparation. What is more, I will have it!'

'What is the "outrageous thing"?' asked the captain.

'I had some despatches to send to New York, to the New York Argus, on whose staff I am.'

'Yes,' said the captain with interest; 'despatches relating to what has happened to the ship?'

'One of them did, the other did not.'

'Well, I hope,' said the captain, 'you have not given an exaggerated account of the condition we are in.'

'I have given no account at all, simply because I was prevented from sending the cablegrams.'

'Ah, indeed,' said the captain, a look of relief coming over his face, in spite of his efforts to conceal it; 'and pray what prevented you from sending your cablegrams? The mate would have taken any messages that were given to him.'

'I know that,' cried the young woman; 'but when I was in my room writing the last of the despatches, a person who is on board as a passenger here—Miss Longworth—came into my room and held me prisoner there until the boat had left the ship.'

The captain arched his eyebrows in surprise.

'My dear madam,' he said, 'you make a very serious charge. Miss Longworth has crossed several times with me, and I am bound to say that a better-behaved young lady I never had on board my ship.'

'Extremely well behaved she is!' cried the correspondent angrily, 'she stood against my door and prevented me from going out. I screamed for help, but my screams were drowned in the cheers of the passengers when the boat left.'

'Why did you not ring your bell?'

'I couldn't ring my bell because she prevented me. Besides, if I had reached the bell, it is not likely anybody would have answered it; everybody seemed to be bawling after the boat that was leaving.'

'You can hardly blame them for that. A great deal depends on the safety of that boat. In fact, if you come to think about it, you will see that whatever grievance you may have, it is, after all, a very trivial one compared with the burden that weighs on me just now, and I should much prefer not to have anything to do with disputes between the passengers until we are out of our present predicament.'

'The predicament has nothing whatever to do with it. I tell you a fact. I tell you that one of your passengers came and imprisoned me in my state-room. I come to you for redress. Now, there must be some law on shipboard that takes the place of ordinary law on land. I make this demand officially to you. If you decline to hear me, and refuse to redress my wrong, then I have public opinion, to which I can appeal through my paper, and perhaps there will also be a chance of obtaining justice through the law of the land to which

160

I am going.'

'My dear madam,' said the captain calmly, 'you must not use threats to me. I am not accustomed to be addressed in the tone you have taken upon yourself to use. Now tell me what it is you wish me to do?'

'It is for you to say what you will do. I am a passenger on board this ship, and am supposed to be under the protection of its captain. I therefore tell you I have been forcibly detained in my state-room, and I demand that the person who did this shall be punished.'

'You say that Miss Longworth is the person who did this?'

'Yes, I do.'

'Now, do you know you make a serious charge against that young lady—a charge that I find it remarkably difficult to believe? May I ask you what reason she had for doing what you say she has done?'

'That is a long story. I am quite prepared to show that she tried to bribe me not to send a despatch, and, finding herself unsuccessful, she forcibly detained me in my room until too late to send the telegram.'

The captain pondered over what had been said to him.

'Have you any proof of this charge?'

'Proof! What do you mean? Do you doubt my word?'

'I mean exactly what I say. Have you anybody to prove the exceedingly serious charge you bring?'

'Certainly not. I have no proof. If there had been a witness there, the thing would not have happened. If I could have summoned help, it would not have happened. How could I have any proof of such an outrage?'

'Well, do you not see that it is impossible for me to take action on your unsupported word? Do you not see that, if you take further steps in this extraordinary affair, Miss Longworth will ask you for proof of what you state? If she denies acting as you say she did, and you fail to prove your allegation, it

161

seems to me that you will be in rather a difficult position. You would be liable to a suit for slander. Just think the matter over calmly for the rest of the day before you take any further action upon it, and I would strongly advise you not to mention this to anyone on board. Then to-morrow, if you are still in the same frame of mind, come to me.'

Thus dismissed, the young woman left the captain's room, and met Fleming just outside, who said:

'Look here, Miss Brewster, I want to have a word with you. You were very curt with me just now.'

'Mr. Fleming, I do not wish to speak to you.'

'Oh, that's all right—that's all right; but let me tell you this: you're a pretty smart young woman, and you have done me one or two very evil turns in your life. I have found out all about this affair, and it's one of the funniest things I ever heard of.'

'Very funny, isn't it?' snapped the young woman.

'Of course it's very funny; but when it appears in full in the opposition papers to the Argus, perhaps you won't see the humour of it—though everybody else in New York will, that's one consolation.'

'What do you mean?'

'I mean to say, Jennie Brewster, that unless you are a fool, you will drop this thing. Don't, for Heaven's sake, let anybody know you were treated by an English girl in the way you were. Take my advice: say no more about it.'

'And what business is it of yours?'

'It isn't mine at all; that is why I am meddling with it. Aren't you well enough acquainted with me to know that nothing in the world pleases me so much as to interfere in other people's business? I have found out all about the girl who kept you in, and a mighty plucky action it was too. I have seen that girl on the deck, and I like the cut of her jib. I like the way she walks. Her independence suits me. She is a girl who wouldn't give a man any trouble,

162

now, I tell you, if he were lucky enough to win her. And I am not going to see that girl put to any trouble by you, understand that!'

'And how are you going to prevent it, may I ask?'

'May you ask? Why, of course you may. I will tell you how I am going to prevent it. Simply by restraining you from doing another thing in the matter.'

'If you think you can do that, you are very much mistaken. I am going to have that girl put in prison, if there is a law in the land.'

'Well, in the first place, we are not on land; and, in the second place, you are going to do nothing of the kind, because, if you do, I shall go to the London correspondents of the other New York papers and give the whole blessed snap away. I'll tell them how the smart and cute Miss Dolly Dimple, who has bamboozled so many persons in her life, was once caught in her own trap; and I shall inform them how it took place. And they'll be glad to get it, you bet! It will make quite interesting reading in the New York opposition papers some fine Sunday morning—about a column and a half, say. Won't there be some swearing in the Argus when that appears! It won't be your losing the despatch you were going to send, but it will be your utter idiocy in making the thing public, and letting the other papers on to it. Why, the best thing in the world for you to do, and the only thing, is to keep as quiet as possible about it. I am astonished at a girl of your sense, Dolly, making a public fuss like this, when you should be the very one trying to keep it secret.'

The newspaper correspondent pondered on these words.

'And if I keep quiet about it, will you do the same?'

'Certainly; but you must remember that if ever you attempt any of your tricks of interviewing on me again, out comes this whole thing. Don't forget that.'

'I won't,' said Miss Jennie Brewster.

And next morning, when the captain was anxiously awaiting her arrival in his room, she did not appear.

CHAPTER XIV.

After all, it must be admitted that George Wentworth was a man of somewhat changeable character. For the last two or three days he had been moping like one who meditated suicide; now when everyone else was anxiously wondering what was going to happen to the ship, he suddenly became the brightest individual on board. For a man to be moody and distraught while danger was impending was not at all surprising; but for a man, right in the midst of gloom, to blossom suddenly out into a general hilarity of manner, was something extraordinary. People thought it must be a case of brain trouble. They watched the young man with interest as he walked with a springy step up and down the deck. Every now and again a bright smile illuminated his face, and then he seemed to be ashamed that people should notice he was feeling so happy. When he was alone he had a habit of smiting his thigh and bursting out into a laugh that was long and low, rather than loud and boisterous. No one was more astonished at this change than Fleming, the politician. George met him on deck, and, to the great surprise of that worthy gentleman, smote him on the back and said:

'My dear sir, I am afraid the other day, when you spoke to me, I answered a little gruffly. I beg to apologize. Come and have a drink with me.'

'Oh, don't mention it,' said Fleming joyously; 'we all of us have our little down-turns now and then. Why, I have them myself, when liquor is bad or scarce! You mightn't believe it, but some days I feel away down in the mouth. It is true I have a recipe for getting up again, which I always use. And that reminds me: do you remember what the Governor of North Carolina said to the Governor of South Carolina?'

'I'm sure I don't know,' said Wentworth; 'you see, I'm not very well versed in United States politics.'

'Well, there wasn't much politics about his remark. He merely said, "It's a long time between drinks;" come in and have something with me. It seems to me you haven't tasted anything in my company since the voyage began.'

'I believe,' said Wentworth, 'that is a true statement. Let us amend it as soon as possible, only in this case let me pay for the drinks. I invited you to drink with me.'

'Not at all, not at all!' cried Fleming; 'not while I'm here. This is my treat, and it is funny to think that a man should spend a week with another man without knowing him. Really, you see, I haven't known you till now.'

And so the two worthy gentlemen disappeared into the smoking-room and rang the electric bell.

But it was in his own state-room that George Wentworth's jocularity came out at its best. He would grasp John Kenyon by the shoulder and shake that solemn man, over whose face a grim smile generally appeared when he noticed the exuberant jollity of his comrade.

'John,' Wentworth cried, 'why don't you laugh?'

'Well, it seems to me,' replied his comrade, 'that you are doing laughing enough for us both. It is necessary to have one member of the firm solid and substantial. I'm trying to keep the average about right. When you were in the dumps I had to be cheerful for two. Now that you feel so lively, I take a refuge in melancholy, to rest me after my hard efforts at cheerfulness.'

'Well, John, it seems to me too good to be true. What a plucky girl she was to do such a thing! How did she know but that the little vixen had a revolver with her, and might have shot her?'

'I suppose she didn't think about it at all.'

'Have you seen her since that dramatic incident?'

'Seen whom? Miss Brewster?'

'No, no; I mean Miss Longworth.'

'No, she hasn't appeared yet. I suppose she fears there will be a scene, and she is anxious to avoid it.'

'Very likely that is the case,' said Wentworth. 'Well, if you do see her, you can tell her there is no danger. Our genial friend, Fleming, has had a talk with that newspaper woman, so he tells me, and the way he describes it is exceedingly picturesque. He has threatened her with giving away the "snap," as he calls it, to the other New York papers, and it seems that the only thing on earth Miss Brewster is afraid of is the opposition press. So she has promised to say nothing more whatever about the incident.'

'Then, you have been talking with Fleming?'

'Certainly I have; a jovial good fellow he is, too. I have been doing something more than talking with him; I have been drinking with him.'

'And yet a day or two ago, I understand, you threatened to strike him.'

'A day or two ago, John! It was ages and ages ago. A day or two isn't in it. That was years and centuries since, as it appears to me. I was an old man then; now I have become young again, and all on account of the plucky action of that angel of a girl of yours.'

'Not of mine,' said Kenyon seriously; 'I wish she were.'

'Well, cheer up. Everything will come out right; you see, it always does. Nothing looked blacker than this matter about the telegram a few days ago, and see how beautifully it has turned out.'

Kenyon said nothing. He did not desire to discuss the matter even with his best friend. The two went up on deck together, and took a few turns along the promenade, during which promenade the eyes of Kenyon were directed to the occupants of the deckchairs, but he did not see the person whom he sought. Telling Wentworth he was going below for a moment, he left him to continue his walk alone, and on reaching the saloon Kenyon spoke to a stewardess.

'Do you know if Miss Longworth is in her stateroom?'

'Yes, sir, I think she is,' was the answer.

'Will you take this note to her?'

John sat down to wait for an answer. The answer did not come by the hand of the stewardess. Edith herself timorously glanced into the saloon, and, seeing Kenyon alone, ventured in. He sprang up to meet her.

'I was afraid,' he said, 'that you had been ill.'

'No, not quite, but almost,' she answered. 'Oh, Mr. Kenyon, I have done the most terrible thing! You could not imagine that I was so bold and wicked;' and tears gathered in the eyes of the girl.

Kenyon stretched out his hand to her, and she took it.

'I am afraid to stay here with you,' she said, 'for fear——'

'Oh, I know all about it,' said Kenyon.

'You cannot know about it; you surely do not know what I have done?'

'Yes, I know exactly what you've done; and we all very much admire your pluck.'

'It hasn't, surely, been the talk of the ship?'

'No, it has not; but Miss Brewster charged me with being an accomplice.'

'And you told her you were not, of course?'

'I couldn't tell her anything, for the simple reason that I hadn't the faintest idea what she was talking about; but that's how I came to know what had happened, and I am here to thank you, Miss Longworth, for your action. I really believe you have saved the sanity of my friend Wentworth. He is a different man since the incident we are speaking of occurred.'

'And have you seen Miss Brewster since?'

'Oh yes; as I was telling you, she met me on the deck. Dear me! how thoughtless of me! I had forgotten you were standing. Won't you sit down?'

'No, no; I have been in my room so long that I am glad to stand anywhere.'

'Then, won't you come up on deck with me?'

'Oh, I'm afraid,' she said. 'I am afraid of a public scene; and I am sure, by the last look I caught in that girl's eyes, she will stop at no scandal to have her revenge. I am sorry to say that I am too much of a coward to meet her. Of course, from her point of view I have done her eternal wrong. Perhaps it was wrong from anybody's point of view.'

'Miss Longworth,' said John Kenyon cordially, 'you need have no fear whatever of meeting her. She will say nothing.'

'How do you know that?'

'Oh, it is a long story. She went to the captain with her complaint, and received very little comfort there. I will tell you all about it on deck. Get a wrap and come with me.'

As Kenyon gave this peremptory order, he realized that he was taking a liberty he had no right to take, and his face flushed as he wondered if Edith would resent the familiarity of his tones; but she merely looked up at him with a bright smile, and said:

'I will do, sir, as you command.'

'No, no,' said Kenyon; 'it was not a command, although it sounded like one. It was a very humble request; at least, I intended it to be such.'

'Well, I will get my wrap.'

As she left for her state-room, a rousing cheer was heard from on deck. She stopped, and looked at Kenyon.

'What does that mean?' she asked.

'I do not know,' was the answer. 'Please get your things on and we will go up and see.'

When they reached the deck they saw everybody at the forward part of the ship. Just becoming visible in the eastern horizon were three trails of black smoke, apparently coming towards them.

The word was whispered from one to the other: 'It is the tug-boats. It is relief.'

Few people on board the steamer knew that their very existence depended entirely on the good weather. The incessant pumping showed everybody, who gave a thought to the matter, that the leak had been serious; but as the subsidence of the vessel was imperceptible to all save experts, no one but the officers really knew the grave danger they were in. Glad as the passengers were to see those three boats approach, the one who most rejoiced was the one who knew everything respecting the disaster and its effects—the captain.

Edith Longworth and John Kenyon paced the deck together, and did not form two of the crowd who could not tear themselves away from the front of the ship, watching the gradually approaching tug boats. Purposely, John Kenyon brought the girl who was with him past Miss Jennie Brewster, and although that person glared with a good deal of anger at Edith, who blushed to her temples with fear and confusion, yet nothing was said; and Kenyon knew that afterwards his companion would feel easier in her mind about meeting the woman with whom she had had such a stormy five minutes. The tug boats speedily took the big steamer in tow, and slowly the four of them made progress towards Queenstown, it having been resolved to land all the passengers there, and to tow the disabled vessel to Liverpool, if an examination of the hull showed such a course to be a safe one. The passengers bade each other good-bye after they left the tender, and many that were on board that ship never saw each other again. One at least, had few regrets and no good-byes to make, but a surprise was in store for her. Jennie Brewster found a cablegram from New York waiting for her. It said 'Cable nothing respecting mines. Letter follows.'

CHAPTER XV.

London again! Muddy, drizzly, foggy London, London, with its well filled omnibuses tearing along the streets, more dangerous than the chariots of Rome, London, with its bustling thoroughfares, with its traffic blocked at the corners by the raised white gloved hand of the policeman, London, with the four wheeled growler piled high with luggage, and the dashing hansom whirling along, missing the wheels of other vehicles by half an inch, while its occupant sits serenely smoking, or motioning his directions to his cabman with an umbrella; London, with its constantly moving procession of every sort of wheeled carriage, from the four-horsed coach to the coster barrow. London, London, London, London! the name seemed to ring in John Kenyon's ears as he walked briskly along the crowded pavement towards the City. The roar of its busy streets was the sweetest music in the world to him, as it is to every man who has once acquired the taste for London. Drink of the fountain of Trevi, and you will return to Rome. Drink of the roar and the bustle of London, and no other metropolis in the world, can ever satisfy the city-hunger in you again. London is London, and John Kenyon loved its very disadvantages as he strode along the streets.

He called at the office of George Wentworth, took that young man with him, and together they went to the place where the adjourned meeting of the London Syndicate was to be held. There were questions to be asked of the two young men, and the directors couldn't quite see why the reports had been so suddenly precipitated upon them, before the arrival of the experts they had sent out. So they had merely read the documents at the former meeting and adjourned until such time as the two young men could appear in person. Most of the directors were there, but, though Kenyon looked anxiously among them, he did not see the face of old Mr. Longworth. Questions were asked Kenyon about the position of the mines, about their output, and such other particulars as the directors wished to know. Then Wentworth underwent a similar examination. He pointed out the discrepancies which he had found in the accounts. He showed that there was an evident desire on the part of the owners of the different mines to make it appear that the properties paid better than they actually did, and he answered in a clear and satisfactory way all the questions asked him. The chairman thanked the young men for the evident care with which they had done their work, and the meeting then went into a private session to consider what action should be taken respecting the mines. When the two friends got out of the building, Kenyon said:

'Well, thank goodness that is over and done with. Now, George, what have you to suggest with reference to the mica-mine?'

'I think,' said Wentworth, 'we had better adjourn to my office and have a talk over the matter quietly there. Let us go into private session as the directors have done. I feel rich after having got my cheque, and the vote of thanks from the chairman; so I will spend a shilling on a hansom and get there with speed and comfort. Actually, since I have got back to London, I am spending all my surplus cash on hansoms. They are certainly the best and cheapest vehicles in the world. Think of what that pirate charged us for a ride from the hotel to the steamer in New York.'

'I don't like to think of it,' said Kenyon; 'it makes me shudder!'

'Do you know, John, I should not be inconsolable if I never saw the great city of New York again. London is good enough for me.'

'Oh, I don't know! New York is all right. I confess there are one or two of her citizens that I do not care much about.'

'Ah,' said Wentworth; then, after a few moments' reflection, he remarked suddenly, apropos of nothing: 'Do you know, John, I was very nearly in love with that girl?'

'I thought you were drifting in that direction.'

'Drifting! It wasn't drifting. It was a mad plunge down the rapids, and it is only lately I have begun to think what a close shave I had of it. The horror of those days, when I thought that despatch was going to New York, completely obliterated any other feeling in regard to her. If I had found she was a hopeless flirt, or something of that kind, who was trifling with me, I should have been very much shocked, of course, but I should have thought about my own feelings. Now, the curious thing is that I never began to think about them till I got to London.'

'Very well, Wentworth; I wouldn't think about them now, if I were you.'

'No, I don't intend to, particularly. The fact that I talk over them with you shows that the impression was not very deep.'

Wentworth drew a long breath that might have been mistaken for a sigh, if he had not just before explained how completely free he was from the thraldom in which Miss Brewster at one time held him.

'Still, she was a very pretty girl, John. You can't deny that.'

'I have no wish to deny it. I simply don't want to think about her at all.'

'No, and we don't need to, thank goodness. But she was very bright and clever. Of course you didn't know her as I did. I never before met anyone who—Well, that's all past and done with. I told her all about our mica-mine, and she gave me much sage advice.'

Kenyon smiled, but held his peace.

'Oh yes, I know what you are thinking of. I spoke of other mines as well; still, that was my folly, and not her fault exactly. She imagined she was doing right, and after all, you know, I think we sometimes don't make enough allowance for another's point of view.'

Kenyon laughed outright.

'It seems to me you are actually defending her. My remembrance is that you didn't make much allowance for her point of view when your own point was that coil of rope in the front of the ship—those days when you wouldn't speak even to me.'

'I admit it, John. No, I'm not defending her. I have succeeded in putting her entirely out of my mind—with an effort. How about your own case, John?'

'My own case! What do you mean?'

'You know very well what I mean.'

'I suppose I do forgive the little bit of affectation, will you? but a man gets somewhat nervous when such a question is sprung upon him. My own case is just where we left it at Queenstown.'

'Haven't you seen her since?'

'No.'

'Aren't you going to?'

'I really do not know what I am going to do.'

'John, that young woman has a decided personal interest in you.'

'I wish I were sure of that, or, rather, I wish I were sure of it and in a position to—But what is the use of talking? I haven't a penny to my name.'

'No; but if our mine goes through, you soon will have.'

'Yes, but what will it amount to? I never can forget the lofty disdain with which a certain person spoke of fifty thousand pounds. It sends a cold chill over me whenever I think of it. Fifty thousand pounds to her seemed so trivial; to me it was something that might be obtained after the struggle of a lifetime.'

'Well, I wouldn't let that discourage me too much if I were you; besides, you see—Oh! here we are. We'll talk about this some other time.'

Having paid the cabman, the two young men went upstairs into Wentworth's room, where they closed the door, and John drew up a seat by the side of his friend.

'Now, then,' said Wentworth, 'what have you done about the mine?'

'I have done absolutely nothing. I have been waiting for this conference with you.'

'Well, my boy, time is the great factor in anything of this sort.'

'Yes, I suppose it is.'

'You see, our option is running along; every day we lose is so much taken off our chances of success. Have you anything to propose?'

'I'll tell you what I thought of doing. You know young Longworth spoke to me a good deal about the mine at one time. His cousin introduced me to him, and she seemed to think he might take some interest in forming the company. I was to have a talk with you, because Longworth gave it as his opinion that the amount should be put at two hundred thousand pounds rather than at fifty thousand pounds.'

Wentworth gave a long whistle.

'Yes, it seems a very large amount; but he claims that if it would pay ten per cent. on that sum—if we could show that there was a reasonable chance of its paying so much—we could put it at two hundred thousand.'

'Well, that looks reasonable. What else did he say?'

'He did not say very much more about it, because I told him I should have to consult you.'

'And why didn't you? On board ship there was one of the best opportunities we could have had of having a talk with him. In fact, the whole matter might perhaps have been arranged there.'

'Oh, well, you know, I couldn't talk to you about it, because a certain circumstance arose, and you spent your time very much in the forward part of the steamer, sitting on a coil of rope and cursing the universe generally and yourself in particular'.

'Ah, yes, I remember, of course—yes. Very well, then, you have not seen young Longworth since, have you?'

'No, I have not.'

'Wouldn't the old gentleman go in for it?'

'His daughter seemed to think he would not, because the amount was too small.'

'Why couldn't he be got to go into it entirely by himself? If we put the

174

price up to one hundred thousand pounds or two hundred thousand pounds, that ought to be large enough for him, if he were playing a lone hand.'

'Well, you see, I don't suppose they thought of going in for it at that, except as a matter of speculation. Of course, if they intended to buy some shares, it is not likely they would propose to raise the price from fifty thousand pounds to two hundred thousand pounds. Young Longworth spoke of dividing the profit. He claimed that whatever we made on fifty thousand pounds would be too small to be divided into three. I told him, of course, that you were my partner in this, and that is why he proposed the price should be made two hundred thousand pounds.'

'I suppose he seemed indifferent on the question whether it should pay a dividend on that amount of money or not?'

'He didn't mention that particularly—at least, he did not dwell upon it. He asked if it would pay a dividend on two hundred thousand, and I told him I thought it would pay ten per cent. if rightly managed; then he said of course that was its price, and we should be great fools to float it at fifty thousand pounds when it was really worth two hundred thousand.'

Wentworth pondered for a few minutes on this, tapping his pencil on the desk and knitting his brow.

'It seems an awful jump, from fifty thousand pounds to two hundred thousand pounds, doesn't it, John?'

'Yes, it does; it has a certain look of swindling about it. But what a glorious thing it would be if it could be done, and if it would pay the right percentage when we got the scheme working!'

'Of course I wouldn't be connected, nor you either, with anything that was bogus.'

'Certainly not. I wouldn't think for a moment of inflating it if I were not positive the property would stand it. I have been making, and have here in my pocket, an elaborate array of figures which will show approximately what the mine will yield, and I am quite convinced that it will pay at least ten per cent., and possible twelve or fifteen.'

'Well, nobody wants a better percentage on their money. Have you the figures with you?'

'Yes, here they are.'

'Very well, you had better leave them with me, and I will go over them as critically as if they were the figures of somebody I was deeply suspicious of, I hope they will hold water; but if they do not, I will point out to you where the discrepancies are.'

'But, you see, George, it is more a question of facts than of figures. I believe the whole mountain is made of the mineral which is so valuable, but I take only about an eighth of it as being possible to get out, which seems to me a very moderate estimate.'

'Yes, but how much demand is there for it? That is the real question. The thing may be valuable enough, but if there is only a limited demand—that is to say, if we have ten times the material that the world needs—the other nine parts are comparatively valueless.'

'That is true.'

'Do you know how many establishments there are in the world that use this mineral?'

'There are a great many in England, and also in the United States.'

'And how about the duty on it in the United States?'

'Ah, that I do not know.'

'Well, we must find that out. Just write down here what it is used for; then I shall try to get some information about the factories that require it, and also what quantities they need in a year. We shall have to get all these facts and figures to lay before the people who are going to invest, because, as I understand it, the great point we make is not on the mica, but on the other mineral.'

'Exactly.'

'Very well, then, you leave me what you know already about it, and I will try to supplement your information. In fact, we shall have to supplement it, before we can go before anybody with it. Now, I advise you to see the Longworths—both old and young Longworth—and you may find that talking with them in the City of London is very different from talking with them on the Caloric. By the way, I wonder why Longworth was not at the directors' meeting to-day.'

'I do not know. I noticed he was absent.'

'He very likely intends to have nothing more to do with the other mines, and so there may be a possibility of his investing in ours. Do you know his address?'

'Yes, I have it with me.'

'Then, if I were you, I would jump into a hansom and go there at once. Meanwhile, I will try to get your figures into shipshape order, and supplement them as far as it is possible to do so. This is going to be no easy matter, John. There are a great many properties now being offered to the public—the papers are full of them—and each of them appears to be the most money-making scheme in existence; so if we are going to float this mine without knowing any particular capitalist, we have our work cut out for us.'

'Then, you would be willing to put the price up to two hundred thousand pounds?'

'Yes, if you say the mine will stand it. That we can tell better after we have gone over the figures together. We ought to be sure of our facts first.'

'Very well. Good-bye; I will go and see Mr. Longworth.'

CHAPTER XVI.

John Kenyon did not take a cab. He walked so that he might have time to think. He wanted to arrange in his mind just what he would say to Mr. Longworth, so he pondered over the coming interview as he walked through the busy streets of the City.

He had not yet settled things satisfactorily to himself when he came to the door leading to Mr. Longworth's offices.

'After all,' he said to himself, as he paused there, 'Mr. Longworth has never said anything to me about the mica-mine; and, from what his daughter thought, it is not likely that he will care to interest himself in it. It was the young man who spoke about it.'

He felt that it was really the young man on whom he should call, but he was rather afraid of meeting him. The little he had seen of William Longworth on board the Caloric had not given him a very high opinion of that gentleman, and he wondered if it would not have been better to have told Wentworth that nothing was to be expected from the Longworths. However, he resolved not to shirk the interview, so passed up the steps and into the outer office. He found the establishment much larger than he had expected. At numerous desks there were numerous clerks writing away for dear life. He approached the inquiry counter, and a man came forward to hear what he had to say.

'Is Mr. Longworth in?'

'Yes, sir. Which Mr. Longworth do you want—the young gentleman or Mr. John Longworth?'

'I wish to see the senior member of the firm.'

'Ah! have you an appointment with him?'

'No, I have not; but perhaps if you will take this card to him, and if he is not busy, he may see me.'

'He is always very busy, sir.'

'Well, take the card to him; and if he doesn't happen to remember the name, tell him I met him on board the Caloric.'

'Very good, sir.' And with that the clerk disappeared, leaving Kenyon to ponder over in his mind the still unsettled question of what he should say to Mr. Longworth if he were ushered into his presence. As he stood there waiting, with the host of men busily and silently working around him, amid the general air of important affairs pervading the place, he made up his mind that Mr. Longworth would not see him, and so was rather surprised when the clerk came back without the card, and said, 'Will you please step this way, sir?'

Passing through a pair of swinging doors, his conductor tapped lightly at a closed one, and then opened it.

'Mr. Kenyon, sir,' he said respectfully, and then closed the door behind him, leaving John Kenyon standing in a large room somewhat handsomely furnished, with two desks near the window. From an inner room came the muffled click, click, click of a type-writer. Seated at one of the desks was young Longworth, who did not look round as Kenyon was announced. The elder gentleman, however, arose, and cordially held out his hand.

'How are you, Mr. Kenyon?' he said. 'I am very pleased to meet you again. The terror of our situation on board that ship does not seem to have left an indelible mark upon you. You are looking well.'

'Yes,' said John; 'I am very glad to be back in London again.'

'Ah, I imagine we all like to get back. By the way, it was a much more serious affair than we thought at the time on board the Caloric.'

'So I see by the papers.'

'How is your friend? He seemed to take it very badly.'

'Take what badly?' asked John in astonishment.

'Well, he appeared to me, at the time of the accident, to feel very

179

despondent about our situation.'

'Oh yes, I remember now. Yes, he did feel a little depressed at the time; but it was not on account of the accident. It was another matter altogether, which, happily, turned out all right.'

'I am glad of that. By the way, have you made your report to the directors yet?'

'Yes; we were at a meeting of the directors to-day.'

'Ah, I could not manage to be there. To tell the truth, I have made up my mind to do nothing with those Ottawa mines. You do not know what action the Board took in the matter, do you?'

'No, they merely received our report; in fact, they had had the report before, but there were some questions they desired to ask us, which we answered apparently to their satisfaction.'

'Who were there? Sir Ropes McKenna was in the chair, I suppose?'

'Yes, sir, he was there.'

'Ah, so I thought. Well, my opinion of him is that he is merely a guinea-pig—you know what that is? I have made up my mind to have nothing more to do with the venture, at any rate. And so they were pleased with your report, were they?'

'They appeared to be. They passed us a vote of thanks, and one or two of the gentlemen spoke in rather a complimentary manner of what we had done.'

'I am glad of that. By the way, William, you know Mr. Kenyon, do you not?'

The young man looked round with an abstracted air, and gazed past, rather than at, John Kenyon.

'Kenyon, Kenyon,' he said to himself, as if trying to recollect a name that he had once heard somewhere. 'I really don't——'

180

'Tut, tut!' said the old man, 'you remember Mr. Kenyon on board the Caloric?'

'Oh, ah, yes; certainly—oh, certainly. How do you do, Mr. Kenyon? I had forgotten for the moment. I thought I had met you in the City somewhere. Feeling first-rate after your trip, I hope.' And young Mr. Longworth fixed his one eyeglass in its place and flashed its glitter on Kenyon.

'I am very well, thanks.'

'That's right. Let me see, your business with the London Syndicate is concluded now, is it not?'

'Yes, it is done with.'

'Ah, and what are you doing? Have you anything else on hand?'

'Well, that is what I wish to see you about.'

'Really?'

'Yes; I—you remember, perhaps, we had some talk about a mica-mine near the Ottawa River?'

'On my soul, I don't. You see, the voyage rather—that was on board ship, I suppose?'

'Yes,' said John, crossing over to the young man's desk and taking a chair beside him. The old gentleman now turned to his own papers, and left the two young men to talk together.

'Do you mean to say you don't remember a talk we had on deck once about a mica-mine?'

Young Longworth looked at him with a puzzled expression, as if he could not quite make out what he was talking about.

'I remember,' he said, 'your telling me that you had been sent over by the London Syndicate to see after certain mines there; but I don't remember anything being said in reference to them.'

'It was not in reference to them at all; it was in reference to another

181

mine, of which I have secured the option. You will, perhaps, recollect that your cousin introduced me to you. You seemed to think at the time that the price at which we were going to offer the mine was too low.'

'By Jove, yes! now I do recollect something about it, when you mention that. Let me see, how much was it? A million, was it not?'

'No, no' said Kenyon, mopping his brow. He did not at all like the turn the conversation had taken. 'Not a million, nor anything like that amount.'

'Ah, I am sorry for that. You see, my uncle and myself rarely touch anything that is not worth while; and anything under a million would be hardly worth bothering with, don't you know.'

'I don't think so; it seems to me that something below a million would be worth spending a little time on; at least, it would be worth my while.'

'That may be very true; but, you see, my uncle takes large interests only in large businesses.'

'If you remember, Mr. Longworth, your uncle was not mentioned in connection with this at all. Your cousin seemed to think you might take some interest in it yourself. You told me, when I said the price at which we wished to offer the mine was fifty thousand pounds, that the sum was altogether too small; at least, it left too little margin to divide amongst three.'

'Well, I think I was perfectly correct in that.'

'And you further said that, if we increased the capital to two hundred thousand pounds, you would take a share in it with us.'

'Did I say that?'

'Yes. It rested with my partner then. I said I would speak to him about it, and, if he were willing, I should be. Circumstances occurred which made it impossible for me to go into details with him on board the ship; but I have spoken to him to-day at his own office, and he is quite willing to offer the mine at two hundred thousand pounds, provided the figures which I have given him show that it will pay a handsome dividend on that sum.'

'Well, it seems to me that, if the mine is really worth two hundred thousand pounds, it is a pity to offer it at fifty thousand pounds. Doesn't it strike you that way?'

'Yes, it does; so I called to see you with reference to it. I wanted to say that Wentworth will go carefully over the figures I have given him, and see if there is any mistake about them. If there is not, and if we find that the mine will bear inflation to two hundred thousand pounds, we shall be very glad of your aid in the matter, and will divide everything equally with you. That is to say, each of us will take a third.'

'If I remember rightly, I asked you a question which you did not answer. I asked you how much you paid for the mine.'

Kenyon was astonished at this peculiar kind of memory, that could forget a whole conversation, and yet remember accurately one detail of it. However, he replied:

'Of course, at that time you had not said you would join us. I recognise that, if you are to be a partner, it is your right to know exactly what we pay for the mine. I may say that we have not paid for it, but have merely got an option on it at a certain price, and of course, if we can sell it for two hundred thousand pounds, we shall have a large amount to divide. Now, if you think you will go in with us, and do your best to make this project a success, I will tell you what our option is on the mica-mine.'

'Well, you see, I can hardly say that I will join you. It is really a very small matter. There ought not to be any difficulty in floating that mine on the London market, except that it is hardly worth one's while to take it up. Still, I should have to know exactly what you are to pay for the property before I went any further in the matter.'

'Very well, then, I tell you in confidence, and only because I expect you to become a partner with us, that the amount the mine is offered to us for is twenty thousand pounds.'

Young Longworth arched his eyeglass.

'It cannot be worth very much if that is all they ask for it.'

'The price they ask for it has really nothing at all to do with the value of the mine. They do not know the value of it. They are not working it, even now, so as to bring out all there is in it. They are mining for mica, and, as I told you, the mineral which they are throwing away is very much more valuable than all the mica they can get out of the mine. If it were worked rightly, the mica would pay all expenses, as well as a good dividend on fifty thousand pounds, while the other mineral would pay a large dividend on one hundred and fifty thousand pounds, or even two hundred thousand pounds.'

'I see. And you feel positive that there is enough of this mineral to hold out for some time?'

'Oh, I am positive of that. There is a whole mountain of it.'

'And do you get the mountain as well as the mine?'

'We get three hundred acres of it, and I think there would be no difficulty in buying the rest.'

'Well, that would seem to be a good speculation, and I am sure I hope you will succeed in forming your company. How much money are you prepared to spend in floating the mine?'

'I have practically nothing at all. My asset, as it were, is the option I have on the mine.'

'Then, how are you going to pay the preliminary fees, the advertising in the newspapers, the cost of counsel, and all that? These expenses will amount to something very heavy in the formation of a company. Of course you know that.'

'Well, you see, I think that perhaps we can get two or three men to go into this and form our company quietly, without having any of those heavy expenses which are necessary in the forming of some companies.'

'My dear sir, when you have been in this business a little longer, you will be very much wiser. That cannot be done—at least, I do not believe it can be done. I do not know of its having been done, and if you can do it, you are a very much cleverer man than I am. Companies are not formed for nothing in the City of London. You seem to have the vaguest possible notion about how

184

this sort of thing is managed. I may tell you frankly I do not think I can go in with you; I have too much else on hand.'

Although Kenyon expected this, he nevertheless felt a grim sense of defeat as the young man calmly said these words. Then he blurted out:

'If you had no idea of going in with us, why have you asked me certain questions about the property which I would not have answered if I had not thought you were going to take an interest in it?'

'My dear sir,' said the other blandly, 'you were at perfect liberty to answer those questions or not, as you chose. You chose to answer them, and you have no one to blame but yourself if you are sorry you have answered them. It really doesn't matter at all to me, as I shall forget all you have said in a day or two at furthest.'

'Very well; I have nothing more to say except that what I have told you has been said in confidence.'

'Oh, of course. I shall mention it to nobody.'

'Then I wish you good-day.'

Turning to the elder gentleman, he said:

'Good-day, Mr. Longworth.'

The old man raised his eyes rather abstractedly from the paper he was reading, and then cordially shook hands with Kenyon.

'If I can do anything,' he said, 'to help you in any matter you have on hand, I shall be very pleased to do it. I hope to see you succeed. Good-day, Mr. Kenyon.'

'Good-day, Mr. Longworth.'

And with that the young man found himself again in the outer office, and shortly afterwards in the busy street, with a keen sense of frustration upon him. His first move in the direction of forming a company had been a disastrous failure; and thinking of this, he walked past the Mansion House and down Cheapside.

CHAPTER XVII.

John Kenyon walked along Cheapside feeling very much downhearted over his rebuff with Longworth. The pretended forgetfulness of the young man, of course, he took at its proper value. He, nevertheless, felt very sorry the interview had been so futile, and, instead of going back to Wentworth and telling him his experience, he thought it best to walk off a little of his disappointment first. He was somewhat startled when a man accosted him; and, glancing up, he saw standing there a tall footman, arrayed in a drab coat that came down to his heels.

'I beg your pardon, sir,' said the footman, 'but Miss Longworth would like to speak to you.'

'Miss Longworth!' cried Kenyon, in surprise; 'where is she?'

'She is here in her carriage, sir.'

The carriage had drawn up beside the pavement, and John Kenyon looked round in confusion to see that Miss Longworth was regarding him and the footman with an amused air. An elderly woman sat in the carriage opposite her, while a grave and dignified coachman, attired somewhat similarly to the footman, kept his place like a seated statue in front. John Kenyon took off his hat as he approached the young woman, whom he had not seen since the last day on the steamer.

'How are you, Mr. Kenyon?' said Edith Longworth brightly, holding out her hand to the young man by her carriage. 'Will you not step in? I want to talk with you, and I am afraid the police will not allow us to block such a crowded thoroughfare as Cheapside.'

As she said this, the nimble footman threw open the door of the carriage, while John, not knowing what to say, stepped inside and took his seat.

'Holborn,' said the young woman to the coachman; then, turning to Kenyon, she continued: 'Will you not tell me where you are going, so that I may know where to set you down?'

'To tell the truth,' said John, 'I do not think I was going anywhere. I am afraid I have not yet got over the delight of being back in London again, so I sometimes walk along the streets in rather a purposeless manner.'

'Well, you did not seem delighted when I first caught sight of you. I thought you looked very dejected, and that gave me courage enough to ask you to come and talk with me. I said to myself, "There is something wrong with the mica-mine," and, with a woman's I curiosity, I wanted to know all about it. Now tell me.'

'There is really very little to tell. We have hardly begun yet. Wentworth is to-day looking over the figures I gave him, and I have been making a beginning by seeing some people who I thought might be interested in the mine.'

'And were they?'

'No; they were not.'

'Then, that was the reason you were looking so distressed.'

'I suppose it was.'

'Well, now, Mr. Kenyon, if you get discouraged after an interview with the first person you think will be interested in the mine, what will you do when a dozen or more people refuse to have anything to do with it?'

'I'm sure I do not know. I am afraid I am not the right person to float a mine on the London market. I am really a student, you see, and flatter myself I am a man of science. I know what I am about when I am in a mine, miles away from civilization; but when I get among men, I feel somehow at a loss. I do not understand them. When a man tells me one thing to-day, and to-morrow calmly forgets all about it, I confess it—well, confuses me.'

'Then the man you have seen to-day has forgotten what he told you yesterday. Is that the case?'

'Yes; that is partly the case.'

'But, Mr. Kenyon, the success of your project is not going to depend upon what one man says, or two, or three, is it?'

'No; I don't suppose it is.'

'Then, if I were you, I would not feel discouraged because one man has forgotten. I wish I were acquainted with your one man, and I would make him ashamed of himself, I think.'

Kenyon flushed as she said this, but made no reply.

The coachman looked round as he came to Holborn, and Miss Longworth nodded to him; so he went on without stopping into Oxford Street.

'Now, I take a great interest in your mine, Mr. Kenyon, and hope to see you succeed with it. I wish I could help you, or, rather, I wish you would be frank with me, and tell me how I can help you. I know a good deal about City men and their ways, and I think I may be able to give you some good advice—at least, if you would have the condescension to consult me.'

Kenyon smiled.

'You are making game of me now, Miss Longworth. Of course, as you said on board ship, it is but a very small matter.'

'I never said any such thing. When did I say that?'

'You said that fifty thousand pounds was a small matter.'

'Did I? Well, I am like your man who has forgotten; I have forgotten that. I remember saying something about its being too small an amount for my father to deal with. Was not that what I said?'

'Yes, I think that was it. It conveyed the idea to my mind that you thought fifty thousand pounds a trifling sum indeed.'

Edith Longworth laughed.

'What a terrible memory you have! I do not wonder at your City man forgetting. Are you sure what you told him did not happen longer ago than yesterday?'

'Yes, it happened some time before.'

'Ah, I thought so; I am afraid it is your own terrible memory, and not his forgetfulness, that is to blame.'

'Oh, I am not blaming him at all. A man has every right to change his mind, if he wants to do so.'

'I thought only a woman had that privilege.'

'No; for my part I freely accord it to everybody, only sometimes it is a little depressing.'

'I can imagine that; in fact, I think no one could be a more undesirable acquaintance than a man who forgets to-day what he promised yesterday, especially if anything particular depends upon it. Now, why cannot you come to our house some evening and have a talk about the mine with my cousin or my father? My father could give you much valuable advice with reference to it, and I am anxious that my cousin should help to carry this project on to success. It is better to talk with them there than at their office, because they are both so busy during the day that I am afraid they might not be able to give the time necessary to its I discussion.'

John Kenyon shook his head.

'I am afraid,' he said, 'that would do no good. I do not think your cousin cares to have anything to do with the mine.'

'How can you say that? Did he not discuss the matter with you on board ship?'

'Yes; we had some conversation about it there, but I imagine that—I really do not think he would care to go any farther with it.'

'Ah, I see,' said Edith Longworth. 'My cousin is the man who "forgot to-day what he said yesterday."'

'What am I to say, Miss Longworth? I do not want to say "Yes," and I cannot truthfully say "No."'

'You need say nothing. I know exactly how it has been. So he does not want to have anything to do with it. What reason did he give?'

'You will not say anything to him about the matter? I should be very sorry if he thought that I talked to anyone else of my conference with him.'

'Oh, certainly not; I will say nothing to him at all.'

'He gave no particular reason; he simply seemed to have changed his mind. But I must say this: he did not appear to be very enthusiastic when I discussed it with him on board ship.'

'Well, you see, Mr. Kenyon, it rests with me now to maintain the honour of the Longworth family. Do you want to make all the profit there is to be made in the mica-mine—that is, yourself and your friend Mr. Wentworth?'

'How do you mean—"all the profit"?'

'Well, I mean—would you share the profit with anyone?'

'Certainly, if that person could help us to form the company.'

'Very well; it was on that basis you were going to take in my cousin as a partner, was it not?'

'Yes.'

'Then I should like to share in the profits of the mine if he does not take an interest in it. If you will let me pay the preliminary expenses of forming this company, and if you will then give me a share of what you make, I shall be glad to furnish the money you need at the outset.'

John Kenyon looked at Miss Longworth with a smile.

'You are very ingenious, Miss Longworth, but I can see, in spite of your way of putting it, that what you propose is merely a form of charity. Suppose we did not succeed in forming our company, how could we repay you the money?'

'You would not need to repay the money. I would take that risk. It is a sort of speculation. If you form the company, then I shall expect a very large reward for furnishing the funds. It is purely selfishness on my part. I believe I have a head for business. Women in this country do not get such chances of developing their business talents as they seem to have in America. In that country there are women who have made fortunes for themselves. I believe in your mine, and I am convinced you will succeed in forming your company. If you or Mr. Wentworth were capitalists, of course there would be no need of my assistance. If I were alone, I could not form a company. You and Mr. Wentworth can do what I cannot do. You can appear before the public and attend to all preliminaries. On the other hand, I believe I can do what neither of you can do; that is, I can supply a certain amount of money from time to time to pay the expenses of forming the company—because a company is not formed in London for nothing, I assure you. Perhaps you think you have simply to go and see a sufficient number of people and get your company formed. I fancy you will find it not so easy as all that. Besides this business interest I have in it, I have a very friendly interest in Mr. Wentworth.'

As she said this, she bent over towards John Kenyon, and spoke in a lower tone of voice:

'Please do not tell him so, because I think that he is a young man who has possibilities of being conceited.'

'I shall say nothing about it,' said Kenyon dolefully.

'Please do not. By the way, I wish you would give me Mr. Wentworth's address, so that I may communicate with him if a good idea occurs to me, or if I find out something of value in forming our company.'

Kenyon took out a card, wrote the address of Wentworth upon it, and handed it to her.

'Thank you,' she said 'You see, I deeply sympathized with Mr. Wentworth for what he had to pass through on the steamer.'

'He is very grateful for all you did for him on that occasion,' replied Kenyon.

'I am glad of that. People, as a general thing, are not grateful for what

191

their friends do for them. I am glad, therefore, that Mr. Wentworth is an exception. Well, suppose you talk with him about what I have said, before you make up your own mind. I shall be quite content with whatever share of the profits you allow me.'

'Ah, that is not business, Miss Longworth.'

'No, it is not; but I am dealing with you—that is, with Mr. Wentworth—and I am sure both of you will do what is right. Perhaps it would be better not to tell him who is to furnish the money. Just say you have met a friend to-day who offers, for a reasonable share of the profits, to supply all the money necessary for the preliminary expenses. You will consult with him about it, will you not?'

'Yes, if it is your wish.'

'Certainly it is my wish; and I also wish you to do it so diplomatically that you will conceal my name from him more successfully than you concealed my cousin's name from me this afternoon.'

'I am afraid I am very awkward,' said John, blushing.

'No; you are very honest, that's all. You are not accomplished in the art of telling what is not true. Now, this is where we live; will you come in?'

'Thank you, no; I'm afraid not,' said John. 'I must really be going now.'

'Let the coachman take you to your station.'

'No, no, it is not worth the trouble; it is only a step from here.'

'It is no trouble. Which is your station—South Kensington?'

'Yes.'

'Very well. Drive to South Kensington Station, Parker,' she said to the coachman; and then, running up the steps, she waved her hand in good-bye, as the carriage turned.

And so John Kenyon, feeling abashed at his own poverty, was driven in this gorgeous equipage to the Underground Railway station, where he took

192

the train for the City.

As he stepped from the carriage at South Kensington, young Mr. Longworth came out of the station on his way home, and was simply dumfounded to see Kenyon in the Longworths' carriage.

John passed him without noticing who he was, and just as the coachman was going to start again, Longworth said to him:

'Parker, have you been picking up fares in the street?'

'Oh no, sir,' replied the respectable Parker; 'the young gentleman as just left us came from the City with Miss Longworth.'

'Did he, indeed? Where did you pick him up, Parker?'

'We picked him up in Cheapside, sir.'

'Ah, indeed;' and with that, muttering some imprecations on the cheek of Kenyon, he stepped into the carriage and drove home.

CHAPTER XVIII.

George Wentworth was a very much better man than John Kenyon to undertake the commercial task they hoped to accomplish. Wentworth had mixed with men, and was not afraid of them. Although he had suffered keenly from the little episode on the steamer, and although at that trying time he appeared to but poor advantage so far as an exhibition of courage was concerned, the reason was largely because the blow had been dealt him by a woman, and not by a man. If one of Wentworth's fellow-men so far forgot himself as to make an insulting or cutting remark to him, Wentworth merely shrugged his shoulders and thought no more about it. On the other hand, notwithstanding his somewhat cold and calm exterior, John Kenyon was as sensitive as a child, and a rebuff such as he received from the Longworths was enough to depress him for a week. He had been a student all his life, and had not yet learnt the valuable lesson of knowing how to look at men's actions with an eye to proportion. Wentworth said to himself that nobody's opinion amounted to very much, but Kenyon knew too little of his fellows to have arrived at this comforting conclusion.

George Wentworth closed his door when he was alone, drew the mass of papers, which Kenyon had left, towards him on his desk, and proceeded systematically to find a flaw in them if possible. He said to himself: 'I must attack this thing without enthusiasm, and treat Kenyon as if he were a thief. I must find an error in the reasoning or something shaky about the facts.' He perused the papers earnestly, making pencil-marks on the margin here and there. At first he said to himself: 'It is quite evident that the mining of the mica will pay for the working of the mine. We can look upon the demand for mica as being in a certain sense settled. It has paid for the working of the mine so far, also a small dividend, and there is no reason to think it should not go on doing so. Now, the uncertain quantity is this other stuff, and the uncertain thing about this uncertain quantity is the demand for it in the markets of the world, also how much the carriage of it is going to cost.' Wentworth had a theory that all things were possible if you only knew a man who knew the man. There is always the man in everything—the man who is the authority on iron; the man who is the authority on mines; the man who is the authority on the currency, and the man who knows all about the printing trade. If you want any information on any particular subject, it was not necessary to know the man, but it was very essential to know a man who can put his finger on the man. Get a note of introduction from a man who knows the man, and there you are!

Wentworth touched his bell, and a boy answered his summons.

'Ask Mr. Close to step in here for a moment, will you, please?'

The boy disappeared, and shortly after an oldish man with a very deferential look, who was perpetually engaged in smoothing one hand over the other, came in, and, in a timid manner, closed the door softly behind him.

'Close,' said Wentworth, 'who is it that knows everything about the china trade?'

'About the china trade, sir?'

'Yes, about the china trade.'

'Wholesale or retail, sir?'

'I want to get at somebody who knows all about the manufacture of china.'

'Ah, the manufacture, sir,' said Close, in a tone that indicated this was another matter altogether; 'the manufacture, sir; yes, sir, I really do not know who could tell everything about the manufacture of china, sir, but I know of a man who could put you on the right track.'

'Very well; that is quite as good.'

'I would see Mr. Melville, if I were you, sir—Mr. Melville, of the great Scranton China Company.'

'And what is his address?'

'His address is——' And here the old man stooped over and wrote it on a card. 'That will find him, sir. If you can drop a note to Mr. Melville, sir, and say you want to learn who knows all about the production of china, he will be able to tell you just the man, sir. He is in the wholesale china trade himself, sir.'

'Would he be in at this hour, do you think?'

'Oh yes, sir, he is sure to be in his office now.'

'Very well, then; I think I will just run over and see him.'

'Very good, sir; anything more, sir?'

'Nothing more, Close, thank you.'

When the valuable Close had departed as softly and apologetically as he had entered, Wentworth picked up one of the specimens of spar which Kenyon had taken from the mine, and put it into his pocket. In two minutes more he was in a cab, dashing through the crowded streets towards Melville's office. By the side of the door of the china company's warehouse, inside the hall, were two parallel rows of names—one under the general heading of 'Out,' the other under the heading of 'In.' It appeared that Mr. Smith was out and Mr. Jones was in, but, what was more to the purpose, the name of Richard Melville happened to be in the column of those who were inside. After a few moments' delay, Wentworth was ushered into the office of this gentleman.

'Mr. Melville,' he said, 'I have been recommended to come to you for information regarding the china trade. The information I want, you will, perhaps, not be able to give me, but I believe you can tell me to whom I should apply for it.' Saying this, he took out of his pocket the specimen of mineral which he had brought with him. 'What I want to know is, how much of this material you use each year in the manufacture of china; what price you pay for it; and I should like to get at an estimate, if possible, of the quantity used in England every year.'

Melville picked up the specimen and turned it round and round, looking at it attentively.

'Well,' he said at last, 'I could tell you anything you wished about the wholesale china trade, but about the manufacture of it I am not so well informed. Where did you get this?'

'That,' said Wentworth, 'is from a mine in which I am interested.'

'Ah, where is the mine situated, may I ask?'

'It is in America,' said Wentworth vaguely.

'I see. Have you considered the question of carriage in proposing to put it on the English market? That, as you know, is an important question. The cost of taking a heavy article a long distance is a great factor in the question of its commercial value.'

'I recognise that,' said Wentworth; 'and it is to enable me to form some estimate of the value of this material that I ask for particulars of its price here.'

'I understand, but I am not able to answer your questions. If you have time to wait and see Mr. Brand, our manager of the works, who is also one of the owners, he could easily tell you everything about this mineral—whether used at all or not. He comes up to London once every fortnight, and to-day is his day. I am expecting him here at any time. You might wait, if you liked, and see him.'

'I do not think that will be necessary. I will write, if you will allow me, just what I want to know, and in two or three minutes he could jot down the information I require. Then I will call again to-morrow, if you don't mind.'

'Not in the least. I will submit the matter to him. You can leave me this piece of mineral, I suppose?'

'Certainly,' said Wentworth, writing on a sheet of paper the questions: 'First, What quantity of this mineral is used in your works in a year? second, What price per ton do you pay for it? third, Will you give me, if possible, an estimate of how much of this is used in England?'

'There,' he said, 'if you will give him this slip of paper, and show him the specimen of mineral, I shall be very much obliged.'

'By the way,' said Melville, 'is this mine in operation?'

'Yes, it is.'

'Is there anyone else beside yourself interested in it in this country?'

'Yes,' said Wentworth, with some hesitation; 'John Kenyon, a mining expert, is interested in it, and Mr. Longworth—young Mr. Longworth of the City.'

'Any relation to John Longworth?'

'His nephew.'

'Ah, well, anything that Longworth has an interest in is reasonably sure of being successful.'

'I am perhaps going too far in saying he has an interest in the mine, but in coming from America he seemed desirous of going in with us. My partner. John Kenyon, of whom I spoke just now, is with him at the present moment, I believe.'

'Very well. I will submit this specimen to Mr. Brand as you desire, and will let you know to-morrow what he says.'

With that Wentworth took his leave, and in going out through the hall he met the manager of the china works, although he didn't know at the time who he was. He was a very shrewd-faced individual, who walked with a brisk business step which showed he believed that time was money.

'Well, Melville,' he said when he entered, 'I am a little late to-day, am I not?'

'You are a little behind the usual time, but not much.'

'By the way——' began the manager, and then his eye wandered to the specimen on the desk before Melville. 'Hello!' he cried, 'where did you get this?'

'That was left here a moment ago by a gentleman whom I wanted to wait until you came, but he seemed to be in a hurry. He is going to call again

198

to-morrow.'

'What is his name?'

'Wentworth. Here's his card.'

'Ah, of a firm of accountants, eh? How did he come to have this?'

'He wanted to get some information about it, and I told him I would show it to you. Here is the note he left.'

The manager turned the crystal over and over in his hand, put on his eyeglasses and peered into it, then picked up the piece of paper and looked at what Kenyon had written.

'Did he say where he had got this?'

'Yes; he says there is a mine of it in America.'

'In America, eh? Did he say how much of this stuff there was?'

'No; he didn't tell me that. The mine is working, however.'

'It is very curious! I never heard of it.'

'I gathered from him,' said Mr. Melville, 'that he wishes to do something with the mine over here. He did not say much, but he told me his partner—I forget his name—was talking at the present moment with young Longworth about it.'

'Longworth—who's he?'

'He's a man who goes in for mines or other investments; that is, his uncle does—a very shrewd old fellow, too. He is always on the right side of the market, no matter how it turns.'

'Then, he would be a man certain to know the value of the property if he had it, wouldn't he?'

'I don't know anybody who knows the value of what he has better than Longworth.'

'Ah, that's a pity,' mused the manager.

'Why? Is it a mineral of any worth?'

'Worth! A quarry of this would be better for us than a gold-mine!'

'Well, it struck me, in talking with Mr. Wentworth, that he had no particular idea of its utility. He seemed to know nothing about it, and that's why he came here for information.'

Again the manager looked at the paper before him.

'I'm not so sure about that,' he said. 'He wants to know the quantity used in a year, how much of it is consumed in England, and the price we pay for it per ton. I should judge, from that, he has an inkling of its value, and wants merely to corroborate it. Yes, I feel certain that is his move. I fear nothing very much can be done with Mr. Wentworth.'

'What were you thinking of doing?'

'My dear Melville, if we could get hold of such a mine, supposing it has an unlimited quantity of this mineral in it, we could control the china markets of the world.'

'You don't mean it!'

'It's a fact, because of the purity of the mineral. The stuff that we use is heavily impregnated with iron; we have to get the iron out of it, and that costs money. Not that the stuff itself is uncommon at all, it is one of the most common substances in Nature; but anything so pure as this I have never seen. I wonder if it is a fair specimen of what they can get out of the mine? If it is, I would rather own that property than any gold-mine I know of.'

'Well, I will see Mr. Wentworth, if you like. He is going to call here about this time to-morrow, and I will find out if some arrangement cannot be made with him.'

'No, I wouldn't do that,' replied the manager, who preferred never to do things in a direct way. 'I think your best plan is to see Longworth. The chances are that a City man like him does not know the value of the property; and, if you don't mind, I will write a letter to Mr. Wentworth and give him my opinion on this mineral.'

'What shall I say to Longworth?'

'Say anything you like; you understand that kind of business better than I. Here are the facts of the case. If we can get a controlling interest in this mine, always supposing that it turns out mineral up to sample—I suspect that this is a picked specimen; of course we should have to send a man to America and see—if we could get hold of this property, it would be the greatest feat in business we have ever done, provided, of course, we get it at a cheap enough price.'

'What do you call a cheap enough price?'

'You find out what Longworth will sell the mine for.'

'But supposing Wentworth owns the mine, or as much of it as Longworth does?'

'I think, somehow, that if you know Longworth you can perhaps make better terms with him. Meanwhile I will send a letter to Wentworth. You have his address there?'

'Yes.'

'Very well.'

Taking his pen, he dashed off the following letter:

'DEAR SIR,

'I regret to say that the mineral you left at our office yesterday is of no value to us. We do not use mineral of this nature, and, so far as I know, it is not used anywhere in England.

'Yours truly,

'ADAM BRAND.'

CHAPTER XIX.

The chances are that, no matter under what circumstances young Longworth and Kenyon had first met, the former would have disliked the latter. Although strong friendships are formed between men who are dissimilar, it must not be forgotten that equally strong hatreds have arisen between people merely because they were of opposite natures. No two young men could have been more unlike each other; and as Longworth recalled the different meetings he had had with Kenyon, he admitted to himself that he had an extreme antipathy to the engineer. The evident friendship which his cousin felt for Kenyon added a bitterness to this dislike which was rapidly turning it into hate. However, he calmed down sufficiently, on going home in the carriage, to become convinced that it was better to say nothing about her meeting with Kenyon unless she introduced the subject. After all, the carriage was hers, not his, and he recognised that fact. He wondered how much Kenyon had told her of the interview at his uncle's office. He flattered himself, however, that he knew enough of women to be sure that she would very speedily refer to the subject, and then he hoped to learn just how much had been said. To his surprise, his cousin said nothing at all about the matter, neither that evening nor the next morning, and, consequently, he went to his office in a somewhat bewildered state of mind.

On arriving at his room in the City, he found Melville waiting for him.

Melville shook hands with young Longworth, and, taking a mineral specimen from his pocket, placed it on the young man's desk, saying;

'I suppose you know where that comes from?'

Longworth looked at it with an air of indecision which made Melville suspect he knew very little about it.

'I haven't the slightest idea, really.'

'No? I was told you were interested in the mine from which this was taken. Mr. Wentworth called on me yesterday, and gave your name as one of those who were concerned with the mine.'

'Ah, yes, I see; yes, yes, I have—some interest in the mine.'

'Well, it is about that I came to talk with you. Where is the mine situated?'

'It is near the Ottawa River, I believe, some distance above Montreal. I am not certain about its exact position, but it is somewhere in that neighbourhood.'

'I thought by the way Wentworth talked it was in the United States. He mentioned another person as being his partner in the affair; I forget his name.'

'John Kenyon, probably.'

'Kenyon! Yes, I think that was the name. Yes, I am sure it was. Now, may I ask what is your connection with that mine? Are you a partner of Wentworth's and Kenyon's? Are you the chief owner of the mine, or is the mine owned by them?'

'In the first place, Mr. Melville, I should like to know why you ask me these questions?'

Melville laughed.

'Well, I will tell you. We should like to know what chance there is of our getting a controlling interest in the mine. That is very frankly put, isn't it?'

'Yes, it is. But whom do you mean by "we"? Who else besides yourself?'

'By "we" I mean the china company to which I belong. This mineral is useful in making china. That I suppose you know.'

'Yes, I was aware of that,' answered Longworth, although he heard it now for the first time.

'Very well, then; I should like to know who is the owner of the mine.'

'The owner of the mine at present is some foreigner whose name and

203

address I do not know. The two young men you speak of have an option on that mine for a certain length of time—how long I don't know. They have been urging me to go in with them to form a company for the floating of that mine for two hundred thousand pounds on the London market.'

'Two hundred thousand pounds!' said Melville. 'That seems to me rather a large amount.'

'Do you think so? Well, the objection I had to it was that it was too small.'

'Those two men must have an exaggerated idea of the value of this mineral if they think it will pay dividends on two hundred thousand pounds.'

'This mineral is not all there is in the mine. In fact, it is already paying a dividend on fifty thousand pounds or thereabouts, because of the mica in it. It is being mined for mica alone. To tell the truth, I did not know much about the other mineral.'

'And do you think the mine is worth two hundred thousand pounds?'

'Frankly, I do not.'

'Then why are you connected with it?'

'I am not connected with it—at least, not definitely connected with it. I have the matter under consideration. Of course, if there is anything approaching a swindle in it, I shall have nothing to do with it. It will depend largely on the figures that the two men show me whether I have anything to do with it or not.'

'I see; I understand your position.' Then, lowering his voice, Melville leaned over towards Longworth, and said: 'You are a man of business. Now, I want to ask you what would be the chance of our getting the mine at something like the original option priced which is, of course, very much less than two hundred thousand pounds? We do not want to have too many in it. In fact, if you could get it for us at a reasonable rate, and did not care to be troubled with the property yourself, we would take the whole ourselves.'

Young Longworth pondered a moment, and then said to Melville:

'Do you mean to freeze out the other two fellows, as they say in America?'

'I do not know about freezing out; but, of course, with the other two there is so much less profit to be divided. We should like to deal with just as few as if possible.'

'Exactly. I see what you mean. I think it can be done. Are you in any great hurry to secure the mine?'

'Not particularly. Why?'

'Well, if things are worked rightly, I don't know but what we could get it for the original option. That would mean, of course, to wait until this first option had run out.'

'Wouldn't there be a little danger in that? They may form their company in the meantime, and then we should lose everything. Our interest in the matter is as much to prevent anyone else getting hold of the mine as to get it ourselves.'

'I see. I will think it over. I believe it can be done without great risk; but, of course, we shall have to be reasonably quiet about the matter.'

'I see the necessity of that.'

'Very good. I will see you again after I have thought over the affair, and we can come to some arrangement.'

'I may say that our manager has written a note to Wentworth, saying that this mineral is of no particular use to us.'

'Exactly,' said young Longworth, with a look of intelligence.

'So, of course, in speaking with Wentworth about the mine, it is just as well not to mention us in any way.'

'I shall not.'

'Very well. I will leave the matter in your hands for the present.'

'Yes, do so. I will think over it this afternoon, and probably see Wentworth and Kenyon to-morrow. There is no immediate hurry, for I happen to know they have not done anything yet.'

With that Mr. Melville took his leave, and young Longworth paced up and down the room, evolving a plan that would at once bring him money and give him the satisfaction of making it lively for John Kenyon.

When he reached home, Longworth waited for his cousin to say something about Kenyon; but he soon saw that she did not intend to speak of him at all. So he said to her:

'Edith, do you remember Kenyon and Wentworth—who were on board our steamer?'

'I remember them very well.'

'Did you know they had a mining property for sale?'

'Yes.'

'I have been thinking about it—in fact, Kenyon called at my office a day or two ago, and at that time, not having given the subject much thought, I could not give him any encouragement; but I have been pondering over it since, and have almost decided to help them. What do you think about it?'

'Oh, I think it would be an excellent plan. I am sure the property is a good one, or Mr. Kenyon would have nothing to do with it. I shall write a note to them, if you think it advisable, inviting them here to talk with you about it.'

'That will not be necessary at all. I do not want people to come here to talk business. My office is the proper place.'

'Still, we met them in a friendly way on board the steamer, and I think it would be nice if they came here some evening and talked over the matter with you.'

'I don't believe in introducing business into a man's home. This would be a purely business conversation, and it may as well take place at my office, or at Wentworth's, if he has one, as I suppose he has.'

'Oh, certainly; his address is——'

'Oh, you know it, do you?'

Edith blushed as she realized what she had said; then she remarked:

'Is there any harm in my knowing the business address of Mr. Wentworth?'

'Oh, not at all—not at all. I merely wondered how you happened to know his address, when I didn't.'

'Well, it doesn't matter how I know it. I am glad you are going to join him, and I am sure you will be successful. Will you see them to-morrow?'

'I think so. I shall call on Wentworth and have a talk with him about it. Of course we may not be able to come to a workable arrangement. If not, it really does not matter very much. But if I can make satisfactory terms with them, I will help them to form their company.'

When Edith went to her own room she wrote a note. It was addressed to George Wentworth in the City, but above that address was the name John Kenyon. She said:

'DEAR MR. KENYON,

'I was certain at the time you spoke that my cousin was not so much at fault in forgetting his conversation as you thought. We had a talk to night about the mine, and when he calls upon you tomorrow, as he intends to do, I want you to know that I said nothing whatever to him of what you told me. He mentioned the subject first. I wanted you to know this because you might feel embarrassed when you met him by thinking I had sent him to you. That is not at all the case. He goes to you of his own accord, and I am sure you will find his assistance in forming a company very valuable. I am glad to think you will be partners.

'Yours very truly,

'EDITH LONGWORTH.'

She gave this letter to her maid to post, and young Longworth met the maid in the hall with the letter in her hand. He somehow suspected, after the foregoing conversation, to whom the letter was addressed.

'Where are you going with that?'

'To the post, sir.'

'I am going out; to save you the trouble I will take it.'

After passing the corner, he looked at the address on the envelope; then he swore to himself a little. If he had been a villain in a play he would have opened the letter; but he did not. He merely dropped it into the first pillar-box he came to, and in due time it reached John Kenyon.

CHAPTER XX.

Although Jennie Brewster arrived in London angry with the world in general, and with several of its inhabitants in particular, she soon began to revel in the delights of the great city. It was so old that it was new to her, and she visited Westminster Abbey and other of its ancient landmarks in rapid succession. The cheapness of the hansoms delighted her, and she spent most of her time dashing about in cabs. She put up at one of the big hotels, and ordered many new dresses at a place in Regent Street. She bought most of the newspapers, morning and evening, and declared she could not find an interesting article in any of them. From her point of view they were stupid and unenterprising, and she resolved to run down the editor of one of the big dailies when she got time, interview him, and discover how he reconciled it with his conscience to publish so dull a sheet every day.

She wrote to her editor in New York that London, though a slow town, was full of good material, and that nobody had touched it in the writing line since Dickens' time; therefore she proposed to write a series of articles on the Metropolis that would wake them up a bit. The editor cabled to her to go ahead, and she went.

Jennie engaged a chaperon, and took great satisfaction in this unwonted luxury. It had been intimated to her that Lady Willow was a sort of society St. Peter, who held keys that would open the gates of the social heaven, if she were sufficiently recompensed. Of all the ancient landmarks of England, none attracted Jennie so much as the aristocracy, and although she had written to New York for letters of introduction that would be useful in London, she was too impatient to await their arrival. Thus she came to secure the services of Lady Willow, the widow of Sir Debenham Willow, who had died abroad, insolvent, some years before, mourned by the creditors he left behind him.

Jennie was suspicious about the title, and demanded convincing proofs of its genuineness before she engaged Lady Willow. She was amazed that any real lady would, as it were, sell her social influence at so much a week;

but, as Lady Willow was equally astonished that an American girl earned her livelihood by writing for the papers, the surprise of the one found its counterpart in the wonder of the other.

Lady Willow thought all American girls were born daughters of millionaires, in accordance with some unexplained Western by-law of nature, and imagined that their sole object in desiring to enter London society was to purchase for themselves a more or less expensive scion of the aristocracy; she was therefore inclined to resent meeting a shrewd young woman apparently determined on getting the value for her money.

'It is not my custom to chaffer about terms,' said Lady Willow with much dignity.

'It is mine,' replied Jennie complacently; 'I always like to know what I am buying, and the price I am to pay for it.'

'You are dealing with me,' said the lady, rising indignantly, 'as if you were engaging a cook. I am sure we would not suit each other at all.'

'Please sit down, Lady Willow, and don't be offended. Let us talk it over in an amicable manner, even if we come to no arrangement. I think a cook an exceedingly important person, and I assure you I would treat one in the most deferential manner; while with you, on the other hand, I talk in an open and frank way, as between friend and friend. I take it that you and I are somewhat similarly situated. We are neither of us rich, and so we have each of us to earn the money we need in our own way. It would be dishonest if I pretended to you that I was wealthy, and then couldn't pay what you expected after you had done all you could for me—now, wouldn't it? Very well, if you have anyone else to chaperon who can afford to pay more than I can, you shouldn't bother about me at all, but secure a richer client.'

Lady Willow remembered that this was not the season when rich clients abounded; so she smothered her resentment, and sat down again.

'That's right,' said Jennie; 'we'll have a nice quiet talk, whatever comes of it. Now, if you like, I could write a lovely article about you in the Sunday Argus, and then all rich girls who come over here would go direct to you.'

210

'Oh dear! oh dear!' cried Lady Willow, evidently inexpressibly shocked at the idea, 'you would surely never do so cruel a thing as that? If my friends knew I chaperoned young ladies and took money for it, I would never be allowed to enter their doors again.'

'Ah, I didn't think of that. Of course it wouldn't do. What a curious thing it is that those who want to be written up in the papers generally never see their names in print; while those who don't want to have anything said about them are the people the reporters are always after.'

'Do you write for the papers, then?'

'For one of them.'

'How dreadful!' said Lady Willow, rising again, with an air of finality about her movement. It was evident that any dealings with this American girl were out of the question.

'Do sit down again, Lady Willow. We will take it that I am hopelessly ineligible, and so say no more about it; but I do want to have a talk with you.'

'But you will write something——'

'I shall not write a word about you or about anything you tell me. You see, your profession is as strange to me as mine is to you.'

'My profession? I have none.'

'Well, whatever you call it. I mean the way in which you make your money.'

Lady Willow sighed, and the tears came into her eyes.

'You little know, my child, to what straits one may come who is left unprovided for, and who has to do the best to keep up appearances.'

Jennie sprang up instantly and took the unresisting hand of the elder woman, smoothing it with her own caressingly.

'Why, of course I know,' she cried, with a little quaver in her voice; 'and there is nothing more terrible on earth than lack of money. If there was a single really civilized country in existence, it would make provision for its women. Every woman should be assured enough to live on, merely because she is a woman. If England had put aside as much for its women as it has spent in the last hundred years on foolish wars, or if America had made a fund of what its politicians have been allowed to steal, the women of both barbarous countries might have been provided with incomes that would at least keep them from the fear of want.'

Lady Willow seemed more alarmed than comforted by the vehemence of Miss Brewster. She said hesitatingly:

'I'm afraid you have some very strange ideas, my dear.'

'Perhaps; but I have one idea that isn't strange: it is that you are going to take charge of a lonesome, friendless girl for a few weeks at least—until the rich pork-packer's daughter from Chicago comes along, and she won't be here for a month or two yet. We won't say a word about terms; I'll pay you all that's left over from my hansom fares.'

'I shall be very happy to do what I can for you, my dear.'

Lady Willow had softened towards her fair client, and had now adopted a somewhat motherly tone with her, which Jennie evidently liked.

'I will try and be very little trouble to you, although I shall probably ask you ever so many questions. All I really want is merely to see the Zoo, hear the animals roar, and watch them being fed. I have no ambition to steal any of them.'

'Oh, that will be easily done,' said Lady Willow in surprise. 'We can get tickets from one of the Fellows of the Zoological Society which will admit us on Sunday, when there are but few people there.'

Jennie laughed merrily.

'I mean the social Zoo, Lady Willow; I have visited the other already. Please do not look so shocked at me, and don't be afraid; I really talk very nicely when I am in society, and I am sure you will not be in the least ashamed of me. You see, I haven't had a soul to speak with since I came to London, so

I think I ought to be allowed a little latitude at first.'

Lady Willow so far relaxed her dignity as to smile, although a little dubiously; and Jennie joyfully proclaimed that their compact was sealed and that she was sure they would be great friends.

'Now you must tell me what I am to do,' she continued. 'I suppose dresses are the most important preliminaries when one is meditating a siege on society. Well, I've ordered ever so many, so that's all right. What's the next thing?'

'Yes, dress is important; but I think the first thing to do is to choose pleasant rooms somewhere. You can't stay at this hotel, you know; besides, it must be very expensive.'

'Yes, it is rather; but it is so handy and central.'

'It is not central for society.'

'Oh, isn't it? I was thinking of Westminster Abbey and Trafalgar Square, and that sort of thing. Besides, there's always a nice hansom right at the door whenever one wants to go out.'

'Oh, but you mustn't ride in hansoms, you know!'

'Why? I thought the aristocracy—the very highest—rode in hansoms.'

'Some of them have private hansoms; but that's a very different thing.'

'And I heard somewhere that most of the hansoms in London are owned by the aristocracy. I am sure I rode in one belonging to the Marquis of Something—I forget his name. I don't suppose the Marquis himself drove it. Perhaps it was driven by his hired man; but the driver was such a nice young fellow, and he gave me a lot of information. He told me that the Marquis owned the hansom; for I asked him whose it was. I thought perhaps it belonged to the driver. I'll give up the hotel willingly, but I don't know about hansoms. I'm afraid to promise; for I feel sure I'll hail a hansom automatically the moment I go out alone. So we will postpone the hansom question until later. Now, where would you recommend me to stay while in London?'

'You could stop with me if you liked. I have not a large house; but there is room for one or two friends, and it is in a very good locality.'

'Oh, that will be delightful. I suppose the correct address on one's notepaper is everything, almost as good as a coat-of-arms—if they use coats-of-arms as letter-heads; and there is a difference between Drury and Park when they precede the word "Lane."'

The two ladies speedily came to an understanding that was satisfactory to each of them, and Lady Willow found, to the no small comforting of her dignity, that, although she came to the hotel in the attitude of one who, if it may be so expressed, sought a favour, the impetuous eagerness of the younger woman had so changed the situation that the elder lady now left with the gratifying self complacency of a generous person who has conferred a boon. Nor was her condescension without its reward, both material and intellectual, for not only did Jennie pay her way with some lavishness, but her immediate social success was flattering to Lady Willow as the introducer of a Transatlantic cousin so bright and vivacious.

So great an impression did Jennie make upon the more susceptible portion of the young men she met under Lady Willow's chaperonage, that even the rumour which got abroad, that she had no money, did not damp the devotion of all of them. Lord Frederick Bingham was quite as assiduous in his attentions as if she were the greatest heiress that ever crossed the ocean to exchange dubiously won gold for a title founded by some thief in the Middle Ages, thus bringing ancient and modern villainy into juxtaposition.

Lady Willow saw Lord Frederick's preference with pleasurable surprise. Although she did not altogether approve of the damsel in her care, she had become very fond of her; but she failed to see why Jennie was so much sought after, when other girls, almost as pretty and much more eligible, were neglected. She hinted delicately to the young woman one day that perhaps her visit to England would not be, after all, so futile.

'I don't think I understand you,' said Jennie.

'Well, my dear, with a little tact on your part, I'm not at all sure but Lord

Frederick Bingham might propose.'

Jennie, who was putting on her gloves, paused and looked at Lady Willow, with a merry twinkle in her eyes, and a demure smile hovering about the corners of her mouth.

'Do you imagine, then, that I have come over here to ensnare some poor unprotected nobleman—with a display of tact? Oh dear me! As if tact had anything to do with it! Never, never, never, Lady Willow! I wouldn't marry an Englishman if he were the last man left on earth.'

'Many Englishmen are very nice, my dear,' protested Lady Willow gently, with a deep sigh, for she thought of her own husband, who, having been all his life an irreclaimable reprobate, had commanded her utmost affection while he lived, and was the object of her tenderest regret now that he had taken his departure from a world that had never appreciated his talents; although its influence was, in the estimation of the widow, entirely to blame for those shortcomings which Sir Debenham had been unable to conceal.

'And yet,' continued Jennie inconsequently, as she buttoned her glove, 'I do adore a title; I wonder why that is? I suppose no woman is ever at heart a republican, and if the United States is to be wrecked, it is the women who will do the wrecking, and start a monarchy. I have no doubt the men would let us proclaim an empire now if they imagined it would please us.'

'I thought you were all sovereigns over there already,' said Lady Willow.

'Oh, we are, but that's just the trouble. There is too much competition in the queen business; there are too many of us, and so we exchange our sovereignty for the lesser titles of duchesses and countesses and all that.

'"It is no trivial thing, I ween,

To be a regular Royal Queen.

No half and half affair, I mean,

But a right down regular, regular regular regular Royal Queen."

I don't know that the words are right, but the sentiment is there. Oh dear me! I'm afraid I'm becoming quite English, you know.'

'I don't see many signs of it,' said Lady Willow, smiling in spite of herself as her voluble companion sang and danced about the room.

'Come, Lady Willow,' cried Jennie, 'get on your things; I am going to a City bank to cash a cheque, and I warn you that I will take a hansom. Lord Freddie agrees with me that a hansom is the jolliest kind of vehicle: please don't frown at me, Lady Willow—"jolliest" is Lord Freddie's word, not mine.'

'What I didn't like,' said Lady Willow, with as near an approach to severity as the kindly woman could assume, 'was your calling him Lord Freddie.'

'Oh, that's his phrase, too! He says everybody calls him Lord Freddie. But come along, and I'll call him Lord—Frederick—Bingham,' with a voice of awe and appropriate pauses between the words. 'He always seems so trivial compared with his name; he reminds me of a salesman at a remnant counter, and I don't wonder everybody calls him Lord Freddie. I'm afraid I'm a disappointed woman, Lady Willow. I suppose the men have retrograded since armour went out of fashion; they had to be big and strong then to carry so much hardware. Of course it makes a difference to a man whether his tailor cuts him a suit out of broadcloth or out of sheet iron. Yes, I begin to suspect that I've come to England several centuries too late.'

Lady Willow was too much shocked at these frivolous remarks to make any reply, so, attempting none, she went to her room to prepare for her trip to the City.

Leaving Lady Willow in the hansom, Jennie entered the bank and got the white notes, generally alluded to in fiction as 'crisp,' stuffing them with greater carelessness than their value warranted into her purse. She took from this receptacle of her wealth a bit of paper on which was written an address, and this she looked at for some moments before leaving the bank. On reaching the hansom, she handed up the slip of paper to the driver.

'Do you know where that is?' she asked.

'Yes, miss; it is just round the corner.'

'Well, drive to the opposite side of the street, and stop where I can see the door of No. 23.'

'Very good, miss.'

Arriving nearly opposite No. 23, the driver pulled up. Jennie looked across at the doorway where many hurrying men were entering and leaving. It was a large building evidently filled with offices; the girl drew a deep breath, but made no motion to leave the hansom.

'Have you business here, too?' asked Lady Willow, to whom the City was an unknown land, the rush and noise of which were unpleasantly bewildering.

'No,' said Jennie, with a doleful note in her voice, 'this is not business; it is pleasure. I want to sit here for a few minutes and think.'

'But, my dear child,' expostulated Lady Willow, 'you can't think in this babel; besides, the police will not allow the hansom to stand here unless one of us is shopping, or has business in an office.'

'Then, dear Lady Willow, do go shopping for ten minutes; I saw some lovely shops just down the street. Here are five pounds, and if you see anything that I ought to have, buy it for me. One must think now and then, you know. Our thoughts are like the letters we receive; we need to sort them out periodically, and discard those that we don't wish to keep. I want to rummage over my thoughts and see whether some of them are to be abandoned or not.'

When Lady Willow left her, Jennie sat with her chin in her hands and her elbows on her knees gazing across at No. 23. The faces of none who went in or came out were familiar to her. Frequently glances were cast at her by passers-by, but she paid no heed to the crowd, nor to the fleeting admiration her pretty face aroused in many a flinty stockbroking breast, if, indeed, she was conscious of the attention she received. She awoke from her reverie when Lady Willow stepped into the hansom.

'What, back already?' she cried.

'I have been away for a quarter of an hour,' said the elder woman reproachfully. 'Besides, the money is all spent, and here are the parcels.'

'Money doesn't go far in the City, does it?' said Jennie.

'Why, what's the matter with you, my dear?' asked the elder woman; 'your voice sounds as if you had been crying.'

'Nonsense! What an idea! This street reminds me so of Broadway that I have become quite homesick, that's all. I think I'll go back to New York.'

'Have you met somebody from over there?'

'No, no. I've seen no one I knew.'

'Did you expect to?'

'Perhaps.'

'I didn't know you had any friends in the City.'

'I haven't. He's an enemy.'

'Really? An enemy who was once a friend?'

'Yes. Why do you ask so many questions?'

Lady Willow took the girl's hand, and said soothingly:

'I am sorry there was a misunderstanding.'

'So am I,' agreed Jennie.

CHAPTER XXI.

When John Kenyon entered the office of his friend next morning, Wentworth said to him:

'Well, what luck with the Longworths?'

'No luck at all,' was the answer; 'the young man seemed to have forgotten all about our conversation on board the steamer, and the old gentleman takes no interest in the matter.'

Wentworth hemmed and tapped on the desk with the end of his lead pencil.

'I never counted much on that young fellow,' he said at last. 'What appeared to be his reason?'

'I don't know exactly. He didn't give any reason. He merely said that he would have nothing to do with it, after having got me to tell him what our option on the mine was.'

'Why did you tell him that?'

'Well, it seemed, after I had talked to him a little, that there was some hope of his going in with us. I told him point-blank that I didn't care to say at what figure we had the option unless he was going in with us. He said of course he couldn't consider the matter at all unless he knew to what he was committed; and so I told him.'

'And what excuse did he make for not joining us?'

'Oh, he merely said he thought he would have nothing to do with it.'

'Now, what do you imagine his object was in pumping you if he had no intention of taking an interest in the mine?'

'I'm sure I don't know. I do not understand that sort of man at all. In fact, I feel rather relieved he is going to have nothing to do with it. I distrust him.'

'That's all very well, John, you are prejudiced against him; but you know the name of Longworth would have a very great effect upon the minds of other City men. If we can get the Longworths into this, even for a small amount, I am certain that we shall have very little trouble in floating the company.'

'Well, all I can say is, my mission to the Longworths was a failure. Have you looked over the papers?'

'Oh yes, and that reminds me. The point on which the whole scheme turns is the availability of the mineral for the making of china, isn't it?'

'That is so.'

'Well, look at this letter; it came this morning.'

He tossed the letter over to Kenyon, who read it, and then asked:

'Who's Adam Brand? He doesn't know what he is talking about.'

'Ah, but the trouble is that he does. No man in England better, I should imagine. He is the manager and part owner of the big Scranton china works. I went to see Melville of that company yesterday. He could tell me nothing about the mineral, but kept the specimen I gave him, and told me he would show it to the manager when he came in. Brand is the manager of the works, and if anybody knows the value of the mineral, he ought to be the man.'

'Nevertheless,' said Kenyon, 'he is mistaken.'

'That is just the point of the whole matter—is he? The mineral is either valueless, as he says, or he is telling a deliberate lie for some particular purpose; and I can't see, for the life of me, why a stranger should not only tell a falsehood, but write it on paper. Now, John, what do you know about china manufacture?'

'I know very little indeed about it.'

'Very well, then, how can you put your knowledge against this man's,

220

who is a practical manufacturer?'

Kenyon looked at Wentworth, who was evidently not feeling in the best of humours.

'Do you mean to say, George, that I do not know what I am talking about when I tell you that this mineral is valuable for a certain purpose?'

'Well, you have just admitted that you know nothing about the china trade.'

'Not "nothing," George—I know something about it; but what I do understand is the value of minerals. The reason I know anything at all about china manufacture is simply because I learned that this mineral is one of the most important components of china.'

'Then why did that man write such a letter?'

'I'm sure I don't know. As you saw the man, you can judge better than I whether he would tell a deliberate falsehood, or whether he was merely ignorant.'

'I didn't see Brand at all; I saw Melville. Melville was to submit this mineral to Brand, and let me know what he thought about it. Of course, everything depends upon the value of it in the china trade.'

'Of course.'

'Very well then, I took the only way that was open to me to find out what practical men say about it. If they say they will have nothing to do with it, then we might as well give up our mining scheme and send back our option to Mr. Von Brent.'

Kenyon read the letter again, and pondered deeply over it.

'You see, of course,' said George once more, 'everything hinges on that, don't you?'

'I certainly see that.'

'Then, what have you to say?'

'I have to say this—that I shall have to take a trip among the china works of Great Britain. I think it would be a good plan if you were to write to the different manufacturers in the United States and find out how much they use of it. There is no necessity for sending the mineral. They have to use that, and nothing else will do. Find out from them, if you can, how much of it they need, what price they will pay for pure material, and what they pay for the impure material they use now.'

'How do you know, John, that there are not a dozen mines with that material in them?'

'How do I know? Well, if you want to impugn my knowledge of mineralogy, I wish you would do so straight out. I either know my business or I do not. If you think I do not, then leave this matter entirely alone. I tell you that what I say about this mineral is true. What I say about its scarcity is true. There are no other mines with mineral so pure as this.'

'I am perfectly satisfied when you say that, but you must remember those who are going to put their money in this company will not be satisfied. They must have the facts and figures down before them, and they are not going to take either your word or mine as to the value of the mineral. Your proposal about seeing the different manufactories is good. I would act upon it at once, if I were you. We must have the opinions of practical men set forth clearly before we can make a move in the matter. Now, how much of this mineral have you got?'

'Only the few lumps I took with me in my portmanteau. The barrel full of it which we got at Burntpine has not arrived yet. I suppose it came by slow steamer and is probably on the ocean still.'

'Very good. Take what specimens you have, go to the North, and see those manufacturers. Get, in some way or another, whether from the principals or from the subordinates, the price they pay for it, and the cost of removing the adulteration from the stuff they employ now; because that is really the material we come into competition with. It is not with their first raw material, but with their material as cleared from the deleterious foreign substances, that we have to deal. Find out exactly what it costs to do

222

this purifying, and then, when you get your facts and figures, I will arrange them for you in the best order. Meanwhile, as you suggest, I will learn what manufactories there are in the States. Nothing can be done except that until you come back, and, if I were you, I should leave at once.'

'I am quite ready. I don't want to lose any further time.'

So John Kenyon departed, and was soon on his way to the North, with a list of china manufactories in his note-book.

That afternoon Wentworth got the letters off by the American mail, and he felt that they were doing business as rapidly as could be expected. Next morning there was a letter for John Kenyon addressed to the care of Wentworth, and by a later mail there came a letter to Wentworth himself from John, who had reached his first district and had had an interview already with the manager of the works. He found the mineral was all he had expected, and they would be glad to take a certain quantity each year at a specified rate. This letter Wentworth filed away with a smile of satisfaction, and then he began again to wonder why Adam Brand, representing such a well-known manufactory, should have written a deliberate falsehood. Before he had time to fathom this mystery, the office-boy announced that a gentleman wished to see him, and handed Wentworth a card which bore the name of William Longworth. Wentworth arched his eyebrows as he looked at it.

'Ask the gentleman to step in, please,' he said; and the gentleman stepped in.

'How are you, Mr. Wentworth? I suppose you remember me, although I did not see much of you on board the steamer.'

'I remember you perfectly,' replied Wentworth. 'Won't you sit down?'

'Thank you. I did not know where to find Mr. Kenyon, and so, being aware that both of you were interested in this mica-mine, I called to see you with reference to it.'

'Indeed! I understood Mr. Kenyon to say that he had called upon you, and that you had decided to have nothing to do with it.'

'I hardly think he was justified in saying anything quite so definite. I got from him such particulars as he cared to give. He is not a very communicative man at the best, but he told me something about it, and I have been thinking over his proposal. I have now concluded to help you in this matter, if you care to have my aid. Perhaps, however, things have got to such a stage that you do not wish any assistance?'

'On the contrary, we have done very little. Mr. Kenyon is just now among the china manufactories in the North, finding out what demand there will be in England for this mineral.'

'Ah, I see. Have you had reports from him yet?'

'Nothing further than a letter this morning, which is very satisfactory.'

'There is no question, then, about the mineral being useful in the china trade?'

'No question whatever.'

'Well, I am glad of that. Now, Mr. Kenyon spoke to me on the steamer of going in share and share alike; that is, you taking a third, he taking a third, and I taking a third. We did not go very minutely into particulars, but I suppose we each share the expense in the same way—the preliminary expenses, I mean?'

'Yes,' said Wentworth; 'that would be the arrangement, I imagine.'

'Well, have you the authority to deal with me in the matter, or would it be better for me to wait until Kenyon comes back?'

'We can settle everything here and now.'

'Very good. Would you have any objection to my seeing the papers that relate to the mine? I should like to get the figures of the output as nearly as possible, and any other particulars you may have that would enable me to estimate the value of the property. Also I should like to see a copy of the option, or the original document by which you hold the mine.'

'Certainly; I shall be very pleased to give you all the information in my power.' Wentworth turned to his desk and wrote for a few moments, then blotted the paper he had been writing, and handed it to Longworth. 'You have no objection, before this is done, to signing this document, have you?'

Longworth adjusted his one eyeglass and looked at the paper, which read: 'I hereby agree to do my best to form a limited liability company for the purpose of taking over the Ottawa Mica-mine. I agree to pay my share of the expenses, and to accept one-third of the profits.'

'No, I don't object to sign this, though I think it should be a little more definite. I think it should state that the liability I incur is to be one-third of the whole preliminary expenses, the other two-thirds to be paid by Kenyon and yourself; and that, in return, I am to get one-third of the profits, the other two-thirds going to yourself and Kenyon. I think it should also state the amount of the capital of the new company; two hundred thousand pounds was suggested, if I remember rightly.'

'Very well,' answered Wentworth; 'I will rewrite that in accordance with your wishes.'

This he did, and Longworth, again adjusting his eyeglass, read it.

'Now,' he said, 'as we are so formal about the matter, perhaps it would be as well for you to give me a note which I can keep, setting forth these same particulars.'

'Undoubtedly,' said Wentworth, 'I shall do that. Probably it would be better for you to write the document to suit your own views, and I will sign it.'

'Oh no, not at all. Write whatever is embodied there, so that you will have one paper and I the other.'

This was done.

'Now then,' said Longworth, 'when does your option run out?'

Wentworth named the date.

'Who is the owner of the mine?'

'It is owned by the Austrian Mining Company, headquarters at Vienna, and the option is signed by a Mr. Von Brent, of Ottawa, who is manager of the mine and one of the owners.'

'You are perfectly certain that he has every right to sell the mine?'

'Yes; Mr. Kenyon's lawyer saw to that while he was in Ottawa.'

'And you are sure, also, that your option is a thoroughly legal instrument?'

'We are sure of that.'

'Has it been examined by a London solicitor?'

'It has been submitted to a Canadian lawyer. The bargain was made in Canada, and it will have to be carried out in Canada, under the laws of Canada.'

'Still, don't you think it would be just as well to get the opinion of an English lawyer on it?'

'I think that would be an unnecessary expense. However, if you wish to have that done, we will do it.'

'Yes; I think we shall need to have the opinion of a good lawyer upon it before we submit it to the stockholders.'

'Very well, I will have it done. Is there anyone whom you wish to give an opinion on it?'

'Oh, it is a matter of indifference to me; your own solicitor would do as well as anyone else. Perhaps, however, it will be better to have a legal adviser for the Mica Mining Company, Limited—we shall have to have one as we go on—and it might be as well to submit the document to whomever we are going to place in that position. It will not increase the legal expenses at all, or at least by only a very trifling amount. Have you anyone to suggest?'

'I have not thought about the matter,' said Wentworth.

'Suppose you let me look up a firm who will answer our purpose? My uncle is sure to know the right men, and that will be something towards my

226

share of forming the company.'

'Very good,' said Wentworth; 'that will be satisfactory to me.'

'Now, there is a good deal to be done in the forming of a company, and it is going to take three men a good deal of time, besides some expense. What do you say to letting me look up offices?'

'Do you think it is necessary to have offices?'

'Oh, certainly. A great deal depends, in this sort of thing, on appearances. We shall need to get offices in a good locality.'

'To tell the truth, Mr. Longworth, Kenyon and I have not very much money, and we do not want to enter into any expense that is needless.'

'My dear sir, it is not needless. This business is one of those things into which, if you go boldly, you win; while if you go gingerly, on the economical plan, you lose everything. Of course, if there is to be a scarcity of cash, I shall have nothing to do with the scheme, because I know how these half-economically worked affairs turn out. I have seen too much of them. We are making a strike for sixty thousand pounds each. That is a sum worth risking something for, and, if you will believe me, you will not get it unless you venture something for it.'

'I suppose that is true.'

'Yes, it is very true. Of course I've had more experience in matters of this kind than either of you, and I know we shall have to get good offices, with a certain prosperous look about them. People are very much influenced by appearances. Now, if you like, I will see to getting the offices and to engaging a solicitor. Every step must be taken under legal advice, otherwise we may get into a very bad tangle and spend a great deal more money in the end.'

'Very well,' said Wentworth. 'Is there anything else you can suggest?'

'Not just at present; nothing need be done until Kenyon comes back, and then we can have a meeting to see what is the best way to proceed.'

Longworth then looked over the papers, took a note of some things mentioned in the option, and finally said:

'I wish you would get these papers copied for me, I suppose you have someone in the office who can do it?'

'Yes.'

'Then just have duplicates made of each of them. Good-morning, Mr. Wentworth.'

Wentworth mused for a few moments over the unexpected turn affairs had taken. He was very glad to get the assistance of Longworth; the name itself was a tower of strength in the City. Then, Kenyon's letter from the North was encouraging. Thinking of the letter brought the writer of it to his mind, so he took a telegraph-form from his desk, and wrote a message to the address given on the letter.

'Everything right. Longworth has joined us, and signed papers to assist in forming company.'

'There,' he said, as he sent the boy out with the message, 'that will cheer up old John when he gets it.'

CHAPTER XXII.

When John Kenyon returned from the North and entered the office of his friend Wentworth, he found that gentleman and young Longworth talking in the outer room.

'There's a letter for you on my desk,' said Wentworth, after shaking hands with him. 'I'll be there in a minute.'

Kenyon entered the room and found the letter. Then he did a very unbusinesslike thing. He pressed the writing to his lips and placed the letter in his pocket-book. This act deserves mention because it is an unusual thing in the City. As a general rule, City men do not press business communications to their lips, and the letter John had received was entirely a business communication, relating only to the mine, and to William Longworth's proposed connection with it. He wondered whether he should write an answer to it or not.

He sat down at Wentworth's desk, and came upon an obstacle at the very beginning. He did not know how to address the young woman. Whether to say 'My dear Miss Longworth,' or 'My dear madam,' or whether to use the adjective 'dear' at all, was a puzzle to him; and over this he was meditating when Wentworth came bustling in.

'Well,' said the latter, as John tore into small pieces a sheet of notepaper and threw the bits into the waste-basket, 'how have you got on? Your letters were very short indeed, but rather to the point. You seem to have succeeded.'

'Yes, I have succeeded very well. I have got all the figures and prices and everything else that it is necessary to have. I succeeded with everybody except Brand, who wrote that letter to you. I cannot make him out at all. He would give me no information, and he managed to prevent everyone else in his works from giving me any. He pooh-poohed the scheme—in fact, wouldn't listen to it. He said it was not usual for men to give away information regarding their business, and in that, of course, he was perfectly justified; but when I tried to argue with him as to whether this mineral was used in his manufactory or not, he would not listen. I asked him what he used in place of it, but he would not tell. All in all, he is a most extraordinary man, and I confess I do not understand him.'

'Oh, it doesn't matter about him in the least. I was speaking with Longworth just now about that curious letter of his, and he agrees with me that it makes no difference. He says, what is quite true, that in every business you find some man with whom it is difficult to deal.'

'Yes, that is so; but, still, he either uses this substance or he does not. I can understand a man who says, "We have no need for that, because we use another material." But that is one of the things Brand does not say.'

'Well, it is not worth while talking about him. By the way, you have all your figures and notes with you, I suppose?'

'Yes, I have everything.'

'Very well. Leave them with me, and I will get them into some sort of shape. Longworth says we shall have to have everything printed relating to this—your statements and all.'

'That will cost a great deal of money, will it not?'

'Oh, not very much. It is necessary, it seems. We must have printed matter to give to those who make application for information. It would be impossible to explain personally to everybody who inquires, and to show them these documents.'

'Yes, I suppose so.'

'Longworth was just now speaking to me about offices he has seen, and he is anxious to secure them at once. He is attending to that matter.'

'Do you think we need an office? Why could not the business be transacted here; or perhaps a room might be had on this floor that would do perfectly well; then we should be close together, and able to communicate when necessary.'

230

'Longworth seems to think differently. He says you must impress the public, and so he is going in for fine offices.'

'Yes, but who is to pay for them?'

'Why, we must, of course—you and Longworth and myself.'

'Have you the money?'

'I have a certain amount. I think we shall have enough to see it through, and if not, we can easily get it, and settle up when we finish the business.'

'Well, you know I have no money to spare.'

'Oh, I know that well enough. Perhaps Longworth will see us through, for, as he says, this sort of thing can be spoilt by niggardliness. He has known, and so have I, many a business go to pieces because of false economy.'

'But it seems to me all this is needless expense. We only want to get a few moneyed men interested in our project, and if they are sensible men, they will look to the probability of getting a good dividend, not at fine offices.'

'Very well, John; you get the men, and I shall be satisfied. I am sure I am as anxious to do this cheaply as you are. If you think you can go out and interest a dozen or twenty-four men in the City, and persuade them to go in for our mine, I will cry "Halt!" on our part until you do it. Will you try that?'

Kenyon pondered for a few minutes, and then said: 'I suppose that would be rather a difficult thing to do.'

'Yes, that is the way it strikes me. I do not know to whom I could go. Longworth is a good man, and we have gone to him. Now it seems to me, having got his assistance, the least we can do, unless we are prepared to produce the men ourselves forthwith, is to act as he wishes.'

'Yes, I quite appreciate that, and I also grasp the fact that too close economy is not the best thing; but, on the other hand, George, how are we to perform our part with Longworth? His ideas of economy and yours may be vastly different. What is a mere trifle to him would bankrupt us!'

'I know that. Well, he is coming here this afternoon at three. Suppose you manage to be in then, and talk with him. Meanwhile, I will go over the papers and get them into tabulated form.'

'Very well; I shall be here at three o'clock.'

It will hardly be credited that a business man like John Kenyon spent most of the time between that hour and three o'clock trying to compose a business letter in answer to the business communication he had received that morning. Yet such was the astonishing fact, and it showed, perhaps more than anything else, how utterly unfit Mr. John Kenyon was to join in a commercial undertaking in a city of hard-headed people. At last, however, the letter was posted, and Kenyon hurried away to be in time for his three-o'clock appointment. He found Wentworth and young Mr. Longworth together, the latter looking more like a young man from the West End than a typical City business man. His monocle was in his eye, and it shone on Kenyon as he entered. It was evident something was troubling Wentworth, and it was equally evident that the something, whatever it was, was not troubling young Longworth.

'You are late, John,' was Wentworth's greeting.

'A little,' he answered. 'I was detained.'

There was silence for a few moments, and Wentworth appeared to be waiting for Longworth to speak. At last Longworth said:

'I have succeeded in getting very nice offices indeed, and I was telling Mr. Wentworth about them. You see, it is not very easy to engage offices in a good part of the City by the week. They do not care to let them in that way, because, while a weekly tenant is occupying them, somebody else, who wants them for a longer time, might have to be sent away.'

'Yes,' said Kenyon in a non-committal manner.

'Well, I have got just the offices we need, and have now set the men at putting gilt lettering on the windows. I have taken the offices in the name of "The Canadian Mica Mining Company, Limited," which I shall have on the plate-glass windows in a very short time. Now, Mr. Wentworth here seems to

232

think the offices rather expensive. I have told him before what my ideas are in the matter of expense. Perhaps, before anything more is said on the subject, we ought to go and look at the rooms.'

'How much are they a week?' asked Kenyon.

Young Mr. Longworth did not answer, because at that moment his monocle fell out of its place and had to be adjusted again; but Wentworth jerked out the two words, 'Thirty pounds.'

'A week?' cried John.

'Yes,' said Longworth, after having succeeded in replacing the round bit of glass—'yes; Mr. Wentworth seems to think that is rather high, but I defy him to get as fine offices in the City for anything less in price. It is merely ten pounds a week for each of us. However, before you can judge of their dearness or cheapness, you must see them. If you ask me, I think they are a bargain.'

'Very well,' said Kenyon. 'Have you the time, George?'

Wentworth, without answering, shoved the papers into his desk and closed it. The three young men went out together, and after a short walk came to large plate-glass windows, where a man on a ladder was chalking the words 'The Canadian Mica Mining Company, Limited,' in a semicircle.

'You see,' said Longworth, 'this is one of the very best situations in the City. As I said before, I doubt if you could get anything like it for the price.'

They could not deny the excellence of the position, or that the plate-glass looked very imposing and the gilt letters exceedingly fine; but the cost of this running on perhaps for two or three months seemed to appal them.

'Come inside,' said young Longworth suavely; 'I am sure you will be pleased with the rooms we have. You see,' he said, entering and nodding to the carpenters who were at work there, 'this will be the front office, where the public is received. Here you have room for an accountant or two and your secretary. The back-room, which you see is also well lighted, is just the spot for our people to meet. We will get in a large long table here, and a number of chairs, and there we are—capital directors' room.'

'Does the thirty pounds a week include the furnishing of the place?' asked Kenyon.

'Oh, bless you, no! You surely couldn't expect that? We shall have to put in the furniture, of course.'

'And do you intend to put in desks and counter and everything of that sort here?'

'Of course. Beside that, we will get in a large safe. There is nothing like a ponderous safe, with the name of the company in gilt letters on it, for impressing the general public.'

'And how much is the furnishing of this place to cost?'

'Really, I don't know that. The men I have engaged will do it very reasonably. They have done work for me before. You don't get it done any cheaper by haggling about the price beforehand—I've found that out.'

'I do not see how we are to pay our share of all this,' said Kenyon.

'Nothing easier, my boy; I've arranged all that. I will pay them my third in cash when it is finished, and, they have agreed to wait three months for the remainder. By that time you will have sixty thousand pounds each, and a little bill like this will be nothing to you.'

Kenyon looked grave.

'It's a little like counting your chickens,' he said.

'Ah, they'll hatch all right,' laughed Longworth. And then his eyeglass dropped out.

CHAPTER XXIII.

It is never wise to despise an enemy, no matter how humble he may be. The mouse liberated the enmeshed lion. Jennie Brewster should have been thankful that circumstances, working in her favour, had rendered her account of the discoveries she made about the mines unnecessary. She was saved the bitterness of acknowledged defeat by the cable despatch that awaited her at Queenstown, telling her not to forward her information. The letter she received from the editor of the Argus later explained the cable message. The Argus had obtained from a different source what purported to be an account of the reports on the mines, and this had been published. If Jennie's contribution corroborated this article, it was unnecessary; if it contradicted what had been already published, then, of course, it was equally unavailable, for the Argus was a paper that never stultified itself by acknowledging an error. So the editor sent his correspondent a short cable message to save the expense of a long and costly despatch that would have been useless when it reached the Argus office.

Instead, however, of being grateful to the stars that fought so well for her, Jennie became bitterly resentful against Fleming, and hardly less so against Miss Longworth. If it had not been for the meddling politician's interference, Wentworth would never have discovered who she was, and the whole train of humiliating events that followed would not have taken place. She would have parted with Wentworth on a friendly basis, at least. She was forced, reluctantly, to admit to herself that she liked Wentworth better than any young man she had ever before met; and now that there was little chance of seeing him again, her regret had become more and more poignant as time went on. He had told her all his hopes about the mica-mine before their unfortunate disaster, and had taken her into his confidence in a way, she felt sure, he had never done with any other woman. She saw the earnest look in his honest eyes whenever she closed her own, and this look haunted her day and night, alternating with the remembrance of that gaze of incredulous reproach with which he regarded her when he discovered her mission, which was even harder to bear than the recollection of his confidence and esteem.

And the sting of the situation lay in the fact that it had all been so useless and unnecessary. She had wounded her friend and humiliated herself all for nothing! The rapid changes that had taken place in the newspaper office since she left, had rendered her sacrifices futile, and while she had buoyed herself up on shipboard by holding that she was merely doing her duty to her employers, even that consolation had been made naught by the editor's letter.

Thus it ever is in that kaleidoscopic, gigantic and fascinating lottery, the modern press. The sensation for which an editor to-day would sell his soul, is to-morrow worthless. The greatest fool in the office will sometimes stumble stupidly upon the most important news of the day, while the cleverest reporter may be baffled in his constant fight against time, for the paper goes to press at a certain hour, and after that, effort is useless. The conductor of a great paper is like the driver of a Roman chariot; he needs a cool head and a strong arm, with a clear eye that peers into the future, and that pays little heed to the victims of the whirling scythe-blades at the hub. He may overturn a Government or be himself thrown, by an unexpected jolt, under the wheels. The fiery steeds never stop, and when one drops the reins, another grasps them, to be in turn lost and forgotten in the mad race, wherein never a glance is cast to the rear. The best brains in the country are called into requisition, squeezed, and flung aside. With a lavish but indiscriminating hand are thrown broadcast fame and dishonour, riches and disaster. Unbribable in the ordinary sense of the word, the press will, for the accumulation of the smallest coins of the realm, exaggerate a cholera scare and paralyze the business of a nation; then it will turn on a corrupt Government and rend it, although millions might be made by taking another course. It is the terror of scoundrels and the despair of honest men.

Jennie Brewster, in the midst of her unavailing regrets, clenched her little fist when she thought of Fleming. It is both customary and consoling to place the blame on other shoulders than our own. Human nature is such an erring quantity, that usually we can find a scapegoat among our fellow-beings, who can be made responsible for any misdeeds or failings which are so much a part of ourselves that they escape recognition. If Fleming had only attended his own business, as a man should, Wentworth would never have known that Jennie wrote for the Argus, and Jennie might have had a friend in London who would have added that spice of interest to her visit which usually accompanies the friendship of an agreeable young man for a girl so pretty and fascinating.

Fleming put up at the hotel that Jennie had at first selected, and now and then she met him in the extensive halls of the great building; but she invariably passed him with the dignity of an offended queen, although the unfortunate man always took off his hat, and once or twice paused as if about to speak with her.

On the last day of her stay at the hotel, she met Fleming oftener than ever before; but it did not occur to her that the unhappy politician was lying in wait for her, never being able to muster up enough courage to address her when his opportunity came. At last a note was brought up to the room she occupied, from Fleming, in which he said that he would like to have a few moments' conversation with her, and would wait for a reply.

'Tell him there is no reply,' said the girl to the messenger.

It is sometimes well to know the point of view, even of an enemy, but Jenny was too angry with him to think of that. However, a politician, to be successful, must not be easily rebuffed, and as a rule he is not.

Fleming, when he got the curt reply to his note, threw away his cigar, put on his hat, took the lift, passed through the long corridor, and knocked at Jennie's door.

The girl's amazement at seeing her enemy there was so great that the obvious act of shutting the door in his face did not occur to her until it was too late, and Fleming had carelessly placed his large foot in the way of its closing.

'How dare you come here, when I refused to see you?' she cried, with her eyes ablaze.

'Oh, I understood the messenger to say I might come,' replied the untruthful politician. 'You see, it's not a personal matter, but the very biggest sensation that ever went under the ocean on a cable, and I thought—Well, you know, I felt I had done you—quite unintentionally—a mean trick on board the Caloric and this was kind of to make up for it, don't you know.'

'You can never repair what you have done.'

'Oh yes, I can, Jennie.'

'I shall be obliged to you if you remember that my name is Miss Brewster,' said the girl, drawing herself up; but Fleming noticed, with relief, that since he had mentioned the sensation she had made no motion to close the door, while the eagerness of the newspaper woman was gradually replacing the anger with which she had at first regarded him.

'All right, Miss Brewster. I meant no disrespect, you know; and, honestly, I would rather give you a big item than anybody else.'

'Oh, you're very honest—I know that.'

'Well, I am, you know, Jen—I mean Miss Brewster; although I tell you it don't pay in politics any more than in the newspaper business.'

'If you only came to speak like that of the newspapers, I don't care to listen to you.'

'Wait a minute. I don't blame you for being angry——'

'Thank you.'

'But, all the same, if you let this item get away, you'll be sorry. I'm giving you the straight tip. I could get more gold than you ever saw for giving this snap away, yet here you're treating me as if I were——'

'A New York politician. Why do you come to me with this valuable piece of information? Just because you have a great regard for me, I suppose?'

'That's right. That's it exactly.'

'I thought so. Very well. There is a parlour on this floor where we can talk without being interrupted. Come with me.'

Jennie closed the door and walked down the passage, followed by Fleming, who smiled with satisfaction at his own tact and shrewdness, as, indeed, he had every right to do.

In the deserted sitting-room was a writing-table, and Jennie sat down beside it, motioning Fleming to a chair opposite her.

'Now,' she said, drawing some paper towards her, and taking up a pen, 'what is this important bit of news?'

'Well, before we begin,' replied Fleming, 'I would like to tell you why I interfered on shipboard and let that Englishman know who you were.'

'Never mind that. Better let it rest.' There was a flash of anger in the girl's eye, but, in spite of it, Fleming continued. He was a persistent man.

'But it has some bearing on what I'm going to tell you. When I saw you on board the Caloric, my heart went down into my boots. I thought the game was up, and that you were after me. I was bound to find out whether the Argus knew anything of my trip or not, and whether it had put you on my track. Only five men in New York knew of my journey across, and as a good deal depended on secrecy, I had to find out in some way whether you were there for the purpose of—well, you know. So I spoke to the Englishman, and raised a hornets' nest about my ears; but I soon saw you had no suspicion of what I was engaged in, otherwise I would have had to telegraph to certain persons then in London, and scatter them.'

'Dear me! And what villainy were you concocting? Counterfeiting?'

'No; politics. Just as bad, I suppose you think. Now, do you know where Crupper is?'

'The Boss of New York? I heard before I left that he was at Carlsbad for his health.'

'He was there,' said Fleming mysteriously; 'but now——'

The politician solemnly pointed downwards with his forefinger.

'What! Dead?' cried Jennie, the ominous motion of Fleming's finger naturally suggesting what all good people believed to be the arch-thief's ultimate destination.

'No,' said Fleming, laughing; 'he's in this hotel.'

'Oh!'

'Yes, and Senator Smollet, leader of the Conscientious Party, is here too, although you don't meet them in the halls as often as you do me. These good men supposed to be political opponents, are lying low and saying nothing.'

'I see. And they've had a conference.'

'Exactly. Now, it's like this.' Fleming pulled a sheet of paper towards him, and drew on it an oval. 'That's New York. We'll call it a pumpkin-pie, if you like, the material of which it is composed being typical of the heads of its conscientious citizens. Or a pigeon-pie, perhaps, for the New Yorker is made to be plucked. Well, look here.' Fleming drew from a point in the centre several radiating lines. 'That's what Crupper and Smollet are doing in London. They're dividing the pie between the two parties.'

'That's very interesting, but how are they going to deliver the pieces?'

'Simple as shelling peas. You see, our great pull is the conscientious citizen—the voter who wants to vote right, and for a good man. If it weren't for the good men as candidates and the good men as voters, New York politics would be a pretty uncertain game. You see, the so-called respectable element in both parties is our only hope. Each believes in his party, thinks his crowd is better than the other fellow's, so all you have to do is to nominate an honest man to represent each party, and then that divides what they call the reputable vote, and we real politicians get our man in between the two. That's all there is in New York politics. Well, Senator Smollet threatened not to put up a good man on the conscientious ticket, and that would have turned the whole unbribable vote of both parties against us, so we had to make a deal with him, and throw in the next Presidential election. Crupper's no hog; he knows when he's had plenty, and New York's good enough for him. He don't care who gets the Presidency.'

'And this conference has been held?'

'That's right. It took place in this hotel.'

'The bargain was made, I suppose?'

'It was. The pie was divided.'

'And you didn't get a slice?'

'Oh, I beg your pardon, I did!'

'Then, why do you come to me and tell me all this—if it's true?'

Honest indignation shone in Fleming's face.

'If it's true? Of course it's true. Why do I come to you? Because I want to be friendly with you, that's why.'

Jennie, nibbling the end of her pen, looked thoughtfully across at him for a few moments, then slowly shook her head.

'If you get me to believe that, Mr. Fleming, I'll not cable a word. No, I must have an adequate motive, for I won't cable anything I don't believe to be absolutely true.'

'I assure you, Jennie——'

'Wait a moment. You say you are promised your share in the new deal, but it is not as big a slice as what you have now. It stands to reason that, if Crupper is to divide with Smollet's rascals, each of Crupper's rascals must content himself with a smaller piece. The greater the number of thieves, the smaller each portion of booty. You didn't see that when you left New York, and therefore you were afraid of publicity. You see it now, and you want a sensational article published, so that Senator Smollet will be forced to deny it, or further arouse the suspicions of the honest men in his party. In either case publicity will nullify the results of the deal, and you will hold the share you have. As you didn't know any of the regular London representatives of the New York papers, you couldn't trust them not to tell on you, and so you came to me. Now that I see a good substantial selfish motive for your action, I am ready to believe you.'

An expression of dismay at first overspread the countenance of the politician, but this gave way to a look of undisguised admiration as the girl went on.

'By Jove, Jennie!' he cried, bringing his fist down on the table when she had finished; 'you're wasted in the newspaper business; you ought to be a politician! Say, girl, if you marry me, I'll be President of the United States yet.'

'Oh no, you wouldn't,' said Jennie, quite unabashed by his handsome, if excited, proposal. 'No corrupt New York politician will ever be President of the United States. You have the great honest bulk of the people to deal with there, and I'm Democrat enough to believe in them when it comes to big issues, however much you may befog them in small; you can't fool all people for all time, Mr. Fleming, as a man who was not in little politics once said. Every now and then the awakened people will get up and smash you.'

Fleming laughed boisterously.

'That's just it,' he said. 'It's every now and then. If they did it every year I would have to quit politics. But will you send the particulars of this meeting to the Argus without giving me away?'

'Yes, I recognise its importance. Now, I want you to give me every detail—the number of the room they met in, the exact hour, and all that. What I like to get in a report of a secret meeting is absolute accuracy in small matters, so that those who were there will know it is not guesswork. That always takes the backbone out of future denials. I'll mention your name——'

'Bless my soul, don't do that!'

'I must say you were present.'

'Why?'

'Why? Dear me! you can't be so stupid as not to see that, if your name is left out, suspicion will at once point to you as the divulger?'

'Yes I suppose that is so.'

'And this man is a ruler in one of the greatest cities in the world! Go on, Mr. Fleming; who else was there besides Crupper, Smollet, and yourself?'

242

The account—two columns and a half—was a bombshell in political New York the morning it appeared in the Argus. Senator Smollet cabled from Paris that there wasn't a word of truth in it, that he wasn't in London on the date mentioned, and had never seen Crupper there or elsewhere. Crupper cabled from Carlsbad that he was ill, and had not been out of bed for a month. He would sue the Argus for libel, which, by the way, he never did. The reporters flocked to meet Fleming when his steamer came in, but of course he knew nothing about it; he had been across the ocean solely on private business that had no connection with politics. He knew nothing of Crupper's whereabouts, but he knew one thing, which was that Crupper was too honest and honourable a man to traffic with the enemy.

Notwithstanding all these denials, the report bore the marks of truth on its face, and everybody believed it, although many pretended not to. The division of the spoils aroused the greatest consternation and indignation among Crupper's own following, and a deputation went over to see the old man.

Meanwhile, the Argus, with much dignity of diction, explained that it stood for the best interests of the people, and in the people's cause was fearless. It defied all and sundry to bring libel suits if they wanted to; it was prepared to battle for the people's rights. And its circulation went up and up, its many web presses being taxed to their utmost in supplying the demand. Thus are the truly good rewarded.

A great newspaper is as lavishly generous as a despotic monarch, to those who serve it well, and the cheque which Jennie cashed when Lady Willow accompanied her to the City lined her purse with banknotes to a fulness that receptacle had never known before.

After a few weeks with Lady Willow, Jennie seemed to tire of the frivolities of society, and even of the sedate company of the good lady with whom she lived. She announced that she was going to Paris for a week or two, but, owing to uncertainty of address, her letters were not to be forwarded. She merely took a hand-bag, leaving the rest of her luggage with Lady Willow, who was thus sustained by the hope that her paying guest would soon return.

Jennie took a hansom to Charing Cross, but instead of departing on the Paris express, she hailed a four-wheeler, and, giving a West End address to the driver, entered the closed vehicle.

CHAPTER XXIV.

On the big plate-glass windows of the new rooms there soon appeared, in gilt letters with black edges, the words, 'Canadian Mica Mining Company, Limited: London Offices.' But the workmen who were finishing the interior were not so quick as the painters and gilders. The new offices took a long time to prepare, and both Kenyon and Wentworth chafed at the delay, because Longworth said nothing could be done until the rooms were occupied.

'It is like this, Longworth,' said Wentworth to him: 'every moment is of value. Time is running on, and we have not for ever in which to form this company.'

'And you must remember,' replied young Mr. Longworth, gazing reproachfully at him through his glittering monocle, 'that I am equally interested in this project with you. It is just as much to my interest to save time as it is to yours. You must not worry about the matter, Mr. Wentworth; everything is all right. The men are doing a good job for us, and it will not be long before their work is completed. As I have told you time and again, a great deal depends on the appearance we present to the public. We have nearly the best offices in the City. The workmen have certainly taken longer than I expected they would, but, you see, they have a great deal of work on hand. When we get this started it will not take long. I, in the meanwhile, have not been idle. At least half a dozen moneyed men are ready to go in with us on this project. The moment the offices are finished we will have a meeting of the proposed shareholders. If they subscribe sufficiently large amounts—and I think they will—all the rest is a mere matter of detail which our solicitors will attend to. But if you imagine that you and Mr. Kenyon can manage everything better than I am doing, you are perfectly at liberty to go ahead. I am sure I have no desire to monopolize all the work. What have you done, for instance? What has Mr. Kenyon done?'

'Kenyon, as I think you know, has got all the facts in reference to the demand for the mineral, and I have arranged them. We have had everything printed as you suggested, and the papers are ready. They were delivered at my office to-day.'

'Very well,' answered young Longworth; 'we are getting on. That is so much done which will not have to be done over again. Perhaps it will be as well to send me some of the printed matter, so that I can give it to the men I was speaking of. Meanwhile, don't worry about the offices; they will be ready in good time.'

Wentworth and Kenyon visited the new offices time and again, but still the work seemed to drag. At last Wentworth said very sharply to the foreman:

'Unless this is finished by next Monday, we will have nothing to do with it.'

The foreman seemed astonished.

'I understood from Mr. Longworth,' he said, 'from whom we take our instructions, that there was no particular hurry about this job.'

'Well, there is a particular hurry. We must be in here by the first of next week, and if you have not finished by that time, we shall have to come in with it unfinished.'

'In that case,' said the foreman, 'I will do the best I can. I think we can finish it this week.'

And finished it was accordingly.

When Kenyon entered his new offices, he found them rather oppressive for so modest a man as himself. Wentworth laughed at his doleful expression as he viewed the general grandeur of his surroundings.

'What bothers me,' said John, 'is knowing that all this has to be paid for.'

'Ah, yes,' answered Wentworth; 'but by the time the debts become due I hope we shall have plenty of money.'

'I must confess I do not understand Longworth in this matter. He seems

246

to be doing nothing; at least, he has nothing to show for what he has done, and he does not appear to realize that time is an object with us; in fact, that our company-forming has really become a race against time.'

'Well, we shall see very shortly what he is going to do. I have sent a messenger for him to meet us here—he ought to be here now—and we must certainly push things. There is no time to lose.'

'Has he said anything to you—he talks more freely with you than he does to me—about what the next move is to be?'

'No; he has said nothing.'

'Well, don't you see the situation in which we stand? We are practically doing nothing—leaving everything in his hands. Now, if he should tell us some fine day that he can have nothing more to do with our project (and I believe he is quite capable of it), here we are with our time nearly spent, deeply in debt, and nothing done.'

'My dear John, what a brain you have for conjuring up awful possibilities! Trust me, Longworth won't act in the way you suggest. It would be dishonourable, and he is, so far as I know, an honourable man of business. I think you take a certain prejudice against a person, and then can see nothing good in anything he does. Longworth told me the other day that he had five or six people who are ready to go into this business with us, and if such is the case he has certainly done his share.'

'Yes, I admit that. Did he give you their names?'

'No, he did not.'

'The thing that troubles me is our own helplessness. We seem, in some way or other, to have been shoved into the background.'

'So far from that being the case,' said Wentworth, 'Longworth told me that, if anything suggested itself to us, we were to go ahead with it. He asked what you had done and what I had done, and I told him. He seemed quite anxious that we should do everything we could, as he is doing.'

'Well, but, don't you see, the situation is this: if we make a move at all, we may do something of which he does not approve. Haven't you noticed that whenever I suggest anything, or whenever you suggest anything, for that matter, he always has something counter to it? And I don't like the solicitors he has engaged for this business. They are what is known as "shady"; you know that as well as I do.'

'Bless me, John! then suggest something yourself if you have such dark suspicions of Longworth. I'm sure I'm willing to do anything you want done. Suggest something.'

Before John could make the required suggestion, the messenger Wentworth had sent to young Longworth returned.

'His uncle says, sir,' began the messenger, 'that Master William has gone to the North, and will not be back for a week.'

'A week!' cried both the young men together.

'Yes, sir, a week was what he said. He left a note to be given to either of you if you called. Here is the note, sir.'

Wentworth took the envelope handed to him and tore it open. The contents ran thus:

'I have been suddenly called away to the North, and may be gone for a week or ten days. I am sorry to be away at this particular juncture, but as it is not likely that the men will have the offices finished before I come back, no great harm will be done. Meanwhile I shall see several gentlemen I have in my mind's eye, men that seldom come to London, who will be of great service to us. If you think of anything to forward the mica-mine, pray go on with it. You can send any letters for me to my uncle, and I shall get them. As there is no hurry in the matter of time, however, I should strongly advise that nothing be done until my return, when we can all go at the business with a will.

'Yours truly,

'WILLIAM LONGWORTH.'

When Wentworth had finished reading this letter, the two young men looked at each other.

'What do you make of that?' said Kenyon.

'I'm sure I do not know. In the first place, he is gone for a week.'

'Yes; that one thing is certain.'

'Well now, John, one of two things has to be done. We have either to trust this Longworth, or we have to go on alone without him. Which is it to be?'

'I am sure I don't know,' answered Kenyon.

'But, my dear fellow, we have come to a point when we must decide. You are, evidently, suspicious of Longworth. What you say really amounts to this: that he, for some reason of his own, which I confess I cannot see or understand, desires to delay forming this company until it is too late.'

'I didn't say that.'

'You say what practically amounts to that. Either he is honest or he is not. Now, we have to decide to-day, and here, whether we are going to ignore him and go on with the forming of the company, or work with him. Unless you can give some good reason for doing otherwise, I propose to work with him. I think it will be very much worse if he leaves us now than if he had never gone into it. People will ask why he left.'

'Probably he wouldn't leave, even if you wanted him to do so. He has your signature to an agreement, and you have his.'

'Certainly.'

'I do not see how we can help ourselves.'

'Then I think these suspicions should be dropped, because you cannot work with a man whom you suspect of being a rascal.'

'I quite admit of the justice of that, so I shall say nothing more. Meanwhile, do you propose to wait until he comes back?'

'I shall write him to-night and ask him what he intends to do. I shall tell him, as I have told him before, that time is pressing, and we want to know what is being done.'

'Very well,' said John; 'I will wait till you get the answer to your letter. In the meantime, I do not see that there is anything to do but occupy this gorgeous office as well as I can, and wait to see what turns up.'

'That is my own idea. I think, myself, it is rather unfair to suspect a man of being a villain when he has really done nothing to show that he is one.'

To this John made no answer.

The next day Kenyon occupied the new offices, and set himself to the task of getting accustomed to them. The first day a few people dropped in, made inquiries about the mine, took some printed matter, and generally managed to ask several questions to which Kenyon was unable to reply. On the second day a number of newspaper men called—advertising canvassers, most of them, who left cards or circulars with Kenyon, showing that unless a commercial venture was advertised in their particular papers it was certain not to be a success. One very swell individual, with a cast of countenance that betokened a frugal, money-making, and shrewd race, asked Kenyon for a private interview. He said he belonged to the Financial Field, the great newspaper of London, which was read by every investor both in the City and in the country. All he wanted was some particulars of the mine.

Had the company been formed yet?

No, it had not.

When did they intend to go to the public?

That Kenyon could not say.

What was the peculiarity about the mine which constituted its recommendation to investors?

Kenyon said the full particulars would be found in the printed sheet he handed him, and with profuse thanks the newspaper man put it in his pocket.

How had the mine paid in previous years?

It had paid a small dividend.

On what amount?

That Kenyon was not prepared to answer.

How long had it been in operation?

For several years.

Had it ever been placed on the London market before?

Not so far as Kenyon was aware.

Who was at present interested in the mine?

That Mr. Kenyon did not care to answer, and he further stated, so far as giving out advertisements was concerned, he was not yet prepared to do any advertising. The visitor, who had taken down these notes, said his object was not to get an advertisement, but to obtain information about the mine. People could advertise in his paper or not, as they chose. The journal was such a well-known medium for reaching investors that everyone who knew his business advertised in it as a matter of course, and so they kept no canvassers, and made no applications for advertisements.

'The chances are,' said the newspaper man, as he took his leave, 'that our editor will write an editorial on this mine, and, in order that there may be no inaccuracy, I shall bring it to you to read, and shall be very much obliged if you will correct any mistakes.'

'I shall be glad to do so,' returned Kenyon, as the representative of the Financial Field took his leave.

The newspaper men were rather hard to please, and to get rid of; but John had a visitor on the afternoon of the second day who almost caused his wits to desert him. He looked up from his desk as the door opened, and was astonished to see the smiling face of Edith Longworth, while behind her came the old lady who had been an occupant of the carriage when John had taken his drive to the west.

'You did not expect to see me here among the investors who have been

251

calling upon you, Mr. Kenyon, did you?'

Kenyon held out his hand, and said:

'I am very pleased indeed to see you, whether you come as an investor or not.'

'And so this is your new office?' she cried, looking round. 'How you have blossomed out, haven't you? These offices are as fine as any in the City.'

'Yes,' said John; 'they are too fine to suit me.'

'Oh, I don't see why you should not have handsome offices as well as anyone else. You have been in my father's place of business, of course. But it is not so grand as these rooms.'

'I think that helps to show the absurdity of ours. Your father's house is an old-standing one, and this gives us an air of new riches which, I must confess, I don't like, especially as we have not the riches.'

'Then, why did you agree to have such offices? I suppose you had something to say about them?'

'Very little, I must own. They were engaged while I was in the North, and after they had been engaged, of course I did not like to say anything against them.'

'Well, and how is the mine getting on? You have not applied to me yet to fulfil my offer, which I think was a very fair one.'

'I have not needed to do so,' said Kenyon.

'Ah, then, subscriptions are coming in, are they? Where is the list?'

'We have no list yet. We are waiting for your cousin, who is in the North.'

'In the North!' said Edith, with her eyes open wide. 'He is not in the North; he is in Paris, and we expect him home to-night.'

'Oh, indeed!' said John, who made no further comment.

252

'Now, where's your subscription-list? Oh, you told me you have none yet. Very well; this sheet of paper will do.' And the young woman drew some lines across the paper, heading it, 'The Canadian Mica-mine.' Then underneath she wrote the name Edith Longworth, and after it—'For ten thousand pounds.' 'There! I am the first subscriber to the new company; if you get the others as easily, you will be very fortunate.'

And, before John could thank her, she laughingly turned to her companion, and said:

'We must go.'

CHAPTER XXV.

When Wentworth dropped in to see if anything had happened, Kenyon told him that young Longworth was not in the North at all, but in Paris. Wentworth pondered over this piece of information for a moment, and said:

'I have written him, but have received no answer. I have just been to see the solicitors, and have told them that time was pressing; that we must do something. They quite agreed it was desirable some action should be taken at once, but, of course, as they said, they merely waited our instructions. They are willing to do anything we ask them to do. However, they advised waiting until Longworth got back, and then they proposed we should have a meeting at the offices here. They said, moreover, that, if Longworth had five or six men who would go at work with a will, the whole affair would be finished in a week at most. They did not appear to be at all alarmed at the shortening time, but said everything depended upon the men Longworth was going to bring with him. If they were the right men, there would be no trouble. So, all in all, they advised me not to worry about it, but to communicate with Longworth, if I could, and get him to come as soon as possible. I had to admit myself that this was the only thing to do, so I called round to see if you had heard anything from him.'

'I have heard nothing about him,' said Kenyon, 'except that he has lied, and has gone to Paris instead of going North.'

'Well,' mused Wentworth, 'I don't know that that is a very important point. He may have business in Paris, and he may have thought it was no affair of ours where he went, in which he was partly right and partly wrong. He thought, no doubt, that if he said he was going North, to see some men who could not be seen without his going there, it would relieve our minds, and make us imagine we were going on all right.'

'That is just what I object to, Wentworth. His whole demeanour seems to show that he wants us to think things are all right when they are not all right.'

'Well, John, as I said before, you've got to do one thing or the other. You have to trust Longworth or to go on without him. Now, for Heaven's sake make up your mind which it is to be, and don't grumble.'

'I am not grumbling. A man that is really honest will not say what is false, even about a small thing.'

'Oh, you are too particular. Wait till you have been in the City ten years longer, and you won't mind a little thing like that.'

'Little things like that, as you call them, are indicative of general character.'

'Sometimes yes, and sometimes no. You mustn't take things too seriously. I do not see that anything can be done until Longworth chooses to exhibit himself. If you can suggest anything better, as I said before, tell me what it is, and I am ready to do my part.'

'I confess I don't see what we can do. We might wait a day or two longer yet, and then, if we hear nothing more from Longworth, dismiss those solicitors he has chosen, and take the gentlemen who act for you.'

'The people Longworth has engaged do not bear a very good reputation; still, I must admit they talk in a very straightforward manner. As you say, it is perhaps better to let matters rest for a day or two.'

And so the days passed. Wentworth wrote again to Longworth at his office, and said they would wait for two days, and if he did not put in an appearance, before that time, they would go on forming the company as if he did not exist.

To this no answer came, and Kenyon and Wentworth again held consultation in the sumptuous offices which had been chosen for them.

'No news yet, I suppose?' said Kenyon.

'None whatever,' was the answer.

'Very well; I have made up my mind what to do——'

But before John Kenyon could say what he had resolved to do, the door opened, and there entered unto them Mr. William Longworth, with his silk hat as glossy as a mirror, a general trim and prosperous appearance about him, a flower in his buttonhole and his eyeglass in its place.

'Good-morning, gentlemen,' he said. 'I thought I should find you here, and so I did not call at your office, Wentworth. Ah,' he cried, looking round, 'this is the proper caper! These offices look even better than I thought they would. I just got back this morning,' he added, turning to his partners.

'Indeed,' said Wentworth, 'we are very glad to see you. How did you enjoy your trip to Paris?'

The young man did not appear in the least abashed by this remark. He merely elevated his eyebrows, shrugged his shoulders, and said:

'Ah, well, as both of you are doubtless aware, Paris is not what it used to be. Still, I had a very good time there.'

'I'm glad of that,' said Wentworth; 'and did you see the gentlemen you expected to meet?'

'I must confess I did not. I did not think it was necessary. I have five or six men interested already, practically pledged to furnish all the capital.' And, saying this, he walked round the desk at which they stood, and sat down, throwing the right leg across the left and clasping his knee in his hands.

'Well, what has been done during my absence? The mine floated yet?'

'No,' said Wentworth; 'the mine is not yet floated. Now, Mr. Longworth, the time has come for plain speaking. You have gone off to Paris without a word of warning to us at a very critical time, and you have not answered any of the letters I sent to you.'

'Well, my dear boy, the reason was that I expected every day to get back here, and each day was detained a little longer.'

'Very good; the point I want to impress upon you is this—time is getting short. If we are going to form this company, we have to set about it at once.'

'My dear fellow,' said Longworth, in an expostulating tone of voice, 'that is exactly what I told myself. The time is getting short, as you say. Of course, as I said when I joined you, I cannot give my whole time to this. We are equal partners, and the fact that I had to leave for a few days should not interrupt the business we have on hand. What did you expect to do if I had not been a partner at all?'

'If you were not a partner,' replied Wentworth with some heat, 'we should have gone on and formed our company, or failed; but the very fact that you are a partner is just what now retards us. We do not feel justified in doing anything until it has your approval, or until we know that it does not run counter with something you have already done.'

'Well, gentlemen, if you feel like that about it, I am quite willing to withdraw. I am ready to give up the paper I hold from you, and receive back the paper you hold from me. Of course we cannot work together if there are to be any recriminations. I have done my best; I have done everything that I promised to do—even more than that; but if you think for a moment you can get on better without me, I am ready at any time to retire.'

'It is easy to say that, Mr. Longworth, now that the time of the option has only a month further to run. You must remember that a great deal of time has been lost, and not through our fault.'

'Ah! do you mean it has been lost through my fault?'

'I mean that if we had been alone something would have been done, whereas we are now in the same position as when we started. We are in a worse position than we were at the beginning, because we have not only spent our money, but are deeply in debt into the bargain.'

'Well, Mr. Wentworth, I did not propose to withdraw until you, as a matter of fact, almost suggested it. I am quite willing and anxious to help, but if I do stay with you it must be understood that we have no such recriminations as these. You must do your best, and I must do my best.'

'Very well, then,' said Wentworth; 'your leaving us at this time is entirely out of the question. Now, will you give me the names of those gentlemen who have offered to go in with us?'

'Certainly.'

And Longworth pulled out a note-book from his inside pocket, while Wentworth took up a pen from the desk and pulled a sheet of paper towards him.

'First, Mr. Melville.'

'Is that the Melville I saw in relation to this mineral?'

'I am sure I do not know. He is at the head of the Scranton China Company.'

'Has he spoken of going in with us?'

'Yes, he seems to think the scheme is a good one. Why do you ask?'

'Well, merely because I took a specimen of the mineral to him and his manager wrote to me that it was of no value. It seems rather remarkable that he should go in for the mine if his manager believes it to be worthless.'

'Oh, he goes in entirely in his own private capacity. He is not at all affected by what the manager says. The manager has nothing to do with Melville's private affairs.'

'Still, it seems very strange, because, when Kenyon saw the manager in the North, he claimed they did not use this material, and said it would be of no benefit whatever to him.'

'That is very singular,' mused Longworth. 'Well, all I can say is, Melville has intimated that he should like to have a share in this mine, so, I take it, he and the manager do not agree as to the value of the mineral. You can set down Mr. Melville's name with perfect confidence. I know him very well, and I know that he's a thorough man of business. Besides, it will be a great advantage to have a man connected with the china trade in with us.'

There was no denying this point, so Wentworth said nothing more. Longworth named five other persons, none of whom Wentworth knew. Then

258

he closed his note-book and put it in his pocket.

'The question now is: Have these gentlemen stated how much they will subscribe?' asked Wentworth.

'No, they have not. Of course, everything will depend on how they are impressed with what we can tell them. The great thing is to get men who are willing even to listen to you. The rest depends on the inducements you offer.'

'Do you expect to get any more men interested?'

'I don't think any more are needed. The best thing to do now is to get those we have together and summon our solicitors here. Then our friend Kenyon, who is a fluent speaker, can lay the case before them.'

Kenyon, who had not spoken at all during the interview, did not even look up, and apparently did not hear the satirical allusion to his eloquence.

'Very well; when would be a good time to call this meeting?'

'As soon as possible, I think,' said Longworth. 'What do you say to Monday, at three o'clock? Men come from lunch about that hour, and are in a good humour. If you send out a letter saying a meeting will be held here in the directors' room at three o'clock, prompt, on Monday, I will see the men and get them to come. Of course they are generally busy, and may have other appointments; still, we must do something, and nothing can be done until we get them together.'

'Right; the invitations to the meeting shall be sent out at once.'

Longworth rose, went to the desk and picked up a paper.

'What is this?' he said.

Kenyon looked up suddenly.

'That,' he said, flushing slightly, 'is our first subscription.'

'Who wrote the name of Miss Edith Longworth here?'

'The young lady herself.'

'Has she been here?'

'She called, and desired to be the first subscriber.'

'Nonsense!' cried Longworth, with a frown; 'we don't want any women in this business;' and, saying that, he tore the paper in two.

Kenyon clenched his fist and was about to say something, when Wentworth's hand came down on his shoulder.

'I don't think I would refuse ten thousands pounds,' said Wentworth, 'from anybody who offered it, woman or man. Perhaps we had better see whether your men will subscribe as much before we throw away a subscription already received.'

'But she hasn't the ten thousand pounds.'

'I fancy,' said Wentworth, 'that whatever Miss Longworth puts her name to, she is ready to stand by;' and with that he placed the two pieces of paper in a drawer. 'Now, I think that is all,' he added; 'we will call the meeting for Monday, and see what comes of it.'

CHAPTER XXVI.

William Longworth had an eye for beauty. One of his eyes was generally covered by a round disc of glass, save when the disc fell out of its place and dangled in front of his waistcoat. Whether the monocle assisted his sight or not, it is certain that William knew a pretty girl when he saw her. One of the housemaids in the Longworth household left suddenly, without just cause or provocation, as the advertisements say, and in her place a girl was engaged who was so pretty that, when William Longworth caught sight of her, his monocle dropped from its usual position, and he stared at her with his two natural eyes, unassisted by science. He tried to speak to her on one or two occasions when he met her alone; but he could get no answer from the girl, who was very shy and demure, and knew her place, as people say. All this only enhanced her value in young Longworth's estimation, and he thought highly of his cousin's taste in choosing this young person to dust the furniture.

William had a room in the house which was partly sitting-room and partly study, and there he kept many of his papers. He was supposed to ponder over matters of business in this room, and it gave him a good excuse for arriving late at the office in the morning. He had been sitting up into the small hours, he would tell his uncle; although he would sometimes vary the excuse by saying that it was quieter at home than in the City, and that he had spent the early part of the morning in reading documents.

The first time William got an answer from the new housemaid was when he expressed his anxiety about the care of this room. He said that servants generally were very careless, and he hoped she would attend to things, and see that his papers were kept nicely in order. This, without glancing up at him, the girl promised to do, and William thereafter found his apartment kept with a scrupulous neatness which would have delighted the most particular of men.

One morning when he was sitting by his table, enjoying an after-breakfast cigarette, the door opened softly, and the new housemaid entered. Seeing him there, she seemed confused, and was about to retire, when William, throwing his cigarette away, sprang to his feet.

'No, don't go,' he said; 'I was just about to ring.'

The girl paused with her hand on the door.

'Yes,' he continued, 'I was just going to ring, but you have saved me the trouble; but, by the way, what is your name?'

'Susy, if you please, sir,' replied the girl modestly.

'Ah well, Susy, just shut the door for a moment.'

The girl did so, but evidently with some reluctance.

'Well, Susy,' said William jauntily, 'I suppose that I'm not the first one who has told you that you are very pretty.'

'Oh, sir!' said Susy, blushing and looking down on the carpet.

'Yes, Susy, and you take such good care of this room that I want to thank you for it,' continued William.

Here he fumbled in his pocket for a moment, and drew out half a sovereign.

'Here, my girl, is something for your trouble. Keep this for yourself.'

'Oh, I couldn't think of taking money, sir,' said the girl, drawing back. 'I couldn't indeed, sir!'

'Nonsense!' said William; 'isn't it enough?'

'Oh, it's more than enough. Miss Longworth pays me well for what I do, sir, and it's only my duty to keep things tidy.'

'Yes, Susy, that is very true; but very few of us do our duty, you know, in this world.'

'But we ought to, sir,' said the girl, in a tone of quiet reproof that made the young man smile.

'Perhaps,' said he; 'but then, you see, we are not all pretty and good, like you. I'm sorry you won't take the money. I hope you are not offended at me for offering it;' and William adjusted his eye-glass, looking his sweetest at the young person standing before him.

'Oh no, sir,' she said, 'I'm not at all offended, and I thank you very much, very much indeed, sir, and I would like to ask you a question, if you wouldn't think me too bold.'

'Bold?' cried William. 'Why, I think you are the shyest little woman I have ever seen. I'll be very pleased to answer any question you may ask me. What is it?'

'You see, sir, I've got a little money of my own.'

'Well, I declare, Susy, this is very interesting. I'd no idea you were an heiress.'

'Oh, not an heiress, sir—far from it. It's only a little matter of four or five hundred pounds, sir,' said Susy, dropping him an awkward little curtsy, which he thought most charming. 'The money is in the bank, and earns no interest, and I thought I would like to invest it where it would bring in something.'

'Certainly, Susy, and a most laudable desire on your part. Was it about that you wished to question me?'

'Yes, if you please, sir. I saw this paper on your desk, and I thought I would ask you if it would be safe for me to put my money in these mines, sir. Seeing the paper here, I supposed you had something to do with it.'

William whistled a long incredulous note, and said:

'So you have been reading my papers, have you, miss?'

'Oh no, sir,' said the girl, looking up at him with startled eyes. 'I only saw the name Canadian Mica-mine on this, and the paper said it would pay ten per cent., and I thought if you had anything to do with it that my money would be quite safe.'

'Oh, that goes without saying,' said William; 'but if I were you, my dear,

263

I should not put my money in the mica-mine.'

'Oh, then, you haven't anything to do with the mine, sir?'

'Yes, Susy, I have. You know, fools build houses, and wise men live in them.'

'So I have heard,' said Susy thoughtfully.

'Well, two fools are building the house that we will call the Canadian Mica-mine, and I am the wise man, don't you see, Susy?' said the young man, with a sweet smile.

'I'm afraid I don't quite understand, sir.'

'I don't suppose, Susy,' replied the young man, with a laugh, 'that there are many who do; but I think in a month's time I shall own this mica-mine, and then, my dear, if you still want to own a share or two, I shall be very pleased to give you a few without your spending any money at all.'

'Oh, would you, sir?' cried Susy in glad surprise; 'and who owns the mine now?'

'Oh, two fellows; you wouldn't know their names if I told them to you.'

'And are they going to sell it to you, sir?'

William laughed heartily, and said:

'Oh no! they themselves will be sold.'

'But how can that be if they don't own the mine? You see, I'm only a very stupid girl, and don't understand business. That's why I asked you about my money.'

'I don't suppose you know what an option is, do you, Susy?'

'No, sir, I don't; I never heard of it before.'

'Well, these two young men have what is called an option on the mine, which is to say that they are to pay a certain sum of money at a certain time and the mine is theirs; but if they don't pay the certain sum at the certain time, the mine isn't theirs.'

'And won't they pay the money, sir?'

'No, Susy, they will not, because, don't you know, they haven't got it. Then these two fools will be sold, for they think they are going to get the money, and they are not.'

'And you have the money to buy the mine when the option runs out, sir.'

'By Jove!' said William in surprise, 'you have a prodigious head for business, Susy; I never saw anyone pick it up so fast. You will have to take lessons from me, and go on the market and speculate yourself.'

'Oh, I should like to do that, sir—I should indeed.'

'Well,' said William kindly, 'whenever you have time, come to me, and I will give you lessons.'

The young man approached her, holding out his hand, but the girl slipped away from him and opened the door.

'I think,' he said in a whisper, 'that you might give me a kiss after all this valuable information.'

'Oh, Mr. William!' cried Susy, horrified.

He stepped forward and tried to catch her, but the girl was too nimble for him, and sprang out into the passage.

'Surely,' protested William, 'this is getting information under false pretences; I expected my fee, you know.'

'And you shall have it,' said the girl, laughing softly, 'when I get ten per cent. on my money.'

'Egad!' said William to himself as he entered his room again, 'I will see that you get it. She's as clever an outside broker.'

When young Longworth had left for his office, Susy swept and dusted out his room again, and then went downstairs.

'Where's the mistress?' she asked a fellow-servant.

'In the library,' was the answer, and to the library Susy went, entering the room without knocking, much to the amazement of Edith Longworth, who sat near the window with a book in her lap. But further surprise was in store for the lady of the house. The housemaid closed the door, and then, selecting a comfortable chair, threw herself down into it, exclaiming:

'Oh dear me! I'm so tired.'

'Susy,' said Miss Longworth, 'what is the meaning of this?'

'It means, mum,' said Susy, 'that I'm going to chuck it.'

'Going to what?' asked Miss Longworth, amazed.

'Going to chuck it. Didn't you understand? Going to give up my situation. I'm tired of it.'

'Very well,' said the young woman, rising, 'you may give notice in the proper way. You have no right to come into this room in this impudent manner. Be so good as to go to your own room.'

'My!' said Susy, 'you can do the dignified! I must practise and see if I can accomplish an attitude like that. If you were a little prettier, Miss Longworth, I should call that striking;' and the girl threw back her head and laughed.

Something in the laugh aroused Miss Longworth's recollection, and a chill of fear came over her; but, looking at the girl again, she saw she was mistaken. Susy jumped up, still laughing, and drew a pin from the little cap she wore, flinging it on the chair; then she pulled off her wig, and stood before Edith Longworth her natural self.

'Miss Brewster!' gasped the astonished Edith. 'What are you doing in my house in that disguise?'

'Oh,' said Jennie, 'I'm an amateur housemaid. How do you think I have acted the part? Now sit down, Miss Dignity, and I will tell you something about your own family. I thought you were a set of rogues, and now I can prove it.'

'Will you leave my house this instant?' cried Edith, in anger. 'I shall not listen to you.'

'Oh yes, you will,' said Jennie, 'for I shall follow your own example, and not let you out until you do hear what I have to tell you.'

Saying which the amateur housemaid skipped nimbly to the door, and placed her back against it.

CHAPTER XXVII.

Jennie Brewster stood with her back to the door, a sweet smile on her face.

'This is my day for acting, Miss Longworth. I think I did the rôle of housemaid so well that it deceived several members of this family. I am now giving an imitation of yourself in your thrilling drama, "All at Sea." Don't you think I do it most admirably?'

'Yes,' said Edith, sitting down again. 'I wonder you did not adopt the stage as a profession.'

'I have often thought of doing so, but journalism is more exciting.'

'Perhaps. Still, it has its disappointments. When I gave my thrilling drama, as you call it, on shipboard, I had my stage accessories arranged to better advantage than you have now.'

'Do you mean the putting off of the boat?'

'No; I mean that the electric button was under my hand—it was impossible for you to ring for help. Now, while you hold the door, you cannot stop me from ringing, for the bell-rope is here beside me.'

'Yes, that is a disadvantage, I admit. Do you intend to ring, then, and have me turned out?'

'I don't think that will be necessary. I imagine you will go quietly.'

'You are a pretty clever girl, Miss Longworth. I wish I liked you, but I don't, so we won't waste valuable time deploring that fact. Have you no curiosity to hear what I was going to tell you?'

'Not the slightest; but there is one thing I should like to know.'

'Oh, is there? Well, that's human, at any rate. What do you wish to know?'

'You came here well recommended. How did you know I wanted a housemaid, and were your testimonials——'

Edith paused for a word, which Jennie promptly supplied.

'Forged? Oh dear no! There is no necessity for doing anything criminal in this country, if you have the money. I didn't forge them—I bought them. Didn't you write to any of the good ladies who stood sponsor for me?'

'Yes, and received most flattering accounts of you.'

'Certainly. That was part of the contract. Oh, you can do anything with money in London; it is a most delightful town. Then, as for knowing there was a vacancy, that also was money. I bribed the other housemaid to leave.'

'I see. And what object had you in all this?'

Jennie Brewster laughed—the same silvery laugh that had charmed William Longworth an hour or two before, a laugh that sometimes haunted Wentworth's memory in the City. She left her sentinel-like position at the door and threw herself into a chair.

'Miss Longworth,' she said, 'you are not consistent. You first pretend that you have no curiosity to hear what I have to say, then you ask me exactly what I was going to tell you. Of course, you are dying to know why I am here; you wouldn't be a woman if you weren't. Now, I've changed my mind, and I don't intend to tell you. I will say, though, that my object in coming here was, first, to find out for myself how servants are treated in this country. You see, my sympathies are all with the women who work, and not with women—well, like yourself, for instance.'

'Yes, I think you said that once before. And how do we treat our servants?'

'So far as my experience goes, very well indeed.'

'It is most gratifying to hear you say this. I was afraid we might not have met with your approval. And now, where shall I send your month's money, Miss Brewster?'

Jennie Brewster leaned back in her chair, her eyes all but closed; an angry light shooting from them reminded Edith of her glance of hatred on board the steamship. A rich warm colour overspread her fair face, and her lips closed tightly. There was a moment's silence, and then Jennie's indignation passed away as quickly as it came. She laughed, with just a touch of restraint in her tone.

'You can say an insulting thing more calmly and sweetly than anyone I ever met before; I envy you that. When I say anything low down and mean, I say it in anger, and my voice has a certain amount of acridity in it. I can't purr like a cat and scratch at the same time—I wish I could.'

'Is it an insult to offer you the money you have earned?'

'Yes, it is, and you knew it was when you spoke. You don't understand me a little bit.'

'Is it necessary that I should?'

'I don't suppose you think it is,' said Jennie meditatively, resting her elbow on her knee and her chin on her palm. 'That is where our point of view differs. I like to know everything. It interests me to learn what people think and talk about, and somehow it doesn't seem to matter to me who the people are, for I was even more interested in your butler's political opinions than I was in Lord Frederick Bingham's. They are both Conservatives, but Lord Freddie seems shaky in his views, for you can argue him down in five minutes, but the butler is as steadfast as a rock. I do admire that butler. I hope you will break the news of my departure gently to him, for he proposed to me, and he has not yet had his answer.'

'There is still time,' said Edith, smiling in spite of herself. 'Shall I ring for him?'

'Please do not. I want to avoid a painful scene, because he is so sure of himself, and never dreams of a refusal. It is such a pity, too, for the butler is my ideal of what a member of the aristocracy should be. His dignity is positively awe-inspiring; while Lord Freddie is such a simple, good-natured, everyday young fellow, that if I imported him to the States I am sure no one would believe he was a real lord. With the butler it would be so different,' added Jennie, with a deep sigh.

'It is too bad that you cannot exchange the declaration of the butler for one from Lord Frederick.'

'Too bad!' cried Jennie, looking with wide-open eyes at the girl before her; 'why, bless you! I had a proposal from Lord Freddie two weeks before I ever saw the butler. I see you don't believe a word I say. Well, you ask Lord Freddie. I'll introduce you, and tell him you don't believe he asked me to be Lady Freddie, if that's the title. He'll look sheepish, but he won't deny it. You see, when I found I was going to stay in England for a time, I wrote to the editor of the Argus to get me a bunch of letters of introduction and send them over, as I wanted particularly to study the aristocracy. So he sent them, and, I assure you, I found it much more difficult to get into your servants' hall than I did into the halls of the nobility—besides, it costs less to mix with the Upper Ten.'

Edith sat in silence, looking with amazed interest at the girl, who talked so rapidly that there was sometimes difficulty in following what she said.

'No, Lord Freddie is not half so condescending as the butler, neither is his language so well chosen; but then, I suppose, the butler's had more practice, for Freddie is very young. I am exceedingly disappointed with the aristocracy. They are not nearly so haughty as I had imagined them to be. But what astonishes me in this country is the way you women spoil the men. You are much too good to them. You pet them and fawn on them, and naturally they get conceited. It is such a pity, too; for they are nice fellows, most of them. It is the same everywhere I've been—servants' hall included. Why, when you meet a young couple, of what you are pleased to call the "lower classes," walking in the Park, the man hangs down his head as he slouches along, but the girl looks defiantly at you, as much as to say, "I've got him. Bless him! What have you to say about it?" while the man seems to be ashamed of himself, and evidently feels that he's been had. Now, a man should be made to understand that you're doing him a great favour when you give him a civil word. That's the proper state of mind to keep a man in, and then you can do what you like with him. I generally make him propose, so as to get it over before any real harm's done, and to give an artistic finish to the episode. After that we can be excellent friends, and have a jolly time. That's the way I did with Lord Freddie. Now, here am I, chattering away as if I were paid for talking instead of writing. Why do you look at me so? Don't you believe what I tell you?'

'Yes, I believe all you say. What I can't understand is, why a bright girl like you should enter a house and,—well, do what you have done here, for instance.'

'Why shouldn't I? I am after accurate information. I get it in my own way. Your writers here tell how the poor live, and that sort of thing. They enter the houses of the poor quite unblushingly, and print their impressions of the poverty-stricken homes. Now, why should the rich man be exempt from a similar investigation?'

'In either case it is the work of a spy.'

'Yes; but a spy is not a dishonourable person—at least, he need not be. I saw a monument in Westminster Abbey to a man who was hanged as a spy. A spy must be brave; he must have nerve, caution, and resource. He sometimes does more for his country than a whole regiment. Oh, there are worse persons than spies in this world.'

'I suppose there are, still——'

'Yes, I know. It is easy for persons with plenty of money to moralize on the shortcomings of others. I'll tell you a secret. I'm writing a book, and if it's a success, then good-bye to journalism. I don't like the spy business myself any too well; I'm afraid England is contaminating me, and if I stayed here a few years I might degenerate so far as to think your newspapers interesting. By the way, have you seen Mr. Wentworth lately?'

Edith hesitated a moment, and at last answered:

'Yes, I saw him a day or two ago.'

'Was he looking well? I think I ought to write him a note of apology for all the anxiety I caused him on board ship. You may not believe it, but I have actually had some twinges of conscience over that episode. I suppose that's why I partially forgave you for stopping the cablegram.'

Edith Longworth was astonished at herself for giving the young woman information about Wentworth, but she gave it, and the amateur housemaid departed in peace, saying, by way of farewell:

'I'm not going to write up your household, after all.'

CHAPTER XXVIII.

One day when Kenyon entered the office, the clerk said to him:

'That young gentleman has been here twice to see you. He said it was very important, sir.'

'What young gentleman?'

'The gentleman—here is his card—who belongs to the Financial Field, sir.'

'Did he leave any message?'

'Yes, sir; he said he would call again at three o'clock.'

'Very good,' said Kenyon; and he began composing his address to the proposed subscribers.

At three o'clock the smooth, oily person from the Financial Field put in an appearance.

'Ah, Mr. Kenyon,' he said, 'I am glad to meet you. I called in twice, but had not the good fortune to find you in. Can I see you in private for a moment?'

'Yes,' answered Kenyon. 'Come into the directors' room;' and into the directors room they went, Kenyon closing the door behind them.

'Now,' said the representative of the Financial Field, 'I have brought you a proof of the editorial we propose using, which I am desired by the proprietor to show you, so that it may be free, if possible, from any error. We are very anxious to have things correct in the Financial Field;' and with this he handed to John a long slip of paper with a column of printed matter upon it.

The article was headed, 'The Canadian Mica Mining Company, Limited.' It went on to show what the mine had been, what it had done, and what chances there were for investors getting a good return for their money by buying the shares. John read it through carefully.

'That is a very handsome article,' he said; 'and it is without an error, so far as I can see.'

'I am glad you think so,' replied the young gentleman, folding up the proof and putting it in his inside pocket. 'Now, as I said before, although I am not the advertising canvasser of the Financial Field, I thought I would see you with reference to an advertisement for the paper.'

'Well, you know, we have not had a meeting of the proposed stockholders yet, and therefore are not in a position to give any advertisements regarding the mine. I have no doubt advertisements will be given, and, of course, your paper will be remembered among the rest.'

'Ah,' said the young man, 'that is hardly satisfactory to us. We have a vacant half-page for Monday, the very best position in the paper, which the proprietor thought you would like to secure.'

'As I said a moment ago, we are not in a position to secure it. It is premature to talk of advertising at the present state of affairs.'

'I think, you know, it will be to your interest to take the half-page. The price is three hundred pounds, and besides that amount we should like to have some shares in the company.'

'Do you mean three hundred pounds for one insertion of the advertisement?'

'Yes.'

'Doesn't that strike you as being a trifle exorbitant? Your paper has a comparatively limited circulation, and they do not ask us such a price even in the large dailies.'

'Ah, my dear sir, the large dailies are quite different. They have a tremendous circulation, it is true, but it is not the kind of circulation we have. No other paper circulates so largely among investors as the Financial Field. It is read by exactly the class of people you desire to reach, and I may say that, except through the Financial Field, you cannot get at some of the best men in the City.'

'Well, admitting all that, as I have said once or twice, we are not yet in a position to give an advertisement.'

'Then, I am very sorry to say that we cannot, on Monday, publish the article I have shown you.'

'Very well; I cannot help it. You are not compelled to print it unless you wish. I am not sure, either, that publishing the article on Monday would do us any good. It would be premature, as I say. We are not yet ready to court publicity until we have had our first meeting of proposed stockholders.'

'When is your first meeting of stockholders?'

'On Monday, at three o'clock.'

'Very well, we could put that announcement in another column, and I am sure you would find the attendance at your meeting would be very largely and substantially increased.'

'Possibly; but I decline to do anything till after the meeting.'

'I think you would find it pay you extremely well to take that half-page.'

'I am not questioning the fact at all. I am merely saying what I have said to everyone else, that we are not ready to consider advertising.'

'I am sorry we cannot come to an arrangement, Mr. Kenyon—very sorry indeed;' and, saying this, he took another proof-sheet out of his pocket, which he handed to Kenyon. 'If we cannot come to an understanding, the manager has determined to print this, instead of the article I showed you. Would you kindly glance over it, because we should like to have it as correct as possible.'

Kenyon opened his eyes, and unfolded the paper. The heading was the same, but he had read only a sentence or two when he found that the mica-mine was one of the greatest swindles ever attempted on poor old innocent financial London!

276

'Do you mean to say,' cried John, looking up at him, with his anger kindling, 'that if I do not bribe you to the extent of three hundred pounds, besides giving you an unknown quantity of stock, you will publish this libel?'

'I do not say it is a libel,' said the young man smoothly; 'that would be a matter for the courts to decide. You might sue us for libel, if you thought we had treated you badly. I may say that has been tried several times, but with indifferent success.'

'But do you mean to tell me that you intend to publish this article if I do not pay you the three hundred pounds?'

'Yes; putting it crudely, that is exactly what I do mean.'

Kenyon rose in his wrath and flung open the door.

'I must ask you to leave this place, and leave it at once. If you ever put in an appearance here again while I am in the office, I will call a policeman and have you turned out!'

'My dear sir,' expostulated the other suavely, 'it is merely a matter of business. If you find it impossible to deal with us, there is no harm done. If our paper has no influence, we cannot possibly injure you. That, of course, is entirely for you to judge. If, any time between now and Sunday night, you conclude to act otherwise, a wire to our office will hold things over until we have had an opportunity of coming to an arrangement with you. If not, this article will be published on Monday morning. I wish you a very good afternoon, sir.'

John said nothing, but watched his visitor out on the pavement, and then returned to the making of his report.

On Monday morning, as he came in by train, his eye caught a flaming poster on one of the bill-boards at the station. It was headed Financial Field, and the next line, in heavy black letters, was, 'The Mica Mining Swindle,' Kenyon called a newsboy to him and bought a copy of the paper. There, in leaded type, was the article before him. It seemed, somehow, much more important on the printed page than it had looked in the proof.

As he read it, he noticed an air of truthful sincerity about the editorial that had escaped him during the brief glance he had given it on Friday. It went on to say that the Austrian Mining Company had sunk a good deal of money in the mine, and that it had never paid a penny of dividends; that they merely kept on at a constant loss to themselves in the hope of being able to swindle some confiding investors—but that even their designs were as nothing compared to the barefaced rascality contemplated by John Kenyon. He caught his breath as he saw his own name in print. It was a shock for which he was not prepared, as he had not noticed it in the proof. Then he read on. It seemed that this man, Kenyon, had secured the mine at something like ten thousand pounds, and was trying to palm it off on the unfortunate British public at the enormous increase of two hundred thousand pounds; but this nefarious attempt would doubtless be frustrated so long as there were papers of the integrity of the Financial Field, to take the risk and expense of making such an exposure as was here set forth.

The article possessed a singular fascination for Kenyon. He read and re-read it in a dazed way, as if the statement referred to some other person, and he could not help feeling sorry for that person.

He still had the paper in his hand as he walked up the street, and he felt numbed and dazed as if someone had struck him a blow. He was nearly run over in crossing one of the thoroughfares, and heard an outburst of profanity directed at him from a cab-driver and a man on a bus; but he heeded them not, walking through the crowd as if under a spell.

He passed the door of his own gorgeous office, and walked some distance up the street before he realized what he had done. Then he turned back again, and, just at the doorstep, paused with a pang at his heart.

'I wonder if Edith Longworth will read that article,' he said to himself.

278

CHAPTER XXIX.

When John Kenyon entered his office, he thought the clerk looked at him askance. He imagined that innocent employee had been reading the article in the Financial Field; but the truth is, John was hardly in a frame of mind to form a correct opinion on what other people were doing. Everybody he met in the street, it seemed to him, was discussing the article in the Financial Field.

He asked if anybody had been in that morning, and was told there had been no callers. Then he passed into the directors' room, closed the door behind him, sat down on a chair, and leaned his head on his hands with his elbows on the table. In this position Wentworth found him some time later, and when John looked up his face was haggard and aged.

'Ah, I see you have read it.'

'Yes.'

'Do you think Longworth is at the bottom of that article?'

John shook his head.

'Oh no,' he said; 'he had nothing whatever to do with it.'

'How do you know?'

Kenyon related exactly what had passed between the oily young man of the Financial Field and himself in that very room. While this recital was going on, Wentworth walked up and down, expressing his opinion now and then, in remarks that were short and pithy, but hardly fit for publication. When the story was told he turned to Kenyon.

'Well,' he said, 'there is nothing for it but to sue the paper for libel.'

'What good will that do?'

'What good will it do? Do you mean to say that you intend to sit here under such an imputation as they have cast upon you, and do nothing? What good will it do? It will do all the good in the world.'

'We cannot form our company and sue the paper at the same time. All our energies will have to be directed towards the matter we have in hand.'

'But, my dear John, don't you see the effect of that article? How can we form our company if such a lie remains unchallenged? Nobody will look at our proposals. Everyone will say, "What have you done about the article that appeared in the Financial Field?" If we say we have done nothing, then, of course, the natural inference is that we are a pair of swindlers, and that our scheme is a fraud.'

'I have always thought,' said John, 'that the capitalization is too high.'

'Really, I believe you think that article is not so unfair, after all. John, I'm astonished at you!'

'But if we do commence a libel suit, it cannot be finished before our option has expired. If we tell people that we have begun a suit against the Financial Field for libel, they will merely say they prefer to wait and hear what the result of the case is. By that time our chances of forming a company will be gone.'

'There is a certain amount of truth in that; nevertheless, I do not see how we are to go on with our company unless suit for libel is at least begun.'

Before John could reply there was a knock at the door, and the clerk entered with a letter in his hand which had just come in. Kenyon tore it open, read it, and then tossed it across the table to Wentworth. Wentworth saw the name of their firm of solicitors at the top of the letter-paper. Then he read:

'DEAR SIR,

'You have doubtless seen the article in the Financial Field of this morning, referring to the Canadian Mica Mining Company. We should be pleased to know what action you intend to take in the matter. We may say that, in justice to our reputation, we can no longer represent your company unless a suit is brought against the paper which contains the article.

280

'Yours truly,

'W. HAWK.'

Wentworth laughed with a certain bitterness.

'Well,' he said, 'if it has come to such a pass that Hawk fears for his reputation, the sooner we begin a libel suit against the paper the better!'

'Perhaps,' said John, with a look of agony on his face, 'you will tell me where the money is to come from. The moment we get into the Law Courts money will simply flow like water, and doubtless the Financial Field has plenty of it. It will add to their reputation, and they will make a boast that they are fighting the battle of the investor in London. Everything is grist that comes to their mill. Meanwhile, we shall be paying out money, or we shall be at a tremendous disadvantage, and the result of it all will probably be a disagreement of the jury and practical ruin for us. You see, I have no witnesses.'

'Yes, but what about the mine? How can we go on without vindicating ourselves?'

Before anything further could be said, young Mr. Longworth came in, looking as cool, calm, and unruffled as if there were no such things in the world as financial newspapers.

'Discussing it, I see,' were his first words.

'Yes,' said Wentworth; 'I am very glad you have come. We have a little difference of opinion in the matter of that article. Kenyon here is averse to suing that paper for libel; I am in favour of prosecuting it. Now, what do you say?'

'My dear fellow,' replied Longworth, 'I am delighted to be able to agree with Mr. Kenyon for once. Sue them! Why, of course not. That is just what they want.'

'But,' said Wentworth, 'if we do not, who is going to look at our mine?'

'Exactly the same number of people as would look at it before the article appeared.'

'Don't you think it will have any effect?'

'Not the slightest.'

'But look at this letter from your own lawyers on the subject.' Wentworth handed Longworth the letter from Hawk. Longworth adjusted his glass and read it carefully through.

'By Jove!' he said with a laugh, 'I call that good; I call that distinctly good. I had no idea old Hawk was such a humorist! His reputation indeed; well, that beats me! All that Hawk wants is another suit on his hands. I wish you would let me keep this letter. I will have some fun with my friend Hawk over it.'

'You are welcome to the letter, so far as I am concerned,' said Wentworth; 'but do you mean to say, Mr. Longworth, that we have to sit here calmly under this imputation and do nothing?'

'I mean to say nothing of the kind; but I don't propose to play into their hands by suing them—at least, I should not if it were my case instead of Kenyon's.'

'What would you do?'

'I would let them sue me if they wanted to. Of course, their canvasser called to see you, didn't he, Kenyon?'

'Yes, he did.'

'He told you that he had a certain amount of space to sell for a certain sum in cash?'

'Yes.'

'And, if you did not buy that space, this certain article would appear; whereas, if you did, an article of quite a different complexion would be printed?'

'You seem to know all about it,' said Kenyon suspiciously.

282

'Of course I do, my dear boy! Everybody knows all about it. That's the way those papers make their money. I think myself, as a general rule, it is cheaper to buy them off. I believe my uncle always does that when he has anything special on hand, and doesn't want to be bothered with outside issues. But we haven't done so in this instance, and this is the result. It can be easily remedied yet, mind you, if you like. All that you have to do is to pay his price, and there will be an equally lengthy article saying that, from outside information received with regard to the Canadian Mining Company, he regrets very much that the former article was an entire mistake, and that there is no more secure investment in England than this particular mine. But now, when he has come out with his editorial, I think it isn't worth while to have any further dealings with him. Anything he can say now will not matter. He has done all the harm he can. But I would at once put the boot on the other foot. I would write down all the circumstances just as they happened— give the name of the young man who called upon you, tell exactly the price he demanded for his silence, and I will have that printed in an opposition paper to-morrow. Then it will be our friend the Financial Field's turn to squirm! He will say it is all a lie, of course, but nobody will believe him, and we can tell him, from the opposition paper, that if it is a lie he is perfectly at liberty to sue us for libel. Let him begin the suit if he wants to do so. Let him defend his reputation. Sue him for libel! I know a game worth two of that. Could you get out the statement before the meeting this afternoon?'

Kenyon, who had been looking, for the first time in his life, gratefully at Longworth, said he could.

'Very well; just set it down in your own words as plainly as possible, and give date, hour, and full particulars. Sign your name to it, and I will take it when I come to the meeting this afternoon. It would not be a bad plan to read it to those who are here. There is nothing like fighting the devil with fire. Fight a paper with another paper. Nothing new, I suppose?'

'No,' said Kenyon; 'nothing new except what we are discussing.'

'Well, don't let that trouble you. Do as I say, and we will begin an interesting controversy. People like a fight, and it will attract attention to the mine. Good-bye. I shall see you this afternoon.'

He left both Kenyon and Wentworth in a much happier frame of mind than that in which he had found them.

'I say, Kenyon,' said Wentworth, 'that fellow is a trump. His advice has cleared the air wonderfully. I believe his plan is the best, after all, and, as you say, we have no money for an expensive lawsuit. I shall leave you now to get on with your work, and will return at three o'clock.'

At that hour John had his statement finished. The first man to arrive was Longworth, who read the article with approval, merely suggesting a change here and there, which was duly made. Then he put the communication into an envelope, and sent it to the editor of the opposition paper. Wentworth came in next, then Melville, then Mr. King. After this they all adjourned to the directors' room, and in a few minutes the others were present.

'Now,' said Longworth, 'as we are all here, I do not see any necessity for delay. You have probably read the article that appeared in this morning's Financial Field. Mr. Kenyon has written a statement in relation to that, which gives the full particulars of the inside of a very disreputable piece of business. It was merely an attempt at blackmailing which failed. I intended to have had the statement read to you, but we thought it best to get it off as quickly as possible, and it will appear to-morrow in the Financial Eagle, where, I hope, you will all read it. Now, Mr. Kenyon, perhaps you will tell us something about the mine.'

Kenyon, like many men of worth and not of words, was a very poor speaker. He seemed confused, and was often a little obscure in his remarks, but he was listened to with great attention by those present. He was helped here and there by a judicious question from young Longworth, and when he sat down the impression was not so bad as might have been expected. After a moment's silence, it was Mr. King who spoke.

'As I take it,' he said, 'all we wish to know is this: Is the mine what it is represented to be? Is the mineral the best for the use Mr. Kenyon has indicated? Is there a sufficient quantity of that mineral in the mountain he speaks of to make it worth while to organize this company? It seems to me that this can only be answered by some practical man going out there and seeing the mine for himself. Mr. Melville is, I understand, a practical man. If he has the time to spare, I would propose that he should go to America, see this mine, and report.'

Another person asked when the option on the mine ran out. This was answered by Longworth, who said that the person who went over and reported on the mine could cable the word 'Right' or 'Wrong'; then there would be time to act in London in getting up the list of subscribers.

'I suppose,' said another, 'that in case of delay there would be no trouble in renewing the option for a month or two?'

To this Kenyon replied that he did not know. The owners might put a higher price on the property, or the mine might be producing more mica than it had been heretofore, and they perhaps might not be inclined to sell. He thought that things should be arranged so that there would be no necessity of asking for an extension of the option, and to this they all agreed.

Melville then said he had no objection to taking a trip to Canada. It was merely a question of the amount of the mineral in sight, and he thought he could determine that as well as anybody else. And so the matter was about to be settled, when Longworth rose, and said that he was perfectly willing to go to Canada himself, in company with Mr. Melville; that he would pay all his own expenses, and give them the benefit of his opinion as well. This was received with applause, and the meeting terminated. Longworth shook hands with Kenyon and Wentworth.

'We will sail by the first steamer,' he said, 'and, as I may not see you again, you might write me a letter of introduction to Mr. Von Brent, and tell him that I am acting for you in this affair. That will make matters smooth in getting an extension of the option, if it should be necessary.'

CHAPTER XXX.

Kenyon was on his way to lunch next day, when he met Wentworth at the door.

'Going to feed?' asked the latter.

'Yes.'

'Very well; I'll go with you. I couldn't stay last night to have a talk with you over the meeting; but what did you think of it?'

'Well, considering the article which appeared in the morning, and considering also the exhibition I made of myself in attempting to explain the merits of the mine, I think things went off rather smoothly.'

'So do I. It doesn't strike you that they went off a little too smoothly, does it?'

'What do you mean?'

'I don't know exactly what I mean. I merely wanted to get your own opinion about it. You see, I have attended a great many gatherings of this sort, and it struck me there was a certain cut-and-driedness about the meeting. I can't say whether it impressed me favourably or unfavourably, but I noticed it.'

'I still don't understand what you mean.'

'Well, as a general thing in such meetings, when a man gets up and proposes a certain action there is some opposition, or somebody has a suggestion to make, or something better to propose—or thinks he has—and so there is a good deal of talk. Now, when King got up and proposed calmly that Melville should go to America, it appeared to me rather an extraordinary thing to do, unless he had consulted Melville beforehand.'

'Perhaps he had done so.'

'Yes, perhaps. What do you think of it all?'

Kenyon mused for a moment before he replied:

'As I said before, I thought things went off very smoothly. Whom do you suspect—young Longworth?'

'I do not know whom I suspect. I am merely getting anxious about the shortness of the time. I think, myself, you ought to go to America. There is nothing to be done here. You should go, see Von Brent, and get a renewal of the option. Don't you see that when they get over there, allowing them a few days in New York, and a day or two to get out to the mine, we shall have little more than a week, after the cable despatch comes, in which to do anything, should they happen to report unfavourably.'

'Yes, I see that. Still, it is only a question of facts on which they have to report, and you know, as well as I do, that no truthful men can report unfavourably on what we have certified. We have understated the case in every instance.'

'I know that. I am perfectly well aware of that. Everything is all right if—if—Longworth is dealing honestly with us. If he is not, then everything is all wrong, and I should feel a great deal easier if we had in our possession another three months' option of the mine. We are now at the fag-end of this option, and, it seems to me, as protection to ourselves, we ought either to write to Von Brent—By the way, have you ever written to him?'

'I wrote one letter telling him how we were getting on, but have received no answer; perhaps he is not in Ottawa at present.'

'Well, I think you ought to go to the mine with Longworth and Melville. It is the conjunction of those two men that makes me suspicious. I can't tell what I distrust. I can give nothing definite; but I have a vague uneasiness when I think that the man who tried to mislead us regarding the value of the mineral is going with the man who has led us into all this expense. Longworth refused to go into the scheme in the first place, pretended he had forgotten all about it in the second place, and then suddenly developed an interest.'

John knitted his brows and said nothing.

'I don't want to worry you about it, but I am anxious to have your candid opinion. What had we better do?'

'It seems to me,' said John, after a pause, 'that we can do nothing. It is a very perplexing situation. I think, however, we should turn it over in our minds for a few days, and then I can get to America in plenty of time, if necessary.'

'Very well, suppose we give them ten days to get to the mine and reply. If no reply comes by the eleventh day then you will still have eighteen or nineteen days before the option expires. Put it at twelve days. I propose, if you hear nothing by then, you go over.'

'Right,' said John; 'we may take that as settled.'

'By the way, you got an invitation to-day, did you not?'

'Yes.'

'Are you going?'

'I do not know. I should like to go and yet, you know, I am entirely unused to fashionable assemblages. I should not know what to say or do while I was there.'

'As I understand, it is not to be a fashionable party, but merely a little friendly gathering which Miss Longworth gives because her cousin is about to sail for Canada. I don't want to flatter you, John, at all, but I imagine Miss Longworth would be rather disappointed if you did not put in an appearance. Besides, as we are partners with Longworth in this, and as he is going away on account of the mine. I think it would be a little ungracious of us not to go.'

'Very well, I will go. Shall I call for you, or will you come for me?'

'I will call for you and we will go there together in a cab. Be ready about eight o'clock.'

The mansion of the Longworths was brilliantly lighted, and John felt rather faint-hearted as he stood on the steps before going in. The chances are he would not have had the courage to allow himself to be announced if his friend Wentworth had not been with him. George, however, had no such qualms, being more experienced in this kind of thing than his comrade. So they entered together, and were warmly greeted by the young hostess.

'It is so kind of you to come,' she said, 'on such short notice. I was afraid you might have had some prior engagement, and would have found it impossible to be with us.'

'You must not think that of me,' said Wentworth. 'I was certain to come; but I must confess my friend Kenyon here was rather difficult to manage. He seems to frown on social festivities, and actually had the coolness to propose that we should both plead more important business.'

Edith looked reproachfully at Kenyon, who flushed to the temples, as was his custom, and said:

'Now, Wentworth, that is unfair. You must not mind what he says, Miss Longworth; he likes to bring confusion on me, and he knows how to do it. I certainly said nothing about a prior engagement.'

'Well, now you are here, I hope you will enjoy yourselves. It is quite an informal little gathering, with nothing to abash even Mr. Kenyon.'

They found young Longworth there in company with Melville, who was to be his companion on the voyage. He shook hands, but without exhibiting the pleasure at meeting them which his cousin had shown.

'My cousin,' said the young man, 'seems resolved to make the going of the prodigal nephew an occasion for killing the fatted calf. I'm sure I don't know why, unless it is that she is glad to be rid of me for a month.'

Edith laughed at this, and left the men together. Wentworth speedily contrived to make himself agreeable to the young ladies who were present; but John, it must be admitted, felt awkward and out of place. He was not enjoying himself. He caught himself now and then following Edith Longworth with his eyes, and when he realized he was doing this, would abruptly look at the floor. In her handsome evening dress she appeared supremely lovely, and this John Kenyon admitted to himself with a sigh, for her very loveliness seemed to place her further and further away from him. Somebody played something on the piano, and this was, in a way, a respite for John. He felt that nobody was looking at him. Then a young man gave a recitation, which was very well received, and Kenyon began to forget his uneasiness. A German gentleman with long hair sat down at the piano with a good deal of importance in his demeanour. There was much arranging of music, and finally, when the leaves were settled to his satisfaction, there was a tremendous crash of chords, the beginning of what was evidently going to be a troublesome time for the piano. In the midst of this hurricane of sound John Kenyon became aware that Edith Longworth had sat down beside him.

'I have got everyone comfortably settled with everyone else,' she said in a whisper to him, 'and you seem to be the only one who is, as it were, out in the cold, so, you see, I have done you the honour to come and talk to you.'

'It is indeed an honour,' said John earnestly.

'Oh, really,' said the young woman, laughing very softly, 'you must not take things so seriously. I didn't mean quite what I said, you know—that was only, as the children say, "pretended"; but you take one's light remarks as if they were most weighty sentences. Now, you must look as if you were entertaining me charmingly, whereas I have sat down beside you to have a very few minutes' talk on business; I know it's very bad form to talk business at an evening party, but, you see, I have no other chance to speak with you. I understand you have had a meeting of shareholders, and yet you never sent me an invitation. I told you that I wished to help you in forming a company; but that is the way you business men always treat a woman.'

'Really, Miss Longworth,' began Kenyon; but she speedily interrupted him.

'I am not going to let you make any explanation. I have come over here to enjoy scolding you, and I am not to be cheated out of my pleasure.'

'I think,' said John, 'if you knew how much I have suffered during this last day or two, you would be very lenient with me. Did you read that article upon me in the Financial Field?'

'No, I did not, but I read your reply to it this morning, and I think it was excellent.'

'Ah, that was hardly fair. A person should read both sides of the question before passing judgment.'

'It is a woman's idea of fairness,' said Edith, 'to read what pertains to her friend, and to form her judgment without hearing the other side. But you must not think I am going to forego scolding you because of my sympathy with you. Don't you remember you promised to let me know how your company was progressing from time to time, and here I have never had a word from you; now tell me how you have been getting on.'

'I hardly know, but I think we are doing very well indeed. You know, of course, that your cousin is going to America to report upon the mine. As I have stated nothing but what is perfectly true about the property, there can be no question as to what that report will be, so it seems to me everything is going on nicely.'

'Why do not you go to America?'

'Ah, well, I am an interested party, and those who are thinking of going in with us have my report already. It is necessary to corroborate that. When it is corroborated, I expect we shall have no trouble in forming the company.'

'And was William chosen by those men to go to Canada?'

'He was not exactly chosen; he volunteered. Mr. Melville here was the one who was chosen.'

'And why Mr. Melville more than you, for instance?'

'Well, as I said, I am out of the question because I am an interested party. Melville is a man connected with china works, and as such, in a measure, an expert.'

'Is Mr. Melville a friend of yours?'

'No, he is not. I never saw him until he came to the meeting.'

'Do you know,' she said, lowering her voice and bending towards him,

291

'that I do not like Mr. Melville's face?' Kenyon glanced at Melville, who was at the other side of the room, and Edith went on: 'You must not look at people when I mention them in that way, or they will know we are talking about them. I do not like his face. He is too handsome a man, and I don't like handsome men.'

'Don't you, really,' said John; 'then, you ought to——'

Edith laughed softly, a low, musical laugh that was not heard above the piano din, and was intended for John alone, and to his ears it was the sweetest music he had ever heard.

'I know what you were going to say,' she said; 'you were going to say that in that case I ought to like you. Well, I do; that is why I am taking such an interest in your mine, and in your friend Mr. Wentworth. And so my cousin volunteered to go to Canada. Now, I think you ought to go yourself.'

'Why?' said Kenyon, startled that she should have touched the point that had been discussed between Wentworth and himself.

'I can only give you a woman's reason—"because I do." It seems to me you ought to be there to know what they report at the time they do report. Perhaps they won't understand the mine without your explanation, and then you see an adverse report might come back in perfect good faith. I think you ought to go to America, Mr. Kenyon.'

'That is just what George Wentworth says.'

'Does he? I always thought he was a very sensible young man, and now I am sure of it. Well, I must not stay here gossiping with you on business. I see the professor is going to finish, and so I shall have to look after my other guests. If I don't see you again this evening, or have no opportunity of speaking with you, think over what I have said.'

And then, with the most charming hypocrisy, the young woman thanked the professor for the music to which she had not listened in the least.

'Well, how did you enjoy yourself?' said Wentworth when they had got outside again.

It was a clear, starlight night, and they had resolved to walk home together.

'I enjoyed myself very well indeed,' answered Kenyon; 'much better than I expected. It was a little awkward at first, but I got over that.'

'I noticed you did—with help.'

'Yes, "with help."'

'If you are inclined to rave, John, now that we are under the stars, remember I am a close confidant, and a sympathetic listener. I should like to hear you rave, just to learn how an exasperatingly sensible man acts under the circumstances.'

'I shall not rave about anything, George, but I will tell you something. I am going to Canada.'

'Ah, did she speak about that?'

'She did.'

'And of course her advice at once decides the matter, after my most cogent arguments have failed?'

'Don't be offended, George, but—it does.'

CHAPTER XXXI.

'What name, please?'

'Tell Mr. Wentworth a lady wishes to see him.'

The boy departed rather dubiously, for he knew this message was decidedly irregular in a business office. People should give their names.

'A lady to see you, sir,' he said to Wentworth; and, then, just as the boy had expected, his employer wanted to know the lady's name.

Ladies are not frequent visitors at the office of an accountant in the City, so Wentworth touched his collar and tie to make sure they were in their correct position, and, wondering who the lady was, asked the boy to show her in.

'How do you do, Mr. Wentworth?' she said brightly, advancing towards his table and holding out her hand.

Wentworth caught his breath, and took her extended hand somewhat limply, then he pulled himself together; saying:

'This is an unexpected pleasure, Miss Brewster.'

Jennie blushed very prettily, and laughed a laugh that Wentworth thought was like a little ripple of music from a mellow flute.

'It may be unexpected,' she said, 'but you don't look a bit like a man suffering from an overdose of pure joy. You didn't expect to see me, did you?'

'I did not; but now that you are here, may I ask in what way I can serve you?'

'Well, in the first place, you may ask me to take a chair, and in the second place you may sit down yourself; for I've come to have a long talk with you.'

The prospect did not seem to be so alluring to Wentworth as one might have expected, when the announcement was made by a girl so pretty, and dressed in such exquisite taste; but the young man promptly offered her a chair, and then sat down, with the table between them. She placed her parasol and a few things she had been carrying on the table, arranging them with some care; then, having given him time to recover from his surprise, she flashed a look at him that sent a thrill to the finger-tips of the young man. Yet a danger understood is a danger half overcome; and Wentworth, unconsciously drawing a deep breath, nerved himself against any recurrence of a feeling he had been trying with but indifferent success to forget, saying grimly, but only half convincingly, to himself:

'You are not going to fool me a second time, my girl, lovely as you are.'

A glimmer of a smile hovered about the red lips of the girl, a smile hardly perceptible, but giving an effect to her clear complexion as if a sunbeam had crept into the room, and its reflection had lit up her face.

'I have come to apologize, Mr. Wentworth,' she said at last. 'I find it a very difficult thing to do, and, as I don't quite know how to begin, I plunge right into it.'

'You don't need to apologize to me for anything, Miss Brewster,' replied Wentworth, rather stiffly.

'Oh yes, I do. Don't make it harder than it is by being too frigidly polite about it, but say you accept the apology, and that you're sorry—no, I don't mean that—I should say that you're sure I'm sorry, and that you know I won't do it again.'

Wentworth laughed, and Miss Brewster joined him.

'There,' she said, 'that's ever so much better. I suppose you've been thinking hard things of me ever since we last met.'

'I've tried to,' replied Wentworth.

'Now, that's what I call honest; besides, I like the implied compliment. I think it's very neat indeed. I'm really very, very sorry that I—that things happened as they did. I wouldn't have blamed you if you had used exceedingly strong language about it at the time.'

'I must confess that I did.'

'Ah!' said Jennie, with a sigh, 'you men have so many comforts denied to us women. But I came here for another purpose; if I had merely wanted to apologize, I think I would have written. I want some information which you can give me, if you like.'

The young woman rested her elbows on the table, with her chin in her hands, gazing across at him earnestly and innocently. Poor George felt that it would be almost impossible to refuse anything to those large beseeching eyes.

'I want you to tell me about your mine.'

All the geniality that had gradually come into Wentworth's face and manner vanished instantly.

'So this is the old business over again,' he said.

'How can you say that!' cried Jennie reproachfully. 'I am asking for my own satisfaction entirely, and not for my paper. Besides, I tell you frankly what I want to know, and don't try to get it by indirect means—by false pretences, as you once said.'

'How can you expect me to give you information that does not belong to me alone? I have no right to speak of a business which concerns others without their permission.'

'Ah, then, there are at least two more concerned in the mine,' said Jennie gleefully. 'Kenyon is one, I know; who is the other?'

'Miss Brewster, I will tell you nothing.'

'But you have told me something already. Please go on and talk, Mr. Wentworth—about anything you like—and I shall soon find out all I want to know about the mine.'

She paused, but Wentworth remained silent, which, indeed, the bewildered young man realized was the only safe thing to do.

'They speak of the talkativeness of women,' Miss Brewster went on, as if soliloquizing, 'but it is nothing to that of the men. Once set a man talking, and you learn everything he knows—besides ever so much more that he doesn't.'

Miss Brewster had abandoned her very taking attitude, with its suggestion of confidential relations, and had removed her elbows from the table, sitting now back in her chair, gazing dreamily at the dingy window which let the light in from the dingy court. She seemed to have forgotten that Wentworth was there, and said, more to herself than to him:

'I wonder if Kenyon would tell me about the mine.'

'You might ask him.'

'No; it wouldn't do any good,' she continued, gently shaking her head. 'He's one of your silent men, and there are so few of them in this world. Perhaps I had better go to William Longworth himself; he's not suspicious of me.'

As she said this, she threw a quick glance at Wentworth, and the unfortunate young man's face at once told her that she had hit the mark. She bent her head over the table, and laughed with such evident enjoyment that Wentworth, in spite of his helpless anger, smiled grimly.

Jennie raised her head, but the sight of his perplexed countenance was too much for her, and it was some time before her merriment allowed her to speak. At last she said:

'Wouldn't you like to take me by the shoulders and put me out of the room, Mr. Wentworth?'

'I'd like to take you by the shoulders and shake you.'

'Ah! that would be taking a liberty, and could not be permitted. We must leave punishment to the law, you know, although I do think a man should be allowed to turn an objectionable visitor into the street.'

'Miss Brewster,' cried the young man earnestly, leaning over the table

297

towards her, 'why don't you abandon your horrible inquisitorial profession, and put your undoubted talents to some other use?'

'What, for instance?'

'Oh, anything.'

Jennie rested her fair cheek against her open palm again, and looked at the dingy window. There was a long silence between them—Wentworth absorbed in watching her clear-cut profile and her white throat, his breath quickening as he feasted his eyes on her beauty.

'I have always got angry,' she said at last, in a low voice with the quiver of a suppressed sigh in it, 'when other people have said that to me—I wonder why it is I merely feel hurt and sad when you say it? It is so easy to say, "Oh, anything"—so easy, so easy. You are a man, with the strength and determination of a man, yet you have met with disappointments and obstacles that have required all your courage to overcome. Every man has, and with most men it is a fight until the head is gray, and the brain weary with the ceaseless struggle. The world is utterly merciless; it will trample you down relentlessly if it can, and if your vigilance relaxes for a moment, it will steal your crust and leave you to starve. Every time I think of this incessant sullen contest, with no quarter given or taken, I shudder, and pray that I may die before I am at the mercy of the pitiless world. When I came to London, I saw, for the first time in my life, that hopeless, melancholy promenade of the sandwich-men; human wreckage drifting along the edge of the street, as if cast there by the rushing tide sweeping past them. They—they seemed to me like a tottering procession of the dead; and on their backs was the announcement of a play that was making all London roar with laughter. The awful comedy and tragedy of it! Well, I simply couldn't stand it. I had to run up a side-street and cry like the little fool I was, right in broad daylight.'

Jennie paused and tried to laugh, but the effort ended in a sound suspiciously like a sob. She dashed her hand with quick impatience across her eyes, from which Wentworth had never taken his own, seeing them become dim, as if the light from the window proved too strong for them, and finally fill as she ceased to speak. Searching ineffectually about her dress for a handkerchief, which lay on the table beside her parasol unnoticed by either, Jennie went on with some difficulty:

'Well, these poor forlorn creatures were once men—men who have gone down—and if the world is so hard on a man with all his strength and resourcefulness, think—think what it is for a woman thrown into this inhuman turmoil—a woman without friends—without money—flung among these relentless wolves—to live if she can—or—to die—if she can.'

The girl's voice broke, and she buried her face in her arms, which rested on the table.

Wentworth sprang to his feet and came round to where she sat.

'Jennie,' he said, putting his hand on her shoulder. The girl, without looking up, shook off the hand that touched her.

'Go back to your place,' she cried, in a smothered voice. 'Leave me alone.'

'Jennie,' persisted Wentworth.

The young woman rose from her chair and faced him, stepping back a pace.

'Don't you hear what I say? Go back and sit down. I came here to talk business, not to make a fool of myself. It's all your fault, and I hate you for it—you and your silly questions.'

But the young man stood where he was, in spite of the dangerous sparkle that shone in his visitor's wet eyes. A frown gathered on his brow.

'Jennie,' he said slowly, 'are you playing with me again?'

The swift anger that blazed up in her face, reddening her cheeks, dried the tears.

'How dare you say such a thing to me!' she cried hotly. 'Do you flatter yourself that, because I came here to talk business, I have also some personal interest in you? Surely even your self-conceit doesn't run so far as that!'

Wentworth stood silent, and Miss Brewster picked up her parasol, scattering, in her haste, the other articles on the floor. If she expected Wentworth to put them on the table again, she was disappointed, for, although his eyes were upon her, his thoughts were far away upon the Atlantic Ocean.

'I shall not stay here to be insulted,' she cried resentfully, bringing Wentworth's thoughts back with a rush to London again. 'It is intolerable that you should use such an expression to me. Playing with you indeed!'

'I had no intention of insulting you, Miss Brewster.'

'What is it but an insult to use such a phrase? It implies that I either care for you, or——'

'And do you?'

'Do I what?'

'Do you care for me?'

Jennie shook out the lace fringes of her parasol; and smoothed them with some precision. Her eyes were bent on what she was doing; consequently, they did not meet those of her questioner.

'I care for you as a friend, of course,' she said at last, still giving much attention to the parasol. 'If I had not looked on you as a friend, I would not have come here to consult with you, would I?'

'No, I suppose not. Well, I am sorry I used the words that displeased you, and now, if you will permit it, we will go on with the consultation.'

'It wasn't a pretty thing to say.'

'I'm afraid I'm not good at saying pretty things.'

'You used to be.'

The parasol being arranged to her liking, she glanced up at him.

'Still, you said you were sorry, and that's all a man can say—or a woman either, for that's what I said myself when I came in. Now, if you will pick up

300

those things from the floor—thanks—we will talk about the mine.'

Wentworth seated himself again, and said;

'Well, what is it you wish to know about the mine?'

'Nothing at all.'

'But you said you wanted information.'

'What a funny reason to give! And how a man misses all the fine points of a conversation! No; just because I asked for information, you might have known that was not what I really wanted.'

'I'm afraid I'm very stupid. I hate to ask boldly what you did want, but I would like to know.'

'I wanted a vote of confidence. I told you I was sorry because of a certain episode. I wished to see if you trusted me, and I found you didn't. There!'

'I think that was hardly a fair test. You see, the facts did not belong to me alone.'

Miss Brewster sighed, and slowly shook her head.

'That wouldn't have made the least difference if you had really trusted me.'

'Oh, I say! You couldn't expect a man to——'

'Yes I could.'

'What, merely a friend?'

Miss Brewster nodded.

'Well, all I can say,' remarked Wentworth, with a laugh, 'is that friendship has made greater strides in the States than it has in this country.'

Before Jennie could reply, the useful boy knocked at the door and brought in a tea-tray, which he placed before his master; then silently departed, closing the door noiselessly.

'May I offer you a cup of tea?'

'Please. What a curious custom this drinking of tea is in business offices! I think I shall write an article on "A Nation of Tea-tipplers." If I were an enemy of England, instead of being its greatest friend, I would descend with my army on this country between the hours of four and five in the afternoon, and so take the population unawares while it was drinking tea. What would you do if the enemy came down on you during such a sacred national ceremony?'

'I would offer her a cup of tea,' replied Wentworth, suiting the action to the phrase.

'Mr. Wentworth,' said the girl archly, 'you're improving. That remark was distinctly good. Still, you must remember that I come as a friend, not as an enemy. Did you ever read the "Babes in the Wood"? It is a most instructive, but pathetic, work of fiction. You remember the wicked uncle, surely? Well, you and Mr. Kenyon remind me of the "Babes," poor innocent little things! and London—this part of it—is the dark and pathless forest. I am the bird hovering about you, waiting to cover you with leaves. The leaves, to do any good, ought to be cheques fluttering down on you, but, alas! I haven't any. If negotiable cheques only grew on trees, life would not be so difficult.'

Miss Brewster sipped her tea pensively, and Wentworth listened contentedly to the musical murmur of her voice. Such an entrancing effect had it on him that he paid less heed to what she said than a man ought when a lady is speaking. The tea-drinking had added a touch of domesticity to the tête-a-tête which rather went to the head of the young man. He clinched and unclinched his hand out of sight under the table, and felt the moisture on his palm. He hoped he would be able to retain control over himself, but the difficulty of his task almost overcame him when she now and then appealed to him with glance or gesture, and he felt as if he must cry out, 'My girl, my girl, don't do that, if you expect me to stay where I am.'

'I see you are not paying the slightest attention to what I am saying,' she said, pushing the cup from her. She rested her arms on the table, leaning slightly forward, and turning her face full upon him: 'I can tell by your eyes that you are thinking of something else.'

302

'I assure you,' said George, drawing a deep breath, 'I am listening with intense interest.'

'Well, that's right, for what I am going to say is important. Now, to wake you up, I will first tell you all about your mine; you will understand thereafter that I did not need to ask anyone for information regarding it.'

Here, to Wentworth's astonishment, she gave a rapid and accurate sketch of the negotiations and arrangements between the three partners, and the present position of affairs.

'How do you know all this?' he asked.

'Never mind that; and you mustn't ask how I know what I am now going to tell you, but you must believe it implicitly, and act upon it promptly. Longworth is fooling both you and Kenyon. He is marking time, so that your option will run out; then he will pay cash for the mine at the original price, and you and Kenyon will be left to pay two-thirds of the debt incurred. Where is Kenyon?'

'He has gone to America.'

'That's good. Cable him to get the option renewed. You can then try to form the company yourselves in London. If he can't obtain a renewal, you have very little time to get the cash together, and if you are not able to do that, then you lose everything. This is what I came to tell you, although I have been a long time about it. Now I must go.'

She rose, gathered her belongings from the table, and stood with the parasol pressed against her. Wentworth came around to where she was standing, his face paler than usual, probably because of the news he had heard. One hand was grasped tightly around one wrist in front of him. He felt that he should thank her for what she had done, but his lips were dry, and, somehow, the proper words were not at his command.

She, holding her fragile lace-fringed parasol against her with one arm, was adjusting her long neatly fitting glove, which she had removed before tea. A button, one of many, was difficult to fasten, and as she endeavoured to put it in its place, her sleeve fell away, showing a round white arm above the glove.

'You see,' she said, a little breathlessly, her eyes upon her glove, 'it is a very serious situation, and time is of immense importance.'

'I realize that.'

'It would be such a pity to lose everything now, when you have had so much trouble and worry.'

'It would.'

'And I think that whatever is done should be done quickly. You should act at once and with energy.'

'I am convinced that is so.'

'Of course it is. You are of too trusting a nature; you should be more suspicious, then you wouldn't be tricked as you have been.'

'No. The trouble is I have been too sceptical, but that is past. I won't be again.'

'What are you talking about?' she said, looking quickly up at him. 'Don't you know you'll lose the mine if——'

'Hang the mine!' he cried, flinging his wrist free, and clasping her to him before she could step back or move from her place. 'There is something more important than mines or money.'

The parasol broke with a sharp snap, and the girl murmured 'Oh!' but the murmur was faint.

'Never mind the parasol,' he said, pulling it from between them and tossing it aside; 'I'll get you another.'

'Reckless man!' she gasped; 'you little know how much it cost, and I think, you know, I ought to have been consulted—in an—in an—affair of this kind—George.'

'There was no time. I acted upon your own advice—promptly. You are

304

not angry, Jennie, my dear girl, are you?'

'I suppose I'm not, though I think I ought to be; especially as I know only too well that I held my heart in my hand the whole time, almost offering it to you. I hope you won't treat it as you have treated the sunshade.'

He kissed her for answer.

'You see,' she said, putting his necktie straight, 'I liked you from the very first, far more than I knew at the time. If you—I'm not trying to justify myself, you know—but if you had, well, just coaxed me a little yourself, I would never have sent that cable message. You seemed to give up everything, and you sent Kenyon to me, and that made me angry. I expected you to come back to me, but you never came.'

'I was a stupid fool. I always am when I get a fair chance.'

'Oh no, you're not, but you do need someone to take care of you.'

She suddenly held him at arm's length from her.

'You don't imagine for a moment, George Wentworth, that I came here to-day for—for this.'

'Certainly not!' cried the honest young man, with much indignant fervour, drawing her again towards him.

'Then it's all right. I couldn't bear to have you think such a thing, especially—well, I'll tell you why some day. But I do wish you had a title. Do they ever ennoble accountants in this country, George?'

'No; they knight only rich fools.'

'Oh, I'm so glad of that; for you'll get rich on the mine, and I'll be Lady Wentworth yet.'

Then she drew his head down until her laughing lips touched his.

CHAPTER XXXII.

Although the steamship that took Kenyon to America was one of the speediest in the Atlantic service, yet the voyage was inexpressibly dreary to him. He spent most of his time walking up and down the deck, thinking about the other voyage of a few weeks before. The one consolation of his present trip was its quickness.

When he arrived at his hotel in New York, he asked if there was any message there for him, and the clerk handed him an envelope, which he tore open. It was a cable despatch from Wentworth, with the words:

'Longworth at Windsor. Proceed to Ottawa immediately. Get option renewed. Longworth duping us.'

John knitted his brows and wondered where Windsor was. The clerk, seeing his perplexity, asked if he could be of any assistance.

'I have received this cablegram, but don't quite understand it. Where is Windsor?'

'Oh, that means the Windsor Hotel. Just up the street.'

Kenyon registered, told the clerk to assign him a room, and send his baggage up to it when it came. Then he walked out from the hotel and sought the Windsor.

He found that colossal hostelry, and was just inquiring of the clerk whether a Mr. Longworth was staying there, when that gentleman appeared at the desk, took some letters and his key.

Kenyon tapped him on the shoulder.

Young Longworth turned round with more alacrity than he usually displayed, and gave a long whistle of surprise when he saw who it was.

'In the name of all the gods,' he cried, 'what are you doing here?' Then, before Kenyon could reply, he said: 'Come up to my room.'

They went to the elevator, rose a few stories, and passed down an apparently endless hall, carpeted with some noiseless stuff that gave no echo of the footfall. Longworth put the key into his door and opened it. They entered a large and pleasant room.

'Well,' he said, 'this is a surprise. What is the reason of your being here? Anything wrong in London?'

'Nothing wrong, so far as I am aware. We received no cablegram from you, and thought there might be some hitch in the business; therefore I came.'

'Ah, I see. I cabled over to your address, and said I was staying at the Windsor for a few days. I sent a cablegram almost as long as a letter, but it didn't appear to do any good.'

'No, I did not receive it.'

'And what did you expect was wrong over here?'

'That I did not know. I knew you had time to get to Ottawa and see the mine in twelve days from London. Not hearing from you in that time, and knowing the option was running out, both Wentworth and I became anxious, and so I came over.'

'Exactly. Well, I'm afraid you've had your trip for nothing.'

'What do you mean? Is not the mine all I said it was?'

'Oh, the mine is all right; all I meant was, there was really no necessity for your coming.'

'But, you know, the option ends in a very short time.'

'Well, the option, like the mine, is all right. I think you might quite safely have left it in my hands.'

It must be admitted that John Kenyon began to feel he had acted with unreasonable rashness in taking his long voyage.

'Is Mr. Melville here with you?'

'Melville has returned home. He had not time to stay longer. All he wanted was to satisfy himself about the mine. He was satisfied, and he has gone home. If you were in London now, you would be able to see him.'

'Did you meet Mr. Von Brent?'

'Yes, he took us to the mine.'

'And did you say anything about the option to him?'

'Well, we had some conversation about it. There will be no trouble about the option. What Von Brent wants is to sell his mine, that is all.' There was a few moments' silence, then Longworth said: 'When are you going back?'

'I do not know. I think I ought to see Von Brent. I am not at all easy about leaving matters as they are. I think I ought to get a renewal of the option. It is not wise to risk things as we are doing. Von Brent might at any time get an offer for his mine, just as we are forming our company, and, of course, if the option had not been renewed, he would sell to the first man who put down the money. As you say, all he wants is to sell his mine.'

Longworth was busy opening his letters, and apparently paying very little attention to what Kenyon said. At last, however, he spoke:

'If I were you—if you care to take my advice—I would go straight back to England. You will do no good here. I merely say this to save you any further trouble, time, and expense.'

'Don't you think it would be as well to get a renewal of the option?'

'Oh, certainly; but, as I told you before, it was not at all necessary for you to come over. I may say, furthermore, that Von Brent will not renew the option without a handsome sum down, to be forfeited if the company is not formed. Have you the money to pay him?'

'No, I have not.'

'Very well, then, why waste time and money going to Ottawa?' Young Mr. Longworth arched his eye-brows and gazed at John through his eyeglass. 'I will let you have my third of the money, if that will do any good.'

'How much money does Von Brent want?'

'How should I know? To tell you the truth, Mr. Kenyon—and truth never hurts, or oughtn't to—I don't at all like this visit to America. You and Mr. Wentworth have been good enough to be suspicious about me from the very first. You have not taken any pains to conceal it, either of you. Your appearance in America at this particular juncture is nothing more nor less than an insult to me. I intend to receive it as such.'

'I have no intention of insulting you,' said Kenyon, 'if you are dealing fairly with me.'

'There it is again. That remark is an insult. Everything you say is a reflection upon me. I wish to have nothing more to say to you. I give you my advice that it is better for you, and cheaper, to go back to London. You need not act on it unless you like. I have nothing further to say to you and so this interview may be considered closed.'

'And how about the mine?'

'I imagine the mine will take care of itself.'

'Do you think this is courteous treatment of a business partner?'

'My dear sir, I do not take my lessons in courtesy from you. Whether you are pleased or displeased with my treatment of you is a matter of supreme indifference to me. I am tired of living in an atmosphere of suspicion, and I have done with it—that is all. You think some game is being played on you—both you and Mr. Wentworth think that—and yet you haven't the "cuteness," as they call it here, or sharpness, to find it out. Now, a man who has suspicions he cannot prove to be well founded should keep those suspicions to himself until he can prove them. That is my advice to you. I wish you a good-day.'

John Kenyon walked back to his hotel with more misgivings than ever. He wrote a letter to Wentworth detailing the conversation, telling him Melville had sailed for home, and advising him to see that gentleman when he arrived. He stayed in New York that night, and took the morning train to Montreal. In due time he arrived at Ottawa, and called on Von Brent. He found that gentleman in his chambers, looking as if he had never left the room since the option was signed. Von Brent at first did not recognise his visitor, but after gazing a moment at him he sprang from his chair and held out his hand.

'I really did not know you,' he said; 'you have changed a great deal since I saw you last. You look haggard, and not at all well. What is the matter with you?'

'I do not think anything is the matter. I am in very good health, thank you; I have had a few business worries, that is all.'

'Ah, yes,' said Von Brent; 'I am very sorry indeed you failed to form your company.'

'Failed!' echoed Kenyon.

'Yes; you haven't succeeded, have you?'

'Well, I don't know about that; we are in a fair way to succeed. You met Longworth and Melville, who came out to see the mine? I saw Longworth in New York, and he told me you had taken them out there.'

'Are they interested with you in the mine?'

'Certainly; they are helping me to form the company.'

Von Brent seemed amazed.

'I did not understand that at all. In fact, I understood the exact opposite. I thought you had attempted to form a company, and failed. They showed me an attack in one of the financial papers upon you, and said that killed your chances of forming a company in London. They were here, apparently, on their own business.'

'And what was their business?'

'To buy the mine.'

'Have they bought it?'

'Practically, yes. Of course, while your option holds good I cannot sell it, but that, as you know, expires in a very few days.'

310

Kenyon, finding his worst suspicions confirmed, seemed speechless with amazement, and in his agony mopped from his brow the drops collected there.

'You appear to be astonished at this,' said Von Brent.

'I am very much astonished.'

'Well, you cannot blame me. I have acted perfectly square in the matter. I had no idea Longworth, and the gentleman who was with him, had any connection with you whatever. Their attention had been drawn to the mine, they said, by that article. They had investigated it and appeared to be satisfied there was something in it—in the mine, I mean, not in the article. They said they had attended a meeting which you had called, but it was quite evident you were not going to be able to form the company. So they came here and made me a cash offer for the mine. They have deposited twenty thousand pounds at the bank here, and on the day your option closes they will give me a cheque for the amount.'

'It serves me right,' said Kenyon. 'I have been cheated and duped. I had grave suspicions of it all along, but I did not act upon them. I have been too timorous and cowardly. This man Longworth has made a pretence of helping me to form a company. Everything he has done has been to delay me. He came out here, apparently, in the interests of the company I was forming, and now he has got the option for himself.'

'Yes, he has,' said Von Brent. 'I may say I am very sorry indeed for the turn affairs have taken. Of course, as I have told you, I had no idea how the land lay. You see, you had placed no deposit with me, and I had to look after my own interests. However, the option is open for a few days more, and I will not turn the mine over to them till the last minute of the time has expired. Isn't there any chance of your getting the money before then?'

'Not the slightest.'

'Well, you see, in that case I cannot help myself. I am bound by a legal document to turn the mine over to them on receipt of the twenty thousand pounds the moment your option is ended. Everything is done legally, and I am perfectly helpless in the matter.'

'Yes, I see that,' said John. 'Good-bye.'

He went to the telegraph-office and sent a cablegram.

Wentworth received the message in London the next morning. It read:

'We are cheated. Longworth has the option on the mine in his own name.'

CHAPTER XXXIII.

When George Wentworth received this message, he read it several times over before its full meaning dawned upon him. Then he paced up and down his room, and gave way to his feelings. His best friends, who had been privileged to hear George's vocabulary when he was rather angry, admitted that the young man had a fluency of expression which was very more terse than proper. When the real significance of the despatch became apparent to him, George outdid himself in this particular line. Then he realized that, however consolatory such language is to a very angry man, it does little good in any practical way. He paced silently up and down the room, wondering what he could do, and the more he wondered the less light he saw through the fog. He put on his hat and went into the other room.

'Henry,' he said to his partner, 'do you know anybody who would lend me twenty thousand pounds?'

Henry laughed. The idea of anybody lending that sum of money, except on the very best security, was in itself extremely comic.

'Do you want it to-day?' he said.

'Yes, I want it to-day.'

'Well, I don't know any better plan than to go out into the street and ask every man you meet if he has that sum about him. You are certain to encounter men who have very much more than twenty thousand pounds, and perhaps one of them, struck by your very sane appearance at the moment, might hand over the sum to you. I think, however, George, that you would be more successful if you met the capitalist in a secluded lane some dark night, and had a good reliable club in your hand.'

'You are right,' said George. 'Of course, there is just as much possibility of my reaching the moon as getting that sum of money on short notice.'

'Yes, or on long notice either, I imagine. I know plenty of men who have the money, but I wouldn't undertake to ask them for it, and I don't believe you would. Still there is nothing like trying. He who tries may succeed, but no one can succeed who doesn't try. Why not go to old Longworth? He could let you have the money in a moment if he wanted to do so. He knows you. What's your security? What are you going to do with it—that eternal mine of yours?'

'Yes, that "eternal mine"; I want it to be mine. That is why I need the twenty thousand pounds.'

'Well, George, I don't see much hope for you. You never spoke to old Longworth about it, did you? He wasn't one of the men you intended to get into this company?'

'No, he was not. I wish he had been. He would have treated us better than his rascally nephew has done.'

'Ah, that immaculate young man has been playing you tricks, has he?'

'He has played me one trick, which is enough.'

'Well, why don't you go and see the old man, and lay the case before him? He treats that nephew as if he were his son. Now, a man will do a great deal for his son, and perhaps old Longworth might do something for his nephew.'

'Yes; but I should have to explain to him that his nephew is a scoundrel.'

'Very well; that is just the kind of explanation to bring the twenty thousand pounds. If his nephew really is a scoundrel, and you can prove it, you could not want a better lever than that on the old man's money-bags.'

'By Jove!' said Wentworth, 'I believe I shall try it. I want to let him know, anyhow, what sort of man his nephew is. I'll go and see him.'

'I would,' said the other, turning to his work.

And so George Wentworth, putting the cablegram in his pocket, went to see old Mr. Longworth in a frame of mind in which no man should see his fellow-man. He did not wait to be announced, but walked, to the astonishment of the clerk, straight through into Mr. Longworth's room. He found the old man seated at his desk.

'Good-day, Mr. Wentworth,' said the financier cordially.

'Good-day,' replied George curtly. 'I have come to read a cable despatch to you, or to let you read it.'

He threw the paper down before the old gentleman, who adjusted his spectacles and read it. Then he looked up inquiringly at Wentworth.

'You don't understand it, do you?' said the latter.

'I confess I do not. The Longworth in this telegram does not refer to me, does it?'

'No, it does not refer to you, but it refers to one of your house. Your nephew, William Longworth, is a scoundrel!'

'Ah!' said the old man, placing the despatch on the desk again, and removing his glasses, 'have you come to tell me that?'

'Yes, I have. Did you know it before?'

'No, I did not,' answered the old gentleman, his colour rising; 'and I do not know it now. I know you say so, and I think very likely you will be glad to take back what you have said. I will at least give you the opportunity.'

'So far from taking it back, Mr. Longworth, I shall prove it. Your nephew formed a partnership with my friend Kenyon and myself to float on the London market a certain Canadian mine.'

'My dear sir,' broke in the old gentleman, 'I have no desire to hear of my nephew's private speculations; I have nothing to do with them. I have nothing to do with your mine. The matter is of no interest whatever to me, and I must decline to hear anything about it. You are, also, if you will excuse my saying so, not in a fit state of temper to talk to any gentleman. If you like to come back here when you are calmer, I shall be very pleased to listen to what you have to say.'

'I shall never be calmer on this subject. I have told you that your nephew is a scoundrel. You are pleased to deny the accusation.'

'I do not deny it; I merely said I did not know it was the case, and I do not believe it, that is all.'

'Very well; the moment I begin to show you proof that things are as I say——'

'My dear sir,' cried the elder man, with some heat, 'you are not showing proof. You are merely making assertions, and assertions about a man who is absent—who is not here to defend himself. If you have anything to say against William Longworth, come and say it when he is here, and he shall answer for himself. It is cowardly of you, and ungenerous to me, to make a number of accusations which I am in no wise able to refute.'

'Will you listen to what I have to say?'

'No; I will not.'

'Then, by God, you shall!' and with that Wentworth strode to the door and turned the key, while the old man rose from his seat and faced him.

'Do you mean to threaten me, sir, in my own office?'

'I mean to say, Mr. Longworth, that I have made a statement which I am going to prove to you. I mean that you shall listen to me, and listen to me now!'

'And I say, if you have anything to charge against my nephew, come and say it when he is here.'

'When he is here, Mr. Longworth, it will be too late to say it; at present you can repair the injury he has done. When he returns to England you cannot do so, no matter how much you might wish to make the attempt.'

The old man stood irresolute for a moment, then he sat down in his chair again.

'Very well,' he said, with a sigh; 'I am not so combative as I once was. Go on with your story.'

316

'My story is very short,' said Wentworth; 'it simply amounts to this: You know your nephew formed a partnership with us in relation to the Canadian mine?'

'I know nothing about it, I tell you,' answered Mr. Longworth.

'Very well, you know it now.'

'I know you say so.'

'Do you doubt my word?'

'I shall tell you more definitely when I hear what you have to say. Go on.'

'Well, your nephew, pretending to aid us in forming this company, did everything to retard our progress. He engaged offices that took a long time to fit up, and which we had at last to take in hand ourselves. Then he left for a week, leaving us no address, and refusing to answer the letters I sent to his office for him. On one pretext or another, the forming of the company was delayed; until at length, when the option by which Mr. Kenyon held the mine had less than a month to run, your nephew went to America in company with Mr. Melville, ostensibly to see and report upon the property. After waiting a certain length of time and hearing nothing from him (he had promised to cable us), Kenyon went to America to get a renewal of the option. This cablegram explains his success. He finds, on going there, that your nephew has secured the option of the mine in his own name, and, as Kenyon says, we are cheated. Now have you any doubt whether your nephew is a scoundrel or not?'

Mr. Longworth mused for a few moments on what the young man had told him.

'If what you say is exactly true, there is no doubt William has been guilty of a piece of very sharp practice.'

'Sharp practice!' cried the other. 'You might as well call robbery sharp practice!'

'My dear sir, I have listened to you; now I ask you to listen to me. If, as

I say, what you have stated is true, my nephew has done something which I think an honourable man would not do; but as to that I cannot judge until I hear his side of the story. It may put a different complexion on the matter, and I have no doubt it will; but even granting your version is true in every particular, what have I to do with it? I am not responsible for my nephew's actions. He has entered into a business connection, it seems, with two young men, and has outwitted them. That is probably what the world would say about it. Perhaps, as you say, he has been guilty of something worse, and has cheated his partners. But even admitting everything to be true, I do not see how I am responsible in any way.'

'Legally, you are not; morally, I think you are.'

'Why?'

'If he were your son——'

'But he is not my son; he is my nephew.'

'If your son had committed a theft, would you not do everything in your power to counteract the evil he had done?'

'I might, and I might not. Some fathers pay their sons' debts, others do not. I cannot say what action I should take in a purely imaginary case.'

'Very well; all I have to say is, our option runs out in two or three days. Twenty thousand pounds will secure the mine for us. I want that twenty thousand pounds before the option ceases.'

'And do you expect me to pay you twenty thousand pounds for this?'

'Yes, I do.'

Old Mr. Longworth leaned back in his office chair, and looked at the young man in amazement.

'To think that you, a man of the City, should come to me, another man of the City, with such an absurd idea in your head, is simply grotesque.'

'Then the name of the Longworths is nothing to you—the good name,

I mean?'

'The good name of the Longworths, my dear sir, is everything to me; but I fancy it will be able to take care of itself without any assistance from you.'

There was silence for a few moments. Then Wentworth said, in a voice of suppressed anguish:

'I thought, Mr. Longworth, one of your family was a scoundrel; I now wish to say I believe the epithet covers uncle as well as nephew. You have had a chance to repair the mischief a member of your family has done. You have answered me with contempt. You have not shown the slightest indication of wishing to make amends.'

He unlocked the door.

'Come, now,' said old Mr. Longworth, rising, 'that will do, that will do, Mr. Wentworth.' Then he pressed an electric bell, and, when the clerk appeared, he said: 'Show this gentleman the door, please, and if ever he calls here again, do not admit him.'

And so George Wentworth, clenching his hands with rage, was shown to the door. He had the rest of the day to ponder on the fact that an angry man seldom accomplishes his purpose.

CHAPTER XXXIV.

The stormy interview with Wentworth disturbed the usual serenity of Mr. Longworth's temper. He went home earlier than was customary with him that night, and the more he thought over the attack, the more unjustifiable it seemed. He wondered what his nephew had really done, and tried to remember what Wentworth had charged against him. He could not recollect, the angrier portions of the interview having, as it were, blotted the charges from his mind. There remained, however, a very bitter resentment against Wentworth. Mr. Longworth searched his conscience to see if he could be in the least to blame, but he found nothing in the recollections of his dealings with the young men to justify him in feeling at all responsible for the disaster that had overtaken them. He read his favourite evening paper with less than his usual interest, for every now and then the episode in his office would occur to him. Finally he said sharply:

'Edith!'

'Yes, father,' answered his daughter.

'You remember a person named Wentworth, whom you had here the evening William went away?'

'Yes, father.'

'Very well. Never invite him to this house again.'

'What has he been doing?' asked the young woman in rather a tremulous voice.

'I desire you also never to ask anyone connected with him—that man Kenyon, for instance,' continued her father, ignoring her question.

'I thought,' she answered, 'that Mr. Kenyon was not in this country at present.'

'He is not, but he will be back again, I suppose. At any rate, I wish to have nothing more to do with those people. You understand that?'

'Yes, father.'

Mr. Longworth went on with his reading. Edith saw her father was greatly disturbed, and eagerly desired to know the reason, but knew enough of human nature to understand that in a short time he would relieve her anxiety. He again appeared to be trying to fix his attention on the paper. At length he threw it down, and turned towards her.

'That man, Wentworth,' he said bitterly, 'behaved to-day in a most unjustifiable manner to me in my own office. It seems that William and he and Kenyon embarked in some mine project. I knew nothing of their doings, and was not even consulted with regard to them. Now it appears William has gone to America and done something Wentworth considers wrong. Wentworth came to me and demanded twenty thousand pounds—the most preposterous thing ever heard of—said I owed it to clear the good name of Longworth. As if the good name were dependent on him, or anyone like him! I turned him out of the office.'

Edith did not answer for a few moments, while her father gave expression to his indignation by various ejaculations that need not be here recorded.

'Did he say,' she spoke at length, 'in what way William had done wrong?'

'I do not remember now just what he said. I know I told him to come again when my nephew was present, and then make his charges against him if he wanted to do so. Not that I admitted I had anything to do with the matter at all, but I simply refused to listen to charges against an absent man. I paid no attention to them.'

'That certainly was reasonable,' replied Edith. 'What did he say to it?'

'Oh, he abused me, and abused William, and went on at a dreadful rate, until I was obliged to order him out of the office.'

'But what did he say about meeting William when he returned, and making the charges against him then?'

'What did he say? I don't remember. Oh yes! he said it would be too late then; that they had only a few days to do what business they have to do, and that is why he made the demand for twenty thousand pounds. It was to repair the harm, whatever the harm was, William had done. I look on it simply as some blackmailing scheme of his, and I am astonished that a man belonging to so good a house as he does should try that game with me. I shall speak to the elder partner about it to-morrow, and if he does not make the young man apologize in the most abject manner he will be the loser by it, I can tell him that.'

'I would think no more about it, father, if I were you. Do not let it trouble you in the least.'

'Oh, it doesn't trouble me, but young men nowadays seem to think they can say anything to their elders.'

'I mean,' she continued, 'that I would not go to his partner for a day or two. Wait and see what happens. I have no doubt, when he considers the matter, he will be thoroughly ashamed of himself.'

'Well, I hope so.'

'Then give him the chance of being ashamed of himself, and take no further steps in the meantime.'

Edith shortly afterwards went to her own room; there, clasping her hands behind her, she walked up and down thinking, with a very troubled heart, of what she had heard. Her view of the occurrence was very different from that taken by her father. She felt certain something dishonourable had been done by her cousin. For a long time she had mistrusted his supposed friendship for the two young men, and now she pictured to herself John Kenyon in the wilds of Canada, helpless and despondent because of the great wrong that had been done him. It was far into the night when she retired, and it was early next morning when she arose. Her father was bright and cheerful at breakfast, and had evidently forgotten all about the unpleasant incident of the day before. A good night's sleep had erased it from his memory. Edith was glad of this, and she did not mention the subject. After he had gone to the City, his daughter prepared to follow him. She did not take her carriage, but hailed a hansom, and gave the driver the number of Wentworth's offices. That young man was evidently somewhat surprised to see her. He had been trying to write to Kenyon an account of his interview with old Mr. Longworth; but after he had finished, he thought John Kenyon would not approve of his zeal, so had just torn the letter up.

'Take this chair,' he said, wheeling an armchair into position. 'It is the only comfortable one we have in the room.'

'Comfort does not matter,' said Miss Longworth. 'I came to see you about the mica-mine. What has my cousin done?'

'How do you know he has done anything?'

'That does not matter. I know. Tell me as quickly as you can what he has done.'

'It is not a very pleasant story to tell,' he said, 'to a young lady about one of her relatives.'

'Never mind that. Tell me.'

'Very well, he has done this: He has pretended he was our friend, and professed to aid us in forming this company. He has delayed us by every means in his power until the option has nearly expired. Then he has gone to Canada and secured for himself, and a man named Melville, the option of the mine when John Kenyon's time is up—that is to say, at twelve o'clock to-morrow, when Kenyon's option expires, your cousin will pay the money and own the mine; after which, of course, Kenyon and myself will be out of it. I don't mind the loss at all—I would gladly give Kenyon my share—but for John it is a terrible blow. He had counted on the money to pay debts which he considers he owes to his father for his education. He calls them debts of honour, though they are not debts of honour in the ordinary sense of the words. Therefore, it seemed to me a terrible thing that—' Here he paused and did not go on. He saw there were tears in the eyes of the girl to whom he was talking. 'It is brutal,' he said, 'to tell you all this. You are not to blame for it and neither is your father, although I spoke to him in a heated manner yesterday.'

'When did you say the option expires?'

'At twelve o'clock to-morrow.'

'How much money is required to buy the mine?'

'Twenty thousand pounds.'

'Can money be sent to Canada by cable?'

'Yes, I think so.'

'Aren't you quite sure?'

'No, I am not. It can be sent by telegraph in this country, and in America.'

'How long will it take you to find out?'

'Only a few moments.'

'Very well. Where is Mr. Kenyon now?'

'Kenyon is in Ottawa. I had a cablegram from him yesterday.'

'Then, will you write a cablegram that can be sent away at once, asking him to wait at the telegraph-office until he receives a further message from you?'

'Yes, I can do that; but what good will it do?'

'Never mind that; perhaps it will do no good. I am going to try to make it worth doing. Meanwhile remember, if I succeed, John Kenyon must never know the particulars of this transaction.'

'He never will—if you say so.'

'I say so. Now, there is six hours' difference of time between this country and Canada, is there not?'

'About that, I think.'

'Very well; lose no time in getting the cable-message sent to him, and tell him to answer, so that we shall be sure he is at the other end of the wire. Then find out about the cabling of the money. I shall be back here, I think, as soon as you are.'

With that she left the office, and, getting into her cab, was driven to her father's place of business.

'Well, my girl,' said the old man, pushing his spectacles up on his brow, and gazing at her, 'what is it now—some new extravagance?'

'Yes, father, some new extravagance.'

His daughter was evidently excited, and her breath came quickly. She closed the door, and took a chair opposite her father.

'Father,' she said, 'I have been your business man, as you call me, for a long time.'

'Yes, you have. Are you going to strike for an increase of salary?'

'Father,' she said earnestly, not heeding the jocularity of his tone, 'this is very serious. I want you to give me some money for myself—to speculate with.'

'I will do that very gladly. How much do you want?'

The old man turned his chair round and pulled out his cheque-book.

'I want thirty thousand pounds,' she answered.

Mr. Longworth wheeled quickly round in his chair and looked at her in astonishment.

'Thirty thousand what?'

'Thirty thousand pounds, father; and I want it now.'

'My dear girl,' he expostulated, 'have you any idea how much thirty thousand pounds is? Do you know that thirty thousand pounds is a fortune?'

'Yes, I know that.'

'Do you know that there is not one in twenty of the richest merchants in London who could at a moment's notice produce thirty thousand pounds in ready money?'

'Yes, I suppose that is true. Have you not the ready money?'

'Yes, I have the money. I can draw a cheque for that amount, and it will be honoured at once; but I cannot give you so much money without knowing what you are going to do with it.'

'And suppose, father, you do not approve of what I am going to do with it?'

'All the more reason, my dear, that I should know.'

'Then, father, I suppose you mean that whatever services I have rendered you, whatever comfort I have given you, what I have been to you all my life, is not worth thirty thousand pounds?'

'You shouldn't talk like that, my daughter. Everything I have is yours, or will be, when I die. It is for you I work; it is for you I accumulate money. You will have everything I own the moment I have to lay down my work.'

'Father!' cried the girl, standing up before him, 'I do not want your money when you die. I do not want you to die, as you know; but I do want thirty thousand pounds to-day, and now. I want it more than I ever wanted anything else before in my life, or ever shall again. Will you give it to me?'

'No, I will not, unless you tell me what you are going to do with it.'

'Then, father, you can leave your money to your nephew when you die; I shall never touch a penny of it. I now bid you good-bye. I will go out from this room and earn my own living.'

With that the young woman turned to go, but her father, with a sprightliness one would not have expected from his years, sprang to the door and looked at her with alarm.

'Edith, my child, you never talked to me like this before in your life. What is wrong with you?'

'Nothing, father, except that I want a cheque for thirty thousand pounds, and want it now.'

'And do you mean to say that you will leave me if I do not give it to you?'

'Have you ever broken your word, father?'

'Never, my child, that I know of.'

'Then remember I am your daughter. I have said, if I do not get that money now, I shall never enter our house again.'

'But thirty thousand pounds is a tremendous amount. Remember, I have given my word, too, that I would not give you the money unless you told me what it was for.'

'Very well, father, I will tell what it is for when you ask me. I would advise you, though, not to ask me; and I would advise you to give me the money. It will all be returned to you if you want it.

'Oh, I don't care about the money at all, Edith. I merely, of course, don't want to see it wasted.'

'And, father, have you no trust in my judgment?'

'Well, you know I haven't much faith in any woman's wisdom, in the matter of investing money.'

'Trust me this time, father. I shall never ask you for any more.'

The old man went slowly to his desk, wrote out a cheque, and handed it to his daughter. It was for thirty thousand pounds.

CHAPTER XXXV.

Edith Longworth, with that precious bit of paper in her pocket, once more got into her hansom and drove to Wentworth's office. Again she took the only easy-chair in the room. Her face was very serious, and Wentworth, the moment he saw it, said to himself. 'She has failed.'

'Have you telegraphed to Mr. Kenyon?' she asked.

'Yes.'

'Are you sure you made it clear to him what was wanted? Cablegrams are apt to be rather brief.'

'I told him to keep in communication with us. Here is a copy of the cablegram.'

Miss Longworth read it approvingly, but said:

'You have not put in the word "answer."'

'No; but I put it in the despatch I sent. I remember that now.'

'Have you had a reply yet?'

'Oh no; you see, it takes a long time to get there, because there are so many changes from the end of the cable to the office where Kenyon is. And then, again, you see, they may have to look for him. He may not be expecting a message; in fact, he is sure not to be expecting any. From his own cablegram to me, it is quite evident he has given up all hope.'

'Show me that cablegram, please.'

Wentworth hesitated.

'It is hardly couched in language you will enjoy reading,' he said.

'That doesn't matter. Show it to me. I must see all the documents in the case.'

He handed her the paper, which she read in silence, and gave it back to him without a word.

'I knew you wouldn't like it,' he said.

'I have not said I do not like it. It is not a bit too strong under the circumstances. In fact, I do not see how he could have put it in other words. It is very concise and to the point.'

'Yes; there is no doubt about that, especially the first three words, "We are cheated!" Those are the words that make me think Kenyon has given up all hope; so there may be some trouble in finding him.'

'Did you learn whether money could be sent by cable or not?'

'Oh yes; there is no difficulty about that. The money is deposited in a bank here, and will be credited to Kenyon in the bank at Ottawa.'

'Very well, then,' said Miss Longworth, handing him the piece of paper, 'there is the money.'

Wentworth gave a long whistle as he looked at it. 'Excuse my rudeness,' he said; 'I don't see a bit of paper like this every day. You mean, then, to buy the mine?'

'Yes, I mean to buy the mine.'

'Very well; but there is ten thousand pounds more here than is necessary.'

'Yes. I mean not only to buy the mine, but to work it; and so some working capital will be necessary. How much do you suppose.'

'About that I have no idea,' said Wentworth. 'I should think five thousand pounds would be ample.'

'Then, we shall leave five thousand pounds in the bank here for contingencies, and cable twenty-five thousand pounds to Mr. Kenyon. I shall expect him to get me a good man to manage the mine. I am sure he will be glad to do that.'

'Most certainly he will. John Kenyon, now that the mine has not fallen

329

into the hands of those who tried to cheat him, will be glad to do anything for the new owner of it. He won't mind, in the least, losing his money if he knows that you have the mine.'

'Ah, but that is the one thing he must not know. As to losing the money, neither you nor Mr. Kenyon are to lose a penny. If the mine is all you think it is, then it will be an exceedingly profitable investment; and I intend that we shall each take our third, just as if you had contributed one-third of the money, and Mr. Kenyon another.'

'But, my dear Miss Longworth, that is absurd. We could never accept any such terms.'

'Oh yes, you can. I spoke to John Kenyon himself about being a partner in this mine. I am afraid he thought very little of the offer at the time. I don't intend him to know anything at all about my ownership now. He has discovered the mine—you and he together. If it is valueless, then you and he will be two of the sufferers; if it is all you think it is, then you will be the gainers. The labourer is worthy of his hire, and I am sure both you and Mr. Kenyon have laboured hard enough in this venture. Should he guess I bought it, the chances are that he will be stupidly and stubbornly conscientious, and decline to share the fruits of his labours.'

'And do you think, Miss Longworth, I am not conscientious enough to refuse?'

'Oh, yes; you are conscientious, but you are sensible. Mr. Kenyon isn't.'

'I think you are mistaken about that. He is one of the most sensible men in the world—morbidly sensible, perhaps.'

'Well, I think, if Mr. Kenyon knew I owned the mine, he would not take a penny as his share. So I trust you will never let him know I am the person who gave the money to buy the mine.'

'But is he never to know it, Miss Longworth?'

'Perhaps not. If he is to learn, I am the person to tell him.'

'I quite agree with you there, and I shall respect your confidence.'

'Now, what time,' said the young woman, looking at her watch, 'ought we to get an answer from Mr. Kenyon?'

'Ah, that, as I said before, no one can tell.'

'I suppose, then, the best plan is to send the money at once, or put it in the way of being sent, to some bank in Ottawa.'

'Yes, that is the best thing to do; although, of course, if John Kenyon is not there——'

'If he is not there what shall we do?'

'I do not exactly know. I could cable to Mr. Von Brent. Von Brent is the owner of the mine, and the man who gave John the option. I do not know how far he is committed to the others. If he is as honest as I take him to be, he will accept the money, providing it is sent in before twelve o'clock, and then we shall have the mine. Of that I know nothing whatever, because I have no particulars except John's cable-message.'

'Then, I can do no more just now?'

'Yes, you can. You will have to write a cheque for the twenty-five thousand pounds. You see, this cheque is crossed, and will go into your banking account. An other cheque will have to be drawn to get the money out.'

'Ah, I see. I have not my cheque-book here, but perhaps you can send this cheque to the bank, and I will return. There will be time enough, I suppose, before the closing hour of the bank?'

'Yes, there will be plenty of time. Of course, the sooner we get the money away the better.'

'I shall return shortly after lunch. Perhaps you will then have heard from Mr. Kenyon. If anything comes sooner, will you send me a telegram? Here is my address.'

'I will do that,' said Wentworth, as he bade her good-bye.

As soon as lunch was over, Miss Longworth, with her cheque-book, again visited Wentworth's office. When she entered he shook his head.

'No news yet,' he said.

'This is terrible,' she answered; 'suppose he has left Ottawa and started for home?'

'I do not think he would do that. Still, I imagine he would think there was no reason for staying in Ottawa. Nevertheless, I know Kenyon well enough to believe that he will wait there till the last minute of the option has expired, in the hope that something may happen. He knows, of course, that I shall be doing everything I can in London, and he may have a faint expectation that I shall be able to accomplish something.'

'It would be useless to cable again?'

'Quite. If that message does not reach him, none will.'

As he was speaking, a boy entered the room with a telegram in his hand. Its contents were short and to the point:

'Cablegram received.

'KENYON.'

'Well, that's all right,' said Wentworth; 'now I shall cable that we have the money, and advise him to identify himself at the bank, so that there can be no formalities about the drawing of it, to detain him.'

Saying this, Wentworth pulled the telegraph-forms towards him, and, after considerable labour, managed to concoct a satisfactory despatch.

'Don't spare money on it,' urged his visitor; 'be sure and make it plain to him.'

'I think that will do, don't you?'

'Yes,' she answered, after reading the despatch; 'that will do.'

'Now,' she said, 'here is the cheque. Shall I wait here while you do all that is necessary to cable the money, or had I better go, and return again to see if everything is all right?'

'If you don't mind, just sit where you are. You may lock this door, if you like, and you will not be disturbed.'

It was an hour before Wentworth returned, but his face was radiant.

'We have done everything we can,' he said, 'the money is at his order there, if the cablegram gets over before twelve o'clock to-morrow, as of course it will.'

'Very well, then, good-bye,' said the girl with a smile, holding out her hand.

CHAPTER XXXVI.

If any man more miserable and dejected than John Kenyon existed in the broad dominion of Canada, he was indeed a person to be pitied. After having sent his cablegram to Wentworth, he returned to his very cheerless hotel. Next morning when he awoke he knew that Wentworth would have received the message, but that the chances were ten thousand to one that he could not get the money in time, even if he could get it at all. Still, he resolved to stay in Ottawa, much as he detested the place, until the hour the option expired. Then, he thought, he would look round among the mines, and see if he could not get something to do in the management of one of them. This would enable him to make some money, wherewith to pay the debts which he and Wentworth would have incurred as a result of their disastrous speculation. He felt so depressed that he did what most other Englishmen would have done in his place—took a long walk. He stood on the bridge over the Ottawa River and gazed for a while at the Chaudière Falls, watching the mist rising from the chasm into which the waters plunged. Then he walked along the other side of the river, among big saw-mills and huge interminable piles of lumber, with their grateful piny smell. By-and-by he found himself in the country, and then the forest closed in upon the bad road on which he walked. Nevertheless, he kept on and on, without heeding where he was going. Here and there he saw clearings in the woods, and a log shanty, or perhaps a barn. The result of all this was that, being a healthy man, he soon developed an enormous appetite, which forced itself upon his attention in spite of his depression. He noticed the evening was closing around him, and so was glad to come to a farmhouse that looked better than the ordinary shanties he had left behind. Here he asked for food, and soon sat down to a plentiful meal, the coarseness of which was more than compensated for by the excellence of his appetite. After dinner he began to realize how tired he was, and felt astonished to hear from his host how far he was from Ottawa.

'You can't get there to-night,' said the farmer; 'it is no use your trying. You stay with us, and I'll take you in to-morrow. I'm going there in the afternoon.'

And so Kenyon remained all night, and slept the dreamless sleep of health and exhaustion.

It was somewhat late in the afternoon when he reached the city of Ottawa. Going towards his hotel, he was astonished to hear his name shouted after him. Turning round, he saw a man, whom he did not recognise, running after him.

'Your name is Kenyon, isn't it?' asked the man, somewhat out of breath.

'Yes, that is my name.'

'I guess you don't remember me. I am the telegraph operator. We have had a despatch waiting for you for some time, a cablegram from London. We have searched all over the town for you, but couldn't find you.'

'Ah,' said Kenyon, 'is it important?'

'Well, that I don't know. You had better come with me to the office and get it. Of course, they don't generally cable unimportant things. I remember it said something about you keeping yourself in readiness for something.'

They walked together to the telegraph-office. The boy was still searching for Kenyon with the original despatch, but the operator turned up the file and read the copy to him.

'You see, it wants an answer,' he said; 'that's why I thought it was important to get you. You will have plenty of time for an answer to-night.'

John took a lead pencil and wrote the cable despatch which Wentworth received. He paid his money, and said:

'I will go to my hotel; it is the —— House. I will wait there, and if anything comes for me, send it over as soon as possible.'

'All right,' said the operator, 'that is the best plan; then we will know exactly where to find you. Of course, there is no use in your waiting here, because we can get you in five minutes. Perhaps I had better telephone to the

335

hotel for you if anything comes.'

'Very well,' said Kenyon; 'I will leave it all in your hands.'

Whether it was the effect of having been in the country or not, John felt that the cablegram he had received was a good omen. He meditated over the tremendous ill-fortune he had suffered in the whole business from beginning to end, and thought of old Mr. Longworth's favourite phrase, 'There's no such thing as luck.'

Then came a rap at his door, and the bell-boy said:

'There is a gentleman here wishes to speak to you.'

'Ask him to come up,' was the answer; and two minutes later Von Brent entered.

'Any news?' he asked.

John, who was in a state of mind which made him suspicious of everything and everybody, answered:

'No, nothing new.'

'Ah, I am sorry for that. I had some hopes that perhaps you might be able to raise the money before twelve o'clock to-morrow. Of course you know the option ends at noon to-morrow?'

'Yes, I know that.'

'Did you know that Longworth was in Ottawa?'

'No,' said Kenyon; 'I have been out of town myself.'

'Yes, he came last night. He has the money in the bank, as I told you. Now, I will not accept it until the very latest moment. Of course, legally, I cannot accept it before that time, and, just as legally, I cannot refuse his money when he tenders it. I am very sorry all this has happened—more sorry than I can tell you. I hope you will not think that I am to blame in the matter?'

'No, you are not in the slightest to blame. There is nobody in fault

336

except myself. I feel that I have been culpably negligent, and altogether too trustful.'

'I wish to goodness I knew where you could get the money; but, of course, if I knew that, I would have had it myself long ago.'

'I am very much obliged to you,' said Kenyon; 'but the only thing you can do for me is to see that your clock is not ahead of time to-morrow. I may, perhaps, be up at the office before twelve o'clock—that is where I shall find you, I suppose?'

'Yes; I shall be there all the forenoon. I shall not leave until twelve.'

'Very good; I am much obliged to you, Mr. Von Brent, for your sympathy. I assure you, I haven't many friends, and it—well, I'm obliged to you, that's all. An Englishman, you know, is not very profuse in the matter of thanks, but I mean it.'

'I'm sure you do,' said Von Brent, 'and I'm only sorry that my assistance cannot be something substantial. Well, good-bye, hoping to see you to-morrow.'

After he had departed, Kenyon's impatience increased as the hours went on. He left the hotel, and went direct to the telegraph-office; but nothing had come for him.

'I'm afraid,' said the operator, 'that there won't be anything more to-night. If it should come late, shall I send it to your hotel?'

'Certainly; no matter at what hour it comes, I wish you would let me have it as soon as possible. It is very important.'

Leaving the office, he went up the street and, passing the principal hotel in the place, saw young Longworth standing under the portico of the hotel as dapper and correct in costume as ever, his single eyeglass the admiration of all Ottawa, for there was not another like it in the city.

'How do you do, Kenyon?' said that young man.

'My dear sir,' replied Kenyon, 'the last time you spoke to me you said you desired to have nothing more to say to me. I cordially reciprocated that sentiment, and I want to have nothing to say to you.'

'My dear fellow,' cried Longworth jauntily, 'there is no harm done. Of course, in New York I was a little out of sorts. Everybody is in New York—beastly hole! I don't think it is worse than Ottawa, but the air is purer here. By the way, perhaps you and I can make a little arrangement. I am going to buy that mine to-morrow, as doubtless you know. Now, I should like to see it in the hands of a good and competent man. If a couple of hundred pounds a year would be any temptation to you, I think we can afford to let you develop the mine.'

'Thank you!' said Kenyon.

'I knew you would be grateful; just think over the matter, will you? and don't come to any rash decision. We can probably give a little more than that; but until we see how the mine is turning out, it is not likely we shall spend a great deal of money on it.'

'Of course,' said John, 'the proper answer to your remark would be to knock you down; but, besides being a law-abiding citizen, I have no desire to get into gaol to-night for doing it, because there is one chance in a thousand, Mr. Longworth, that I may have some business to do with that mine myself before twelve o'clock to-morrow.'

'Ah, it is my turn to be grateful now!' said Longworth. 'In a rough-and-tumble fight I am afraid you would master me easier than you would do in a contest of diplomacy.'

'Do you call it diplomacy? You refer, I suppose, to your action in relation to the mine. I call it robbery.'

'Oh, do you? Well, that is the kind of conversation which leads to breaches of the peace; and as I also am a law-abiding subject, I will not continue the discussion any further. I bid you a very good evening, Mr. Kenyon.'

The young man turned on his heel and went into the hotel. John walked to his own much more modest inn, and retired for the night. He did not sleep

338

well. All night long, phantom telegraph-messengers were rapping at the door, and he started up every now and then to receive cablegrams which faded away as he awoke. Shortly after breakfast he went to the telegraph-office, but found that nothing had arrived for him.

'I am afraid,' said the operator, 'that nothing will come on before noon.'

'Before noon!' echoed John. 'Why?'

'The wires are down in some places in the East, and messages are delayed a good deal. Perhaps you noticed the lack of Eastern news in the morning papers? Very little news came from the East last night.' Seeing John's look of anxious interest, the operator continued: 'Does the despatch you expect pertain to money matters?'

'Yes, it does.'

'Do they know you at the bank?'

'No, I don't think they do.'

'Then, if I were you, I would go up to the bank and be identified, so that, if it is a matter of minutes, no unnecessary time may be lost. You had better tell them you expect a money-order by cable, and, although such orders are paid without any identification at the bank, yet they take every precaution to see that it does not get into the hands of the wrong man.'

'Thank you,' said Kenyon. 'I am much obliged to you for your suggestion. I will act upon it.'

And as soon as the bank opened, John Kenyon presented himself to the cashier.

'I am expecting a large amount of money from England to-day. It is very important that, when it arrives, there shall be no delay in having it placed at my disposal. I want to know if there are any formalities to be gone through.'

'Where is the money coming from?' said the clerk.

'It is coming from England.'

'Is there anyone in Ottawa who can identify you?'

'Yes; I know the telegraph operator here.'

'Ah!' said the cashier somewhat doubtfully. 'Anybody else?'

'Mr. Von Brent knows me very well.'

'That will do. Suppose you get Mr. Von Brent to come here and identify you as the man who bears the name of Kenyon. Then the moment your cablegram comes the money will be at your disposal.'

Kenyon hurried to Von Brent's rooms and found him alone.

'Will you come down to the bank and identify me as Kenyon?'

'Certainly. Has the money arrived?'

'No, it has not; but I expect it, and want to provide for every contingency. I do not wish to have any delay in my identification when it does come.'

'If it comes by cable,' said Von Brent, 'there will be no need of identification. The bank is not responsible, you know. They take the money entirely at the sender's risk. They might pay it to the telegraph operator who receives the message! I believe they would not be held liable. However, it is better to see that nothing is left undone.'

Going over to the bank, Von Brent said to the cashier: 'This is John Kenyon.'

'Very good,' replied the cashier. 'Have you been at the telegraph-office lately, Mr. Kenyon?'

'No, I have not—at least, not for half an hour or so.'

'Well, I would go there as soon as possible, if I were you.'

'That means,' said Von Brent, as soon as they had reached the door, 'that they have had their notice about the money. I believe it is already in the bank for you. I will go back to my rooms and not leave them till you come.'

John hurried to the telegraph-office.

340

'Anything for me yet?' he said.

'Nothing as yet, Mr. Kenyon; I think, however,' he added with a smile, 'that it will be all right. I hope so.'

The moments ticked along with their usual rapidity, yet it seemed to Kenyon the clock was going fearfully fast. Eleven o'clock came and found him still pacing up and down the office of the telegraph. The operator offered him the hospitality of the private room, but this he declined. Every time the machine clicked, John's ears were on the alert, trying to catch a meaning from the instrument.

Ten minutes after eleven!

Twenty minutes after eleven, and still no despatch! The cold perspiration stood on John's brow, and he groaned aloud.

'I suppose it's very important,' said the operator.

'Very important.'

'Well, now, I shouldn't say so, but I know the money is in the bank for you. Perhaps if you went up there and demanded it, they would give it to you.'

It was twenty-five minutes past the hour when John hurried towards the bank.

'I have every belief,' he said to the cashier, 'that the money is here for me now. Is it possible for me to get it?'

'Have you your cablegram?'

'No, I have not.'

'Well, you know, we cannot pay the money until we see your cablegram. If time is of importance, you should not leave the telegraph-office, and the moment you get your message, come here; then there will be no delay whatever. Do you wish to draw all the money at once?'

'I don't know how much there is, but I must have twenty thousand pounds.'

'Very well, to save time you had better make out a cheque for twenty thousand pounds; that will be———'

And here he gave the number of dollars at the rate of the day on the pound. 'Just make out a cheque for that amount, and I will certify it. A certified cheque is as good as gold. The moment you get your message I will hand you the certified cheque.'

John wrote out the order and gave it to the cashier, glancing at the clock as he did so. It was now twenty-five minutes to twelve. He rushed to the telegraph-office with all the speed of which he was capable, but met only a blank look again from the chief operator.

'It has not come yet,' he said, shaking his head.

Gradually despair began to descend on the waiting man. It was worse to miss everything now, than never to have had the hope of success. It was like hanging a man who had once been reprieved. He resumed his nervous pace up and down that chamber of torture. A quarter to twelve. He heard chimes ring somewhere. If the message did not come before they rang again, it would be for ever too late.

Fourteen minutes—thirteen minutes—twelve minutes—eleven minutes—ten minutes to twelve, and yet, no—

'Here you are!' shouted the operator in great glee, 'she's a-coming—it's all right—"John Kenyon, Ottawa."' Then he wrote as rapidly as the machine ticked out the message. 'There it is; now rush!'

John needed no telling to rush. People had begun to notice him as the man who was doing nothing but running between the bank and the telegraph-office.

It was seven minutes to twelve when he got to the bank.

'Is that despatch right?' he said, shoving it through the arched aperture.

The clerk looked at it with provoking composure, and then compared

342

2

222

2

it with some papers.

'For God's sake, hurry!' pleaded John.

'You have plenty of time,' said the cashier coolly, looking up at the clock and going on with his examination. 'Yes,' he added, 'that is right. Here is your certified cheque.'

John clasped it, and bolted out of the bank as a burglar might have done. It was five minutes to twelve when he got to the steps that led to the rooms of Mr. Von Brent. Now all his excitement seemed to have deserted him. He was as cool and calm as if he had five days, instead of so many minutes, in which to make the payment. He mounted the steps quietly, walked along the passage, and knocked at the door of Von Brent's room.

'Come in!' was the shout that greeted him.

He opened the door, glancing at the clock behind Von Brent's head as he did so.

It stood at three minutes to twelve.

Young Mr. Longworth was sitting there, with just a touch of pallor on his countenance, and there seemed to be an ominous glitter in his eyeglass. He said nothing, and John Kenyon completely ignored his presence.

'There is still some life left in my option, I believe?' he said to Von Brent, after nodding good-day to him.

'Very little, but perhaps it will serve. You have two minutes and a half,' said Von Brent.

'Are the papers ready?' inquired John.

'All ready, everything except putting in the names.'

'Very well, here is the money.'

Von Brent looked at the certified cheque. 'That is perfectly right,' he said, 'the mine is yours.'

Then he rose and stretched his hand across the table to Kenyon, who grasped it cordially.

Young Mr. Longworth also rose, and said languidly 'As this seems to be a meeting of long-lost brothers, I shall not intrude. Good-day, Mr. Von Brent.'

Then, adjusting his eyeglass in a leisurely manner, he walked out of the room.

CHAPTER XXXVII.

When Edith Longworth entered the office of George Wentworth, that young gentleman somewhat surprised her. He sprang from his chair the moment she entered the room, rushed out of the door, and shouted at the top of his voice to the boy, who answered him, whereupon Wentworth returned to the room, apparently in his right mind.

'I beg your pardon, Miss Longworth,' he said, laughing; 'the fact was, I had just sent my boy with a telegram for you, and now, you see, I have saved sixpence.'

'Then you have heard from Canada?' said the young lady.

'Yes; a short message, but to the point.' He handed her the cablegram, and she read:

'Mine purchased; shall take charge temporarily.'

'Then, the money got there in time,' she said, handing him back the telegraphic message.

'Oh yes,' said George, with the easy confidence of a man who doesn't at all know what he is talking about. 'We had plenty of time; I knew it would get there all right.'

'I am glad of that; I was afraid perhaps we might have sent it too late. One can never tell what delays or formalities there may be.'

'Evidently there was no trouble. And now, Miss Longworth, what are your commands? Am I to be your agent here, in Great Britain?'

'Have you written to Mr. Kenyon?'

'Yes, I wrote to him just after I sent the cable message.'

'Of course you didn't——'

'No, I didn't say a word that would lead him to suspect who was the mistress of the mine. In my zeal I even went so far as to give you a name. You are hereafter to be known in the correspondence as Mr. Smith, the owner of the mine.'

Miss Longworth laughed.

'And—oh, by the way,' cried Wentworth, 'here is a barrel belonging to you.'

'A barrel!' she said, and, looking in the direction to which he pointed, she saw in the corner of the room a barrel with the head taken away. 'If it is my property,' continued the young woman, 'who has taken the liberty of opening it?'

'Oh, I did that as your agent. That barrel contains the mineral from the mine, which we hope will prove so valuable. It started from Canada over three months ago, and only arrived here the other day. It seems that the idiot who sent it addressed it by way of New York, and it was held by some Jack-in-office belonging to the United States Customs. We have had more diplomatic correspondence and trouble about that barrel than you can imagine, and now it comes a day behind the fair, when it is really of no use to anyone.'

Miss Longworth rose and went to the barrel. She picked out some of the beautiful white specimens that were in it.

'Is this the mineral?' she asked.

Wentworth laughed.

'Imagine a person buying a mine at an exorbitant price, and not knowing what it produces. Yes, that is the mineral.'

'This is not mica, of course?'

'No, it is not mica. That is the stuff used for the making of china.'

'It looks as if it would take a good polish. Will it, do you know?'

'I do not know. I could easily find out for you.'

'I wish you would, and get a piece of it polished, which I will use as a

346

paper-weight.'

'What are your orders for the rest of the barrel?'

'What did you intend doing with it?' said the young woman.

'Well, I was thinking the best plan would be to send some of it to each of the pottery works in this country, and get their orders for more of the stuff, if they want to use it.'

'I think that an extremely good idea. I understand from the cablegram that Mr. Kenyon says he will take charge of the mine temporarily.'

'Yes; I imagine he left Ottawa at once, as soon as he had concluded his bargain. Of course, we shall not know for certain until he writes.'

'Very well, then, it appears to me the best thing you could do over here would be to secure what orders can be obtained in England for the mineral. Then, I suppose, you could write to Mr. Kenyon, and ask him to engage a proper person to work the mine.'

'Yes, I will do that.'

'When he comes over here, you and he can have a consultation as to the best thing to do next. I expect nothing very definite can be arranged until he comes. You may make whatever excuse you can for the absence of the mythical Mr. Smith, and say that you act for him. Then you may tell Mr. Kenyon, in whatever manner you choose, that Mr. Smith intends both you and Mr. Kenyon to share conjointly with him. I think you will have no trouble in making John—that is, in making Mr. Kenyon—believe there is such a person as Mr. Smith, if you put it strongly enough to him. Make him understand that Mr. Smith would never have heard of the mine unless Mr. Kenyon and you had discovered it, and that he is very glad indeed to have such a good opportunity of investing his money; so that, naturally, he wishes those who have been instrumental in helping him to this investment to share in its profits. I imagine you can make all this clear enough, so that your friend will suspect nothing. Don't you think so?'

'Well, with any other man than John Kenyon I should have my doubts, because, as a fabricator, I don't think I have a very high reputation; but with John I have no fears whatever. He will believe everything I say. It is almost a pity to delude so trustful a man, but it's so very much to his own advantage that I shall have no hesitation in doing it.'

'Then, you will write to him about getting a fit and proper person to manage the mine?'

'Yes. I don't think there will be any necessity for doing so, but I will make sure. I imagine John will not leave there until he sees everything to his satisfaction. He will be very anxious indeed for the mine to prove the great success he has always believed it to be, even though, at present, he does not know he is to have any pecuniary interest in its prosperity.'

'Very well then, I shall bid you good-bye. I may not be here again, but whenever you hear from Mr. Kenyon, I shall be very glad if you will let me know.'

'Certainly; I will send you all the documents in the case, as you once remarked. You always like to see the original papers, don't you?'

'Yes, I suppose I do.' Miss Longworth lingered a moment at the door, then, looking straight at Wentworth, she said to him, 'You remember you spoke rather bitterly to my father the other day?'

'Yes,' said Wentworth, colouring; 'I remember it.'

'You are a young man; he is old. Besides that, I think you were entirely in the wrong. He had nothing whatever to do with his nephew's action.'

'Oh, I know that,' said Wentworth. 'I would have apologized to him long ago, only—well, you know, he told me I shouldn't be allowed in the office again, and I don't suppose I should.'

'A letter from you would be allowed in the office,' replied the young lady, looking at the floor.

'Of course it would,' said George; 'I will write to him instantly and apologize.'

348

'It is very good of you,' said, Edith, holding out her hand to him; the next moment she was gone.

George Wentworth turned to his desk and wrote a letter of apology. Then he mused to himself upon the strange and incomprehensible nature of women. 'She makes me apologize to him, and quite right too; but if it hadn't been for the row with her father, she never would have heard about the transaction, and therefore couldn't have bought the mine, which she was anxious to do for Kenyon's sake—lucky beggar John is, after all!'

CHAPTER XXXVIII.

When the business of transferring the mine to its new owner was completed, John Kenyon went to the telegraph-office, and sent a short cable-message to Wentworth. Then he turned his steps to the hotel, an utterly exhausted man. The excitement and tension of the day had been too much for him, and he felt that, if he did not get out of the city of Ottawa and into the country, where there were fewer people and more air, he was going to be ill. He resolved to leave for the mine as soon as possible. There he would get affairs in as good order as might be, and keep things going until he heard from the owner. When he reached his hotel, he wrote a letter to Wentworth, detailing briefly the circumstances under which he had secured the mine, and dealing with other more personal matters. Having posted this, he began to pack his portmanteau, preparatory to leaving early next morning. While thus occupied, the bell-boy came into his room, and said:

'There is a gentleman wants to see you.'

He imagined at once that it was Von Brent, who wished to see him with regard to some formality relating to the transfer, and he was, therefore, very much astonished—in fact, for the moment speechless—when Mr. William Longworth entered and calmly gazed round the rather shabby room with his critical eyeglass.

'Ah,' he said, 'these are your diggings, are they? This is what they call a dollar hotel, I suppose, over here. Well, some people may like it, but, I confess, I don't care much about it, myself. Their three or four dollars a day hotels are bad enough for me. By the way, you look rather surprised to see me; being strangers together in a strange country, I expected a warmer greeting. You said last night, in front of the Russell House, that it would please you very much to give me a warm greeting; perhaps you would like to do so to-night.'

'Have you come up here to provoke a quarrel with me?' asked Kenyon.

'Oh, bless you, no! Quarrel! Nothing of the sort. What should I want to quarrel about?'

'Perhaps you will be good enough to tell me why you come here, then?'

'A very reasonable request. Very reasonable indeed, and perfectly natural, but still quite unnecessary. It is not likely that a man would climb up here into your rooms, and then not be prepared to tell you why he came. I came, in the first place, to congratulate you on the beautiful and dramatic way in which you secured the mine at the last moment, or apparently at the last moment. I suppose you had the money all the time?'

'No, I had not.'

'Then you came in to Von Brent just as soon as you received it?'

'Well, now, I don't see that it is the business of anyone else but myself. Still, if you want to know, I may say that I came to Mr. Von Brent's room at the moment I received the money.'

'Really! Then it was sent over by cable, I presume?'

'Your presumption is entirely correct.'

'My dear Kenyon,' said the young man, seating himself without being asked, and gazing at John in a benevolent kind of way, 'you really show some temper over this little affair of yours. Now, here is the whole thing in a nutshell——'

'My dear sir, I don't wish to hear the whole thing, in a nutshell. I know all about it—all I wish to know.'

'Ah, precisely; of course you do; certainly; but, nevertheless, let me have my say. Here is the whole thing. I tried to—well, to cheat you. I thought I could make a little money by doing so, and my scheme failed. Now, if anybody should be in a bad temper, it is I, not you. Don't you see that? You are not acting your part well at all. I'm astonished at you!'

'Mr. Longworth, I wish to have nothing whatever to say to you. If you have anything to ask, I wish you would ask it as quickly as possible, and then

351

leave me alone.'

'The chief fault I find with you, Kenyon,' said Longworth, throwing one leg over the other, and clasping his hands round his knee—'the chief fault I have to find is your painful lack of a sense of humour. Now, you remember last night I offered you the managership of the mine. I thought, certainly, that by this time to-day I should be owner of it, or, at least, one of the owners. Now, you don't appear to appreciate the funniness of the situation. Here you are the owner of the mine, and I am out in the cold—"left," as they say here in America. I am the man who is left——'

'If that is all you have to talk about,' said Kenyon gravely, 'I must ask you to allow me to go on with my packing. I am going to the mine to-morrow.'

'Certainly, my dear fellow; go at once and never mind me. Can I be of any assistance to you? It requires a special genius, you know, to pack a portmanteau properly. But what I wanted to say was this: Why didn't you turn round, when you had got the mine, and offer me the managership of it? Then you would have had your revenge. The more I think of that episode in Von Brent's office, the more I think you utterly failed to realize the dramatic possibilities of the situation.'

Kenyon was silent.

'Now, all this time you are wondering why I came here. Doubtless you wish to know what I want.'

'I have not the slightest interest in the matter,' said Kenyon.

'That is ungracious, but, nevertheless, I will continue. It is better, I see, to be honest with you, if a man wants to get anything from you. Now, I want to get a bit of information from you. I want to know where you got the money with which you bought the mine?'

'I got it from the bank.'

'Ah, yes, but I want to know who sent it over to you?'

'It was sent to me by George Wentworth.'

'Quite so; but now I want to know who gave Wentworth the money?'

'You will have a chance of finding that out when you go to England, by asking him.'

'Then you won't tell me?'

'I can't tell you.'

'You mean by that, of course, that you won't.'

'I always mean, Mr. Longworth, exactly what I say. I mean that I can't tell you. I don't know myself.'

'Really?'

'Yes, really. You seem to have some difficulty in believing that anybody can speak the truth.'

'Well, it isn't a common vice, speaking the truth. You must forgive a little surprise.' He nursed his knee for a moment, and looked meditatively up at the ceiling. 'Now, would you like to know who furnished that money?'

'I have no curiosity in the matter whatever.'

'Have you not? You are a singular man. It seems to me that a person into whose lap twenty thousand pounds drops from the skies would have some little curiosity to know from whom the money came.'

'I haven't the slightest.'

'Nevertheless, I will tell you who gave the money to Wentworth. It was my dear friend Melville. I didn't tell you in New York, of course, that Melville and I had a little quarrel about this matter, and he went home decidedly huffy. I had no idea he would take this method of revenge; but I see it quite clearly now. He knew I had secured the option of the mine. There was a little trouble as to what our respective shares were to be, and I thought, as I had secured the option, I had the right to dictate terms. He thought differently. He was going to Von Brent to explain the whole matter; but I pointed out that such a course would do no good, the option being legally made out in my name, so that the moment your claim expired mine began. When this dawned upon him, he took the steamer and went to England. Now, I can see his hand in this artistic finish to the affair. It was a pretty sharp trick of Melville's, and I give him credit for it. He is a very much shrewder and cleverer man than I thought he was.'

'It seems to me, Mr. Longworth, that your inordinate conceit makes you always underestimate your friends, or your enemies either, for that matter.'

'There is something in that, Kenyon; I think you are more than half right, but I thought, perhaps, I could make it advantageous to you to do me a favour in this matter. I thought you might have no objection to writing a little document to the effect that the money did not come in time, and consequently, I had secured the mine. Then, if you would sign that, I would take it over to Melville and make terms with him. Of course, if he knows that he has the mine there will not be much chance of coming to any arrangement with him.'

'You can make no arrangements with me, Mr. Longworth, that involve sacrifice of the truth.'

'Ah, well, I suspected as much; but I thought it was worth trying. However, my dear sir, I may make terms with Melville yet, and then, I imagine, you won't have much to do with the mine.'

'I shall not have anything to do with it if you and Melville have a share in it; and if, as you suspect, Melville has the mine, I consider you are in a bad way. My opinion is that, when one rascal gets advantage over another rascal, the other rascal will be, as you say, "left."'

Longworth mused over this for a moment, and said:

'Yes, I fear you are right—in fact, I am certain of it. Well, that is all I wanted to know. I will bid you good-bye. I shan't see you again in Ottawa, as I shall sail very shortly for England. Have you any messages you would like given to your friends over there?'

'None, thank you.'

'Well, ta-ta!' And John was left to his packing. That necessary operation concluded, Kenyon sat down and thought over what young Longworth had told him. His triumph, after all, had been short-lived. The choice between the two scoundrels was so small that he felt he didn't care which of them owned the mine. Meditating on this disagreeable subject, he suddenly remembered a request he had asked Wentworth to place before the new owner of the mine. He wanted no favour from Melville, so he wrote a second letter, contradicting the request made in the first, and, after posting it, returned to his hotel, and went to bed, probably the most tired man in the city of Ottawa.

CHAPTER XXXIX.

This chapter consists largely of letters. As a general rule, letters are of little concern to anyone except the writers and the receivers, but they are inserted here in the hope that the reader is already well enough acquainted with the correspondents to feel some interest in what they have written.

It was nearly a fortnight after the receipt of the cablegram from Kenyon that George Wentworth found, one morning, on his desk two letters, each bearing a Canadian postage-stamp. One was somewhat bulky and one was thin, but they were both from the same writer. He tore open the thin one first, without looking at the date stamped upon it. He was a little bewildered by its contents, which ran as follows:

'MY DEAR GEORGE,

'I have just heard that Melville is the man who has bought the mine. The circumstances of the case leave no doubt in my mind that such is the fact; therefore, please disregard the request I made as to employment in the letter I posted to you a short time ago. I feel a certain sense of disappointment in the fact that Melville is the owner of the mine. It seems I have only kept one rascal from buying it in order to put it in the hands of another rascal.

'Your friend,

'JOHN KENYON.'

'Melville the owner!' cried Wentworth to himself. 'What could have put that into John's head? This letter is evidently the one posted a few hours before, so it will contain whatever request he has to make;' and, without delay, George Wentworth tore open the envelope of the second letter, which was obviously the one written first.

It contained a number of documents relating to the transfer of the mine. The letter from John himself went on to give particulars of the buying of the property. Then it continued:

'I wish you would do me a favour, George. Will you kindly ask the owner of the mine if he will give me charge of it? I am, of course, anxious to make it turn out as well as possible, and I believe I can more than earn my salary, whatever it is. You know I am not grasping in the matter of money, but get me as large a salary as you think I deserve. I desire to make money for reasons that are not entirely selfish, as you know. To tell you the truth, George, I am tired of cities and of people. I want to live here in the woods, where there is not so much deceit and treachery as there seems to be in the big towns. When I reached London last time, I felt like a boy getting home. My feelings have undergone a complete change, and I think, if it were not for you and a certain young lady, I should never care to see the big city again. What is the use of my affecting mystery, and writing the words "a certain young lady"? Of course, you know whom I mean—Miss Edith Longworth. You know, also, that I am, and have long been, in love with her. If I had succeeded in making the money I thought I should by selling the mine, I might have had some hopes of making more, and of ultimately being in a position to ask her to be my wife; but that and very many other hopes have disappeared with my recent London experiences. I want to get into the forest and recover some of my lost tone, and my lost faith in human nature. If you can arrange matters with the owner of the mine, so that I may stay here for a year or two, you will do me a great favour.'

George Wentworth read over the latter part of this letter two or three times. Then he rose, paced the floor, and pondered.

'It isn't a thing upon which I can ask anyone's advice,' he muttered to himself. 'The trouble with Kenyon is, he is entirely too modest; a little useful self-esteem would be just the thing for him.' At last he stopped suddenly in his walk. 'By Jove!' he said to himself, slapping his thigh, 'I shall do it, let the consequences be what they may.'

Then he sat down at his desk and wrote a letter.

'DEAR Miss LONGWORTH' (it began),

'You told me when you were here last that you wanted all the documents pertaining to the mine, in every instance. A document has come this morning that is rather important. John Kenyon, as you will learn by reading the letter, desires the managership of the mine. I need not say that I think he is the best man in the world for the position, and that everything will be safe in his hands. I therefore enclose you his letter. I had some thought of cutting out a part of it, but knowing your desire to have all the documents in the case, I take the liberty of sending this one exactly as it reached me, and if anyone is to blame, I am the person.

'I remain, your agent,

'GEORGE WENTWORTH.'

He sent this letter out at once, so that he would not have a chance to change his mind.

'It will reach her this afternoon, and doubtless she will call and see me.'

It is, perhaps, hardly necessary to say she did not call, and she did not see him for many days afterwards; but next morning, when he came to his office, he found a letter from her. It ran:

'DEAR MR. WENTWORTH,

'The sending of Mr. Kenyon's letter to me is a somewhat dangerous precedent, which you must on no account follow by sending any letters you may receive from any other person to Mr. Kenyon. However, as you were probably aware when you sent the letter, no blame will rest on your shoulders, or on those of anyone else, in this instance. Still, be very careful in future, because letter-sending, unabridged, is sometimes a risky thing to do. You are to remember that I always want all the documents in the case, and I want them with nothing eliminated. I am very much obliged to you for forwarding the letter.

'As to the managership of the mine, of course I thought Mr. Kenyon would desire to come back to London. If he is content to stay abroad, and really wants to stay there, I wish you would tell him that Mr. Smith is exceedingly pleased to know he is willing to take charge of the mine. It would not look businesslike on the part of Mr. Smith to say that Mr. Kenyon is to name his own salary, but, unfortunately, Mr. Smith is very ignorant as to what a proper salary should be, so will you kindly settle that question? You know the usual salary for such an occupation. Please write down that figure, and add two hundred a year to it. Tell Mr. Kenyon the amount named is the salary Mr. Smith assigns to him.

'Pray be very careful in the wording of the letters, so that Mr. Kenyon will not have any idea who Mr. Smith is.

'Yours truly,

'EDITH LONGWORTH.

When Wentworth received this letter, being a man, he did not know whether Miss Longworth was pleased or not. However, he speedily wrote to John, telling him that he was appointed manager of the mine, and that Mr. Smith was very much pleased to have him in that capacity. He named the salary, but said if it was not enough, no doubt Mr. Smith was so anxious for his services that the amount would be increased.

John, when he got the letter, was more than satisfied.

At the time Wentworth was reading his letters, John had received those which had been sent when the mine was bought. He was relieved to find that Melville was not, after all, the owner; and he went to work with a will, intending to put in two or three years of his life, with hard labour, in developing the resources of the property. The first fortnight, before he received any letters, he did nothing but make himself acquainted with the way work was being carried on there. He found many things to improve. The machinery had been allowed to run down, and the men worked in the listless way men do when they are under no particular supervision. The manager of the mine was very anxious about his position. John told him the property had changed hands but, until he had further news from England, he could not tell just what would be done. When the letters came, John took hold with a will, and there was soon a decided improvement in the way affairs were going. He allowed the old manager to remain as a sort of sub-manager; but that individual soon found that the easy times of the Austrian Mining Company were for ever gone.

Kenyon had to take one or two long trips in Canada and the United States, to arrange for the disposal of the products of the mine; but, as a general rule, his time was spent entirely in the log village near the river.

When a year had passed, he was able to write a very jubilant letter to Wentworth.

'You see,' he said, 'after all, the mine was worth the two hundred thousand pounds we asked for it. It pays, even the first year, ten per cent. on that amount. This will give back all the mine has cost, and I think, George, the honest thing for us to do would be to let the whole proceeds go to Mr. Smith this year, who advanced the money at a critical time. This will recoup him for his outlay, because the working capital has not been touched. The mica has more than paid the working of the mine, and all the rest is clear profit. Therefore, if you are willing, we will let our third go this year, and then we can take our large dividend next year with a clear conscience. I enclose the balance-sheet.'

To this letter there came an answer in due time from Wentworth, who said that he had placed John's proposal before Mr. Smith; but it seemed the gentleman was so pleased with the profitable investment he had made that he would hear of no other division of the profits but that of share and share alike. He appeared to be very much touched by the offer John had made, and respected him for making it, but the proposed rescinding on his part and Wentworth's was a thing not to be thought of. This being the case, John sent a letter and a very large cheque to his father. The moment of posting that letter was, doubtless, one of the happiest of his life, and this ends the formidable array of letters which appears in this chapter.

CHAPTER XL.

Wentworth had written to Kenyon that Mr. Smith absolutely refused to take more than one-third of the profits of the mine. It was true that the offer had been declined, but Wentworth never knew how much tempted the Mistress of the Mine had been when he made it. Her one great desire was to pay back the thirty thousand pounds to her father, and she wanted to do it as speedily as possible. At the end of the second year her profits from the mine, including the return of the five thousand pounds which had been sent to Ottawa as working capital, was still about five thousand pounds under the thirty thousand pounds. She looked forward eagerly to the time when she would be able to pay the thirty thousand pounds to her father. Old Mr. Longworth had never spoken a word to his daughter about the money. She had expected he would ask her what she had done with it, but he had never mentioned the subject. Her conscience troubled her very frequently about the method she had taken to obtain that large amount. She saw that her father had changed in his manner towards her since that day. He had given her the money, but he had given it, as one might say, almost under compulsion, and there was no doubt that, generous as he was, he did not like being coerced into parting with his money. Edith Longworth had paid more for the mine than the amount of cash she had deposited in Ottawa. She had paid for it by being cut off from her father's confidence. Now he never asked her advice about any of his business ventures, and, for the first time in many years, he had taken a long sea-voyage without inviting her to accompany him. All this made the girl more and more anxious to obtain the money to pay back her indebtedness, and, if Wentworth had made the same offer at the end of the second year which he had made at the close of the first, she would have accepted it. The offer, however, was not made, and Miss Longworth said nothing, but took her share of the profits and put them into the bank.

The plan of placing all one's eggs into the same basket is a good one—until something happens to the basket! It is said that lightning never strikes twice in the same place, and, as the small boy remarked, 'it never needed to.'

In Mr. Longworth's affairs lightning struck in three places, and in each of those strokes it hit a large basket. A new law had been passed in one part of the world that vitally affected great interests he held there. In another part of the world, at the same time, there occurred a revolution, and every business in that country stopped for the time being. In still another part of the world there had been a commercial crisis; and, in sympathy with all these financial disasters, the money market in London was exceedingly stringent.

Everybody wanted to sell, and nobody wished to buy. This unfortunate combination of circumstances hit old Mr. Longworth hard. It was not that he did not believe all his investments were secure, could he only weather the gale, but there was an immediate need of ready money which it seemed absolutely impossible to obtain. Day by day his daughter saw him ageing perceptibly. She knew worry was the cause of this, and she knew the events that were happening in different parts of the world must seriously embarrass her father. She longed to speak to him about his business, but one attempt she made in this direction had been very rudely rebuffed, and she was not a woman to tempt a second repulse of that kind. So she kept silent, and saw with grief the havoc business troubles were making with her father's health.

'The old man,' said young Longworth, 'seems to be in a corner.'

'I do not want you ever again to allude to my father as "the old man"— remember that!' cried the girl indignantly.

Young Longworth shrugged his shoulders, and said:

'I don't think you can insist on my calling him a young man much longer. If he isn't an old man, I should like to know who is?'

'That doesn't matter,' said Edith. 'You must not use such a phrase again in my hearing. What do you mean by saying he is in a corner?'

'Well,' returned the young man, 'I don't know much about his business. He does not take me into his confidence at all. In fact, the older he grows, the closer he gets, and the chances are he will make some very bad speculation before long, if he has not done so already. That is the way with old men, begging your pardon for using the phrase. It is not levelled against your father in this instance, but at old men as a class, especially men who have been successful. They seem to resent anybody giving them advice.'

One day Edith received a telegram, asking her to come to the office in the City without delay. She was panic-stricken when she read the message, feeling sure her father had been stricken down in his office, and was probably dying—perhaps dead. She had feared some such result for a long time, because of the intense anxiety to which he had been subjected, and he was not a man who could be counselled to take care of himself on the plea that he was getting old. He resented any intimation that he was not as good a business man as he had ever been, and so it was extremely difficult to get him to listen to reason, if anyone had the courage to talk reason to him.

Edith, without a moment's delay, sprang lightly into a hansom, and went to the District Railway without waiting for her carriage. From the Mansion House Station another cab took her quickly to her father's office.

She was immensely relieved, as she passed through, to see the clerks working as if nothing particular had happened. On entering her father's room, she found him pacing up and down the apartment, while her cousin sat, apparently absorbed in his own affairs, at his desk. Her father was evidently greatly excited.

'Edith,' he cried the moment she entered, 'where is that money I gave you two years ago?'

'It is invested,' she answered, turning slightly pale.

Her father laughed—a hoarse, dry laugh.

'Just as I thought,' he sneered—'put in such shape that a person cannot touch a penny of it, I suppose. In what is it invested? I must have that money.'

'How soon do you need it, father?

'I want it just now, at this moment; if I don't have that money I am a ruined man.'

'This moment. I suppose, means any time to-day, before the bank closes?'

Her father looked at her for a moment, then said:

'Yes that is what it means.'

'I will try and get you the money before that time.'

'My dear girl,' he said bitterly, 'you don't know what you are talking about. If you have that money invested, even if your investment is worth three times now what it was then, you could not get a penny on it. Don't you know the state of the London money market? Don't you know how close money is? I thought perhaps you might have some portion of it yet, not sunk in your silly investment, whatever it is. I have never asked you what it was. You told me you would tell me, but you never have done so. I looked on that money as lost. I look on it still as lost. If you can get me a remnant of it, it will help me now more than the whole amount, or double the amount, would have done at the time I gave it to you. What have you done with the money? What is it invested in?'

'It is invested in a mine.'

'A mine. Of all things in the world in which to sink money, a mine is the worst. Just what a woman or a fool would do! How do you expect to raise money on a mine in the present state of the market? What, in the name of wonder, made you put it into a mine? Whose mine did you buy?'

'I do not know whose it was, father, but I was willing to tell you all I knew at the time you asked me and if you ask me now what mine I bought, I will tell you.'

'Certainly I ask you. What mine did you buy?'

'I bought the mine for which John Kenyon was agent.'

The moment these words were said, her cousin sprang to his feet and glared at her like a man demented.

'You bought that mine—you? Then Wentworth lied to me. He said a Mr. Smith had given him the money.'

'I am the Mr. Smith, William.'

'You are the Mr. Smith! You are the one who has cheated me out of that mine!'

'My dear cousin, the less we say about cheating, the better. I am talking to my father just now, and I do not wish to be interrupted. Will you be so kind as to leave the room until my interview with him is over?'

'So you bought the mica-mine, did you! Pretending to be friendly with me, and knowing all the time that you were doing your best to cheat——'

'Come, come!' interrupted the old gentleman; 'William, none of this. If anyone is to talk roughly to Edith, it will be me, not you. Come, sir, leave the room, as she has asked you to do. Now, my daughter,' he continued, in a much milder tone of voice, after young Longworth had left the office, 'have you any ready money? It is no use saying the mine is worth a hundred thousand pounds, or a million, just now, if you haven't the ready money. Edith, my child,' he cried, 'sit down with me a moment, and I will explain the whole situation to you. It seems to me that ever since I stopped consulting you things have gone wrong. Perhaps, even if you have the money, it is better not to risk it just now; but one pound will do what two pounds will not do a year hence, or perhaps six months from now, when this panic is over.'

Edith sat down beside her father and heard from him exactly how things stood. Then she said:

'All you really need is about fifteen thousand pounds?'

'Yes, that would do; I'm sure that would carry me over. Can you get it for me, my child?'

'Yes, and more. I will try to get you the whole amount. Wait for me here twenty minutes or half an hour.'

George Wentworth was very much surprised when he saw Edith Longworth enter his office. It had been many months since she was there before, and he cordially held out his hand to the girl.

'Mr. Wentworth,' she began at once, 'have you any of the money the mica mine has brought you?'

The Heralds of Fame & A Woman Intervenes

'Yes. I invested the first year's proceeds, but, since I got the last amount, things have been so shaky in the City that it is still at the bank.'

'Will you lend me—can you lend me five thousand pounds of it?'

'Of, course I can, and will; and very glad I am to get the chance of doing so.'

'Then, please write me out a cheque for it at once, and whatever papers you want as security, make them out, and I will see that you are secured.'

'Look here, Miss Longworth,' said the young man, placing his hands on his hips and gazing at her, 'do you mean to insult me? Do you not know that the reason I am able to write out a cheque for five thousand pounds, that will be honoured, is entirely because you trusted your money to me and Kenyon without security? Do you think I want security? Take back the word, Miss Longworth.'

'I will—I will,' she said; 'but I am in a great hurry. Please write me out the cheque, for I must have it before the bank closes.'

The cheque was promptly written out and handed to her.

'I am afraid,' she said, 'I am not very polite to-day, and rather abrupt; but I will make up for it some other time.'

And so, bidding the young man good-bye, she drove to the bank, deposited the cheque, drew her own for thirty thousand pounds, and carried it to her father.

'There,' she said, 'is thirty thousand pounds, and I still own the mine, or, at least, part of it. All the money is made from the cheque you gave me, or, rather, two-thirds of it, because one-third was never touched. Now, it seems to me, father, that, if I am a good enough business woman to more than double my money in two years, I am a good enough business woman to be consulted by my father whenever he needs a confidant. My dear father, I want to take some of the burden off your shoulders.'

There were tears in her father's eyes as he put his arm round her waist and whispered to her:

'There is no one in all London like you, my dear—no one, no one. I'll have no more secrets from you, my own brave girl.'

CHAPTER XLI.

Kenyon's luck, as he said to himself, had turned. The second year was even more prosperous than the first, and the third as successful as the second. He had a steady market for his mineral, and, besides, he had the great advantage of knowing the rogues to avoid. Some new swindles he had encountered during his first year's experience had taught him lessons that he profited by in the second and third. He liked his home in the wilderness, and he liked the rough people amongst whom he found himself.

Notwithstanding his renunciation of London, however, there would now and then come upon him a yearning for the big city, and he promised himself a trip there at the end of the third year. Wentworth had been threatening month after month to come out and see him, but something had always interfered.

Taking it all in all, John liked it better in the winter than in the summer, in spite of the extreme cold. The cold was steady and could be depended upon; moreover, it was healthful and invigorating. In summer, John never quite became accustomed to the ravages of the black fly, the mosquito, and other insect pests of that region. His first interview with the black fly left his face in such a condition that he was glad he lived in a wilderness.

At the beginning of the second winter John treated himself to a luxury. He bought a natty little French Canadian horse that was very quick and accustomed to the ice of the river, which formed the highway by which he reached Burntpine from the mine in the cold season. To supplement the horse, he also got a comfortable little cutter, and with this turn-out he made his frequent journeys between the mine and Burntpine with comfort and speed, wrapped snugly in buffalo robes.

If London often reverted to his mind, there was another subject that obtruded itself even more frequently. His increased prosperity had something to do with this. He saw that, if he was to have a third of the receipts of the mine, he was not to remain a poor man for very long, and this fact gave him a certain courage which had been lacking before. He wondered if she remembered him. Wentworth had said very little about her when he wrote, for his letters were largely devoted to enthusiastic eulogies of Jennie Brewster, and Kenyon, in spite of the confession he had made when his case seemed hopeless, was loath to write and ask his friend anything about Edith.

One day, on a clear sharp frosty winter morning, Kenyon had his little pony harnessed for his weekly journey to Burntpine. After the rougher part of the road between the mine and the river had been left behind, and the pony got down to her work on the ice, with the two white banks of snow on either side of the smooth track, John gave himself up to thinking about the subject which now so often engrossed his mind. Wrapped closely in his furs, with the cutter skimming along the ice, these thoughts found a pleasant accompaniment in the silvery tinkle of the bells which jingled around his horse's neck. As a general thing, he met no one on the icy road from the mine to the village. Sometimes there was a procession of sleighs bearing supplies for his own mine and those beyond, and when this procession was seen, Kenyon had to look out for some place by the side of the track where he could pull up his horse and cutter and allow the teams to pass. The snow on each side of the cutting was so deep that these bays were shovelled out here and there to permit teams to get past each other. He had gone halfway to the village, when he saw ahead of him a pair of horses which he at once recognised as those belonging to the hotel-keeper. He drew up in the first bay and awaited the approach of the sleigh. He saw that it contained visitors for himself, because the driver, on recognising him, had turned round and spoken to the occupants of the vehicle. As it came along, the man drew up and nodded to Kenyon, who, although ordinarily the most polite of men, did not return the salutation. He was stricken dumb with astonishment on seeing who was in the sleigh. One woman was so bundled up that not even her nose appeared out in the cold, but the smiling rosy face of the other needed no introduction to John Kenyon.

'Well, Mr. Kenyon,' cried a laughing voice, 'you did not expect to see me this morning, did you?'

'I confess I did not,' said John, 'and yet——.' Here he paused; he was going to say, 'and yet I was thinking of you,' but he checked himself.

Miss Longworth, who had a talent for reading the unspoken thoughts of John Kenyon, probably did not need to be told the end of the sentence.

'Are you going to the village?' she asked.

'I was going. I am not going now.'

'That's right. I was just about to invite you to turn round with us. You see, we are on our way to look at the mine, and, I suppose, we shall have to obtain the consent of the manager before we can do so.'

Miss Longworth's companion had emerged for a moment from her wraps and looked at John, but instantly retired among the furs again with a shiver. She was not so young as her companion, and she considered this the most frightful climate she had ever encountered.

'Now,' said John, 'although your sleigh is very comfortable, I think this cutter of mine is even more so. It is intended for two; won't you step out of the sleigh into the cutter? Then, if the driver will move on, I can turn, and we will follow the sleigh.'

'I shall be delighted to do so,' said the young woman, shaking herself free from the buffalo robe, and stepping lightly from the sleigh into the cutter, pausing, however, for a moment, before she did so, to put her own wraps over her companion. John tucked her in beside himself, and, as the sleigh jingled on, he slowly turned his pony round into the road again.

'I have got a pretty fast pony,' he said, 'but I think we will let them drive on ahead. It irritates this little horse to see anything in front of it.'

'Then we can make up speed,' said Edith, 'and catch them before they get to the mine. Is it far from here?'

'No, not very far; at least, it doesn't take long to get there with a smart horse.'

'I have enjoyed this experience ever so much,' she said; 'you see, my father had to come to Montreal on business, so I came with him, as usual, and, being there, I thought I would run up here and see the mine. I wanted,' she continued, looking at the other side of the cutter and trailing her well-gloved fingers in the snow—'I wanted to know personally whether my manager was conducting my property in the way it ought to be conducted, notwithstanding the very satisfactory balance-sheets he sends.'

'Your property!' exclaimed John, in amazement.

'Certainly. You didn't know that, did you?' she replied, looking for a moment at him, and then away from him. 'I call myself the Mistress of the Mine.'

'Then you are—you are——'

'Mr. Smith,' said the girl coming to his rescue.

There was a moment's pause, and the next words John said were not at all what she expected.

'Take your hand out of the snow,' he commanded, 'and put it in under the buffalo robe; you have no idea how cold it is here, and your hand will be frozen in a moment.'

'Really,' said the girl, 'an employee must not talk to his employer in that tone! My hand is my own, is it not?'

'I hope it is,' said John, 'because I want to ask you for it.'

For answer Miss Edith Longworth placed her hand in his.

Actions speak louder than words. The sleigh was far in advance, and there were no witnesses on the white topped hills.

'Were you astonished?' she said, 'when I told you that I owned the mine?'

'Very much so indeed. Were you astonished when I told you I wished to own the owner of the mine?'

'Not in the slightest.'

'Why?'

'Because your treacherous friend Wentworth sent me your letter applying for a situation. You got the situation, didn't you, John?'

THE END

About Author

Robert Barr (16 September 1849 – 21 October 1912) was a Scottish-Canadian short story writer and novelist.

Early years in Canada

Robert Barr was born in Barony, Lanark, Scotland to Robert Barr and Jane Watson. In 1854, he emigrated with his parents to Upper Canada at the age of four years old. His family settled on a farm near the village of Muirkirk. Barr assisted his father with his job as a carpenter, and developed a sound work ethic. Robert Barr then worked as a steel smelter for a number of years before he was educated at Toronto Normal School in 1873 to train as a teacher.

After graduating Toronto Normal School, Barr became a teacher, and eventually headmaster/principal of the Central School of Windsor, Ontario in 1874. While Barr worked as head master of the Central School of Windsor, Ontario, he began to contribute short stories—often based on personal experiences, and recorded his work. On August 1876, when he was 27, Robert Barr married Ontario-born Eva Bennett, who was 21. According to the 1891 England Census, the couple appears to have had three children, Laura, William, and Andrew.

In 1876, Barr quit his teaching position to become a staff member of publication, and later on became the news editor for the Detroit Free Press. Barr wrote for this newspaper under the pseudonym, "Luke Sharp." The idea for this pseudonym was inspired during his morning commute to work when Barr saw a sign that read "Luke Sharp, Undertaker." In 1881, Barr left Canada to return to England in order to start a new weekly version of "The Detroit Free Press Magazine."

London years

In 1881 Barr decided to "vamoose the ranch", as he called the process of immigration in search of literary fame outside of Canada, and relocated to London to continue to write/establish the weekly English edition of the Detroit Free Press. During the 1890s, he broadened his literary works, and started writing novels from the popular crime genre. In 1892 he founded the magazine The Idler, choosing Jerome K. Jerome as his collaborator (wanting, as Jerome said, "a popular name"). He retired from its co-editorship in 1895.

In London of the 1890s Barr became a more prolific author—publishing a book a year—and was familiar with many of the best-selling authors of his day, including :Arnold Bennett, Horatio Gilbert Parker, Joseph Conrad, Bret Harte, Rudyard Kipling, H. Rider Haggard, H. G. Wells, and George Robert Gissing. Barr was well-spoken, well-cultured due to travel, and considered a "socializer."

Because most of Barr's literary output was of the crime genre, his works were highly in vogue. As Sherlock Holmes stories were becoming well-known, Barr wrote and published in the Idler the first Holmes parody, "The Adventures of "Sherlaw Kombs" (1892), a spoof that was continued a decade later in another Barr story, "The Adventure of the Second Swag" (1904). Despite those jibes at the growing Holmes phenomenon, Barr remained on very good terms with its creator Arthur Conan Doyle. In Memories and Adventures, a serial memoir published 1923–24, Doyle described him as "a volcanic Anglo—or rather Scot-American, with a violent manner, a wealth of strong adjectives, and one of the kindest natures underneath it all".

In 1904, Robert Barr completed an unfinished novel for Methuen & Co. by the recently deceased American author Stephen Crane entitled The O'Ruddy, a romance.Despite his reservations at taking on the project, Barr reluctantly finished the last eight chapters due to his longstanding friendship with Crane and his common-law wife, Cora, the war correspondent and bordello owner.

Death

The 1911 census places Robert Barr, "a writer of fiction," at Hillhead, Woldingham, Surrey, a small village southeast of London, living with his wife, Eva, their son William, and two female servants. At this home, the author died from heart disease on 21 October 1912.

Writing Style

Barr's volumes of short stories were often written with an ironic twist in the story with a witty, appealing narrator telling the story. Barr's other works also include numerous fiction and non-fiction contributions to periodicals. A few of his mystery stories and stories of the supernatural were put in anthologies, and a few novels have been republished. His writings have also attracted scholarly attention. His narrative personae also featured moral and editorial interpolations within their tales. Barr's achievements were recognized by an honorary degree from the University of Michigan in 1900.

His protagonists were journalists, princes, detectives, deserving commercial and social climbers, financiers, the new woman of bright wit and aggressive accomplishment, and lords. Often, his characters were stereotypical and romanticized.

Barr wrote fiction in an episode-like format. He developed this style when working as an editor for the newspaper Detroit Press. Barr developed his skill with the anecdote and vignette; often only the central character serves to link the nearly self-contained chapters of the novels. (Source: Wikipedia)

NOTABLE WORKS

In a Steamer Chair and Other Stories (Thirteen short stories by one of the most famous writers in his day -1892)

"The Face And The Mask" (1894) consists of twenty-four delightful short stories.

In the Midst of Alarms (1894, 1900, 1912), a story of the attempted Fenian invasion of Canada in 1866.

From Whose Bourne (1896) Novel in which the main character, William Brenton, searches for truth to set his wife free.

One Day's Courtship (1896)

Revenge! (Collection of 20 short stories, Alfred Hitchcock-like style, thriller with a surprise ending)

The Strong Arm

A Woman Intervenes (1896), a story of love, finance, and American journalism.

Tekla: A Romance of Love and War (1898)

Jennie Baxter, Journalist (1899)

The Unchanging East (1900)

The Victors (1901)

A Prince of Good Fellows (1902)

Over The Border: A Romance (1903)

The O'Ruddy, A Romance, with Stephen Crane (1903)

A Chicago Princess (1904)

The Speculations of John Steele (1905)

The Tempestuous Petticoat (1905–12)

A Rock in the Baltic (1906)

The Triumphs of Eugène Valmont (1906)

The Measure of the Rule (1907)

Stranleigh's Millions (1909)

The Sword Maker (Medieval action/adventure novel, genre: Historical Fiction-1910)

The Palace of Logs (1912)

"The Ambassadors Pigeons" (1899)

"And the Rigor of the Game" (1892)

"Converted" (1896)

"Count Conrad's Courtship" (1896)

"The Count's Apology" (1896)

"A Deal on Change " (1896)

"The Exposure of Lord Stanford" (1896)

"Gentlemen: The King!"

"The Hour-Glass" (1899)

"An invitation" (1892)

" A Ladies Man"

"The Long Ladder" (1899)

"Mrs. Tremain" (1892)

" Transformation" (1896)

"The Understudy" (1896)

" The Vengeance of the Dead" (1896)

"The Bromley Gibbert's Story" (1896)

" Out of Thun" (1896)

"The Shadow of Greenback" (1896)

"Flight of the Red Dog" (fiction)

"Lord Stranleigh Abroad" (1913)

"One Day's Courtship and the Herald's of Fame" (1896)

"Cardillac"

"Dr. Barr's Tales"

"The Triumphs of Eugene Valmont"